DATE DUE

QUEST

RICHARD BEN SAPIR

QUEST

E. P. DUTTON | NEW YORK

Published in the United States by
E. P. Dutton, a division of NAL Penguin Inc.,
2 Park Avenue, New York, N.Y. 10016.

Published simultaneously in Canada by
Fitzhenry and Whiteside Limited, Toronto.

Library of Congress Cataloging-in-Publication Data
Sapir, Richard.
Quest.
I. Title.
PS3569.A59Q4   1987   813'.54   86-31904
ISBN 0-525-24548-0

COBE

Designed by Mark O'Connor

10 9 8 7 6 5 4 3 2 1

First Edition

For Richard Lynn Fogel,
who meant so much to so many,
especially Mimi, Dan, and Fred.

Acknowledgments

I would like to thank Joan Mandarin and Jerry Lorig of the NYPD; Tarnia Prater of Great Britain; Chris Moylan of Roslindale; Ben Kupferman, Boston jeweler and sculptor; Ward Damio; Joyce Engelson; Sumner Dorfman; and, as always, my first editorial reader and advisor, P. K. Chute from South Portland, Maine.

A ruby dealer asked his name not be used.

QUEST

I

She was gold, fifty pounds of it used mostly for bulking. She was five square-cut pink topazes, a mere ten karats each, atop the backs of jade lions rampant. She was a magnificent night-blue sapphire the size of a palm, engraved with Poseidon enthroned. She was six diamonds—polished, not cut—the smallest at least twenty karats by weight, set around the thick round base as a border. Garnet brilliants embroidered her upper lips, and lapis lazuli as bright as summer rain speckled her thick gold bosom, reserved for the awesome Christ's head ruby, as purely red as His blood itself.

Simon Sedgewick, of London's Worshipful Company of Goldsmiths, polished the base one last time, waiting to implant his maker's mark. This he would not do until Her Majesty Elizabeth, Queen of England, France, Ireland, and Virginia, had seen it and approved the work.

It was a saltcellar, a proper three feet high, but made under the strangest circumstances. Her Majesty herself insisted goldsmith Sedgewick not only work alone but construct everything here in Tilbury

[1]

Field in the center of her army waiting for the invasion of the Spanish Armada.

For Sedgewick the impending doom of the massive Spanish fleet was only the least of his problems. Here, he was deprived not only of his bellowed furnaces but of the apprentices to work them. A slow and difficult thing it had been, using hollowed-out logs for fire and layering the gold in sheets as in the old days before the skills of England's smiths became famous. He had burned his hands countless times, and now it was done, done as well, he told himself, as human hands could form it, considering Her Majesty's inviolate orders.

For the first time in two and a half months, he stepped out into the sunlight that burned his eyes and took a good lung of fresh English air from the rich salt marsh surrounding the field. The tents of the thirty thousand were gone, and now only a few stood to house those who guarded him in his labors. The Spanish Armada was no more either, divine winds, they said, having blown the great heavy ships into disorder and disaster in the English Channel.

A captain of the guard did not let Sedgewick walk far.

"Done?" he asked.

"Ready for presentation to Her Majesty and my maker's mark," said Sedgewick.

"You've used every piece given?"

"You may search the tent. There is nothing left but my tools," said Sedgewick. He felt good. He had done something that would make his name live at royal dinners as long as the royals used salt, which was another way of saying forever.

The captain not only searched the tent, accounting for everything in it, but had the cellar crated. Then, without waiting for either Sedgewick or his maker's mark, he took the crate and his entire company away from Tilbury Field, leaving Sedgewick only a Queen's purse and the fresh salt air and sunlight, which now graced a newly powerful England, conqueror of the greatest fleet ever assembled.

Sedgewick would hear the cellar went not to Her Majesty's residence in Greenwich but to Windsor Castle, where it was locked and stored away even from most noble eyes, never to grace the royal table or hold one grain of salt.

Generations of English schoolboys would learn of it as the Tilbury Cellar, commemorating the survival and triumph of an island nation against only one of its awesome foes.

.   .   .

"All right, Jack, it's all over. Slow 'er down," said the man with the gun.

The engineer thought pistols should not have barrels that big. It looked like a dark tunnel at the end of the man's hand, a tunnel the engineer imagined filling with a flash and then a large slug. It would be the last thing he would see.

"What're you doin'?" asked the engineer.

"What's it look like I'm doin'. I'm robbin' the bloody train. Slow 'er down, mate."

The pistol was close and the barrel was so big, and the thought of that big lead slug going into his brain so vivid, the engineer didn't even try to sudden brake to throw the lone robber off balance. Instead he slowed the 8:10 as directed to a railway crossing where three lorries waited, their engines running, exhausts coughing cheap smoke and dripping discharge.

"This is a troop train, mate. You crazy?" asked the engineer. "Those boys back there kicked Jerry's arse through Africa, Italy, France, right back into Germany. You can't rob this train. We got a load of armed veterans."

"They're through. We're through. We're gettin' ours, an you're through too, Jack, if you open 'er up again," said the man with the big barrelled gun.

The engineer waited for the first shots. He was going to fall down and get close to the reinforced steel plates. He didn't even think of going for the gun at any opportunity. The war was over. England was no longer desperate. It had arms and allies, and he didn't want to be the last man killed in some line of duty when there were so many soldiers on board. He waited for the shots and he heard laughter. Lots of laughter.

The man with the gun looked out of the engine cab.

"There's your troops, Jack," he said.

Careful not to get too close to the robber to appear threatening, the engineer peered out of the cab back down the tracks. A young subaltern, his face tender as market plums, his new uniform still holding some supply-room creases, ran beside the cars yelling, his face getting redder and his hands getting wilder the more the veterans laughed.

It would shock all England, tired from a brutal war in which this island nation stood alone for so long against what had seemed like invincible legions of darkness.

While three lorries of thieves unloaded an entire car of national treasures that had been stored in bunkers outside of London for the duration of the war, the veterans, a bit boisterous from beer on this warm spring day and the giddy knowledge that no one would be shooting at them again, cheered on the thieves. Three bobbies who had counted on the veterans stood helplessly by. The subaltern tried to save a copy of the Magna Carta with his body but was brushed aside.

The point was not that the thieves had gotten away with so much. Most of it was recovered within days. After all, who would risk jail for owning the standard that had flown over Hastings Field, and where would one sell it? What so shattered the reading public was what one newspaper termed the "loss of the spirit that brought us through."

Later, there were rumors that some valuables were indeed missing, such as the Tilbury Cellar. Scotland Yard was supposed to have been sent at first on a desperate all-points search, then for some reason, never to be fully explained, was told not to look for it at all. Then later there was a newspaper article about how the Tilbury Cellar, like the royal family itself during the blitz, had never left Windsor Castle but remained in the vault where the Virgin Queen had placed it in the early days of the British Empire.

NEW YORK CITY, THE PRESENT

"You can't sell it like that," said Geoffrey Battissen, owner of the Battissen Galleries of Fifth Avenue. "It not only isn't done, it can't be done."

"It's the only way I'm gonna do it," said Vern Andrews of Carney, Ohio, with the righteous twang of a mule trader.

"He'll never agree to it," said Battissen. He shook his balding head as though he had locks that would quiver glamorously.

"Then he won't buy it," said Andrews. "I am not going to get myself killed or robbed."

"Mr. Andrews, Battissen Galleries has been here on Fifth Avenue for twenty-two years and—"

"That's the fourth time I heard that, Mister. I don't care how rich people are supposed to be, or how important they're supposed to be. People have killed for a lot less."

To Vern Andrews everything seemed artistic in this gallery, except the paintings and sculptures. There were marble bench seats, expensive and dramatic track lighting, exotic plants in austere white holders, and Geoffrey Battissen himself, in a cream beige jacket of his own design, which matched his shoes and was tolerably close to the color of his pancake makeup. He was in his mid fifties, fleshy, dramatic, and seeming always about to throw a kiss or spit depending on his moods. He had a redheaded assistant who wore a black dress and white pearls with the kind of body only a homosexual could ignore.

[4]

Andrews wore a plain blue suit he had bought in Columbus, which was good enough for business in New York, Frankfurt, London, and Tokyo. He wasn't going to be bullied. He wasn't going to be rushed. He crossed his arms and leaned against a piece of rusted junk priced at more than many Carney homes and which no self-respecting Carney yard would allow uncollected. Andrews was at least ten years older than Battissen, but with more energy in his large body, a strong squarish face that showed a willingness to battle, and disdain for the pressure he was receiving now.

"Battissen Galleries cannot sell any piece, no matter how valuable, unless it has the trust and respect of the client, especially not to a prospective buyer of such importance. The man is a surgeon. He has homes in Switzerland and Italy. He is a member of society on both continents."

"Well, then I'll go back to my hotel and look for another broker, Mr. Battissen. Thank you, kindly." Andrews turned to the door. He wasn't sure what he would do if the art dealer let him reach it. He had to make this sale, and do it in a few days, or the cash wouldn't matter. He was in his sixties and he had made these turns away from deals many times, possibly with as much riding on it at other times, and always it felt like the world would end if he reached that door. It gave life flavor.

"I will try," said Battissen.

"No," said Andrews. "You'll do it."

With a navel-deep sigh of resignation, Battissen excused himself to make a phone call, and Vern Andrews struck up a conversation with the red-haired assistant.

"Some of these pictures are real nice," he said.

"I think they're shit, too," she answered and they both laughed. If Vern Andrews had brought his wife along on this trip or almost anyone else, he would have made an excuse to be free that evening for this redhead. But Claire was with him, and she was his daughter and she was something else. He would never cancel a dinner with Claire, even for a business deal.

Battissen returned bubbling.

"Forgive me if I boast, but I don't think Dr. Martins would ever endure such strange proscriptions for a purchase unless it was Battissen Galleries that had put its reputation on the line. We have been here twenty-two years and earned the trust of people like Dr. Martins, even if we don't have yours, Mr. Andrews."

"Sorry," said Andrews in a clipped sunshine way that cut away mists of remorse.

"He has agreed to look at it, but I am sure he will not purchase it under such conditions."

"Well, let's find out," said Andrews, and leaving the galleries he winked to the redhead, and almost put a hand on Battissen's shoulder, something he normally did to maneuver people during a sale.

They walked toward Madison Avenue in the whip of the October winds through the tall buildings, with Battissen struggling to keep up with the strong pace of the larger and older man. Battissen talked of Dr. Martins's reputation in the business of gems, something that would be needed in this sale. Battissen thought Andrews had chosen well in the Battissen Galleries because while Battissen Galleries never dealt in anything of inherent value like gems and gold, Battissen Galleries did understand major purchases and sales.

Vern Andrews hardly listened. He thought of how enormous prices were asked for even the shabbiest building he passed. He was a businessman with a share in many businesses, and he understood all price was only a matter of opinion and all opinion was a matter of timing. He remembered times in his life when he didn't have a quarter for a sandwich, and his mother had remembered not having a nickel for a sandwich, and he was sure his grandmother remembered doing without for lack of three cents. But his daughter Claire never knew hunger or even denying herself anything because of price. And she never would.

The branch of the International Bank and Trust Company was on the corner of Madison Avenue and Fiftieth Street, a place of two-story-high glass windows showing a vast interior of polished steel safes, marble floors, and cold stone teller windows.

An elegant man in a parked forest-green Jaguar waited in front of the bank. Battissen fairly flew to him.

"That's him," said Battissen.

Dr. Martins looked as elegant as his fashionable car. The overcoat fit with the clean lines of careful hand tailoring. Every small detail of collar, shirt, tie, and gloves seemed to be perfection, like an excellence above ordinary men. Even his features seemed a bit too perfect, and only the uneven graying around the temples broke the symmetry of gray suit, tweed coat, gray gloves, and that perfect face. The hands seemed ready for an operating room.

Battissen hovered around the Jaguar door as though waiting to offer his Dr. Martins his back to step out on.

"He wouldn't change his mind," said Battissen. "I tried."

"You want to see it?" said Andrews.

"I'm here at this point," said Dr. Martins with a soft guttural molding the consonants.

"Where's the money?" asked Andrews. "I said there's got to be money."

"He's been like this since the beginning, Dr. Martins. But I guarantee, everything is worth it. And again forgive me the manner in which we are going to have to do the viewing."

Dr. Martins spoke directly to Vern Andrews.

"I am not in the habit of bringing money before I know what I am buying."

Vern Andrews stuck his hands in his pants pockets.

"Terms still the same. No money, no piece."

"Let's see this thing. What is it?" asked Dr. Martins.

"You'll see," said Andrews.

"It's breathtaking," said Battissen. "I thought only you, when I saw the gems. I didn't even think of anyone else."

"Hardly puts pressure on him, fella," said Andrews, smiling. Dr. Martins refused to acknowledge the humor, and Battissen attempted to be above it, as the three men entered the branch office of the International Bank and signed in for access to the safety deposit boxes. Andrews noticed that Dr. Martins signed in as James Smith.

A bank official led them through a large burnished steel door in the rear of the bank. A guard opened the first door and the official's key opened the second. The room was lined with burnished steel drawers the size of filing cabinets, each with double key slots. Overhead a harsh fluorescent lamp glared down on a plain gray-topped table with two chairs. Andrews had used all the pull he had with his bank back home to get this New York bank to rent him a deposit box on short notice.

The bank official inserted her key into one of the locks in front of the shoulder-high box, and Andrews inserted his. Then they turned both simultaneously, and the steel door swung open showing a large square black drawer with a handle. Only when the bank official had left them alone did Vern Andrews, with a grunting effort, pull out the drawer and clunk it down on the gray table at which Dr. Martins sat disdainfully removing his gray gloves. Battissen hovered over him.

Andrews smiled to both and unhinged the top of the large black box, revealing a burlap sack inside. With a grunt, Vern Andrews lifted the sack out so that it stood upright, about three feet high and two feet wide. Dried dirt from the sack cast pale dust on the gray table top. Battissen stretched across the table to wipe it with a beige handkerchief as Dr. Martins leaned away from it.

Andrews's large fingers untied the top, and then like a stripper in a Dayton burlesque house, he slowly undraped the piece, showing first the golden bowl on top, and then the thickness of her gold shoulders, with dark chips of stone, and the heads of the jade lions. With a jerk he exposed the big red stone full in the rounded center, and after Dr. Martins had gotten an eyeful, then revealed the larger blue sapphire just beneath. Finally, at her feet, were six tubular water-clear diamonds. It was almost three feet of a solid chunky fire hydrant of gold, laced with scrollwork and booming precious stones out of its middle and base. She was like a hefty woman with bumps instead of curves, because nothing dipped in anywhere. But what a fat waist. All the fat was gold and the bumps were a mouthful of ruby and a plush palm-sized blue sapphire, both engraved. The diamonds were thick as thumbs. Vern Andrews knew what he had.

"I told you it was worth it," said Battissen.

Dr. Martins signaled with his hand that he wanted the rest of the burlap removed completely. From his coat pocket he took a black metal jeweler's loupe, and inserting it into his right eye he stood up and leaned toward the ruby, crooking a finger for Vern Andrews to tilt back the piece so Dr. Martins could get a different light on it.

"This is an absurd way to examine a gem," said Dr. Martins, signaling he wanted a different tilt to the piece. "All right. Back," he said.

He circled the ruby, like a bee considering a petal, and then he moved to the sapphire. On the sapphire he only nodded, and then moved down to the diamonds, signaling for the big trunk of gold to be turned for each one.

"Well," said Dr. Martins, "we certainly can't sell all these wonderful gems like this. Can't be done."

"I told him that. I told him it couldn't be done that way," said Battissen.

Vern Andrews placed a hand on the dish at the top.

"I'll tell you again what I told Geoff here. When you bring three million dollars, this here piece goes with you and the three million goes in this box. That's it. No deals."

"Where did you get it?" asked Dr. Martins.

"You tell me, I'll give you a thousand dollars."

"I'm sure it's genuine and legitimate. We just haven't located its general area or form," said Battissen.

"It's a saltcellar," said Dr. Martins.

Andrews nodded. He had thought it was some kind of royal pedestal for something.

"Yes, now that you mention it," said Battissen. "And most real."

"I'll buy the diamonds if you wish. I might give you some sort of price on the sapphire, but what am I going to do with that ruby?"

"That's your problem," said Andrews.

"No, it's not. It's yours. That is a major gem. I believe that is a pigeon's blood ruby, but I can't tell you its quality. I can only guess."

"Then what's going on here?" asked Andrews. "Are you buying, yes or no?"

"You don't understand the market you're trying to reach. This is not like some Hollywood movie with a chest of colored stones as a treasure. People don't buy gems that way, a half dozen large rubies and a dozen emeralds. You'll never sell this."

"I told him there was a way it was done," said Battissen. "Now maybe he'll listen to you. Of course it has to be broken up."

"No," said Vern Andrews.

"Then I can't do anything for you. I'm sorry."

"So am I," said Andrews, pulling up the sack. More dried dirt sprayed out onto the table. This time Dr. Martins did not back away but reached for Andrews's hand. He had seen the sapphire, well over a hundred karats and even in this fluorescent light screaming its greatness from its bowels. He couldn't let this bumpkin play these games with such a gem. It offended him that a man who talked like that, wore those sorts of suits, and had that outrageous haircut, would own such a valuable piece, so many valuable pieces.

"Look. I think I know someone who could buy the ruby. I'd like to bring him."

"He better not be six foot five and carry a knife," said Andrews.

"What do you think we are?" asked Dr. Martins. "This is ridiculous. This is no way to sell major gems, under a fluorescent light of a vault. Are you some sort of criminal?"

"Three million dollars cash is a great way to get yourself killed. When someone gives me my three million, I will just have it transferred from down here in this box to a teller upstairs and wired to my home," said Andrews. "And that's the way it's gonna be, especially with people who sign their names in as Smith."

"Battissen Galleries will give you a receipt," said Battissen. Andrews laughed and pushed away the hand Dr. Martins had on the burlap sack.

"Mr. Andrews, the only man I know who could purchase the ruby correctly would not tolerate doing business in a vault," said Dr. Martins. "He is known to museum curators throughout the world. Anyone who deals in major rubies knows of him, and he probably is one of fewer than five people who could properly sell that ruby you have. Please."

"If he sees it, he sees it here," said Andrews.

An hour later, a man who didn't look as though he had the price of a pair of shoes showed up in a suit that had to be twenty years old and was worn around the sleeves. He had a face like a collapsed rubber bag with lines that formed a perpetual scowl. He could have been called elderly except he was too spry.

He did not say hello. He did not sit down. He said: "Where is it?"

His name was Norman Feldman. He had signed in as such. Dr.

Martins watched the older man's face the way Battissen watched Dr. Martins. So there was a hierarchy among these people, thought Vern Andrews.

Andrews stripped the burlap from the golden shoulders, quickly down to the diamond feet.

"What am I supposed to look at?" asked Feldman.

"That's not a real ruby?" asked Battissen.

"Who's he?" asked Feldman, glancing at Battissen.

"He introduced me to the seller," said Dr. Martins. Andrews leaned back against the wall of safety deposit boxes in a gesture more reminiscent of a farmer leaning against a fence, tucked a thumb under his belt, and let them all know if he wasn't going to be bowled over by the other two, he certainly wasn't going to be moved by this man.

"Of course that's a real ruby," said Feldman. "But I'm not going to look at it in this light. This is fluorescent light. You need north light. This is shit. What are we, a bunch of crooks? Meeting in a vault. Is it going to be midnight in an alley? What goes on here?"

"Is that or is that not a magnificent ruby?" asked Dr. Martins.

"Of course it is, and I'm not buying it in some basement with a fluorescent light."

"It ain't moving, buddy," said Andrews.

"Any reason you want to keep it hidden?" asked Feldman.

"I don't want to be robbed," said Andrews.

"You think it's stolen. You wouldn't be selling it like this if you didn't," said Feldman. "Someone like you would be in Tiffany's instead of with these gonifs. Don't tell me you're going to be robbed there."

"I have reasons that are my own," said Andrews.

"I've never seen that ruby. That's a very big pigeon's blood ruby. I've never heard of it," said Feldman. His voice whined. So there really was a very narrow market for a ruby this size, thought Andrews, if this man could think it was odd he didn't know of it.

"It's a saltcellar," said Battissen.

"Then why aren't there scratches in the bowl on top?" asked Feldman, peering across the table and down at the bowl on top.

"Perhaps they were careful," said Battissen. "It's a magnificent piece."

"If that's gold it will scratch with salt and it has no scratches in it," said Feldman.

"Oh god, maybe it's not gold?" gasped Battissen.

"Of course it's gold. You don't set those stones in chopped liver," said Feldman. "I'll give you a half million dollars just to get that ruby out of this crowd and into good north light."

"Three million for the whole thing," said Andrews.

"I don't want the whole thing. Six hundred thousand."

"Three million. You break it up."

"I don't deal in diamonds. Seven hundred thousand."

"I'll add three hundred thousand for the sapphire," said Dr. Martins. "That's a million dollars for the two gems alone. You've got fifty pounds of gold, diamonds, things you can sell more easily—"

"Hold it," said Feldman, nodding to Andrews. "I am dealing with this man. I will be happy to pay you a commission. But I am not going into business with you."

"Any way you people want to work it out. I'm not breaking her down," said Andrews.

"If you want to bring the ruby into the north light, I can go nine hundred thousand dollars. Maybe a million," said Feldman. "I don't know why you won't show it in a legitimate setting unless you know something I don't know."

"A quarter of a million dollars more just to look at it in a different light? Who are you kidding?" Andrews laughed.

"Sonny, you have never seen the power inside a great ruby. And you can't see that power in this light. Power is what the great gems are about. Holding it. Owning it. Here, I couldn't tell you anything more than she is a big pigeon's blood. In a north light I would know what I am buying."

"And I'm supposed to carry that thing on me to some place under the sun so's you can look at it in a better light?" asked Andrews. He didn't like being called "sonny" and he knew this New York Jew didn't care whether he liked it or not.

"Sonny. When and if you sell this thing, tell the buyer that if he brings it to Norman Feldman, he may get a million dollars for it if he is willing to deal like a human being. I don't need this shit, not even for that."

"Then what'd you come in here for?" asked Andrews.

"To see a great ruby. And I'd still like to see it. Now, let me out of here. I don't want to stay here. This isn't for me," said Feldman.

"You're pretty damned touchy," said Andrews.

"Just wrap up your toy, and let's get out of here."

"Tell him he's never going to sell that cellar whole," said Dr. Martins.

"You want to reason with a fool, you reason with a fool," said Feldman.

"Is it possible you don't want to sell the cellar?" asked Battissen. "Maybe you have an attachment to it that's emotional. I've seen it in art. Somebody wants to sell a piece but can't give it up."

"You're right. I do have an attachment. But I am going to sell it. I've got a buyer for the whole thing. And unless you fellas come up with my price, I'll give it to him."

"You're lying," said Dr. Martins. He almost made a grab for the cellar.

"Mr. Andrews, please be reasonable for once," said Battissen.

"Why are you two assholes wasting your time with another one?" asked Feldman.

Outside, Geoffrey Battissen commented what a shame it was that such a hayseed should have something so valuable.

"He doesn't know what he has. He just knows a price," said Dr. Martins.

Norman Feldman trotted quickly across the street. He didn't want to be on the same sidewalk with the other two. He was certain the dying was going to begin.

"Dad, there's a telephone call for you. Some very British gentleman wants to buy something of yours," said Claire Andrews, getting up from the sofa of the parlor of their Waldorf suite. She put down her book and went to kiss her father. She wore a light pink bathrobe.

"You didn't go out, not for anything?" asked Vern Andrews, glancing at the book.

"It's New York, Dad. I'd rather go out with you," said Claire. "You know how I feel about New York."

"You felt that way about Paris and Rome and London too."

"But not as bad as New York," said Claire. She was a beautiful woman with striking sharp features and sheer blond hair; she looked like a movie actress Vern Andrews always considered the ideal, possibly because the actress looked like Claire: the late Grace Kelly, who died a princess. But unlike that Philadelphia beauty Claire did not consort with princes. She was twenty-eight years old, unmarried, and went out occasionally with a local fellow so mealy even she could push him around.

The Andrewses had tried sending her to Radcliffe, but instead she chose Ohio State so she could come home weekends.

Andrews had left her here in the suite that morning with an admonition to buy anything in New York City she wanted. From the leftovers on a plate yet to be removed by Waldorf room service, he could tell she had settled for a tuna fish sandwich.

"I don't know why I'm trying to earn all this money, Claire, if you're not going to spend any of it."

"I don't know why either, Dad."

"Peanuts, am I ever going to win an argument with you?"

Claire Andrews smiled at her father, and he knew all of it, every bit of it, no matter what it was, was worth it for that smile he had loved since she was four months old.

The British caller had not left a number but said he would get back. He did. And Andrews took the call in his own bedroom.

"Mr. Andrews, I am interested in a piece you are selling out of an International Bank branch office. Is it still available?" came the voice, very clipped, very British, very dry. There were no unnecessary words.

"Only if you have money," said Andrews.

"The asking price is three million dollars, yes?"

"Cash. I'm not looking for talk. I'm looking for buyers."

"If it is what we want, I'll pay on the spot."

Vern Andrews knew not to jump up and yell hot diggity dog. He also knew when he had a live one.

"How did you hear about it?"

"It's late today. What about ten in the a.m. tomorrow when the bank opens."

"Sure. Will Battissen be there?"

"I don't know any Battissen."

"Wonderful, neither do I," said Andrews and hung up, whistling. He wouldn't even have to pay a commission. He composed himself before he went out to see Claire again. She didn't have to know anything about business; all she had to know was to enjoy herself and let her father sometimes know how happy she was.

"What's so crucial? What's so exciting? What's so mysterious?" asked Claire as soon as he entered the parlor.

"Just some business, peanuts."

"It's not just business, Dad. What is it?" She put down her book again.

"Nothing you have to know. But maybe something you should know," he said. A hotel suite didn't seem the right place, so he waited until dinner, at a good New York restaurant. Just before they ordered, with drinks in their hands so things would be calm, he explained to her the seriousness of his last heart attack, a year ago. He had not wanted her to know how bad it had been. It was the worst of them, and he realized he didn't have all that much time. More than anything, he wanted to leave a fortune so immense, Claire would be one of the richest women in the country. He wanted to do this last thing for his baby.

"I know you didn't want that much. But I wanted it for you. Do you understand? I needed to leave you this great fortune."

"I do, Dad," she said. She thought he was the most beautiful man in the restaurant. If she could find one like him, half like him, she would marry tomorrow.

"I leveraged heavily. No risks, no gain. I ran into a cash-flow problem, and I couldn't let any of my creditors know how badly I needed the money or all of them would have come down on me. We would have lost everything. So I came to New York and very quietly and very discreetly put something valuable up for sale. In fact, damned secretly."

"You're valuable, Dad," she said. "Things are just objects. People make them valuable because of what they think and feel. That you did it is the important thing to me. In my view."

Vern Andrews, a powerful man, with a strong face and strong hands stretching out of white cuffs with glistening gold links, felt his eyes water as his beautiful Claire touched his hands with hers. She would always be rich enough to believe such crap.

II

The Englishman was waiting for him with a suitcase the next day at the bank. He had no requests to see the cellar in a special light. He was a bland sort of fellow who seemed too pale for sunlight and too dour for private business. He introduced himself as James. He carried a valise.

"What's that?" asked Andrews.

"Money, if you have what I want," said the man. The vowels seemed to resonate in the back of his throat, that sort of superior British sound, but the man did not give any of those sorts of airs. He could have been waiting for a bus on some street corner.

Inside the bank, he sat down at the gray-topped table, and as though going to work pulled out a notebook and a pair of callipers as Vern exposed the golden saltcellar with the luxurious gems. The man showed neither joy nor lust, but the sense of a burdensome job. He didn't speak, and seemed to have places on the cellar to look at, checking with his notebook every now and then. He measured the major gems like a clerk making sure a count was correct.

When he was done, he opened the dark valise with a combination lock, exposing rows of orderly one-hundred-dollar bills.

"Three million. Your asking price. Count it."

The valise had a nice fresh odor of cash. Vern Andrews looked at the money that he could infuse that very afternoon as lubrication into the dry joints of his investment empire. He looked at the man with the valise wide open. He was obviously just a messenger, but the messenger carried a note Vern Andrews had been able to read since he cadged nickles and dimes by helping drunks home from Carney bars when he was young. The message said, "There is more where this comes from." It said: "Push me. We're good for it."

He could have taken what was there in front of him, but if Vern Andrews had taken just what was there in his life, he would have ended up working for the McCaffertys in Carney, instead of marrying one of them. He would never have gotten this piece if he had been like most men, who only took what was there. He would have been afraid of the old American gold laws, of the U.S. Army, of losing it all. He would have been afraid to go for more.

In the safety deposit vault, he could still remember how he had found it. He remembered the troop ship coming back from Europe, the smells of sweat and rotting pieces of food soldiers always kept by them for snacks, the quart of Scotch smuggled on board and selling for fifty dollars, a fortune at the time, more than a man could expect for a weekly salary. Because he had always been a good gambler, the sail home was like a three-week bonus to World War II.

They were on a large, slow British tramp steamer converted for the duration to a troop ship, and they were boarded with several other companies. Before they sighted America, Vern had won eighteen thousand dollars, mostly at poker, none of which came from his own platoon, which he was really using for bodyguards. He knew that if a man didn't have friends to protect him, that much money in cash could get him thrown overboard real easy.

One of the British sailors heard about the winnings and wanted to sell something for "every penny you got, mate."

It was the first time Vern saw Lucky. She was in a seaman's duffel, under a bunk. The sailors crowded around him, shielding sight of the duffel from the rest of the hold. She looked like some sort of tall footstool on which somebody had thrown designs and jewels without thinking.

"There she is, mate. Solid gold, and them stones gotta be real too."

"How do I know?"

"Just lift her."

"So she's heavy. Lead's heavy."

"Mate, this is a fortune. It's real."

"Where'd you get her?"

" 'Ey, c'mon now, mate."

"What am I going to do with it? Gold's illegal in America. Where could I sell it?"

"You could break her down. Sell off the gold alone for a bloody fortune. Save the jewels. Cut the jewels."

"Why don't you do it?"

"'Cause we can't agree as to who gets what. There's been hard feelin's since before Liverpool."

"Since bloody Cheltham," said one sailor, who got a dirty look.

"She's too big for us. We ain't used to somethin' like her," said another, and still another said they were all assholes and shouldn't sell her at all. There was a bit of shoving even then, and Vern backed off from the deal until just before they docked in Bayonne, New Jersey, when he heard one of the sailors had been found with his throat slit. That was enough of a gold assay for Vern Andrews.

He bought it for almost every dollar he had and stuffed it into his duffel, and as the band played "Stars and Stripes Forever" Vern Andrews debarked with a rifle, a helmet, and a fortune he didn't as yet know what to do with. He didn't know how he would sell it. He didn't know who would buy it. All he knew was that it was something great, something a boy like him from Carney, whose father had never been more than a janitor with a drinking problem, could never aspire to. It represented things that were beyond Carney. Eighteen thousand dollars had been money. You could buy the best house in Carney for that.

But this great gold thing was more. To own it was to dare beyond anyone in his world. He had seen the value of gold as he had trudged through a ruined Europe. It outlasted the mere paper money. It was wealth, and in daring he separated himself from everyone he had known.

He had to go AWOL to avoid surrendering illegal gold at mustering out. He knew this would mean a court-martial of some sort. He would pay that price. It was just too much wealth not to have. If worse came to worst, he could always melt down pieces of it and sell it to dentists, or take it into Canada or Mexico.

But he never had to take it apart, and his luck seemed to begin right there. The court-martial he expected when he returned to Fort Dix never materialized. In an army disbanding itself after a victorious war, everyone wanted to go home, especially his company commander, who would have had to stay in order to testify against one of his men, a man who had gone through the same hell with him without one previous bad mark.

Perhaps it was his first experience trusting himself on such a large scale, but it came to represent his luck to Vern Andrews himself. And believing it, he had it. So that when he stood in that bank vault ready to sell Lucky, he was a wealthy, powerful man, who only needed immediate cash, a man who by this time found pushing for more to be second nature. And when he got his first demand, he shook his head and put a pained expression on his face, and in his most hayseed manner allowed as how things were kind of different now.

The British gentleman, his hand on a stack of one-hundred-dollar bills as thick as a historical novel, looked up startled.

"Sorry," said Andrews. "Three million was the price before I had other bidders. I'm thinking these stones will sell better separately, know what I mean? I got bidders now."

"I see. And what is your new price?" asked the man.

"Well, I want to sell this thing stone by stone now. People are bidding like that, you know," said Vern Andrews, as happy as a pebble tinkling around inside a tin can. He liked this. He would rather be doing this than being dragged through some museum by Claire or eating at the best restaurant in the world.

"I am only prepared to offer on the entire piece."

"Well then, I'm real sorry. I stopped thinking of her as a whole."

"Yes, well, try, if you would, please," said the Briton.

"Sure will. I'll just find what the stones are bringing. I sure was surprised to see how valuable these little fellers are. These things are worth fortunes," Vern said, pulling up the burlap and lifting Lucky back into her box.

"Well, I'm not sure our offer will still be here. Just how much are you asking now?"

"I'd have to say five million now."

BRITISH FOREIGN OFFICE
SOURCE: NEW YORK CITY

CLASSIFICATION: MAXIMUM SECURITY, FOREIGN OFFICE, RATE ONE

ESTABLISHED CONTACT WITH SELLER VERN ANDREWS, 62, AMERICAN CITIZEN, HONORABLE DISCHARGE US ARMY JUNE 1945, SGT. FIRST DIVISION. IRS AUDIT 1984, PAID $57,000 TAXES ON INCOME OF $2.8 MILLION. PASS AUDIT. PIECE VERIFIES. NEW ASKING PRICE $5 MILLION. SUSPECT PRICE WILL RISE WITH AVAILABLE OFFER. WHAT PROCEED?

NEW YORK
SOURCE: FOREIGN OFFICE—LONDON

CLASSIFICATION: MAXIMUM SECURITY, FOREIGN OFFICE, RATE ONE

APPARENT YOU USING US GOVERNMENT ASSISTANCE. DESIST IMMEDI-
ATELY. NO ONE BUT YOU TO KNOW. ACCESS NO ONE NOT EVEN EMBASSY
STAFF NO MATTER WHAT CLEARANCE. FUNDS NO PROBLEM. TIE HIM
DOWN TO A PRICE. BUT UNDER NO CIRCUMSTANCES AND AT ALL COSTS
DO NOT LET CELLAR GO TO ANYONE ELSE.

BRITISH FOREIGN OFFICE
SOURCE: NEW YORK CITY

CLASSIFICATION: MAXIMUM SECURITY, FOREIGN OFFICE, RATE ONE

DEFINE ALL COSTS, PLEASE. DOES THIS INCLUDE RISKING EXPOSURE,
USE OF FRIENDLY ASSISTANCE, FORCE, WHAT? PREVIOUS MESSAGE CON-
TRADICTORY.

NEW YORK
SOURCE: FOREIGN OFFICE—LONDON

CLASSIFICATION: MAXIMUM SECURITY, FOREIGN OFFICE, RATE ONE

REPEAT AS GIVEN TO FOREIGN OFFICE: OBTAIN CELLAR AT ALL COSTS,
AVOID EXPOSURE AT ALL COSTS. SORRY, COULD NOT GET ONE OR THE
OTHER AS PRIORITY.

"I think five is a bit much for me," said the man.

They met in Central Park. The wind played uncomfortably through
the man's hair. Vern Andrews suspected the man rarely went without
his bowler. They sat on a park bench looking at a stone bridge over
which joggers puffed and lovers strolled and a vendor with a pink wagon
sold large salty pretzels and peanuts.

"All right, let's try six," said Vern, cracking open a peanut. The
man was trying to dicker, and he really didn't know how. If he expected
Vern to come back and ask how much would be all right, he had to be
a total stranger to business.

"Do you really want to sell it?"

"Course," said Vern.

"I'm trying to establish a price you're going to live with. I wish to
buy your piece, but I gather if I say ten you say eleven and so on. So
what is your real price?"

"Six," said Vern.

"I'll give you four."

"Hell, I got it sold already. Don't bother bidding," said Vern.

The man jumped up from the bench.

"Wait. Wait a minute. You didn't say you had it sold. I'm bidding
on it."

"I've got a six million bid and I'm going to sell it this afternoon. I just can't wait any longer. Bye," said Vern and the man actually ran after him.

He actually followed him down several blocks, and Vern just kept tightening the screws, and with every demand that was met, Vern kept adding on a condition. It was like running through an open field. Everything he asked was met. So he kept pushing.

And to excavate the absolute ultimate, the final offer, he stopped in the middle of one of those crowded side streets of New York City, where cars were parked three deep, only barely distinguishable from the slow traffic, and said to the man, now red-faced and on the verge of frothing: "I not only want my price. If I don't have it in a half an hour, that baby is gone and sold, and good-bye."

"You can't do that," said the man.

"Good-bye," said Vern. He was standing in front of an alley. And, hysterical, the man went at him.

Claire Andrews wondered why Dad was knocking instead of using his key, when she answered the door and saw a policeman who asked her who she was and then told her father was dead.

At first she thought he had told her that Dad was dead, and she asked him to say that again. And he told her that her father had been stabbed to death in an alley off Fifth Avenue, and would she identify the body.

"No," said Claire. She had been in the midst of reading a book and Dad was expected back any minute. And now someone was saying Dad's body had been found in an alley.

"No," she screamed. The policeman and a policewoman stood there in the doorway, repeating this, and no matter how angry she got, they refused to admit they had made a mistake. She hated their telling such a horrible lie, and only when they told her they had already been in contact with people in Carney who had offered to fly to New York to identify the body did she understand that they really meant Dad was dead. It was not a mistake. She apologized for being rude to them, and they kept saying she had done nothing wrong.

Dad had been stabbed to death. His pockets had been turned out, indicating he had been robbed, and yet, the killer or killers had left his wallet and, strangely, his expensive watch and a good deal of cash. Did Miss Andrews feel capable of identifying the body.

If not, there were others in Carney who could do it. She could get a sedative, and perhaps find someone to take her home.

"No," Claire heard herself say. "He's my father. I'm his daughter. I'll take him home."

Was she really saying that? Did she know what it meant? Was she really going to go to a morgue and see Dad, and take him home by herself? She didn't even go out in this city alone. She never traveled alone except driving to Columbus or around Carney.

But she knew the world couldn't do anything worse to her now. There was nothing out there to harm her now. The harm had been done.

And maybe they had made a mistake about Dad, and then he would be alive, and seeing him alive, she would cry and tell him the horror she was going through now.

She grabbed any dress and put on a coat and made sure her hair was combed because that was what she was supposed to do and if she combed her hair, it would be that much time before she would know whether Dad was really dead.

And then there was nothing else to do but go with the police to a large building that was a morgue, and there in a room that wasn't as cold as people said morgues were was Dad, on a pull-out shelf with his face so twisted in pain she thought it didn't look like him, that maybe it wasn't him. But it was.

And then she cried, and people were giving her a sedative and telling her there were folks back in Carney who would come out for her. They had been in touch with her hometown.

"No. I don't want to leave him here. He's got family, you know. We're from Ohio. People love him, you know. I'm taking him home now. We're going home."

And then she was on the plane going home, and someone, not Dad, of course, sat down next to her. The very strangeness of the person told her Dad would never be there again beside her, going somewhere, seeing the world. And when the person asked her if anything were wrong, she found herself saying "nothing" and turning away into her own tears, because if she started to tell anyone about Dad, she would come apart. There would be nothing left of her. There was nothing left of her, she knew. It was just that if she didn't talk about it, she could keep that nothing together until she got home.

Mother and Bob Truet met her at the airport, saying they would take over, telling her how brave she was. But she wasn't brave. She just didn't know what else to do.

They drove her from the Columbus airport back to Carney, with the black hearse following along the autumn roads that she had once traveled with Dad and that he was now going home on.

The large white Victorian house with the great wrapping porch on

Maple Hill was not the same when she got there. It was home without Dad. The whole house without him. Every room was without him and something he had done or said in that room. Every moment was without him.

He was buried in the McCafferty lot just outside town, and there, finally, Mother cried with her.

Bob Truet, who owned the *Carney Daily News*, could assure them that his reporters wouldn't bother them, but he could do nothing about the Columbus papers. He sent over an assistant to help them handle the outside press because the New York murder of the wealthiest man in Carney was a big story in the state.

Ralph Caswell, the funeral director, brought something over to the house that the police had missed in New York City. Inside Dad's sock was a key. It was an old army trick for keeping valuables, Mr. Caswell explained. He did not say what he told Frank Broyles, the police chief, or Bob Truet, that the trick was used when soldiers wanted to protect something while visiting places where they took off their pants.

At first, Claire thought the key might have been to their Waldorf suite, but it wasn't. Those keys were labeled. This key had only a number.

A New Yorker called to give his condolences. His name was Geoffrey Battissen and he sounded like a flagrant homosexual. He really wasn't interested in condolences, of course.

"Your father and I were working on a business arrangement, and while I know how painful it must be to think about such things, I know he was most interested in pursuing the sale of an item I was brokering for him."

"Yes," said Claire. She didn't know how much she should tell him. She didn't know if she should let him know how little she knew of what Dad was doing.

"We were about to conclude our business when the unfortunate event happened," said the New York art dealer. "If I didn't love this city, I would leave. It is so dangerous. The nicest people get killed in this random violence for no reason. It's awful."

"Yes," said Claire.

"I would like to make the sale, at your convenience of course."

"Then go ahead. Bring me back an offer."

"I need you. Your father kept the piece in a safety deposit box. He kept the key."

Looking at the yard where the golden leaves had covered the tulip beds, and where the white lawn furniture was still out waiting for Jed the handyman to put it back into the garage until spring, Claire wondered why Dad had hidden that key. Her hesitation carried all the way to New York.

"I am Geoffrey Battissen of the Battissen Galleries in New York. I am on Fifth Avenue. Please do come in to my gallery and let me show you that your concerns are unfounded. I know how tragic your father's loss is. I am aware of the circumstances. I don't wish to appear especially cruel, my dear, but the random senseless violence that took Vern's life is unfortunately most commonplace in our city. We New Yorkers transcend it if we are to survive. That is the truth. You may contact me whenever you wish. I will be here as Battissen Galleries has been here on Fifth Avenue for twenty-two years. You have my deepest sympathies."

Claire had the key, and Dad was not here to finish what he had started. She decided to go to New York City and do this last thing that Dad wanted done. Everywhere was painful. New York didn't matter anymore.

"Claire, we have lawyers to do those sort of things," said her mother, Lenore McCafferty, a statuesque woman of high cheekbones, soft brown hair, and dark eyes that seemed young for middle age.

"What else am I going to do? Attend the garden club? Shop? Play tennis? Dad's dead. He's dead. He did everything. I never did anything. I'm going to do something, Mother. And I'm going to do it now."

"Do you think you should, in the state you're in?"

"It's the only state I would go to New York City in. Yes."

"I'm grieving, too, dear," said her mother, and Claire was furious at that and didn't know why.

Bob Truet came over offering to go with her to New York. Mother had obviously phoned him.

"Bob, thank you, no. Please," she said.

"I have contacts in New York. I can help."

"Yes, I know, Bob. Please." She didn't want to be angry with him. He was older by four years. She had known him since high school, when he had come back from college to take her to the senior prom, and everyone thought they were going to be married—the local newspaper to the local fortune. Everyone thought it would have been right, including her. Except when she compared Bob Truet, decent Bob Truet, to Dad, he just seemed so much like a boy. He was good-looking, too. Clean features, brown hair, and soft brown eyes, jogger, tennis player, golfer, publisher of the *Carney Daily News* and a boy with his daddy's money and his daddy's paper, and Claire just thought she could do better. There had to be better. Even though he was so damned nice, so damned nice all the time.

"I'll be in New York as briefly as possible," she told him. "I'm just going to sell something and be back."

"I'm here for you. I want you to know that. I'll always be here for you."

She kissed him on the cheek, thanked him for being so supportive, and left for New York City alone in a gray suit with a simple pearl brooch her grandmother had given her. The suit was the most businesslike thing she had.

New York was every bit as dirty and harsh as she remembered it, cold and drizzly. The Battissen Galleries seemed quite impressive, with a window from floor to ceiling and elegant benches and lighting throughout.

Mr. Battissen himself seemed suitably high art, and his somewhat officious and delicately precise manner reassured Claire that business would be done with the least amount of unpleasantness.

Apparently, Mr. Battissen knew where the bank vault was and that too was reassuring. Blake Comstock, Dad's lawyer, had said Dad's affairs were so tangled at this point because of heavy borrowing that he couldn't imagine what Vern Andrews might be selling or which New York bank. And of course Mother didn't know. She kept her business affairs separate with McCafferty lawyers. What made this even more curious was that Dad was selling this thing through an art dealer. She knew Dad never dealt in art. He only bought paintings when she liked them.

Geoffrey Battissen taxied them to a bank on Madison Avenue and introduced her to an officer, explaining that Claire was an heir of the late Mr. Andrews and how the bank could get verification of Miss Andrews's right to access. It took forty minutes for both Carney banks to verify Claire's identity and rights to access. It was also made easier by the fact that Claire had possession of the key.

Inside the vault, Mr. Battissen went to the box to help her.

"It's too heavy for a woman, alone," he said.

They both grunted getting it to the table. And she helped him lift a heavy burlap sack out of the box, and set it upright. As soon as she started to pull down the rough cloth she saw a gold bowl on top and knew what it was. It was Lucky.

The last time she'd seen it had been twenty years ago, just after Dad had had his first heart attack. He had taken her down to the cold cellar where the family stored potatoes and squash in the old-fashioned way above a packed dirt floor. He had dug into the dirt himself and hauled out this very burlap sack and then showed her this magnificent big gold thing with the shiny stones.

"You're a big girl now. And I want to share a big girl's secret with you. No one else in the entire world knows this secret," he had said.

"Not even Mommy?"

"No one else, honey. This is mine. It's very valuable. No one knows it's here but you and me. If anything should ever happen to me, remember where this is. It's ours. Yours and mine. But you must never ever tell anyone about it. All right? Just keep it. It's lucky. I call her Lucky."

"Why do you keep her here?"

"Cause I don't want anyone to steal her. She's special."

"Could you lock her in the biggest bank possible?" Claire had asked.

"I want to keep her near me, not in some vault somewhere. I know she is in the safest bank in the world, because no one knows where she is but me, and now you. So that's what makes it such a big promise. You're my locks."

It was the biggest promise she had made to that point in her life, and she treasured it. She understood later that he had told her this because he thought he might die, and he didn't want Lucky accidentally sold with the house or never discovered at all. Funny, she had forgotten about it at his death, just the time she should have remembered.

"It's an elegant saltcellar," said Mr. Battissen. "But of course it was never used as that."

"How do you know?"

"Obvious. Look at the bowl on top. This is gold. Salt will pockmark gold. Your great saltcellars will never be used, rather displayed such as this. Vern and I were certain of a sale. It's certainly special in its environment, don't you think?" said Mr. Battissen, putting the empty drawer back into the wall of steel doors. It reminded Claire of the morgue shelf. She didn't know what he meant by "special in its environment."

"I see. Well, I'm not really sure I want to sell it. You see, it was Dad's special property, and I think I'd like to keep it now."

"Oh, we can't do that. We have a sale. We have a commitment— your father made it."

"I don't know, really. I don't want to sell it."

"But it's sold. Your father already sold it. Now all that remains is delivery and money transfer. We can't back out now. And truthfully, with what I know of Vern, I am sure he would not want to change things now. This was the last decision he made."

Claire looked at the big red stone with the carving. It had looked so much larger back in Carney. Everything was larger to a small girl.

"All right," she said softly. It was what Dad had wanted.

He gave her a receipt on Battissen Galleries stationery before they left the vault, and outside he said that he would have the sale completed shortly and that he wouldn't need her for a few hours.

"These things are best done when buyer and seller are separate. It is a discreet business," he said with such consummate assurance that Claire thought it would be improper to disagree.

"Go out to a very good restaurant. You deserve it this day, and treat yourself to the very best meal you can buy. When you meet me at the Battissen Galleries, everything will have been completed. Your father would be happy with the way this is turning out."

Claire chose the closest restaurant with tablecloths. She didn't enjoy the meal. She sat by the kitchen and had a hard time getting a waiter. Dad would have been furious at this treatment, but all she wanted was to get out. This only reminded her that Dad was no longer here, and she had had enough of that already. She didn't eat. The waiter, who had not put her at this table, asked her if there was anything wrong with her meal, and she said no.

"Ah, you have lost a lover," said the waiter.

"No . . . Yes. I guess, yes. Yes, I have," said Claire.

"There will be others for a beautiful young woman."

"Not like him," she said.

"It always feels like that," said the waiter. "When you come back again, and you bring someone, I will see to it that we make up for what you have passed by today."

"I won't be coming back. I'm leaving the city tonight."

"You must come back. We owe special service."

"Thank you, but I think I will go to any city in the world but this one. Not this one. Not for a long time at least."

At the gallery, Mr. Battissen had her check ready. It was all so smooth and elegant, she felt almost embarrassed to look at the numbers on the check. It seemed too crude for a place so fine. The check was from Battissen Galleries but it was wrong.

"This is for thirty thousand dollars," she said.

"As you know, one never gets what one wants on a sale one wants to conclude quickly. Yet we at Battissen Galleries feel secure in this price. And your father would have been pleased. It was the upper-limit figure your father thought we could get."

"Dad wouldn't come to New York City for a week to make thirty thousand dollars. He was involved in a big deal. He spent more than that on his cars."

"That's all we received, minus of course my commission, which was five thousand dollars. I think I deserved that at least for finding a buyer."

"He never would sell it for that. I can't take that. I'll take the saltcellar back. I'll take it home."

"It's gone."

"I didn't sell it. I never sold it to you. I have your receipt that you took it. But I never authorized a sale for that price. You've got to get it back. Who did you sell it to? I'll see him. I'm not taking this money."

"This isn't how we do business at Battissen."

"You're telling me you don't know who you sell things to, is that it? Is that what you're telling me, Mr. Battissen?"

"I am telling you your father entrusted us with this sale and we completed it."

"Maybe the police would like to know about what goes on here."

"Fine. We have been here for twenty-two years, and we certainly would be most happy to talk to the police if you wish," said Mr. Battissen, snatching back the check before Claire could get a hand on it. She couldn't believe he had done that.

"I have your receipt. I have your signature," she said.

"Excuse me," said Mr. Battissen, fanning imaginary dust off his mocha suit, "but I don't like this sort of display. I wouldn't give you a Battissen check at this moment. I don't want anything more to do with you than I have to. I don't even want my commission. When you calm down I would be happy to give you thirty-five thousand dollars in cash for your receipt that really doesn't explain anything. It's either that or nothing. It's that clear."

"Maybe you think you're dealing with some New Yorker for whom everything has a price, but you're not, Mr. Battissen. That was my father's cellar, and I'm not giving it up."

"I have lived twenty-two years in the art business, my good girl, and I am tough too, so let's not get into a cat fight."

"If there is one thing that isn't over, it's this. I wouldn't sell you this receipt for a half million dollars. I'm going to get back that saltcellar and I am going to make you pay for this."

Mr. Battissen seemed so content in his mocha suit, like a little bundle of pudding, that Claire wanted to scratch his eyes out. Of course, she thought, he probably would win a scratching fight.

She knew something he didn't. She knew she was never going to let him get away with this. She didn't know where she was going to sleep that night. She didn't know the full range of things she would do, but she was an Andrews and they didn't give up on things like this. She could outwait Dad, and Dad was the toughest man in Carney, everyone said.

"I am going to the police," said Claire.

"Please do," said Mr. Battissen, and because he seemed so sure of himself, she yelled it while going out of the gallery. Unfortunately, only his redheaded assistant was there at the time.

Police headquarters was a skyscraper, One Police Plaza, and it was so big it had its own zip code. It probably had more people than Carney, she thought. They checked her bag and checked her body with a metal detector in a line at a desk. It was a gloomy building, and the fraud

[27]

squad was located in a large, barn-sized office. A good-looking young man with black curly hair, a bit too hoodlumish for Claire's taste, came up to her and asked her what her problem was.

He handed her a pamphlet with the seven most common fraud crimes in the city and asked her to read it and then tell him which one was most like the one that fit the crime perpetrated against her.

His name was Detective Arthur Modelstein.

"I am sure, Detective Modelstein, that even in a city as big as New York this crime has got to be unique."

"Yeah, well they all are, you know. If it happens to you, it's special. Match it up as close as you can, okay?" said Detective Modelstein.

"I'd like to just tell you about it. I can express myself."

"It's not you, lady. These things kind of give us a framework, so you don't have to go wandering around for an hour. Ninety percent of all the fraud crimes are right there. And the other ten percent are partly there. Okay?"

"I have been swindled by a supposedly legitimate businessman. Is that routine? Is it normal to be robbed by a supposedly high-class merchant?"

"Hey, those are the best kind," said the detective. Claire could have sworn he was glancing down her blouse.

III

The foreign officer entered Buckingham Palace through the small arches of the East Gate. A Union Jack flew from the second floor. The Queen was in residence. He did not use the Privy Purse entrance with the room containing the guest book, thus avoiding the waiting rooms. He was not going to wait.

He was not visiting. He had been summoned to report what had happened in New York City. His name was Jenkins, and he was the one who had received the contradictory messages from Buckingham Palace and relayed them to New York. A servant led him up a grand staircase to a long passageway without windows. A curving skylight almost two stories high gave an eerie white light to the long journey of the two lone men down the polished marble floor. Their feet beat with the sound of timpani.

They walked past yards and yards of large paintings in massive gilt frames, neither of them bothering to look up at all the outsized heroism and grandeur.

At the end of the corridor, Jenkins was brought into a large drawing room done in cream white, gold, and crimson. The doors were shut behind him, and he was alone. Large pale drapes shielded the room from what the foreign officer judged were the gallery gardens. He didn't sit.

But it was not Her Majesty who entered. It was her secretary, Sir Anthony Witt-Dawlings, who had been dealing with the Foreign Office in this matter on Her Majesty's behalf. He was in his late fifties, and although his face was fleshy and loose, the folds seemed to hang with furious gravity.

"There have been some serious problems with Her Majesty's request. We're going to need the help of the Americans," said Jenkins.

"No. Absolutely not," said Witt-Dawlings.

"An American national has been killed in America."

"That's not our problem. That's not our main concern."

"We care very much. America is our most important ally."

"Then they'll have to understand."

"Sir, how can we help them understand if the Foreign Office doesn't understand itself? We don't understand. What could be so important about a jeweled piece to disharmonize our relationship with the Americans? This is especially puzzling since Her Majesty has already the largest private and public jewelry collection in the world, and according to someone in our office, he believes she already has a similar cellar at Windsor, one no one to his knowledge even bothers to look at."

"You were not supposed to discuss this with anyone," said Her Majesty's secretary.

"The confusing and contradictory nature of your instructions, your insistence on withholding information to protect Her Majesty, has led to this difficulty. We had to withdraw our special man from America, with the deepest hopes and expectations that this incident will never be noticed. We are all holding our breath."

"You just abandoned the cellar? You didn't get it?"

"We are responsible for our international relations."

"Disaster," said Anthony Witt-Dawlings. "Bloody disaster. How could you do that? With men like you, no wonder England struggles on her knees. How dare you? How could you?"

Desk Officer Jenkins saw Witt-Dawlings redden with rage. Witt-Dawlings was of a type more royal than the Queen, more regimental than the Guards, the sort of Eton graduate who thought the United Kingdom was still the major player in the world. Sir Anthony enjoyed some quite diluted royal blood, and would get his peerage at the end of his service, and would be sure that he had performed some vital service to his nation and his crown by exaggerating the importance of an appointment calendar for Her Majesty.

But Witt-Dawlings lived in a world that was no more, a little world of palaces and parades, while outside there were riots in the streets, bobbies being shot, a secret service so riddled with foreign agents no reasonable ally would trust it, an army that had all it could do to beat Argentina, and an industrial base that had seen its last dominance in the age of coal and steam.

Sir Anthony could rage at the Foreign Office, but unless the Crown could somehow enlist the support of the Prime Minister in this affair his angry noise would mean no more than the tunes of a parade that had passed forty years before.

"We are removing you from this . . . this quest. We will call upon other services more skilled and more loyal to serve Great Britain in her desperate hours."

"Very good, sir," said Desk Officer Jenkins, and he left Buckingham Palace the way he had entered, back down the long corridor with the footstep-echoing marble walkway. This time he glanced at the portraits, many of them royals, some mounted on horseback, all so terribly important in the days they were painted. He didn't even know the names of many of them, but was sure the likes of Sir Anthony Witt-Dawlings had memorized them all in first form.

Her hair was neat. That's what Artie Modelstein noticed first. She had that neat sort of way about her. A sharp light gray suit with a peach-colored silk shirt that opened never enough revealed the upper part of a slightly freckled chest, which unfortunately was encased in a bra. Her face had those clean magazine sort of features, where everything was right, naturally right. Nothing dramatic. Small upturned nose, not that upturned. Blue eyes, not washed out, and an even open jaw. He wondered what it all would look like in excruciating orgasm. He wondered if she had orgasms.

The voice, of course, carried a twang that could saw brick. She was from the midwest somewhere. She did not have a place to stay that night.

These were the things ascertained by Detective Sergeant Arthur Modelstein, Frauds/Jewels, as the pretty lady from the midwest worked on matching her fraud with the list. Another thing to be noted from a glance at the calf of the leg was that she probably had an exceptional body.

Her name was Claire Andrews and she had a number three, a switch as it was called, whereby one con man promises a lot of money but he needs security, and then he never returns with the security.

"Where did it happen?" asked Artie, who now only had to fill in a few blanks on his report. She sat beside his desk in the bank of Fraud desks, a proper lady in a paper-cluttered squadroom with unwashed walls and a sense of disordered grayness.

"It happened at two places. It happened at the bank—"

"Name . . ."

"The International Bank of New York, I think."

"Branch?"

"Madison and Fiftieth."

"And how much did you withdraw from the bank?"

"It wasn't cash. It was a very, very valuable cellar."

"What, the cellar? You dug it up, or what?"

"No, a saltcellar."

"A cellar full of salt?" Detective Modelstein lifted his hands from the keys of his manual typewriter and made a very New York sort of shrug. He was a handsome man with a strong nose and full lips and dark brown eyes that spoke of laughter in bedrooms and places Claire would not want to go but might love to hear about.

"No. They were fancy, very fancy holders of salt. I imagine they were put on the tables where important people ate."

"I think I heard of them," said Detective Modelstein.

"Benvenuto Cellini sculpted a fancy one in Paris, I read somewhere, but I don't know what it looked like. My father's was two and a half to three feet tall."

"How much was it worth?" asked Detective Modelstein, turning the complaint form a notch on his typewriter to get the amount square underneath the keys.

"I couldn't imagine my father personally coming into New York to sell it for less than a million dollars. A million dollars. This man, Geoffrey Battissen, tried to give me a check for thirty thousand dollars. My father would never, never have sold it for that. I'm not trying to impress you but . . ."

Detective Modelstein made sure he had room for six zeroes, typed in the number, and then interrupted her.

"Where does your father fit in? What's he doing? Why were you dealing this thing and not him?"

"He's dead," said Clare quickly, and she almost got to another sentence. But her body became rigid and the next word stuck in her mouth, and tears cascaded down her clean white cheeks, and Detective Modelstein couldn't find the tissues fast enough. He slapped his pockets, rummaged through his desk, looked on other desks, and almost tore the complaint out of the typewriter to soak up the tears. He had stepped in it. He had stepped into her tragedy, and now it was flooding him, and he felt awful. He knew he was not supposed to get involved emotionally because there was just too much tragedy in a career for a cop to handle emotionally. But this one had come suddenly out of left field. He was in the midst of a routine report before he realized he was in one of those things.

The young woman refused to reach for a tissue herself, just stayed there with her mouth open, sobbing, and he had done it. He had triggered it all over himself.

And if Detective Modelstein tried to avoid anything in his life, it was human pain. This was partly how he had gotten into Frauds/Jewels. There were, of course, accidents in his service that he could not avoid, like the time he had been nearby a plane crash at Kennedy, and the central dispatcher had located his car and ordered it to the scene. He had been temporarily put in charge of the detail handling grief-stricken relatives and the few survivors, making sure no one got in the way of the ambulances and ground crews. He was depressed for weeks. He knew then that if they ever transferred him to Homicide, he would quit. His older sister had said he never should have been a policeman in the first place.

"You joined because it was the easiest damned thing to do. You're always taking the easy course, Artie, and you'll pay for it. In the end, everyone pays for it," his older sister had said. If Esther were here, she would be lecturing this poor girl on getting her just deserts for not putting the affair into the hands of the proper people, for taking shortcuts by doing it herself. There were no random events in his older sister's life, only laziness or cupidity punished by God, and that not strongly enough.

When the young lady from Ohio could talk again, she explained that her father had died, she believed, trying to set her up for life. Detective Modelstein thought this was beautiful. He felt uneasy having thoughts about her body. But not that uneasy. He tried to be gentle. Other detectives had walked by the sobbing. He never could.

"Did his killing have anything to do with this, do you think? Did anyone think?" he asked.

She shook her head. Her eyes were red now.

"It was one of those accidents. It was a mugging. A stabbing. Someone or some boys pushed him into an alley and stabbed him. Senseless. They didn't even get all the money."

"These things happen. No one knows why. Senseless," said Detective Modelstein. He was glad to see she had found a handkerchief.

The man who had pulled the swindle, he found out, was Geoffrey Battissen, who owned a gallery on pricey Fifth Avenue. She had given up this cellar for a receipt that she showed with righteous justification. All it said was that Geoffrey Battissen had received a gold piece.

"Anything else you have?" he asked. "Is that it?"

"That's it. That's his signature. I saw him sign it."

Detective Modelstein made sure the tissues were close before he told her what her situation was.

"Miss Andrews," said Detective Modelstein, "when you let Battissen take that cellar, you as much as gave it to him."

"What about my receipt? He gave me a receipt."

"Even if it said 'saltcellar with jewels,' that wouldn't be a receipt. You want to see a receipt, a real one? It has the gem prints. It has size and weight and grade. That's a receipt. You got a piece of paper."

"I have his signature. I have my testimony. I can at least damage his reputation. He said he has been on Fifth Avenue for twenty-two years. I imagine that requires a degree of trust, Detective Modelstein. Let's see how he feels about his reputation and a long court suit." Claire pushed herself forward, her eyes wide, her nostrils flaring.

"I'm sorry. You're not someone who can hurt him. I'm sorry. If you had a lot of friends who bought art in that crowd, you might hurt him."

"You mean to say, Detective Modelstein, that because I am from Carney, Ohio, and because I trusted him, because I was defenseless, he is getting away with this?"

Detective Modelstein didn't answer. And he had a hard time looking into the clear blue of those eyes, the ones demanding an answer he was not giving.

"No," said the young lady. It was clear. It was sharp. It did not get modified, but hung there, sure as sunrise and just as bright. She would not accept this.

"I don't know what we can do," said the detective.

"You can arrest him. I am willing to swear out a complaint."

"I have to have evidence."

"You're a policeman, aren't you? You're supposed to get evidence. Search his place. Don't you have people who tell you if hot goods are for sale?"

"What do you think I'm gonna find?"

"You don't know if you don't look, do you?"

"Look, that cellar doesn't exist anymore. They melt down the gold first thing. They'd market the jewels anywhere. Hell, they don't even have to cut the gems again. Lady, you don't have a description."

"The ruby was like a goose egg," said Claire Andrews very firmly to the New York detective.

"Yeah. Okay. I'm sorry, lady, that's not a description. It isn't."

"I could identify it if I saw it again. It was carved. I saw the head of Christ on it. I remember that from the basement when I was a child. And I remember the blue stone too. Daddy said it was a man with a spear and it was a funny spear 'cause it had three prongs."

"Okay, a red stone and a blue stone. With pictures. Wonderful.

You don't even know if they're really gems. That guy could come back with colored glass and you couldn't prove it wasn't yours. Please already."

"The spear was a trident. That's what three prongs are. A trident. Put that in the description. I am pressing charges, Officer Modelstein."

"And the proof that you own it?"

"It's ours."

"Okay. Get the bill of sale, and maybe that's got the gem prints and we maybe got something to begin with. Not much, but better than that," said Artie, nodding to the receipt from Battissen Galleries on clean gray dramatic paper.

"We have had it for years. It's my father's lucky piece."

"But what about the bill of sale?"

"I don't know of one. Maybe he had it. I don't know where he kept it. I suspect he may not have had one," said Claire. "He kept it in our basement at home. It was a personal possession."

"In the basement?" asked Detective Modelstein. If she weren't so firm in her conviction, and so fragile, he would have laughed.

"Yes, that's where he kept it."

"And he didn't come here to some big auction house to sell it but to this guy Battissen who I never heard of."

"He had to be discreet for business reasons."

"Well, you know you love him, and I'm sure your father's honest and you're sure your father's honest, but some people might think that a thing he kept in the basement all his life and then tried to sell so quietly might not be his in the first place."

"Of course it's his."

"Yeah, but you got to have proof it's yours; otherwise, if you press a criminal complaint against someone, you might run into problems that really come down on your head hard. Real hard. Do you know what I mean?"

"It was my father's and I want it back."

"You want to press charges, press charges," said Modelstein. "But I'd like to see some proof of ownership."

"My father was a hard businessman, but an honest one. Do you think in Carney, Ohio, people would let my father get away with even the slightest hint of shadiness? We have a wrong side of the tracks in Carney, and he came up from that, and no one, least of all—"

Modelstein put his hands over his ears. When she stopped grinding at his head, he said: "Okay. Okay. It's your business. You're pressing charges. Charges being pressed." He typed up the report as she talked on about her father and Carney, more information than he wanted to know about any place west of Bayonne, New Jersey, and east of California. She said it was important to her that Detective Modelstein understand who her father was, because then he would know that he earned everything he ever had in his life. Nothing ever came easy for him. And he wouldn't steal just because so many people would be happy to see him get caught. Carney was like that.

For a moment Artie Modelstein thought Carney, Ohio, was like his sister Esther.

"Look, I never accused him of anything. I don't even want to accuse this guy Battissen," said Artie. "What's your value on the piece?"

"Say a million and a half dollars as of now."

"A million and a half," said Modelstein, typing it into the form. "And it's a saltcellar, right?"

"I don't know for sure," said Claire.

"You don't know for sure."

"I thought it was. Geoffrey Battissen said it was. He seems to be an expert on them."

"So we will call it a large gold piece with jewels?"

"All right. We'll do that," said Claire Andrews, burning.

Detective Modelstein finished the report and handed her a statement to sign.

Claire poised the ballpoint pen over the form and looked to the darkly handsome detective. He couldn't be right about Geoffrey Battissen just getting away with things. Maybe being raised in New York had dulled him to a sense of justice. Maybe he didn't understand how determined she was.

She must have waited with the pen a long time because Detective Modelstein began talking to her about how the city was cruel at times, and how it seemed there was no justice in the world, but he knew that the loss of her father had to be greater than any financial loss, that perhaps it was her father's death that was really motivating these charges. He wasn't a psychologist, he admitted. But he did know the city and did know jewel fraud, and maybe it was so that her father had acted in only the best traditions, but it wouldn't appear that way to the public necessarily. They didn't know her father. He didn't know her father.

"What are you saying?"

"If I were offered some money, even though it wasn't what I wanted, or even if it wasn't fair, more importantly, I'd take it if I didn't have a chance of getting anything else."

"Take the money?"

"I'm a cop. I can't give advice."

"You're saying I don't have a chance."

"Listen, you come from a nice town. It's clean. People care what other people do. You're somebody there. I've seen a town like that once. Everybody was nice. What do you need this for? See if you can get a check from the guy. Don't carry cash. And go home. Thirty-five grand was his nuisance payoff, you said. If he gives you any trouble with that, call me. I think we can get you your money."

"Make a deal?"

"Go home. Banging your head against a wall doesn't move a wall. It gets your brains hurt."

Detective Arthur Modelstein saw the little half-smile on the pretty lady's face. He was sure maniacs had just that sort of smile before they shot up a restaurant full of strangers.

She signed the complaint.

"I think that says it all," she said. "I don't make deals with criminals and this is what I learned from my father."

Artie took the complaint and filed it with the computer system. In the old days it was called entering something on a blotter. Now it was faster. There would be a warning sent to major jewelers, which would be useless because even if they got any of the stones, there wasn't a description that would hold up in any court of law. In fact, the claim of a swindle of a million and a half dollars would probably not even get a paragraph in any New York newspaper. It could open Claire Andrews up to a charge of slander, but she did have her receipt. If she got a civil lawyer, the whole thing might end up, after some hefty fees, with Battissen settling out of court for no more than the nuisance money he was going to pay her to begin with.

The only people who would get excited about this would be those in her hometown, where people were going to start asking questions about what her father was doing all those years keeping secret a big gold thing worth over a million dollars.

The pretty lady from Carney, Ohio, had taken a big swing at the forces of injustice, which would probably deck only her father's reputation.

"All right, what happens now?" she asked.

"Now I get supper. I eat, you know."

"Aren't you going to arrest Mr. Battissen?"

"I got enough to talk to him. Not to arrest him. If I had enough to arrest him, he would have offered you more. Everybody knows what's goin' on here but you."

"But if you get a search warrant you can move now."

"I don't have enough to get a search warrant. That's what I been tellin' ya. Besides, it ain't there. It ain't anywhere anymore. If it did have those gems, it was broken down into separate stones before you finished that fancy meal he sent you out on. That gold is something else now. You been had. It's what I'm tellin' ya."

"That's horrible."

"Right," screamed Artie.

"Don't yell," said Claire.

Artie Modelstein gave up. He engineered his chair away from her and rose from his desk.

"I will be back here in the morning. I am going to eat," he said.

She came to supper with him.

She didn't know where else to go. She didn't want to leave things like this, just with a report going into a computer. She was pretty enough to get glances at Farnies restaurant, two blocks from Artie's Nineteenth Street apartment (which contained his bedroom). He offered to buy her supper. She said she wasn't hungry and then absentmindedly picked from his plate.

She talked on about her father and what he meant in Carney, someone who had risen from a very wrong section of the town to the top of it. She was beautiful but Artie sensed she was not truly aware of this. He also sensed she might be crazy, and crazy could outdo beautiful anyday. He had enough crazy in his life. Life was crazy. The purpose of life was to avoid grief. He had become a policeman in a futile effort to avoid personal grief. Granted, that had not been too successful, but it was better than other things.

Artie was six foot two and had been an all-city linebacker for DeWitt Clinton High School in the Bronx. He had gotten a scholarship to a Texas university with a promise that they would put him through law school. It seemed a lot easier than struggling for grades, and he had plans on cramming for the bar with special help later. He had plotted a course with the least amount of uncertainty and difficulty, financial and academic.

And then he got down to freshman football camp, and the two-a-day drills, and the special sweat drills to separate the men from the boys. Down in Texas they took football with a seriousness that he was not used to. He walked out on the second day.

"You know, Modelstein," said the linebacker coach, "you got everything it would take to make an all-American except guts. You don't have it here." The linebacker coach had pointed to his chest.

"Right," Artie had said.

The coach had never heard that answer before, especially from someone who was eighteen years old. The coach said that Artie had wasted a scholarship the university could have used on someone who wanted to play ball.

"You don't play football. This is war," said Artie.

"You quit here and you'll quit on everything in your life, Modelstein."

"Fine," said Artie, who had plenty of preparation in staying away from his sister's assaults. This coach was an amateur.

"The thing I like about the Israelis is they got guts. If the likes of you were over there, Modelstein, they'd all be a hind end on a camel."

The implication was clear: the linebacker coach could accept Israeli Jews but not New York ones, which was all right with Artie because he had no intention of staying in Texas, let alone that university. He quit the Texas university, enrolled at City College in New York, found out he could become a policeman and get the NYPD to help pay for his school, which he also quit because he really didn't need a college degree once he got in Frauds/Jewels. He belonged there. He knew the dealers on Forty-seventh Street. He knew the new crowd from Iran. He knew where everyone was and everyone knew where he was, and unless there was some accident, life was good and even modestly challenging. He had taken easily to the jewels. He liked the people. They liked him.

And now this young lady, who reminded him so very much of that linebacker coach in Texas with her talk about not giving up, was pushing herself into his life, specifically into his garlic bread.

She had asked if he minded. He really couldn't say no. It was still very possible that she would wind down, have a drink, come with him down the street to his apartment, and then take off her clothes.

She talked about her childhood, about being protected by her father, and about her natural reluctance to face a city like this alone. She talked of aloneness.

Artie thought of soft blondish pubic hair. Claire talked about how inhospitable New York City was and about how perhaps that was inevitable with a city this size.

Artie thought of running a hand down the silk blouse and what the nipple would feel like when it hardened.

Claire said that people were a lot kinder when you got to know them, that she didn't think they would pass you by in New York City if you passed out on the street, as people said they would.

"No, they'd strip you of your belongings," said Artie. He wondered what she would sound like having an orgasm. Would she be a yeller? Would she groan? Would she complain that she didn't want to? Complaining could be very exciting if they really didn't mean it.

She always kept coming back to her father.

"It doesn't matter what the odds against you are, it matters how you make them work for you, Dad always said. That's why I know we are going to win."

"Uh huh," said Artie, digging into his steak and spaghetti.

"You are only beaten," said Claire, "when you say you're beaten."

[39]

The harsh twangy voice seemed to go with something like that. So would a Texas linebacker coach. To boot, she stressed how retiring she ordinarily was.

"But you are going to get hurt anyway even if you stay in your room and do nothing. You might as well go out and face the worst of it. That's what I learned from Dad's death."

She started sharing his spaghetti.

"You've got to learn from everything. That's what Dad said. You can always learn. His death taught me."

"Can I get you an order of spaghetti?"

"No. I'm not hungry."

"Sure. You ate mine."

"Did I?" said Claire, putting a hand over her mouth. "I am so sorry. Sometimes I just pig out. You've got to let me pay for it."

Artie refused. He had a better idea. Why not get some rich dessert and eat it at his place with some good coffee and brandy? His pad was two blocks away on Nineteenth Street.

Claire looked at her watch.

"Oh my god. I missed my plane. I didn't make a reservation at a hotel. I don't know what to do."

Artie offered his apartment.

"No. Thank you," said Claire. "I'll get a hotel, but I love talking with you. I appreciate your interest. I really couldn't expect caring like this in New York from a policeman."

Artie dismissed it as nothing, but restaurants were not a place to talk about such things. Apartments were better. And he knew a wonderful bakery for dessert.

"You don't have to do that," said Claire.

"No. I want to," said Artie.

"You are really kind," said Claire.

"Nah. I'm not that kind," said Artie.

"You are. You don't know it. I know people. I can tell. You think maybe you're slick and all that, but I know a kind person when I meet one."

Artie bought two large whipped cream—topped pastries even though Claire said she didn't want one. She said she found New York City less frightening with Detective Modelstein. He said she didn't have to feel obliged to go to a hotel that night. She still preferred one.

"Just so that you'll know it's here for you if you should need it," said Artie, hanging up her jacket and getting them both brandies to go with the whipped cream pastry. She sat on the sofa in front of his large color television. That was good. There was space there for him.

Coffee was supposed to be involved in this sort of thing, too, but for Artie two out of three was more than good enough.

With a smooth motion, he emptied an ashtray with lipsticked cigarette butts behind his back and sat down next to her. To discard evidence of another woman was not a lie, but simply removal of something that would lend a bad atmosphere.

Artie was the atmosphere. He moved close. She put a hand on his. Good.

"They may think they're getting away with this. But what they don't know is they're not," said Claire. "What they don't know, and what's going to defeat them in the end, is that we're not giving up. They have not counted on us. They have counted on the normal way business is done. You see, that's our strength. That they would think like you had thought," said Claire.

"Well," said Artie, who wanted to get away from insanity and back to body as smoothly and as quickly as possible.

"Do you think I'm wrong? Say it if you think I'm wrong. I'm not wrong, you know. What are you thinking?"

"I'm thinking you're beautiful," said Artie.

"Thank you. What do you think about our position?"

"Wished it were as attractive as you," said Artie. She thought that was funny. And then the door to the apartment opened and a handsome woman in her twenties with auburn hair, and a face set for combat, entered with her own key.

"Am I interrupting?" she asked.

"No," said Artie.

"He's working on a case with me," said Claire.

"Trudy Gerson, this is Claire Andrews. Claire, Trudy Gerson."

"Artie, we had a date tonight."

"You can still have it. We're just having dessert that he was kind enough to get. It's a complicated case," said Claire.

"Excuse me, miss," said Trudy, her voice barbed with venom. "I've never heard Detective Modelstein carry work one second past quitting time. If he can't eat it or screw it, he is generally not interested in it."

"But that's not so. He has been every bit a gentleman with me. He has restored my faith in the decency of people. I was alone here, and friendless, and he left work hours ago."

"Oh Artie, you're *so* good to the girl," said Trudy.

"It's true," said Artie, cloaking himself in nobility. He knew he couldn't sell that one to Trudy, not with this blonde's good looks.

"Artie, you haven't had a nonsexual thought since you found out you could do more with it than wet your diapers," said Trudy, loosing a final bitter laugh. She threw the keys on the floor and left, slamming the door with all the force of a woman who wished it were closing on the head of Arthur C. Modelstein.

"I hope I haven't damaged your relationship. Were you living to-gether?"

"No. I don't believe in living together. People get on each other's nerves. I believe that everyone is free to do what he or she wants. It makes life easier, you know." He glanced at the door.

He knew it was a nice try, but the evening was really over on two fronts. Trudy was gone, and by vicious circumstance he had been trapped into a posture of decency he had to carry through.

Two hours later they shook hands good night.

"I hope I didn't ruin anything between you and your friend."

"Nah," said Artie. "That's okay. Remember, stay in the cab until you reach the hotel, and you'll be fine."

"You're a dear, Arthur," she said and gave him a quick kiss on the cheek. He washed it off before he went to bed.

In the morning, when normal people were still struggling to adjust to the day, to accept the cold of the morning, to ease eyes to sunlight and the body to the necessary movement of work and remorseless society, when coffee was a labor and juice too cold for a warm tongue nurtured properly in hours of rest and comfort, Arthur C. Modelstein encountered at the front door of his Nineteenth Street apartment a boisterous and happy yellow-haired woman, ready for a touchdown cheer.

"Arthur, I found the way. I found the way we're going to get this criminal and proof of my father's ownership. Everything we want is in here."

"Did you sleep?"

"No. I had trouble with that. But look. This is it," said Claire. Artie stared at the bound notebook, the kind schoolchildren used to use in New York City. The cardboard cover had phony imitation mar-bling on it for a reason so ancient in the school system no one could re-member it.

"How's that gonna do anything?"

"Maybe the trail is faint. Maybe the trail is long. But I am going to record everything. Everything leaves a trail. And if you write it down, and never give up, you'll find that trail."

She opened the book for Artie. He noticed, of course, she had a neat handwriting. Artie would have been surprised if it weren't. There was yesterday's date, and there was the time and place of the cellar exchange, and Geoffrey Battissen's name, and his gallery address, under the title "stolen from the Andrewses this date."

Vindication gleamed in the lady's blue eyes.

"I'm going to find out how and when Dad got it, how and when it came into being. Who sold it to whom, and when. You may not be able to arrest Geoffrey Battissen for a long while, but I am never going to let this go, and that is why we're going to win."

"Well, yeah," said Artie. "Good. I'll let you know everything that happens here. I'm going to stay on this, I promise. I've got a couple of ideas of my own. No guarantees, but I'm with this for you."

"You are decent, Arthur. Don't let anybody tell you otherwise."

"It's my job. What flight do you have? I'll take you to the airport."

"I don't know if I should leave now without things settled."

"I think you shouldn't stay here," said Artie.

"Are you going to speak to Geoffrey Battissen today?"

"Sure," said Artie.

"You didn't say it like you meant it, Arthur."

"I mean it," said Detective Modelstein, noticing that it wasn't even nine A.M. yet and this major promise had been extracted from him.

"Well, if you really mean it, I can go home."

"I mean it," said Artie. "I mean it."

"Good, then I can go home. Honestly, I never really wanted to stay here in the first place," said Claire. "I'm really quite relieved to know I can leave everything in good hands."

"Good hands," said Artie, thinking coffee, thinking chair, thinking, perhaps later in the morning, a cherry danish and coffee with cream, and thinking what price he was going to have to pay Trudy Gerson if he were to make amends.

IV

"If it were not the Queen, Sir Anthony, we would have ended this little talk at the beginning," said the little man in the stuffy car. Word had gone out discreetly to the proper quarters of government that Her Majesty had a serious situation, which needed a special solution, all of the utmost confidentiality and dispatch. No middle level government clerks need apply.

The answer to the crown plea, came in a large black chauffeur-driven car with darkened windows that picked up Witt-Dawlings on a crowded London street corner. The dark-haired little man apparently did not need to verify who Sir Anthony was, nor would he introduce himself.

They rode south of London in aimless circles in the countryside, making peculiar turns and stops and twists without any discernible reason. The chauffeur could not hear their conversation and could only be reached by a little intercom in the back seat. The windows cast a greyish tint over lane and highway. People could not look in. They could also not eavesdrop on this sedan with modern electronics, the dark-haired little man assured Sir Anthony.

"I suppose all this precaution is necessary," said Sir Anthony. The car looked plush on the outside. But the upholstery felt tinny in a way, with severe ribbing that made sitting definitely uncomfortable. The little man smoked a foul pipe.

Sir Anthony coughed.

The man ignored that.

"Would you be so kind as to please open the window?" asked Sir Anthony.

"No," said the little man.

This, nowadays was what defended England at the highest levels of Intelligence, Witt-Dawlings thought.

"Sir Anthony, the precautions correspond to the demands of the Crown. You do not wish Her Majesty in any way to be associated with this. So we did not discuss this anywhere near Buckingham Palace, and picked you up on a street corner. If you don't wish the Crown involved in any way, as I was instructed, then you don't meet at Buckingham Palace or at any other royal residence. It's not complicated. Now, the more you tell us, the better we can help."

"We are looking for something which I do not have the authority to disclose to you at this time."

The little man put the tar-smelling pipe into Sir Anthony's hands.

"There. That's something. If you're not more specific, then I feel our group has done its work. We have given you something."

Sir Anthony put the pipe firmly back into the little man's hands.

"It's not a pipe," he said.

"Is it bigger than a bread box?" asked the man.

"I would appreciate less ridicule, thank you," said Sir Anthony. What could he tell the man? That Her Majesty's first question when informed the Tilbury was lost again, was not whether they could recover it but whether it had become common knowledge the Crown was after it in the first place?

Gratefully, he had told her no. Gratefully, he had been able to tell her that at no time was the Foreign Office informed it was the Tilbury. In fact, he had been forbidden to rely on American help, lest another party even know Britain was looking for a jeweled cellar.

Granted, it was almost inconceivable that despite her most generous willingness to pay any price for the saltcellar, they had not been able to secure it. But that was because middle-level clerks were sent on an errand that needed firmer and more resourceful stuff, he had said.

The Foreign Office had been the wrong choice. Sir Anthony had taken the blame for that, although it had been through the Foreign

Office that the first report of a jeweled saltcellar had come to Buckingham Palace. A wealthy British subject had heard of a great jeweled saltcellar for sale under questionable circumstances in New York City. He believed he might have read something about such a cellar in connection with the crown, but could neither place the cellar nor where he had read about it, this despite an entire afternoon he had spent personally trying to look up such a reference in the great New York Public Library.

On the chance he might have been correct, he notified the embassy in America, which routinely forwarded the information to Buckingham Palace. It was on that day that Sir Anthony Witt-Dawlings became the first nonroyal to learn the real secret of the Tilbury Cellar in four centuries, and then only because he had to know.

From that moment on he had thought of little else, and had twice mentioned to Her Majesty on different occasions that perhaps it was more than coincidence that the Tilbury resurfaced at such a time of despair in England's history.

Now it was lost again, and Sir Anthony had to explain to a cold Intelligence sort, without telling too much, that keeping a secret was possibly even more important than getting the object itself back.

"All right, you cannot tell me what you're looking for, but you want a whole organization to look for it."

"We will tell the person you select, and only him, what he has to know. And that, I am afraid, has to be all," said Witt-Dawling.

"There are many different kinds of people with different talents, and abilities. Do we need an electronics engineer?"

"No," said Sir Anthony.

"Do we need someone daring?"

"Yes."

"Why?"

"Because of the importance of what we're looking for. But even more important, he must be discreet."

"Why not you?"

"If I were younger, I might."

"So we need someone young, possibly athletic."

"Yes, I would say that might be called for."

The little man lit his pipe again. Sir Anthony coughed. The little man inhaled deeply. The whole backseat tasted of rotted tar.

"All right, but let me warn you, in the real world, systems find things, secure things, protect things, get things. One man alone, despite all fairy tales, ancient and modern, has got to be considered severely restricted, possibly even to the point of uselessness. Are you sure it must be one man?"

"That is, I believe, the most certain way to discretion."

"Yes. I agree. Information is at risk in geometric proportion to the number of people who know about it."

"Then one person has to do, preferably one who treasures England and what we are and have been. We want one person alone."

"Ah well," said the little man. "I sense I could be more help if I knew more. I do so feel I am doing the wrong thing for Her Majesty, but if that is what she wants, and you are her secretary and you do know, then I will comply."

"It most certainly is Her Majesty's desire."

"Then I will provide you your lone knight," said the little man, who now that the topic was done, rolled down the windows allowing in cool moist air.

And on hearing the word "knight" Sir Anthony wondered if he somehow hadn't told too much already.

There was a message for Harry Rawson back at the English consulate. The radio operator on the cutter of the sultanate of Banai brought the word to the commander, who said Captain Rawson should be given the message.

The operator folded it over as though he had not read it. These were after all British messages, and he knew it was a bad thing for the British to see others reading their mail. So with an air of someone who had respected privacy, he delivered the message folded, with his eyes straight ahead, his feet stamping on the floor in proper salute, his right hand quivering adjacent to his forehead.

"Sir. Message for you, sir," said the radio operator.

Captain Rawson sat on a lounge chair in front of the main cabin, an Uzi machine gun in his lap. He had not left this door since Ahmadabad in India, and now they were almost a day out into the Arabian Sea.

"What is it, Hamid?" said Rawson, a campaign hat over his eyes.

"It is confidential."

"Read it to me anyhow."

"Sir, I cannot do that, sir. It is for your eyes only."

"Very good," said Rawson, and without taking the hat from his eyes, held out his hand for the message. The Royal Navy had trained Hamid just as it had trained his captain, just as the Royal Air Force had trained the two fighter pilots who made up the Banai Air Force and the British Army had trained the two regiments that made up the Banai Defense Forces.

They had learned their salutes very well, their weapons modestly, and when British officers were about they could be counted on not to run or, if things went the other way, not to pillage and rape. They were mostly bedouins hired by the Sultanate, an old trading family that had moved pearls and slaves across the Arabian Sea for three centuries. Only in this century did anyone think to call the family's city and the surrounding desert a country. Her Majesty's government had always considered Banai vital since it was a good port on the trade routes to western India. When the Empire lost India, the British advisors stayed. The excuse then was oil, even though the world was awash in it. Harry Rawson suspected it was a chance to still play empire.

The sun over the Arabian Sea rose like a single red wound splitting the dark waters from the sky. It would be a scorcher of a day, but it was always a scorcher of a day even though nights could approach freezing. Rawson read the message and then stuffed it under his hat.

The radio operator waited half an hour by the Japanese watch he had been given by the sultan himself, then went to the bridge.

"Captain Rawson is not messaging London," said the operator.

"He will not leave the cabin door," said the commander.

"But it is urgent. He is to contact London immediately about his return. It is an order. It is a secret order. It is a top secret urgent message."

"Captain Rawson does what he does," said the commander, and so another tale of the handsome Captain Rawson made its way to the palace in Banai even before Harry Rawson returned there, how Captain Rawson received a message from his government but ignored it in favor of serving his friend the sultan, how he waited in front of the cabin door with the gun until they were docked and the sultan's women came to claim the girl inside. By this uninterrupted act of visible presence in front of the girl's cabin door, he had publicly assured that whatever virginity the girl had brought from India was delivered to the sultan certifiably intact. And this was added to the tale of what he had already done to protect the girl in India itself from those who sought to capture her and ultimately steal the sultan's throne, to bring down Banai, to change everything everyone had known for so long.

All of these tales reached the throne in Banai along with the fact that Captain Rawson's orderly had packed his bags and all his belongings. Captain Rawson was leaving.

"I'll change that," said Sultan Abdul Al Haj Al Hadir. "They are not taking my Harry away from me."

Hadir, thirty-five, no older than Harry, was so certain this was all a mistake that he took the prize Harry had protected for him before even calling the British ambassador.

She had skin as light as heavily creamed coffee and smooth as soft duck down. Her breasts were buds, her limbs were willing. She was the best of all worlds, most assuredly a virgin, and trained to please a man. This one might please him so much over the years, he might marry her.

She would of course become a Muslim immediately. He would not keep a Hindu in his palace.

That young girls were bought in India and brought to the Arabian Peninsula was not new. It had been going on since the Hadir family had taken control of the port, centuries before. What was new was that revolutionary elements from Banai had joined with revolutionary elements from India in a plan to seize the girl and, they hoped, use her to embarrass both India and the Sultanate of Banai.

But no one had counted on the sultan's Harry Rawson, and Abdul Al Haj Al Hadir was almost as interested in hearing Harry's version of what had happened as he was in taking first pleasure with the girl. Of course, Harry was British. One could never get the really good details from him. But with enough good Scotch whiskey and enough good time, his majesty Abdul Al Haj Al Hadir, sultan of Banai, would coax enough details out of an evening's meal to make it worthwhile. The problem with the British was not modesty. It was that they had no poetry in their souls, Hadir believed. They could not listen to the beauty of a story for the beauty itself. Words for them were like microscopes, thought best when precisely accurate.

It had been a hard two years at Sandhurst for Abdul Al Haj Al Hadir, but there he had met his friend Harry and insisted he be the one assigned as British Army representative in Banai, Harry, who always knew where the best whores were, the best whiskey, and most of all the safe places to enjoy these things. Harry, the stunning shot with a pistol, who arranged with his own skill for the prince to pass marksmanship. Harry, who on every field maneuver was at the head of the class. Harry, the best adviser a ruler could have. He was not going to give him up.

But when Captain Rawson appeared for dinner at the palace, he was not in evening clothes but in a plain summer suit, with regimental tie from the regiment he had been assigned to but never served in, the Royal Argyle Sutherlanders.

"Harry, what is the matter?"

"I'm leaving, sir, within two hours."

"No. No. That will never be," said the sultan, extending an arm to the pillow beside him. The table was barely a foot off the floor, and a Waterford decanter of what the sultan knew was Harry's favorite whiskey sat on the table with two Waterford tumblers. There would be food later, hours later. But now there was drinking. That a citizen in this Muslim land could be flogged for doing what the sultan and Harry were going to do did not matter. Alcohol was all right in the palace, not the public streets.

The sultan gave the proper stipends to the mullahs, consulted them on what was said and done officially, and virtually gave them the lives of the citizens, provided he retained the palace, the armed forces, and foreign affairs. It was an arrangement heartily endorsed by his British friends.

He himself poured a drink for Harry and half filled a glass for himself. He did not like servants pouring his whiskey. It seemed to rob it of its English flavor.

"Harry, you're not going and that's that. I will break relations with Her Majesty's government. I will sever them. This is an act of an unfriendly power. Finish your drink."

"I am afraid I must go, Your Majesty. I am a British subject."

The sultan angrily hit the pillow next to him. Harry lowered himself to the table.

"What would be so important as to risk losing our friendship?"

"I don't know yet, Your Majesty."

"So this is the end, Harry?"

"For now, perhaps," said Rawson. The winds off the Arabian Sea, softened by the sun, met the cold night desert air here in this room open in a vast circle. It was a pleasant place and time, surrounded by so much discomfort. He could smell the flowers imported from Africa and made to bloom by skilled German hands in the sultan's gardens. The whiskey lingered on his tongue. Ten years here were over, ten years of unrest, intrigue, and dangerous political and religious winds blowing outside this kingdom on the rest of the Arabian peninsula. His Majesty had survived. A friend of Britain had survived. A port on the route to an India Britain no longer controlled was still available for British warships, and now oil was that much more secure. Of course, Britain now had her own North Sea oil. But Harry Rawson had done his duty, not bearing a pike for Henry VIII as his ancestors had done, but doing what was assigned, what was expected of him. And he had done it well, even if it required a variation of pimping on behalf of the United Kingdom.

"Harry, tell me about it. They say you actually stopped an attack using a knife. Just a knife."

"A rather exceptional situation. I didn't run at machine guns with it, you know." He saw the sultan finish his tumbler of whiskey and pour himself another.

"But how you used it. You must tell me if it was true."

"Bit of a botch, sir. The revolutionaries had gotten into the car with your lovely prize. She had panicked, thinking the leader was you, and began to perform some acts."

"She was not touched by him?" asked Hadir with alarm.

"No. You were the first, as far as my custody went. I made sure of that."

"I heard you stayed in front of her door all trip."

"It was important to you she was a virgin. I assume now that is a condition that you have altered."

"Harry," said Hadir, grinning and slapping the back of his friend.

"Your enemy happened to be exposed at the time. If I used a gun, I think we would have had a gun battle. I used a knife, explaining to him that his cohorts might get my life, but I would take his manhood with me. Funny thing about that sort of thing, Your Majesty. Some men would rather give up their lives than that. He cooperated, and here we all are, another day in the reign of Abdul Al Haj Al Hadir."

"I would have loved to have served with you at Waterloo or Dieppe, or Balaclava. Or Hastings. I would have made a good general, don't you think, Harry?"

"A great one or a dead one, Your Majesty."

"You see what I like about you, Harry, is that you are honest in your way. You can tell me I am too rash, and yet you yourself will use a simple pocketknife."

"We both learned at the old place that you fight wars with what you have, not what you think you should have."

"We should sweep across the desert and into Europe and you should come down from your island empire and meet us in one grand battle for the ages," said Hadir. He finished his drink and emptied the decanter into his glass, while reaching into a drawer set into the table for another bottle of Laphroaig, a strong malt whiskey he had developed a taste for in England.

"We will humble the Jews and you will break the French."

"That will not happen. You will never sweep out of the Arabian Peninsula again, and we will never leave our island."

"We have oil, we have Islam," said Hadir. He looked into his glass. "We have the souls of warriors. We should destroy the Jews. They have humiliated us."

"This might be their time. I don't know. Your time has passed. When an empire is gone, it never returns. Each people has a time on stage, and when it is gone, it is gone. It never comes back." England was gone, too. Banai would never be needed again for a fueling stop on the way to India. The whole relationship between Britain and Banai was the appendix of British foreign policy, a vestigial organ.

"If you have the will, Harry. If you have the memory of what you were, then you know in your mind what you have to be again."

"No, friend," said Harry Rawson. The sultan was spilling his Laphroaig now. It would not be long before he would go to sleep on the pillows, and Harry would leave, and the servants would clean up the bottles and put His Majesty to bed.

[51]

"Support your premise. I demand it," said Hadir.

"Look at the Mongols. There wasn't an army that could stand against them. How many did they kill in Baghdad alone? They took Asia, much of the Arab world, and were on their way into Europe when Kublai Khan died. Now look at them. They ride around on horses in an area that is a dot on the map. The Romans conquered Europe, and they are a city with a second-rate sewer system. Where are the Hittites? Where are the Persians? And what about the Spanish empire?"

"It will happen to all Europeans too," said Hadir angrily.

"Of course. And when it does, we will never rise again. When it is over, it is over."

"Why?"

"That I do not know. But it is up to the Americans and Russians now, and their time will go also."

"You must know why, Harry. You're so damned smart. Why, Harry?"

Rawson straightened out His Majesty's glass. It would not be long now. It was a good question, and he didn't have an answer. In a few moments the sultan would be talking about dying at the head of his troops storming Jerusalem. Of course that would mean leaving his capital unguarded, something he would never do. Perhaps it was internal treachery that tore the Arab empire apart almost as soon as it was formed. But then where was the treachery of the Mongols? Perhaps it was life. Everything that was born died. And yet the same peoples still lived. Same genetics. Same race. Same language and culture. What was it about the passing of empires that made it so they never came back?

"If you believe that Britain is done for, why the hell, why the hell, Harry, do you do any damned thing to keep Banai a healthy friend of Britain? Answer me that. Answer it. That's an order. I'll cut off your tongue if you don't tell me." The sultan laughed. "I would never harm you, my friend."

"One doesn't choose the time one is born in; one only chooses how one will live it. Do you understand, Your Majesty?"

"No," said the sultan happily. "Not a bloody word. Let me die at the gates of Jerusalem." He was weaving and laughing. His father had said the same thing to cheering crowds and other visiting Arab dignitaries. His one great wish was to pray at Al Aksa mosque before he died. No one ever mentioned that he had never bothered to go there when Jordan controlled it.

The problem with Israel was not Jerusalem; it wasn't even Palestine, much less the Palestinians. The problem was that that little country, run by people they had considered of no warrior account, reminded every Arab of what the Arabs had been and no longer were. It stopped their revered poets in the very first stanzas about the prowess of their tribes, the strength of their weapons, the courage of their men.

The sultan leaned forward on the table and went to sleep and Harry Rawson left to catch his plane. Before he was out of the main palace, a cousin to the prince, commander of the Banai Navy, presented Harry with a jeweled dagger in thanks for his service.

At the embassy, Rawson hurriedly gave his final report. Rawson had the sort of British good looks popularized more by actors than by British men. He had sharp features and a longish nose, with haughty blue eyes and soft blondish hair. He was over six feet and did not allow fat to collect on his well exercised body. He could have served in a Guards regiment if national service had not required him to be a pimp among other things.

The ambassador said, "This is rather hurried, Captain. What's your assessment of Abdul Al Haj Al Hadir?"

"Better start grooming a successor. He's got a drinking problem," said Rawson.

"You're his friend. Couldn't you warn him? Couldn't you stop him? I know he's a sultan, Captain, but you are there to advise. And he has trusted you ever since Sandhurst."

"It's not that he's sultan. It's that he's a bloody alcoholic."

"Well, tell him then."

"You're serious about that?"

"Bloody right, Captain."

"You don't tell that to an alcoholic. They wouldn't be alcoholics if advice worked."

"So what are we supposed to do now that you're leaving us in the lurch?"

"Find his successor."

"Who?"

"Stay cozy with his brothers and his cousins and whichever one successfully stabs him in the back first, present your credentials and wax on a bit about our historic friendship."

"That's rather cold, Captain, even for intelligence," said the ambassador.

"We're supposed to be, you know," said Rawson, flashing a quick smile. But he had lied. He had warned Hadir about his drinking several times. The last time, the sultan had slapped him in the face, and because he was drunk, forgotten it the next morning.

London was suitably damp and suitably cold and suitably home. Every return to London meant a visit to the family tailor, the family bootmaker, and some time with the family. Usually a dinner. But Father was at the country place, and Mother was in Italy. Had been for the last year, according to his father's secretary. And Rawson had an urgent order to report to an apartment in Belgravia for his instructions. So family was out.

Belgravia, an exclusive area in the heart of London, near Victoria Station, still maintained a residue of blue and orange flowers tough enough to survive an English autumn in the many little block-sized parks around which the Georgian homes had been built. There were many small streets, alleys, and mews. The French Embassy was here. The Danish Embassy was here. Harrod's was nearby.

On Chapel Street, near Grosvenor Place, a short trot from Buckingham Palace Gardens, Rawson found the address his unit chief had given him. It was a Georgian townhouse with a stucco ground floor and red-brick upper floors. A slender balcony girdled the second floor.

A butler answered the ringing bell.

"I am Captain Rawson. Here for Sir Anthony Witt-Dawlings," said Rawson.

He was taken to a sitting room in the rear of the narrow townhouse, where pale curtains were drawn over ceiling-high windows, letting in only light. Crossed swords were mounted above a white painted hearth. The room smelled stale somehow, cared for but not lived in.

Anthony Witt-Dawlings entered the room quietly, shutting the door behind him. He was shorter than Rawson, his body surrendering decently to a sixty-year-old paunch. He looked like he had just witnessed his first execution.

He wore a small campaign ribbon Rawson could not place. He introduced himself, including the ribbon on his lapel. He asked what Rawson knew about the situation.

"Your name and the address," said Rawson.

"They didn't tell you this was for the Queen?"

"No. They said it was urgent. They did not say it was for the Queen."

"Good. I am the Queen's secretary. I was quite a few years ahead of you at Eton. Didn't choose Sandhurst, though. Missed the war, but saw some action later at Suez. Seventh Hereford. I have been with Her Majesty for thirty years."

Rawson nodded.

"I asked your people for a man who was discreet above all, calculating, daring if necessary, and knew his way around."

"Around what?" asked Rawson.

"Around the world, Captain. In all levels. Can you deal with criminals while maintaining the highest integrity? Can you be trusted with millions? Can you operate totally on your own without waiting for someone to give you an order, without needing people to make judgments for you? That's what Her Majesty asked for. Have we gotten that man?"

"I would imagine I am about as good as any," said Rawson.

"Could you search for something forever until you found it?"

"Would depend on that something, wouldn't it?" asked Rawson.

"A treasure, a piece of England," said Witt-Dawlings.

"Possibly—I certainly have done worse," said Rawson.

Sir Anthony left the large fireplace and approached the young captain. Rawson still had not been invited to sit.

"Captain, it is not unappreciated that your father is Lord Rawson."

"I don't understand," said Rawson.

"Captain, do you think we are going to send some greengrocer's son off into the world with a blank chit for millions of pounds and a fiat from Her Majesty to use his own judgment?"

Rawson didn't answer that. He knew he wouldn't be withdrawn from Banai for some royal social function. It wasn't done in this age, although the whole royal scene was a form of lunacy, joyously participated in by the nation. And he was, after all and in the beginning, an Englishman.

"We also asked for someone who understands our history."

"If this is going to take some time, may I sit?" asked Rawson.

"Please," said Sir Anthony. Rawson chose an overstuffed chair by a mahogany lampstand.

"All right, what are we looking for?"

"You are going to regain the Tilbury Cellar, for England," said Witt-Dawlings, his voice resonating like a trumpet call to knights about to battle for their God and king.

Rawson took a small leather notepad from his pocket and with a pen wrote down the words. When he glanced up, he saw Sir Anthony's face steam crimson, the eyes glowering darkly. Rawson wondered if he had done something wrong.

"You have heard of the Tilbury?" said Sir Anthony coldly.

"No," said Rawson.

"Perhaps you have heard of the Armada and Elizabeth the First."

"Oh, you mean Tilbury Field, where she gave the speech to her troops. Yes, I have," said Captain Rawson.

"And what have you heard?" said Sir Anthony.

"Elizabeth's army was encamped there. She had been languishing in Winchester, now Whitehall, for months while the kingdom was virtually dissolving in despair at the approach of the Spanish. One day she left Whitehall with only three lords escort and enough fight in her to start an empire. She went right to Tilbury Field, where she delivered the classic military speech. We still study it at Sandhurst. Wonderful speech—explained the rightness of her cause, the sureness of victory, and the accountability of all those involved. No one ever improved on that speech. Of course, one still does wonder how facing such odds she could assure victory, but that's what you're supposed to do in a military speech, yes?"

Sir Anthony's glower set into his face like stone. If he was not going to explain his disapproval, Rawson was certainly not going to go mining for it with his own ego as pick and shovel.

"Especially interesting because of the religious strife," said Rawson brightly. If Sir Anthony wanted someone who knew British history, Rawson would give him some. "So much suspicion of Catholic lords being disloyal, favoring the Spanish over Protestant Elizabeth, which of course didn't turn out to be true in the main. But that didn't bother the Protestant extremists, who were also a problem. There was a big fear of royal assassination from all sides, so you can imagine what courage it took to go into her countryside with only three lords as though heaven and earth were there to protect her."

"Then you haven't heard of the Tilbury Cellar?" said Sir Anthony.

"No," said Rawson. "I can't say I have."

Captain Rawson's bright clear answer sat in the dark-curtained room like an insult, and that insult was all over the red face of Sir Anthony Witt-Dawlings. The room was quiet, no honks or engine grates of London traffic coming in, and Rawson assumed the room was secured for sound by the drapes themselves.

Witt-Dawlings spoke with the slow icy cadence of bitter tolerance: "Elizabeth the First had fashioned there on Tilbury Field to commemorate England's great victory a saltcellar with 'jewels of such glorious nature as befit one's gratitude to divine providence in protecting this island kingdom in its darkest hour.' "

"I take it that's a quote, Sir Anthony. I seem to retain quotes way beyond their usefulness, but I am hard-pressed to identify that one," said Rawson.

"Schoolbooks. In our generation before the war, we all read of the Tilbury."

"It was not in ours," said Rawson.

"I take it that like so much it passed with the war, a war we won."

"This cellar, I presume, plays an important part in something."

"It was stolen. We want it back. We want you to get it back for England. It is England's, as surely as fields and country lanes and a cottage small beside a field of grain. It is Runnymede and Balaclava. It is England, Captain."

"When was it stolen?" asked Rawson, putting the pen to the pad and not looking up.

"In 1945 in one of the most heinous and disreputable robberies in the history of England."

"Oh, the Cheltham. Thought they got everything back."

"We did not get back the Tilbury."

"I see. I guess I was wrong."

"We kept it from the world."

"No wonder you never got it back. Was there any reason not to announce it publicly? Then you would have had a chance of its discovery."

"We were war-weary. It was a tired England that emerged from the war we won."

"So you just said bosh it all and let it go?"

"Yes."

"But now you wish to invest if need be the unlimited time of what I arrogantly assume is a highly qualified agent?"

"Yes. The Tilbury was seen again in New York City and we almost had her back, except the Foreign Office bungled it horribly. We told them spare no price, spare no effort, and they lost it."

"And what do the American security people say, police, FBI?"

"Didn't say anything, thank God. They're not to know. They were never to know, and no matter what shall never know. They are out of it, even if there weren't a killing."

"What?"

"The Foreign Office killed someone. Not sure of the details."

"Not an American national? Not within American borders?" asked Captain Rawson. He looked up.

"I imagine he was an American national," said Witt-Dawlings.

"America is our major ally," said Rawson.

"Yes, well, that's why we have to keep everything quiet."

"What could be worth a rupture in our relationship with America?"

"Well, it doesn't have to be, you see. That's why we asked for you, a man of impeccable credentials and experience in these things. Never should have trusted the Foreign Office chaps. Bunch of pensioners. Might as well be French."

Captain Rawson paused. He stifled a deep sigh and pressed Witt-Dawlings to explain further, as though he had not heard someone dismiss the killing of an American national within American borders as a minor inconvenience on the way to regaining some royal artifact.

"During World War Two, when we were expecting an invasion by the Hun, the Tilbury and other treasures of our history were buried in deep bunkers outside London. Didn't trust them to be shipped to Canada because of U-boats. Bombing was heavy, if you do remember that. Keep them safe in England. We needed our traditions most sorely during those days. Need them more now, if you ask me."

Captain Rawson nodded.

"Fortunately, before the Tilbury was removed from Windsor, where it had sat in the same dungeon place for four centuries, modern jewelers took dimensions of the stones and I believe gem prints. They're all in that folder."

Rawson checked the bound black packet. He saw numbers and sizes and didn't understand a one of them. There were diamonds, a ruby, a sapphire, lesser stones, and upward of fifty pounds of gold, all making up a saltcellar. Inside, apparently as a frame of some sort for the whole works, was "a poorish bowl." Undoubtedly the latter description was provided by Elizabeth I, who had ordered the cellar crafted.

"Do you have a picture of this cellar?"

"Absolutely not. Aren't any."

"What about your schoolbooks?"

"None. Just the phrases commemorating our deliverance."

"Without a picture?"

"If you showed me a picture of it, I probably wouldn't be able to help you. Why are you making such a fuss over a picture? I daresay if you circulated that picture from Cornwall to Glasgow no one would recognize it. Why are you so deucedly interested in a picture of it?"

"Because someone who has seen it would recognize it."

"Well, we don't have one. We have the gems described by, as you'll see, different jewelers, none of whom was allowed to see the entire piece."

"You have gem prints but not the picture, and you wouldn't allow any one jeweler to see the whole thing—may I ask why?"

"Precautions."

"Against what, for God's sake, man?" asked Rawson.

"Dangers. We value this cellar; presumably, that's why we have you here, Captain Rawson."

"If I am to find this cellar, I have got to have some rational answers to work with."

"Your Queen commands it. That should be answer enough."

"For a butler or a secretary, but not for someone who is supposed to invest his blood in finding this artifact. Why are there no pictures?"

"Because Elizabeth never bothered, and we see no reason to change tradition. She kept this most valuable piece locked in Windsor, where it stayed for four centuries. It's the least we can do to honor her."

Harry Rawson knew when to retreat. Undoubtedly, there were good reasons why Elizabeth I kept a fortune locked up in some dungeon instead of displayed. But he was certain he could not get a rational explanation from the likes of Witt-Dawlings, who thought of that cunning monarch as some sort of Brittanic saint and the peculiar Tilbury Cellar another unquestioned example of her holiness. Rawson knew that Elizabeth I did everything with blade-sharp reason, whereas Witt-Dawlings obviously believed that if she did something, it needed no reason.

Besides, Captain Rawson already had the answer he needed as to why he was here. He was sure he had landed with Sir Anthony through some accident of command, not an impossibility, especially when the name of Her Majesty was involved.

That afternoon in a plain-faced building in a modest section of London, which looked to the world like just another drab office, Captain Rawson checked with his former command control as to the accuracy of the transfer to service under Sir Anthony Witt-Dawlings.

"Not only have you been transferred, old boy, but you shouldn't even be talking to me anymore. Captain Rawson, you are with the Crown for the rest of your natural life."

V

"We was quite put out by that, sir. Yes, that's the old list. I remember her. Gems and all that. I'll tell you what I told His Majesty. War was over, you know, Captain Rawson, just about. I was given this list not by my superior, but by His Majesty, George the Sixth himself. Well, there I was an inspector in the Yard, and we still had our hands full with this war, and I am brought personally to His Majesty, who was acting like you would think he was a local constable in charge of apprehending some criminal."

"This right after the Cheltham robbery?" asked Rawson.

"The day of it. The very day. I wasn't even allowed to stay at the scene. But that's not the strangest part."

The old man with the ruddy face in the pillowed oak chair sat by the window of his cottage with the good South Downs sun on the harvested autumn barley fields outside, taking peaceful pleasure in his last days, and special joy that now he was duly authorized to air a royal duty almost a half century under wraps.

It was also the sort of cottage Witt-Dawlings had rhapsodized about in quoting the poem that said there would always be an England.

"But what specifically did he say about the cellar?" asked Rawson. "The Tilbury was a saltcellar. The Crown has many saltcellars. You can visit some at the Tower of London. The Crown has many jewels. It has the largest gem collection in the world. Why the Tilbury? Why would you have an audience with the king over just one piece from the Cheltham train robbery?"

"Don't rightly know, Captain. But himself was as close as me to you, sir, 'cepting I wasn't sitting in his presence so to speak."

"And he talked about nothing else but the Tilbury?" asked Rawson. The solid dark wood chair he sat on was more charming to eyes than buttocks. Rawson missed the pillows of the Gulf and felt like some crusader must have, back from the oriental refinement of the Holy Land to the crude hard joys of England. The cottage had the rich crusty smell of many oak log fires.

"They didn't tell you why you were having an audience with the king?"

"Nossir. It was the end of the war. You did things without asking questions. I was the investigating inspector of the Cheltham, and I'm brought to Buckingham Palace like I'm some field marshal, taken right into His Majesty's presence."

"And?"

"And he gives me a list like what you showed me."

"And?"

"And I give His Person my regrets, but I must inform His Majesty the Tilbury Cellar undoubtedly no longer exists."

"Why?"

"Thieves won't sell the bloody thing whole. They'll sell the gold. They'll sell the gems—each stone separate. That's how they do it with gems in big pieces like necklaces and such."

Rawson felt relief, like warm clean air out of the desert. This was the first logical, rational, the-world-as-Rawson-knew-it fact to surface in this Tilbury affair. Unfortunately, the fact was not so. Somehow the Tilbury toward which the Crown acted so strangely had remained whole, at least until recently in New York City.

"Is there anything else His Majesty or anyone said about the Tilbury?" asked Rawson.

"Yes. Strangest part, Captain. I'm scarce on the job so to speak, when I'm told forget everything I heard. A gentleman comes, takes back the list, and I don't hear another word about it for more than forty years until I'm informed that a captain of the Royal Argyle Sutherlanders had official clearance on the matter of the Cheltham."

"I remember reading briefly about the robbery. It was the end of the war, and the soldiers on the train were tired. It happens after an intense effort that there has to be a letdown," said Rawson.

"You're right, Captain. Called it the 'loss of the spirit that brought us through.' Thing was, right as soon as they call me off for no reason I read where the Tilbury has never left Windsor. You would think that a king would know that. What do you think? Do you think we could have lost her in some bureaucratic shuffle and such? Seems like an awful lot to lose, but don't they lose more every day?"

"Did anyone ever show you a picture of the Tilbury?"

"No. I asked for one myself."

"Thank you," said Rawson and left the cottage small in the still thriving agricultural belt of southern England. One man, at least, had seen the Tilbury, or at least something that matched the gems list.

He was the employee of the Foreign Office who, panicked by Witt-Dawlings's contradictory and hysterical orders, had done the stabbing in New York City.

The Foreign Office had retired the poor chap fifteen years early to a flat in the city of Liverpool, a cindered wretched remnant of the refuse of England's industrial age. Riots had left some areas worse off than the Blitz had left parts of London, and unemployment was so bad that this man on an early pension was considerably better off than the gangs of men who lounged around the bleak broken pavements. Industrial England, which had powered the need for empire, had died here, leaving corpses of cities throughout the north. No one would write a poem about this England, that it would always be. This England had the stink of the dead, waiting for the grace of years to clean its bones for archeologists who would only then begin digging up clues to England's empire, why it rose and why it fell.

The man's name was Paul Hawkins. He was pale and thin, and his eyes were red. He was forty-two and looked twenty years older. He wore a striped cotton bathrobe and slippers and held on to a tumbler of whiskey as if it were a parachute ripcord. He lived in a modest flat, a bachelor. Only in the last generation had the British Foreign Office begun taking people from the lower-middle-class, to which Hawkins had now been returned.

He couldn't talk about the stabbing without crying.

"I don't know what happened. I couldn't rely on anyone. I was ordered not to rely on anyone. I was ordered to pay any price to get it. And every price only convinced him to ask for more. It was horrid. I wasn't trained for this. I was ordered under no circumstances to lose this cellar."

"They didn't tell you more about the cellar?"

"No. Just gave me a list of gems. Every price I offered he made higher, until I saw I had lost it. He was going to sell it somewhere else, he said, and I don't know what happened. I started stabbing him with a penknife, and once I started I just had to keep going. I ran. I offered to confess everything, and they just shipped me back here. And you're the first person I've talked to about it since, except of course the doctors. But they don't count. Do they?"

"You did see the cellar?" asked Rawson.

"Yes."

"What did it look like?"

"Oh, Lord. I can't remember. All I can see is this man's face. He was so surprised when I stabbed him. He looked at me as though he wanted to say 'What are you doing? What are you doing?' "

"How tall was the cellar?" asked Rawson softly.

Hawkins held his hand in front of him at the height of a toddler.

"And where were the stones? The red one?"

"It matched, you know. It matched the list. They all matched the list. Was I not supposed to tell you about the list? I'm so confused now."

"I have the list myself. Where was the ruby?" asked Rawson. He gave Hawkins a thin pen and put a clean white pad into his hands.

"It was horrid," said Hawkins.

"Yes," said Rawson. "Was the red stone in the middle or at the bottom, or where?"

"It was in the bottom. No. In the middle. In the middle."

"And the sapphire?"

"Wait. That was in the middle. No. They were both in the middle. There were lots of stones."

"Draw me a picture of it."

Hawkins put the ballpoint tip on the paper, and the pen did not move.

"Anything. Draw anything," said Rawson.

The pen rose and then came down hard on the paper, stabbing and stabbing and stabbing, until Rawson took the pen out of the poor man's hand.

"Hawkins," Rawson said, trying to make eye contact with the man, lowering himself almost to a squat. "Look at me. Listen. You may not be able to allow yourself to understand this now, but you were not at fault. You were given bad orders in a strange situation for which no one trained you or prepared you."

"I didn't have to stab someone."

"Oh, yes you did. And worse. It was not your mistake."

"Don't try to help, please," said the man, turning his head away.

Rawson left, thinking there were now two victims from the New

York incident. He didn't intend to become the third. When he went off, he would know what he was really looking for. He suspected but was not certain that the Crown should not be that concerned over just a cellar, even one with great gems, even the Tilbury. But he didn't know.

If Witt-Dawlings could issue hysterical and contradictory orders for this Elizabeth, Rawson was certain no one did for the first Elizabeth. She was a great monarch in a treacherous time. If she had commissioned a cellar with gems in it and then locked it up, there had to have been a reason. There had to be good cause why the cellar was not royally brandished on some state occasion to add to the appearance of her power. It was Elizabeth I who had decided to hide something in the first place, he was sure. And this was confirmed when some quick research turned up little more than a few sentences in old, outdated schoolbooks. There were no pictures of the Tilbury. No royal decrees about the Tilbury. All those gems and all that gold, locked away like some blemish under the heavy makeup of a castle.

Four hundred years away from human sight, and supposedly still there, according to the cover story. Why did England want everyone to believe they had never lost it?

"I do think you are wasting your time, Captain. No one is allowed into that section of the Round Tower. That's where the Tilbury Cellar is," said the deputy governor of Windsor Castle.

He had met Rawson at the Norman Gate and escorted him past the quartz-white heathstone walls of the castle. It rose 165 feet over the Thames, dominating the river and the great valley beneath it. He brought Rawson to a small drawing room, too busy with Louis XIV chairs, and portraits in massive gilded frames, and a rug so bare and worn, Rawson knew it had to have some ancient and royal history. Otherwise, it wouldn't have covered a hallway in Liverpool.

The phone on the lap-sized desk was just plain old, a big black clunker of a phone.

"I am sure if you reach Anthony Witt-Dawlings he will authorize access," said Rawson.

"I would be most surprised," said the deputy governor, a man in a plain gray suit, with a plain grayish face, and very neat white hair. The hands were blue-veined. He lifted the heavy receiver and asked an operator simply for "Sir Anthony."

When he hung up, he said, "I'm sorry, there must be some misunderstanding, Captain. Sir Anthony can't recall you."

"Excuse me," said Rawson and grabbed the receiver and asked for Sir Anthony.

"You can't do that, Captain," said the deputy governor.

"Just did," said Rawson. "Hello, Sir Anthony, Harry Rawson here."

"What are you doing? What on earth are you doing?" came Sir Anthony's voice. He was blazing.

"Going about the Queen's business," said Rawson.

"Why aren't you in New York City? What are you doing there? You were supposed to be discreet. You're dragging our name into things. We were promised someone who was discreet, Captain."

"Dragging the Queen's name into Windsor Castle, Sir Anthony?"

"Your name with it, Rawson."

"I am here. If you are not going to at least give me access in Windsor, I really can't go on."

"You gave your word."

"Let's strike this bargain, Sir Anthony. You give me one remotely logical reason why I should be denied access to special sections of the Round Tower and I will be on a Concorde to New York City before dusk."

"Because no one is to know anything is amiss."

"Well, good. Why?"

Sir Anthony paused. Finally, he said: "There will be someone for you tomorrow at the Round Tower. I am most disappointed in you. Most disappointed that you would bargain in Windsor itself."

Rawson thought otherwise. It was a most proper place to bargain. When knights pledged themselves to their sovereigns, there were always obligations on both sides. If the Queen's secretary refused relevant information, Harry Rawson would refuse to do the Queen's bidding, and what a wonderful place to do it in, Windsor Castle, the most royal of all castles in England, first built by William the Conqueror because legend had said this was where King Arthur and the Round Table had met. But more properly built because it controlled the Thames River and was a day's foot march to London for its garrison. There were reasons for things, and just because Sir Anthony considered tradition some irrational form of holy worship didn't mean that Harry Rawson, who knew better, had to support it. Sir Anthony had gotten someone steeped in history because he really didn't understand history. What he really wanted was someone steeped in myth, and oblivious to history.

Rawson was met at the cruel hour of 8:00 A.M. by an elderly sergeant major who took him into the massive three-story Round Tower and then gave him a set of old iron keys to an iron-studded oak door that was blackened with age.

"I'll be here, sir, when you get out," said the sergeant major.

The door was heavy, and swinging it open felt like wrenching a boulder. The sergeant major not only didn't help, he didn't even bother to look. Apparently, he had lived at Windsor a while. Passageways, unexplained visitors, and tradition were like the weather to him.

Rawson tried to adjust his eyes, to see something. The passageway was dark as a stone womb, without a single wire promising some switch somewhere to modern lighting installed as a convenience in later ages. Luckily, Rawson had carried a little pocketknife and penlight since he was twelve, when his governess thought it was a good idea that he always be prepared for the little nuisances in life.

The massive heathstone blocks dressed almost a thousand years before were dark gray under his small beam, unrefreshed by the rains that made the exterior of Windsor sparkle almost quartz-white-new with each downpour. The stones were dank from the nearby well of the tower, now boarded over, so Rawson had read, but vital for early defense. No castle or city built without access to water ever survived a siege. The dark, narrow passage felt as though it were closing in on him. The leather of his feet on stone made a soft shuffle like an old man, and he realized he walked this way because he was stooped. He was over six feet and this passage was built for the normal height of a knight, five foot five. It smelled like the moist warren of underearth, and his elbows could touch the sides so that he not only stooped but tended to walk sideways. His light hit a metal gate ahead of him. He ran the penlight up and down both sides and did not see a keyhole large enough for anything the sergeant major back in the light of the twentieth century had given him.

So he gave the gate a good shove with his shoulder and felt something gritty smash into his eyes. He could not blink it free. Carefully, he wiped his eyes with a handkerchief and then shone the light on the cloth. Orangish streaks stained the white linen. Rust. The gate had been rusted through.

Rawson stepped over the gate, crushing some of the weak fragments of iron underfoot. To his right was a small stone room, with wood petrified black and iron parts rusted orange and decayed. It looked like a small printing press, with some of the pieces obviously removed. They lay in a mound to the right. It was not, of course, a printing press. Such a thing wasn't in use in England then.

But the rising central bar of the platform told Rawson it was a thing totally appropriate for its age. They called it a "scavenger's daughter" back then. You placed the person over the bar and then folded him back until his spine snapped, an old torture device probably left unused once the area was designated for the Tilbury.

But why hide such a glory in a torture chamber? Rawson pressed on until his light hit a stone wall. There was only one entrance to this passage. The Round Tower was Windsor's castle keep, which meant it was the last redoubt if the castle were falling. It had no entrance on any ground level but would force attackers to mount narrow stairs on the side. It had the thickest walls of any part of Windsor, and in this safest stone hole of this safest tower, with only one entrance, Elizabeth had placed the Tilbury.

Harry Rawson was standing in what had once been the absolutely safest place in England. His light hit a round gold fog, glistening back at him. It was knee-high and horizontal, on a black rock pedestal, probably basalt.

The pedestal was set into the center of a five-by-five-foot room, on the same side of the passage as the scavenger's daughter. Rawson flashed his beam back down the passage. There were only two rooms in the passage.

He stepped into the room, lowering himself to a knee. The golden haze on the basalt block was unmistakable, like the imprint of a round yellow pan, a foot and a half in diameter. On this part, they hadn't deceived him. Something gold probably did sit here for four hundred years. Gold in contact with another substance for centuries transferred molecules. Here was its four-hundred—year golden fingerprint. They weren't lying.

And what would they do with the Tilbury if Rawson should recover it? Put it back here? Was that what a captain in Her Majesty's Royal Argyle Sutherlanders was supposed to devote his life to, pouring in his painfully learned skills and, if need be, his blood?

He shone his light on the walls. It was a small cell, probably previously used to keep those to be tortured. A cell with a black basalt block in the middle. The block did not seem set into the floor but placed on it. Small chisel marks bit neatly into the heathstone floor at its base, like some irregular border.

Rawson felt something sharp cut through the tweed of his slacks where he knelt. He lifted the knee and duck-waddled backward.

He shone the light down in front of him to see what had caused the pain. Of course. The heathstone floor had been cut there. He had been kneeling with all the pressure of his body on one point, and that point held chiseled stone words.

This belongs to England forever. I leave it to sovereign and subject alike, that England should rule free and strong—Elizabeth R.

It was a royal request that just might explain why different royal houses had left such a valuable piece untouched, specifically Charles II, who had to flee the country. There was not an unbroken line between the Elizabeths, but much turmoil, including the beheading of one monarch.

Rawson read the words again and then shone the light back to the irregular border beneath the basalt. It wasn't a border. Those had to be letters also, the bottoms of letters, hidden under the basalt pedestal.

He leaned forward and rammed the basalt block with his shoulder at a low point, like some rugby player in scrum. The block moved only three inches. His shoulder throbbed. Basalt, as it always had been, was stronger than flesh and bone. Rawson hit it again with the other shoulder. He got another three inches and could see there was still more writing, so he offered up his poor left shoulder for another blow and, with searing pain, got it back to where there was space above a carved line: the top of the inscription.

The square space was paler where the basalt had protected it from centuries of air. It was Latin, but the quotation, which Rawson translated to himself, was not from Rome.

You shall reign over all things, whatsoever the air touches.

"No," bellowed Rawson in the little cell and almost hit his head standing up. "No. It couldn't be. It has to be." He almost laughed. He almost danced. He almost cried and shouted hosannahs to the close hard walls. But all he said was "no," again here in this logically safest place in all Elizabethan England.

He had read a hidden sentence every educated person would have recognized in Elizabeth's age. It had come from a Bavarian minnesinger, Wolfram von Eschenbach. But he was only one of scores of poets who wrote about this.

It was the very thing of Arthurian myths, of Galahad and Lancelot and that great quest in search of it. There were as many tales, it seemed, as there were societies in Europe: the French and German and Celtic versions; the supposition that a follower, Joseph of Arimathea, had brought it to Glastonbury in England, where it was later lost; the rumor that it had originally come to Southern France, a tale that had prompted the German Gestapo during World War II to sweep those provinces in search of it. But then Hitler always was an absurd romantic, a mass murderer who ached for legitimacy.

It was more than just the most important Christian relic. It had been elevated to a level of salvation only accorded Christ Himself. It was the great myth of the Middle Ages and for centuries thereafter.

No wonder they covered the inscription with a basalt block. No wonder each monarch left its container, the Tilbury, for the next. No wonder even George VI in modern times would be concerned only about the loss of the Tilbury in the Cheltham train robbery.

You shall reign over all things, whatsoever the air touches.

The words were meaningless today. But every learned person who would naturally speak Latin, as the Bavarian naturally composed in it, would understand the translation, where it had come from and what it meant.

It was von Eschenbach in *Parzival*, meaningless to most people today but instantly recognizable to the successors of Elizabeth I. That's how they knew, and that's why they left it for England.

Bent over, his eyes tearing from iron rust, his shoulders aching from his body battle with the basalt block, his head aching from the strain of following a penlight down a narrow stone passage in the deepest safe place of England's most royal castle, Harry Rawson of the Queen's Argyle Sutherlanders, a proud and noble regiment, of Eton and Sandhurst, son of Lord Rawson, whose ancestor had carried a pike with William the Conqueror, for which he earned a goodly patch of Saxon land and a minor knighthood, understood it all. He knew a lifetime was the least he could devote to this search, and he knew that what the Tilbury Cellar hid was perhaps the only object in the sixteenth century that could inspire a despairing monarch to brace her nation with her new fierce soul against the greatest fleet ever assembled, a fleet so vast that it would give its name to every large battle fleet thereafter. The Armada.

WINCHESTER, ENGLAND, 1588

Her Most High, Mighty, and Magnificent Empress Elizabeth, by the Grace of God Queen of England, France, Ireland, and Virginia, Defender of the Faith, refused her normal summer duties, despite pleas from her closest lords.

Now more than ever, she was needed to make her routine summer sojourns to her lords, spending time in their manors, reaffirming their loyalty and her sovereignty.

The Spanish empire had assembled more than ninety galleons, full galleons cannoned and manned to the portholes, and half again as many smaller ships. An enormous war fleet never before seen in a world where a nation would consider itself well equipped to have five galleons in its war fleet. It was the Armada and it was coming against England and her Queen to punish them for "their reformist heresy and insolence."

There was hardly a subject who did not understand punishment in a time when people were boiled alive in pitch, pulled apart by plough horses driven in opposite directions, bent backward until the spine cracked, and brought to painful death as "was torture itself to Christian ears to hear it."

And against this vengeful behemoth was a small English fleet, some of it little more than pirates who had been raiding Spanish wealth in the Americas and even sacking a city or two along the Spanish coast, further infuriating Phillip II, His Most Catholic Majesty of Spain. And worse, many of the lords and soldiers of England needed to repel Spain were themselves Catholics who warily watched the more radical Protestants gaining strength.

If ever a land needed an active monarch to hold it together it was fair England. And Elizabeth had not moved from Winchester while the army that stood between London and the Channel languished near the salt marshes of Tilbury field.

And Her Most High, Mighty, and Magnificent Empress Elizabeth, by the Grace of God Queen of England, France, Ireland, and Virginia, Defender of the Faith, danced with young ladies in her residence at Winchester and drank the light wines of the countryside, and played with her handsomest lords as though, some said, she was determined to enjoy her last days. Even if it were not so, the rumors of such folly did enough damage to demand they be refuted in the person of Elizabeth herself.

Thus, when the Duke de Cota, Luis y Gonzalez y Gonzalez y Cota, arrived in Plymouth on a small bark requesting sanctuary and an audience with the Queen, the last thing any of her Protestant lords wanted was for her to be exposed to some deceitful compromise in her weakened state. This had to be a trick to get to her alone with de Cota, known to be among the most virulently intolerant of Papists, his very name the symbol of what Protestants would suffer should Spain triumph.

It did not matter that a British privateer had verified that no less than seven Spanish ships of the line had been chasing this de Cota. It did not matter that he swore he was not even Catholic anymore or that he had a jeweled chalice for Her Majesty.

Such was the state of England looking at the doom gathering in the Spanish ports that many thought this was all some Spanish trick for Phillip II to sneak the Duke de Cota into Elizabeth's chambers and there personally break her will, which, in these dreadful summer months, too many lords feared could happen to their Virgin Queen.

But as in other times of crisis, courage, dressed as cold reason, prevailed among Englishmen at Plymouth Harbor.

"The Spanish think themselves above such base endeavors as the use of spies. They not only do not know the mind of Her Majesty, I doubt from their last message they even care," said one lord who had counseled Her Majesty. "But if they did, it would not be for the likes of the Duke de Cota to swindle a hidden plea for surrender. He is more the measure of the man who would be sent to crucify our pathetic Protestant remnants should we lose."

And besides, he pointed out, the duke had taken his family with him.

The Duke de Cota was a Spanish grandee to his very breath, and even the cart they insisted he ride in did not diminish his bearing. He sat on the plain wood as though it were a damask-covered seat in one of his castles and rode that way to Winchester. It was not lost on the British lords that the duke himself owned more lands than their own queen, or that English castles, while grand in size and adornments, were looked upon as barbarities by the more refined Spaniards familiar with the graceful and more civilized architecture of the Muslim East.

What looked strange for His Grace was that he carried a gray cloth bundle in hands that normally touched nothing other than gold utensils or swords. But to carry that bundle containing the rumored chalice was his one and only demand. He must bring it himself to Elizabeth.

The Duke de Cota did not miss the fact that the walls lacked tapestry at Winchester Palace. It was true what they said about her, then. She preferred her walls bare and crude.

The room he waited in smelled heavily of different perfumes, which obliterated the freshness that might otherwise come from the nearby Thames or gardens. A waxed sheen covered the pale wood of the room's wainscoting, and the duke surmised this was the British oak he had heard so much about.

There were no carpets but a woven rush covering for the feet. The fireplace was huge, ornate to distraction with grotesque circle quatrefoils and lozenges. It was the first thing he saw because it faced the door.

A woven wool design covered the sparse trestle table. And there he waited with his bundle until Her Majesty arrived. He gave a low and courtly bow, greeting her properly in English. She was accompanied by young women who wore pure white gowns interlaced with pearls, and the duke noticed he had not seen a man.

It occurred to him there, in shock, that this crude room was Her Majesty's privy chamber itself. Life, he thought, is going to be hard in England, if it is life I will still retain.

But he and his family had decided that even death was better than life with all the slaves and wealth. For man himself was far more valuable than any of the things he valued. Thus had spoken the great rabbi Maimonides, who himself more than a century before had chosen to leave Spain rather than convert to Catholicism as the duke's ancestors had.

"We are told, de Cota, 'tis a strange thing to witness thee without an army at thy back," said Her Majesty. She did not sit, but allowed one of the young women to support an arm.

"What Jew has an army, Your Highness?"

"What grandee is a Jew?" countered the Queen.

"There was a time in the glory years when the Empire began its growth that many were."

De Cota knew the Queen hesitated to use the Spanish word for those Jews who secretly remained Jews while professing Catholicism. So he used it himself.

"Indeed, we had come to believe we were *Maranos* for abandoning our souls for wealth and power," said de Cota.

"Not a thing, Your Grace, unknown for those who worship at Canterbury. It is but one of the things that worries this prince," said the Queen.

It was not an unwelcome sign that she had recognized him as a duke even though he had told her he was a Jew. The reference to Canterbury was clear, for this was the seat of her father's church that broke from Rome. But then she added the shrewdest and most pointed of questions.

"Why does your soul suffer these pangs at this moment, my good lord?"

De Cota knew she spoke six languages and could, it was said, conspire in every one of them. She had not grown up free of treachery against her, not the least from the Spanish throne. For she was the issue of Anne Boleyn, that woman for whom Henry VIII had put aside Catherine of Aragon and the Holy Roman Catholic Church. It had been a dangerous way for the young woman Elizabeth to succeed to the throne of England.

De Cota chose his words carefully. But he always chose his words carefully. It was a thing in the blood of those called Maranos.

"Deceit always weighs heavy on the soul. Perhaps when my ancestors chose this way they assumed the kingdoms of Spain would return to enlightenment. But you are right, I do choose this moment. And for a reason. I do not think Spain must win."

And then he asked a daring question. He asked to be alone with Her Majesty, a thing unheard of under normal circumstances and impossible under these.

"I trust my ladies," said Her Majesty.

"With what you know now, Your Highness. I do not think you would wish to trust them with this, and I am clearly wagering my life on that belief."

"You have already bet that sum, de Cota," said Elizabeth, but with a laugh dismissed her ladies, even when they protested that someone with a sword should stand beside her in the face of this Spaniard, if not as protection for her modesty, then at least for her life.

The Duke de Cota offered the bundle, but Elizabeth's painted face hardened.

"Are we to take that in our own hands?" asked Elizabeth.

"I beg your pardon, Your Majesty. But this is one thing that should never escape your hands."

And with a formal bow taking leave to move to the wool-covered table, the Duke de Cota put the bundle on the coarse covering and, himself unfamiliar with knots of cloth, managed to undrape a gold chalice with six polished diamonds at its base and one large sapphire with Poseidon enthroned set into its bosom, a strange adornment for an instrument of the Mass. For Poseidon was, as they both knew, a pagan god.

"A handsome cup," said Elizabeth.

"Worth an empire. Worth a half dozen Spanish men o' war chasing me toward Plymouth, as you must know. Worth my belief that you will harbor me and my descendants forever."

"Still but a handsome cup."

"You see only the disguise."

"And what does it cover? What could it cover?"

"It covers, Your Majesty, what the Spanish kingdoms seized from the Moors, who seized it from the Christians, when first they rose. From the moment one small Christian kingdom on the Iberian Peninsula owned it, the Moors did not win one battle. Christian forces swept through Spain."

"Magic?"

"All life is magic, Your Majesty," said de Cota. He knew that Her Highness, like her father, despite protesting Catholic idolatry, maintained one of the largest collections of relics in Europe, not an insignificant thing in his calculations.

"Your Majesty," he said, "name me a drinking cup of such worth as I would wager a life that Spain having lost it would lose a war and you having gained it would win one?"

He saw what he thought was anger in her brooding eyes. She stared at him as though trying to take the flesh off his countenance to see what was underneath. He knew this was the moment he had feared above all moments.

She reached out her hands and took the chalice.

"The cup is covered by gold?"

"Yes."

"What does it look like underneath?"

"I am not sure."

"If this be it, de Cota, then why have none of us in Christendom heard of its Spanish possession?"

"Show me a wall, no matter how mighty, that has forever protected from thieves. What a thief does not know, he cannot steal."

"But you claim to know," said Elizabeth. She looked under the chalice, squinting to see if there were any special marks. There were none.

"Yes," said de Cota. Was that a smile on her face, or was it a crease in the heavy whitening creams she employed?

"If you know, why not other lords, and if other lords know, we would have heard."

"It was not a thing confided in us by His Most Catholic Majesty Phillip II. We were there when first it came back to Christianity."

"And how do you know it is inside that fine chalice?"

"It was not a chalice when it came, nor did it have those diamonds given by my family later toward that worshipful piece."

"But if you are a Jew you do not believe in these sacred things. And neither did your family."

"That is why we are Jews. But you are not. And neither is Phillip."

"Then why do you think we would win?" She lowered the chalice and looked directly at de Cota.

"The Armada is poorly commanded of many ungainly ships, manned by many seamen already ill."

"Still it is vast," said Elizabeth.

"They are fighting for conquest, you are fighting for your lives."

"Still it is vast," said Elizabeth.

"But you, Your Majesty, believe it and so did Phillip who sent no fewer than seven men o' war not to bring some disguised Jew back to Spain who had left all earthly goods there."

And then there came the smile, and better than a smile. A quote in Latin, and its meaning lit de Cota's heart with the sun.

"You shall reign over all things, whatsoever the air touches. All creatures, tame and wild, shall serve you and the utmost power and riches shall be yours."

It was from a German work, called *Parzival*, one of so many romances written about the Holy Grail.

The Grail was not just another relic. It was the most prized and powerful relic of the Christian world. This was the cup that Christ used at the Last Supper and in it some thought his blood too was caught later from the cross. This was the cup only the pure, according to legend, were supposed to obtain. Some thought he who had it would be blessed with neverending sustenance. Others claimed that to own it was to rule whatever one's eyes set on. More had been sung and rhapsodized about this relic than any Christian object in Europe. Not even the bones of St. Peter himself were considered as holy.

De Cota answered as only a learned man would. "Be assured that your prowess as a knight will avail you nothing unless the Holy Ghost first paves your way in all the adventures you meet with," he said, quoting from the most famous work in the English language, the magnificent tale of Sir Thomas Malory, *Morte d'Arthur*. It had swept all of England with its splendor and nothing was considered its match. The quoted line referred to Galahad's search for this Holy Grail.

"It is heavy," she said with a sudden vigor and joy that astonished her guest. "And only Heaven knows its truth. But better in Canterbury than Glastonbury."

And with the mention of those two towns, Duke de Cota understood that it had now been accepted into reformist hands. Glastonbury was the old seat of Catholic England, which, according to one Grail tradition, had held that holiest relic in Christendom brought by Joseph of Arimathea from Jerusalem, only to lose it again as the Grail always was lost. But this was the Grail not of poems or of legends, but something a monarch could hold in her hands and dedicate, grinning, to Canterbury, the seat of Protestant England. The de Cotas had found a rare home where they could practice neither faith. The next day Elizabeth, with only three lords, each ordered not to wear plumes so that her people and her soldiers could see her, rode out to Tilbury, her army, and her destiny.

VI

There will come a man pure all the days of his life and at the end will be marvelous in virtue above all mortal knights.

—*Grand Saint Grail* (French tradition of the late twelfth century).

"I'm certainly not Galahad, and I daresay my virtues are narrow, but you're in luck, Sir Anthony. They are the ones you need in this modern world. Chastity and faith just won't do."

Witt-Dawlings fell into a seat as though a cannonball had been shot into his midsection. His mouth opened and said nothing. He was quiet for a long while in his Belgravia study.

Harry Rawson assumed a crystal decanter on a copper stand was port and asked if he might have a glass. Not getting an answer, he poured one for each of them and held Sir Anthony's under his nose until the Queen's secretary took it.

"First, a lone knight galloping off with his virtue to regain the Holy Grail for England is fine for Sir Thomas Malory, Chrétien de Troyes, or von Eschenbach, and even later for our Alfred, Lord Tennyson. But those are the myths of the Holy Grail. We are after a real 'poorish bowl' in the center of the Tilbury, or what may have been the Tilbury."

Witt-Dawlings stared blankly at his glass of port.

"Look, I am delighted to be on this quest for the Holy Grail, and

I have good news for you. I am not looking for the unattainable myth. We have a splendid go at getting her back. I'm going to use the Foreign Office and Intelligence in very discreet ways. What is the matter, Sir Anthony? Drink your port."

Sir Anthony grunted weakly.

"Take a sip of the port. It will activate your intestines. Good for you," said Rawson.

Sir Anthony shook his head. He closed his mouth and put down the crystal goblet on the edge of an elegant small Chippendale lamp table by his left elbow. Rawson leaned toward him to center the glass, which at any moment might otherwise end up in the Queen's secretary's lap. Sir Anthony looked as though half of London's electrical current had just been diverted to his brain.

"I know it's the Holy Grail, Sir Anthony, or at least Elizabeth believed it, as did her successors. So please, let's get on with it. There is a real poorish bowl out in the world that bloody well may be in some garbage heap somewhere already if professionals have gotten hold of the Tilbury."

Sir Anthony raised a hand and took several deep lungfuls of air. Blood came back to his face and he swallowed. Steadied, he accepted the crystal wine glass and finished off the port as if it were a gulp of medicine. Rawson refilled the glass.

"How did you find out?" asked Sir Anthony.

"We'll get to that later. Don't worry about that," said Rawson. He kept his left hand in his jacket pocket. It was bandaged, and the many sharp little cuts on the fingers and palm still ached.

"That's all I worry about. It is better that we never regain it than that the world find out we had it and lost it, especially at the time we did."

"I understand," said Rawson. "We had the Grail when our greatness began and when we lost the Grail we lost our empire and seem to be losing more every day. I do understand your concern for secrecy about the Grail."

"Please don't even refer to it by name again. If it became known when we had the Grail, I am sure there would be those who would say England is through."

"They're saying it already, Sir Anthony. Don't you pass the book-stalls?"

"Yes, but this would be even further and greater proof. Those last of us who are truly England may lose hope. The very best of us may despair. We can't afford that wound to the great British heritage. It was bad enough when it was stolen in 1945. We were still an empire."

"Is that why they stopped looking?"

"It was the end of the war. We had lost so much. The Crown reasoned that if we couldn't get it back right away, then what harm to just pretend we had it and forget about it. There was so much else to do after all. And it was gone, probably to pieces, they believed, and after all who would know it was gone? But then no one foresaw what would happen, that from the end of the war it would be a constant slide. You would have thought we had lost the war. Maybe we should have. Look at Germany and Japan. But when it reappeared whole, we had the hindsight to know we should get it back and to make bloody well sure no one, anyone would ever suspect we had it for those dates and lost it."

"I can see your concern, Sir Anthony."

"You understand now that it is more important that no one finds out what we lost and when we lost it than even your regaining it?"

"I understood," said Rawson, his left hand still aching. "Don't worry about that."

"But you found out."

"No one else will," said Rawson. "There is nothing for them to find out with."

"But how did you find out without being told?"

"I read an inscription beneath a basalt block, Sir Anthony," said Rawson, taking his left hand out of his pocket and with it chips of quartz-white heathstone.

"Your hand, what happened?" asked Sir Anthony, wincing. Many small cuts, some shredding the skin, had ground into the palm as though some rodent had gnawed on it. It was bloated.

"Had to hold the hand close to the penknife blade to catch the stone as I chipped enough of the inscription away. Undoubtedly, it was Elizabeth who had that line put there, but to anyone familiar with that body of literature about our—possession, it was an advertisement for what rested above it," said Rawson. He was sure he knew why Elizabeth had done it.

The cellar disguised the bowl, with the gems being a proper honor for such a relic. But it was ordered crafted before England's victory over the Spanish. Afterward she probably had little doubt it was of some immense power. But what to do? Melt it down again? Take away the jewels? Not for her Grail. She placed it in the safest place in England, and then so successors of this childless monarch would know what it was, she had the inscription cut into the stone. Who covered it with the basalt pedestal? Who knew? It could have been Elizabeth I. But she had indeed entrusted it to her nation for the future. That was what it was doing hidden in Windsor for four centuries.

"Thought you might like to have the chips if for some reason in the future our Sovereign wishes to restore that inscription with the original stone," said Rawson. "Be painstaking, but I am sure it can be done by some stonemason who wouldn't recognize what he was trying to restore. Stonemasons are not notoriously literate. More useful, perhaps, than an Oxford don, but most certainly less literate. Her Majesty's secret is safe."

"I must have your pledge on that. That is absolutely first priority."

"You do."

"You'll make sure of that."

"There is no way now that anyone can find out. I chipped out the last physical evidence. It was four hundred years old, hidden in the bowels of the Round Tower in a locked passageway with only one entrance, and now even that stone message, which I daresay few would understand, is gone."

"Then get her back for England," said Sir Anthony. And this time he took a sip of port like a gentleman. And enjoyed it. "You know I believe we really did have the actual cup of the Last Supper."

"Really?" asked Rawson. He put his hand back in his pocket.

"Yes. Relics at that time were notoriously forged. Notorious. Vials of Mary's milk that were mercury. Straw from the manger that was gold and silver. Enough wood from the one true cross, they said, to build a fence around the Vatican. But ours was a poorish bowl, just the kind Our Lord might use. Now if that doesn't convince you it was real, I don't know what will." Sir Anthony shook his head with conviction.

"Then you believe," said Rawson.

"I do. I believe, Captain, you may well be searching for our greatness. Get her back. Get her back for England. For everything we are and always were. For England, Captain."

"Save the chips," said Rawson cheerily. "You'll need them when I return our bowl. And don't worry. I should be the only one who has a chance of finding it. I'm the only one after it who knows how valuable our poorish bowl is, and undoubtedly I am the only one who has a nation behind him."

It wasn't the lady's looks, or even some of the unique stones, that got Detective Modelstein moving that day, putting the word out in the right places that there was an interest in some large colored stones that might be moving hot.

It was the damned little imitation marble-covered notebook she had bought and filled with her own neat handwriting, the kind of notebook in which Arthur Modelstein of P.S. 19 and millions of other New York City schoolchildren learned to write their first letters, and the kind in which they learned that neatness counted and that honesty was rewarded and that they lived in the greatest country in the world where everyone was created equal.

Claire Andrews had been neat. She had all that faith that, having written everything down neatly, persevering as she was told, justice would prevail. The rightness of her cause would win. Her father was innocent as all daddies had to be, and in the course of time, justice would out.

It was beautiful. Artie wanted to kiss her. On the cheek, no less. More than that, he wanted her at home in Carney, and maybe telling bad stories about the horrible city, and getting married to another Wasp in Carney, Ohio, and raising other little Wasps who would become chairmen of the Joint Chiefs of Staff or run big banks or the country itself, and noticing spring coming with the flowers instead of an absence of slush. Of Claire Andrews, Artie thought she would never have a plastic pumpkin on Halloween as he did.

Claire Andrews was real pumpkin, with her mother making pie from the insides instead of insisting Artie wrap them in the *New York Post* and get rid of them immediately. He had only bought a real pumpkin once, and his mother threw it out when it began to sag three days before Halloween.

Claire Andrews was all the innocent hope that was in a fresh notebook that always began a school year. She was Artie before he got out of the first grade. She was the girl in the schoolbooks chasing perfectly round red and yellow balls across color-box green fields with a very happy dog who never made in the gutter or got run over.

Artie moved out that morning into his world of fences and informers, crooks and merchants, dealers and con men, and he began the almost impossible task of getting back something he knew didn't exist from people who had no reason to return it.

All he had was that the lady would not lie. The word on Battissen was that he lived in the gray area of the law, dealing forgeries but in such a way that he was not really vulnerable. He sold forgeries on the side, but the people who bought them knew they were forgeries and if they didn't and complained, he would buy them back at the sale price. The fact was everyone knew there was a market for forgeries and the only time they became criminal cases was when someone foolishly sold one of them at an original's price. Then the person who paid $150,000 for a Picasso that wasn't went to the police.

Battissen, according to the book on him, was never one of those.

He would gum but he would never bite, and the last thing he would ever do was steal something worth a million—this was the word from fences, thieves, and forgers.

It was worth a push on Geoffrey Battissen, who didn't, as the word went, like trouble.

Detective Modelstein found Battissen Galleries a quiet, expensive establishment with an elegant presence that made him regret not spending more on his tie. It had rugs that devoured sound and elegant white fabric walls that encouraged whispers.

So Artie yelled as though fighting for attention in a Bronx candy store.

"Detective Arthur Modelstein from Fraud," Artie boomed in the middle of the gallery. Everyone looked around. A slick young woman in severe black hurried over to him. He flashed his badge. "I'd like to see Geoffrey Battissen."

The voice was louder than it had to be. So was the repetition. A middle-aged gay man in a robin's egg blue blouse walked desperately quickly from the back, looking as though someone had nailed a bee into his crotch.

Mr. Battissen suggested strongly they discuss this matter in his office, and Artie loudly talked about hot goods all the way to the back.

"I got a complaint against you about some stolen goods. I'm talking grand larceny. Grand larceny, Mr. Battissen. It doesn't look good."

Battissen listened. His pinkish face paled, but he didn't break.

"Are you going to charge me with something, officer?" said Battissen, cleaning imaginary dust off the corner of a glass table.

"I'm gonna ask you questions. I'd like some answers."

"Am I a suspect?"

"Sure," said Artie.

"Then talk to my lawyer," said Battissen.

"I'm talking to you. I'm talking to you about a young lady who trusted you with a gold saltcellar. I'm talking about switch. I wouldn't try to move stuff like that if I were you."

"Officer Modelstein, are you going to charge me with something?"

"I'm wondering how real those pictures are out in the gallery. You think art experts would say there aren't some forgeries here?"

"Is somebody pressing charges?" asked Battissen.

The man was right. Artie couldn't touch him. Almost no one ever pressed a charge for buying forgeries. If they pressed charges, they would have to prove the painting they owned was phony. That would definitely make their property less valuable while only offering the possibility that they might win a lawsuit that might recover the money. On the other hand, if they kept their mouths shut, they could pass on the forgery, often for a modest profit. And Artie was sure they would just as soon use Battissen again, because he had a proven ability to sell forgeries.

So Battissen knew there probably wasn't anyone around who was going to press charges, which meant Artie was flapping his tongue in this very expensive place on Fifth Avenue.

"I'll be back," said Artie, letting the dealer know there would be more crude noise amidst this quiet sophistication. Which was all he was doing in the first place. If Artie could increase the nuisance value to the owner of Battissen Galleries, then it might mean a few thousand more to the lady from Ohio. Of course, that implied that Claire Andrews of the pure white notebook, and perfect daddy, would settle for a few thousand more.

Artie had lunch in the back room of a diamond cutter on Forty-seventh Street, where he felt comfortable again. He was accepted by these people so much that he could entertain the illusion that he was part of the cutting trade, but he knew he wasn't. He would always be a policeman even though he could eat a pastrami sandwich next to one hundred thousand dollars worth of uncut diamonds, careful not to let the coleslaw drip on the wax paper that held them. They looked like a handful of bumpy caramels. But in the hands of Dov Katzman and his son they would be cleaved in planes to sparkle and glisten under "the light," that special banking of lights that made diamonds jump with so much life that people buying rings would sometimes wonder where the luster went the minute they left the store. That luster was the cleaved reflection of light. Without cleaved planes, a diamond had none of that sparkle in any light. Artie wondered why anyone would ever polish a diamond instead of cutting it. He asked that of the Katzmans. He did not mention that Claire's cellar had about a half dozen of them.

"It's the old way," said Katzman, offering Artie a glass for his diet cream soda. "They only discovered cleaving in the seventeen hundreds. You'll never see a stone like that today."

"Maybe you will," said Artie. He said nothing more and finished his sandwich.

He could not put the word out that large uncleaved stones were stolen because then he would have to admit he did not have a description or gem prints, and that would have been tantamount to announcing there was no provable claim on them. Diamonds that might have been eschewed by dealers as hot, treated as hot, with possible rumors to that effect, would become as free and open as sunlight. And this despite the famed honor of "the street."

A dealer's word on Forty-seventh Street to another dealer was bond, even with religious overtones of rabbinical courts deciding disputes. If it should ever be found that someone knowingly dealt hot stones, his word would no longer be accepted for a deal. And without that handshake from one diamond merchant to another, more legally binding for them than any contract between banks or nations, a man could not buy or sell on the street or in Tel Aviv, London, or Antwerp.

But the moment Artie advertised that five or six large uncuts without parentage could not be traced, the diamonds in the big gold piece could have moved out of sight like rain into the Hudson. Even the honor of the street might not protect them.

If diamonds were a generally closed business around the world, rubies were so exclusive there were only a few people in any city who even knew the name of a dealer.

Artie not only knew one, but he was a friend to one, perhaps the man's only friend.

He had not seen him for a year when he knocked on the plain office door that had no sign. Norman Feldman did not want anyone coming to his office who did not know him already.

His space was in a morose and somewhat seamy office building on Forty-eighth Street. It could have been anywhere, because the only thing Feldman needed was good north light, the only proper light in which to examine a ruby. Feldman chose midtown Manhattan and its high prices because being there saved him time getting around the city. The only way money really mattered to Feldman was as a way to keep score, a way to record he had gotten a good deal, and a way in selling to know he had made one also. It was, to Feldman, a question of doing things right. So while he could pay fifty thousand dollars a year for a rental that would save him some time, he would also save paper clips from letters in a small white wood box, because wasting money was not doing things right either.

Artie knew Feldman looked down on the diamond dealers, many of them Hasidic Jews. He also looked down on all rabbis, as well as priests, ministers, merchants, museum curators, the Internal Revenue Service, and speculators.

Norman Feldman, like the Catholic Church, believed in original sin. Unlike the Church, Norman Feldman did not believe God provided any sort of solution to it.

"A large ruby the size of a goose egg. Hear about it?" asked Artie, entering the sparse office with the good north light. He did not say hello. Feldman would only have asked him what he wanted without replying anyhow. Feldman did not believe in small talk like hello.

Feldman sat behind a large oak desk with five black telephones on it. His hands stayed on the arms of the old oak swivel chair, which probably had the button that unlocked the door and let Artie in. One of the telephones was ringing. Feldman did not answer it. He did this sometimes, why Artie was not sure, but he suspected it was Feldman's way of insuring privacy from answering services or machines, anything that might leave information around as to who had tried to contact him. Because of this, Artie was never sure when Feldman was in.

Behind Feldman was a small scale, set up on a plain wood shelf. There were no books or pictures. The phone stopped ringing.

"What are you talking about?" asked Feldman.

"I am talking about a large red stone the size of a goose egg. It may be a ruby. Could be a ruby."

"And if it were a ruby would you know what you are talking about?"

"I would hope so. You taught me," said Artie.

"No, I didn't," said Feldman. "So don't act like an idiot."

"I sat in this chair in this room with that north light and looked into your ruby. Here."

"Right," said Feldman.

"So?" said Artie.

"So you don't know what you're talking about."

"I'm talking about a damned ruby I saw, and another one I may be looking for."

"You saw my ruby. Right. Twenty karats. Rare. Pigeon's blood. A beautiful stone. You saw that."

"Right."

"When you're talking goose egg—that is, if you ever saw a goose egg in your life, a real one I mean—you are talking in the size of rubies, a great gem. A great gem. Not a good one. You saw a good one."

"So it's larger."

"Artie, don't break my heart by saying these things. You really think that a four-karat ruby is four times more valuable than a one-karat ruby?"

"I know that it's not," said Artie.

"So if we are not dealing in an arithmetical progression, and you see a twenty-karat stone that is a rare gem, what would one four times that size be?"

"A hundred times more valuable? I don't know."

Feldman shook his head. "Of that size you do not know. It's nothing I have ever talked to you about. Even the crown of England doesn't have a real ruby—it's a spinel. Don't come in here talking great rubies. Please," said Feldman with disgust.

"I'm listening," said Artie. He was not going to cower at Feldman's disapproval.

"You don't need to know."

"It may be stolen," said Artie.

"Go back to the gonifs on Forty-seventh Street. Play with the diamonds. Put them in wristwatches. Go. Chase necklaces of emeralds. Get out of here."

"I'm asking a question. There's been a big swindle in this town."

"You don't know what you're doing. I spent all this time talking to you about stones, teaching you about stones, and you come in here with silly questions about great rubies."

"I'm asking if the damned thing has come to you for sale."

"The problem today is every gonif, everyone with a dollar in his pants, thinks he belongs in great gems. It's a whole other world. A whole other thing. You've got nothing to do with it."

"I'm talking about stolen property."

"You steal a car, that's stolen property. You steal a country, that's a historical event. Go chase stolen cars. I hate to hear you talking this foolishness. I hate people who don't know what they're doing."

"Stealing is stealing, Norman."

"Artie, if you hung around me for a couple of years and did nothing else, you might get to suspect what I'm talking about."

"How did you learn?"

"Lucky to be alive is how I learned. Really great gems are a whole other world. There are no courts and things like that. Stay where you know what you're doing."

It was then that Artie realized Feldman had not taught him a vast amount about his business. He had omitted what may have been a way of life, and Artie had never suspected this over all these years. Was that the world ringing on the phones Feldman did not answer?

"You mean I could get killed?"

"No. Never. You won't get close enough."

"Don't bet on it."

"If you had something to bet with, I would wager everything in my life, idiot. I would form consortiums to raise money to bet. Bet? Get me that bet."

"Has a man named Geoffrey Battissen tried to sell you a ruby that size?"

"You can bet him, too."

"What can I bet?"

"That he doesn't belong with a stone like that anymore than you. You don't understand, you are not going to understand, so how have you been in the last year since I've seen you?"

"Okay. And you, Norm?"

"The same. How can I be in a world of idiots?"

That night, because they hadn't seen each other in so long, they had dinner together. They did not discuss business anymore. Artie had lasagna and calamari salad at the fine Italian restaurant. Feldman, who Artie knew was a millionaire many times over, ate a bologna sandwich on white bread. A single slice. Calories, as he said, were calories, and all special cooking was just another form of fraud and a waste of time.

[85]

"If you do run across that stone, let me know. Okay?" said Artie at the end of the evening.

"You ask one more stupid question like that," said Feldman, "and I really am not going to talk to you again. Ever. I mean it. What is the point?"

"Why is it stupid?"

"If I told you I saw it, it wouldn't make any difference. If I told you it was in the middle of your lasagna, it wouldn't make any difference."

"Why not?"

"Because it would only be on its way toward where it belongs."

"And where's that?"

"Not with you and probably not with anyone who is looking for it."

Claire didn't know why all the phones were ringing and why the man Bob Truet sent over from the *Carney Daily News* had to answer them all. Mother said Bob was just helping out.

"But why is it so important?" Claire asked as they ate so terribly alone in the large dining room with the fresh breakfast orange juice Dad used to love so much.

"The Columbus papers have less sensitivity, dear," said Lenore McCafferty Andrews, calmly, as though if she attempted to keep everything normal it might be as if nothing had happened. She unfolded her white linen napkin and placed it slowly beneath the table.

Claire was afraid to ask, but sensed Mother might not be grieving much. She had not cried at the funeral and didn't talk much about Dad. There had never been the closeness Claire felt she had had with her father. For breakfast, Mother was dressed bright and fresh in a yellow print dress, as though the only thing that had changed was one less setting of pale blue Wedgwood china on the white linen tablecloth. Even the pink autumn chrysanthemums were the same. The problem, and what made Claire so angry, was that she didn't know what to be angry about. Did she want them both to wear black and drape the house in black? Yes. And make the world drape black too? But of course, the world did not and that was why Claire asked why the papers were still calling from Columbus.

"The killing was a week ago," said Claire. She had not touched her napkin. Her right fist rested on top of it. Her egg sat unopened in the throne of the Wedgwood cup.

"Claire, we shouldn't blame ourselves for the crazy things other people do or say." Mrs. Andrews delicately chipped away at the top of her egg with a spoon, concentrating on every shell chip as though she were performing brain surgery.

"I cannot take a Lenore McCafferty Andrews life popsicle for an answer. I've got to have a direct clear answer as though I am a twenty-eight-year-old woman," said Claire.

She threw her napkin on top of her damned egg in the damned cup and it didn't even knock it over. She wanted to cry about that. She wanted to cry about anything. About Dad. She pushed the triumphant egg and her plate away. She wasn't hungry, and she resented the fact that her mother was eating her toasted English muffin and one soft boiled egg just as she had when Dad was alive. Of course, what could Claire demand? That her mother should fast? There was so much soul-consuming anger with no legitimate place to go.

"Apparently, when you attempted to sell Dad's property two days ago, and when it was stolen, you filed a report with the New York City police," said her mother.

"I had no way of knowing the art dealer was a thief. Anyone could have been misled by him. He was very effective, I told you," said Claire.

"I'm not blaming you, dear."

"I told you, the man knew so many things about Dad and the saltcellar."

"I'm not blaming you, dear. We don't need the money to survive."

"I don't care who you blame. You're always blaming someone for something. I'm just explaining," said Claire, and knew she was being unreasonable, and knew that Mother knew it and was overlooking it, making Claire feel childish, and all Claire had wanted was an answer to what the latest commotion was about.

"Because of that report, for which I am in no way blaming you, dear, the wire services sent out a single-paragraph story about the complaint, according to Bob Truet. What the papers in Columbus did was put reporters on the story because, while it wasn't important in New York or the rest of the world, it was here in Ohio, especially with large papers that circulate here."

"What are you trying to tell me?"

"The implication is that your father was trying to sell something through less than reputable sources, something that could be considered what they call hot goods."

"That's ridiculous. What did you say to the papers?"

"Bob Truet says the story will blow over in a few days, it always does," said Lenore.

"You did deny everything to the papers, of course," said Claire.

"What could we deny? I never even knew he had a saltcellar. He kept it hidden."

"It was his lucky piece, Mom. I saw it. I want to talk to the newspapers."

"Bob Truet thinks that would only prolong things," said Lenore, breaking off a piece of the English muffin and, before it could get cold, dunking it into the yellow egg yolk.

"You ought to be ashamed of yourself," said Claire, livid.

"What do you honestly want from me, dear?" asked her mother.

"Oh, that is so like you," said Claire, feeling her whole body boil, snarling at Mother, who did not look up from that damned egg. "I'm not going to let this go. I'm not letting anything go. We're going to get back that cellar, too. I have a New York detective on that situation. I am not giving up. I'm not letting everything of Dad's go just like that because he's not here to defend it."

Claire turned over her eggcup and cracked it down hard on her plate. The plate, thank God, broke. Her mother paused, looked up, and placid as a pond returned to her breakfast. Claire knew this would not even be mentioned again.

She went by herself to the family lawyer, Blake Comstock, who immediately cancelled all appointments for the morning and sat with her on the soft leather couch of his dark warm office with the funny cartoons of lawyer business behind his desk and the degrees from Ohio State and Harvard on the wall. She had been here with Dad a few times. Mr. Comstock had been at the funeral. She had phoned him from New York City when the cellar was stolen.

She explained what was happening now. Mr. Comstock was younger than her father, but looked older because of his white hair and the layers of fat around his face. Ordinarily analytic, he would lay out options for things and what they could do and others could do.

This time, he told her bluntly, a libel suit against the Columbus newspapers for the damage to Dad's reputation was absolutely inadvisable. Absolutely.

"For one I don't have any tangible evidence Vern owned the salt-cellar. He did sell it from a bank vault quite discreetly."

"He couldn't let his creditors know how much he needed cash."

"Claire, you asked me for some receipts, some bills of sale in a phone call from New York City. Nowhere in Vern's estate is there any evidence that he owned a saltcellar."

"What are you saying? I want it clear and direct," said Claire. She wore an autumn sweater and a dark wool skirt, her hair hanging loose, looking almost like she had in high school. She leaned forward in the couch, a very hard thing to do with so much soft leather around her. Mr. Comstock sat on the other end of the couch.

"Vern Andrews knew what he was doing. While Bob Truet wouldn't even hint at it in his *Carney Daily News,* I think most of us, without thinking any the worse of Vern, have to acknowledge that he was trying to sell something that was to all intents and purposes stolen or at least questionable."

"How could you not think the worse of him in that case? I would. But I don't. Because both you and I know Dad would never do anything illegal."

Mr. Comstock looked pained, and in his most comforting manner said: "Claire, I considered Vern not only a client but a friend. I knew him, perhaps in ways that a daughter didn't. I liked him. I trusted him and I also knew he played in the fast lane and he wasn't afraid to cut corners. He amassed quite a fortune. Even the collapse has left enough rubble for you to live on for the rest of your life. Comfortably. Here. You come from a good family, the McCaffertys . . ."

Claire pulled back in the sofa. She could not believe this man, who went out of his way so often to tell her how wonderful her father was just on the chance it might get back to Dad, now felt so free without any evidence to slander him.

"I don't think he trusted you enough to confide in you as to the purchase of the cellar."

"I wouldn't put it that way."

"But it is a fact that there were many deals he made that you were not privy to."

"Yes."

"So it is possible that he had purchased this cellar as an investment and never told you, which does not mean he was dealing in stolen property."

"It's very hard, Claire, for someone to see one's own father in a less than ideal light. A suit for libel first of all has to show allegations are false. The Columbus newspapers only reported facts that would make people suspicious. Can we disprove that you said he kept it hidden in a cellar until he chose an art dealer to sell it on the quiet?"

The couch, like the whole office, felt sticky. Claire sat rigid, her hands squeezing the life out of her little white purse.

"Doesn't right mean anything anymore in the world? Do you have to be assured of winning before you try? Is that what we're down to?"

"It's the world, Claire.

"It's only the world if you let it be. My father was killed while trying to sell his property. I am going to not only get it back, but prove eventually that he acted as he lived, honestly and decently. I would have hoped that I could have had your support."

"You do. The best support I can tell you is to let this go. It's too bad Vern was killed. It's too bad all this came out the way it did, but it did. I am your friend. Let me be that."

She left Mr. Comstock's office forcing herself to be civil. At the bank, at the shoe store, at the magazine vendors, no one mentioned Dad as they had just after his death. Even her once closest friend from high school, Mary Beth Hayes, now Mrs. Mary Thornburgh, talked about everything but Dad when they met outside Prangle's Market.

Mary Beth had two boys, seven and eight, and they were tearing up the family station wagon.

"Do you think my father was dishonest, Mary Beth? Do you?" asked Claire.

"I don't believe the papers," said Mary Beth.

"Do you believe Dad would deal in something that was stolen. You've always been honest. Be honest now. Please. I want to know. I have to know. What do you honestly think?"

Mary Beth warned one of her boys to act mannerly.

"What do you think, Mary Beth?" asked Claire.

Her friend looked pained and drew in a good solid breath.

"No one blames you, Claire. Everyone likes you, Claire. You and your mother will always be considered the best part of this town," said Mary Beth and had to drive off because the boys were just too much, leaving Claire alone in front of the market, and knowing she alone not only believed her father innocent, but also knew that he belonged with the best of Carney. No, he was better than they were because he had come so far with his life, while all Mother's family had to do was be born.

I don't want to live among these people, thought Claire. I don't even think I can anymore.

By the time she got home, Mother had heard from Mr. Comstock about her plans to prove Vern Andrews's innocence. Mother had Bob Truet there in a casual sports jacket, which meant he was going to stay for dinner. Bob was explaining how difficult facts were to unearth for trained professionals much less someone who did not have much experience. Mother nodded as the town's publisher delivered the McCafferty line for the McCafferty convenience. Claire heard him through, then went upstairs to pack.

She was going to New York.

Finally, that got to Mother.

"You can't do that. You hate New York."

"I do," said Claire. It felt good. It felt so deliciously, perfectly good because it was beyond reason. Even her bloodstream knew it was good, and she didn't stop to make sure she had everything. In front of Bob and her mother, she phoned her airline reservations.

Bob begged her to wait a day to think it over.

Claire ignored him. Her mother didn't know what to say. But Mother never knew what to say. She just stood there quiet, making Claire feel guilty and stupid and then childish and furious about feeling all those things.

Mother asked a stupid question about whether Claire had enough clothes, and Claire answered that she could buy whatever she needed in New York. They did sell clothes there just as on Main Street.

"You don't have to prove anything to anyone, dear," said her mother.

"Oh, but I do. And most of all to you. I will always have to prove something to you, but I never thought it would be that Dad wasn't a crook."

Bob Truet offered to drive her to the airport, and she refused. Then, to add to the craziness of it all, in the parlor overlooking the east garden, Bob, in begging her once more not to go, proposed marriage. Again.

"Thank you. No," said Claire, just about the same way she had rejected the ride, with gratitude and aversion.

Claire Andrews left Carney alone in a taxicab to Columbus through the cornfields whose yellowed stalks were being plowed under for the winter, past the stadium on a street named for an All-American who had played there and had the bad taste not to make it in the pros but returned to a job selling cars right up on Troy Road, and every year the *Carney Daily News* asked his opinion on the new Carney High School team and every year they were the best bunch of boys he had ever seen. Quickly she moved away from all that she had ever known, past the fairgrounds, and farms, and wood fences, and the Miami River quiet and low now, waiting to ice over later in the year.

She flew to New York and because it was late spent the first night in a hotel room. But the next day, she rented an apartment in the borough of Queens.

It was the first lease she had ever signed in her life, and the rent was exorbitant, but much less than Manhattan, which was unreal. And the street seemed somewhat nice. It had trees on it. The apartment had a single bedroom and a large living room that could be turned into an office to conduct her work. She did not know how she would begin or even where. She knew this great city had to have more libraries and lawyers and people who could find out things than practically anywhere on earth. And it was here that Dad's cellar was stolen, and here he died, possibly even was murdered, she thought now, by those who had swindled her. She didn't know. She only knew that here she had to start.

She signed a two-year lease and phoned her mother to send her personal furniture, but even then she did not feel as though she had left. Only at 3:00 A.M., when sleeping on a bare mattress she had purchased quickly, did she realize she had really left home. She had awakened and thrown her feet out over the bed and there was no bed, only floor that rudely smacked her feet.

It was dark and there was no one to call and no one to help, and she was alone. Cars honked outside on the street, and she didn't know where the light switch was at first. On her knees she crawled to a wall and then stood up.

She was twenty-eight years old and realized she had been sleeping on a mattress, waiting for furniture, and this was going to be her life. It would be as good as she would make it or as bad as she would make it, but she would have to make it herself.

And in her twenty-eighth year, this was her first real night alone. And it scared her bone-numb just shy of weeping. All her noble promises of vindicating her father and seeing justice done seemed emptier than the night. How could she do all those things? She didn't even feel secure enough now to make it to morning.

She walked out into the living room that she had planned with such certainty to become a headquarters. The walls were fresh white and bare. The floor was polished, and there was nothing on it. And she didn't even have a teabag or a cup or any place to sit. The only thing in this room was her.

This is the lowest point in my life, she thought. And then she thought that if it were, things could only get better. It did not reassure her. It only made sense.

She didn't want to return to the bedroom because she knew she couldn't fall asleep now, but she didn't want to stay in the living room, this supposed headquarters of her mission, because that reminded her of how really helpless she was in the world. She looked at the walls. Barren.

She could remain standing all night feeling helpless, or she could do something. She had to fill up the night with something besides her fear, she knew. From her suitcase, she took out her notebook, a pen, and a roll of tape she had purchased in the hotel. She tore a sheet out of the notebook and facing the longest blank wall taped a piece of square white paper at eye level near the right side.

"That represents the last two weeks," she said. It was a piece of white paper on a white wall. But it was something. The wall was not barren anymore. The paper was the time in which Dad came to New York to sell the cellar, when he was killed by the mugger, and when the cellar was stolen by the Battissen Galleries with that twenty-two-year reputation for integrity. Then, on the extreme left of the blank wall, she taped another piece of paper. She did not have a date for that, but wrote that this was the day the cellar was made.

She stepped back and looked at her two points in time. In between, it had to have been bought and sold and traded. The wall was very white. There was so much space. She added another piece of paper, next to the one on the extreme right. That was twenty years ago, when she had seen it in the basement.

She wrote down a schedule for herself for the next day. First, there was the New York Public Library. Then there was a telephone call to Detective Modelstein. She decided she would need a separate book for the criminal aspect of the cellar. So she put down getting more stationery supplies as the third most important thing.

Then she again reviewed the questions she had written down in that fresh notebook, the ones she had asked Detective Modelstein. She decided that now was the best time to make as good a drawing of the cellar as she could remember.

It was an awful drawing. She used a pencil and none of it was quite right. The more she drew, the more she realized she was forgetting what it looked like. Suddenly, she tore out pages of the notebook and laid them flat until they were roughly the size of the cellar. And then she made a dot where the ruby was, and another dot where the sapphire was, and a dot where she remembered what looked like topaz, and the jade lions and the polished clear diamonds around the base. Then she shut her eyes and tried to imagine the cellar as she had seen it in the vault, and as soon as she opened her eyes, she made a circle the size of the ruby around the dot exactly as she had remembered it. She knew this was inaccurate as all getout, but it was something. There were borders of reality. Once it got down on paper she was no longer dealing with infinity. There were limits. And in those limits fear and doubt could not get out of hand.

She had never been to a business school and would have been surprised if anyone had told her she was establishing direction and parameters, a prerequisite for any operation. Nor would she have been impressed that what she had done was cut infinity down to size by taking the first steps toward determining where the cellar had been, and, she hoped, where it was.

All she knew was that if she did not do these things, she would open herself up to despair without borders.

She got sleepy before dawn and went back into the bedroom with the lone mattress in it and went to sleep. When she woke up, right there in her living room was a life-sized picture of the cellar and, from wall to wall, the time in which it had been created. She was not wandering around in space anymore. She had a beginning. Dad's cellar had a time and a place, and she was going to find it, find all about it, even who sold it to him.

VII

You are aware that this quest was undertaken to glean some knowledge
of the mysteries of the Holy Grail, which Our Lord has promised to
reveal to the true knight who shall transcend in chivalry and virtue
his fellows past and future.   —WALTER MAP
Queste del Saint Graal, 1225

A jeweler's graver, a short triangle
of a blade at the end of a round wood pommel, dug into her soft gold
waist. It cut ugly wedges into the elegant scrollwork of Simon Sedgewick,
most late of London's Worshipful Company of Goldsmiths. With short
hard chops, like tears around an eye, it gashed away from the blue
Poseidon, never toward, until the magnificent stone stood raised away
from the cellar, as though set high in a wound.

Drops of perspiration fell from the cutter's forehead to his hand,
and he ignored them. He delicately severed the last gold tendons to the
blue stone with a dental probe, plucking out the sapphire into a soft
white bathroom towel.

In the same way, the Christ's head ruby left the Tilbury's breast,
and the diamonds left her base one by one, revered and treasured by the
hands that desecrated the scrolling and carelessly chipped the jade lions
when getting into the cellar's bosom. Even her adornments of topaz
brilliants suffered as fulcrums for tools, and yet this was the only time

since the cellar left the tent in Tilbury field that this work of Goldsmith Simon Sedgewick was appreciated.

All the great stones were held by bezels, thin strips of gold with seats for the gems, cross sections of which looked like wires shaped like the letter L. For centuries now, machines had made them, but the ones in the cellar were perfectly crafted by hand, first flattened by some other metal, then cut so perfectly that only the jeweler's loupe showed a human hand had almost matched a machine, which never could, on the other hand, produce such intricate grandeur as the scrolling on this awesome monument of gold.

Even more revealing of the talent that had made this cellar was evidence that the sapphire and ruby were removed once by different hands, hands less careful than those that had set them. It might have been to replace them with less valuable stones, but even under the fluorescent lights, even in their original places, the ruby and sapphire virtually screamed their magnificent worth.

Poseidon with his familiar crown and trident sat on a backless throne, well carved, perhaps too well carved because some of the sapphire had to be removed to make that raised image. The Christ's head, Christ in thorns and apparently weeping, was crude but crude with purpose. It left the ruby with maximum stone.

For some reason the diamonds had not been removed. This was clear in the careful way they remained in their bezels, without a ripple or a bubble in their gold settings, most clearly seen in a cross section, when they, too, were shorn.

Even gouged of her major gems, the cellar stood with the dignity Simon Sedgewick's pride of work had given her in Tilbury Field. But she could not withstand the thin German blade that hacked her into quarters, more manageable for the acetylene torch waiting to melt away the last sign that she had ever been an English cellar.

Perhaps the cutter worked too quickly, now that the major cash gems were free, but he found his blade spewing pink powder for a while before he noticed it. He withdrew the saw and wedged in with the graver. This was not a frame set into the solid gold, because it held up nothing. It was a fired clay of some sort, easily seen as the gold came off, protected by a cloth that fell away when exposed to the air. He cracked several topaz brilliants cutting toward that strange thing in the center.

What was it doing there? He freed it easily because kiln-fired clay did not adhere to gold. It took some crude hacking to get to it, but finally it was out, missing a little chip he had just made. Of common kiln-fired clay, the bowl was a little larger than his palm, with some sort of undistinguished black lacquer at the base. The bowl had no reason to be there structurally, and yet it was there, right in the middle, almost as though it had worn the cellar itself. So as to protect that bowl, the gold around it had been folded plates, not melted into form like the rest.

He put it aside quickly. He did not have time for it now. He freed the rest of the gold in manageable chunks and lit the acetylene torch. The ugly sulphur smell in the small room nauseated him, but the work was quick. He only needed 1,800 degrees to melt gold, and the blue flame of the acetylene far exceeded that. He held the chunks with a ring clamp, a design from ancient Egypt, still used to this very day. In four thousand years nothing better had been invented. Two separate bars of wood were bound in the middle by a simple ring. When a wedge pressed in one side, it clamped down the other side. No screws, no gears, one simple thrust of a wedge in one end and the gold was held in the other.

He held the gold over a large, specially treated block of charcoal. The gold melted into yellow rivers that flowed down the funnels of the charcoal into one-ounce molds. He had to be careful. Molten gold could go right through flesh and bone like a burning penny through butter.

In such a way, ounce by ounce, did the cellar disappear into its sellable parts. More than eight hundred single ounces of gold, six yet to be cut gem-grade diamonds, a blue sapphire of roughly one hundred and fifty karats, and an awesome pigeon's blood ruby of at least eighty.

Lying among the jade lions and topaz pieces waiting for disposal was the strange piece of clay. These were the least worthy items, not worth the bother on the slight possibility one might be recognized.

The room now reeked of sulphur as he wrapped the ruby in one felt bag and the sapphire in another, and the diamonds first in wax paper and then in boxes. Of all the stones, the ruby was the most delicate. A drop on a table could shatter it.

He dumped the jade lions and the topazes and the pink-baked clay into a canvas sack, ready to hammer into rubble, but as the hammer raised, he wondered just who could identify a bowl in the center of a mass of gold? And clearly, the bowl had been set in some special way, otherwise something as crude as that clay would have been like a common pebble in a crown. There had to be some reason behind it, and if that were the case, it might have a worth in itself. Or it might be nothing. In any case, unlike the jade lions and the square-cut topazes, it was certainly not going to be remotely identifiable because it had to have disappeared from human sight centuries before the invention of the camera. And certainly the bumptious Vern Andrews didn't know of it. He didn't even know it was a saltcellar he was selling.

The clay bowl came out of the canvas bag and was placed to the side of the valuable pieces. With a crack the hammer came down on the jade and topazes and lapis lazuli, once bright as summer rain, smashing rhythmically until there was only the soft sound of sand. The cutter rushed to get out of the foul-smelling room. The gems were now viewable in proper light, and most sellable. Treasures freed after centuries.

Claire Andrews almost ran from the stone lions in front of the New York Public Library. She had passed here once with her father and had said that some day she would like to go in, just to see what it was like.

Now she had to go in, and she felt the city was swallowing her. She couldn't count the people who passed her as she stood in the mild autumn day at the base of the steps that went on several layers above her to that mass of a building, that thing so large its shelves expanded every year by miles, greater than the distance of the entire Carney shopping district. And this by the spines of the books. She knew that fact. She had read it somewhere.

What frightened her most, perhaps, was that everyone who passed did not know her. She had wanted all her life not to be treated well just because she was a McCafferty or Vern Andrews's daughter. And here she had it more than anywhere in the world. She was nobody. She didn't even have a library card.

What would happen if she made a fool of herself trying to find a book on saltcellars? What if there weren't any? What if there never had been? Ridiculous. If anyone knew anything about them, that knowledge had to have been written down somewhere, and if there were a place in the world that would have a good lead, she was looking up at it.

Did it matter that she would make a fool of herself? Of course it did. It mattered to her. But didn't people make fools of themselves all the time in libraries? And how different was this from Ohio State? She knew how to research. You couldn't get out of Ohio State without knowing how to use a library. And how different was State's library from this? And what was she really afraid of?

She was not ever going to be more afraid than last night, knowing she was alone for the first time, the realization that made people grown-ups. There was nothing up ahead of her that could possibly be worse than the 3:00 A.M. of the night before in that bare apartment with only herself.

Could she turn back? Go back where? It was all gone. Dad was gone. Back was Carney. And she couldn't go there, and she couldn't make herself move up the steps to the cavernous mouth of that library with the thousands of people all around, none of whom knew her. Or cared.

She wanted to be able to stand there forever, not going back to Carney, but not going forward either. She waited for someone to jostle her, perhaps try to pick her up, and thus motivate her to move. But no one did that for her.

People weren't even looking at her as strange for just standing there between the big cement lions of the New York Public Library.

And then she moved a single step because she already knew she had taken the first step before. It was last night when, instead of being overwhelmed by the infinity of a blank wall, she pasted up a piece of paper, and in doing so she had attacked it. Claire Andrews of Carney, Ohio, in her twenty-eighth year mounted the high steps of the New York Public Library, clutching her notebook and purse from pickpockets she was sure abounded in New York City.

She went through a turnstile and a check of her bag going in, and then she was confronted by more cavernous hallways, and she had to ask someone where the reference library was.

The words stuck in her throat. She never remembered stammering before, but she was doing it now, even speaking to a guard. It took her twenty minutes to find the main reference library—God, there was more than one—and another five minutes waiting in line to speak to a librarian while her palms sweated and her mouth felt dry, and she was sure she was perspiring.

"I wonder if you might help me look for this thing I'm looking for," she said when she got to the front of the line. The man wore eyeglasses. He had a nameplate on his checkered shirt that said *Grassi*.

"I'm not from New York, but I rent an apartment in Queens," she added. "I don't have a card yet."

"Whadya lookin' for?"

"Saltcellars. The cellars salt goes into. They were an old form of salt holders."

"I know what saltcellars are," said Grassi. He sent her to a room that had card files that seemed to stretch hundreds of yards. She had to walk to the S's. People read on pale oak tables illuminated by quiet green covered lights. There were twenty drawers of just the letter S.

She pulled open the drawer, and it came out in her hand because it was meant to be leafed through on adjacent tables.

Claire Andrews, she told herself, are you insane? Do you think the New York alphabet is different from the one you had in Carney?

Her fingers moved through the cards, at first uneasily, but then she found her first reference. There was no book on saltcellars, but there was a book on medieval dinnerware that had two chapters on saltcellars, which led her to another book on sculptors who made them.

She filled her notepads, found the copying machine, waited in line, and got reproductions of saltcellars.

The Cellini cellar was like a bowl with an incredibly graceful Neptune on it. She remembered the carving on the blue stone as being Poseidon, which was Neptune. Neptune was the Roman version of Poseidon. She wondered if there were any connection. There didn't seem to be. This Cellini cellar seemed graceful, a thing of delicate and magnificent form.

Dad's cellar was a big trunk of gold.

There was nothing in the Italian section remotely like it. But saltcellars definitely were European, according to the books. The German saltcellars seemed like boats, boats of salt for the table.

Was it possible Dad's piece was not a saltcellar? After all, she had only heard that it was one from Geoffrey Battissen. Would he have lied about that, too?

She waited on line to get a book on English silversmiths. There never seemed to be lines like this in Carney, and if there were lines she always knew the person behind her or ahead of her. She was glad she didn't have to talk to anyone. There was too much on her mind. Too much to think about. Too many steps to organize. Why was the line moving so slowly?

"Hey. What's holding it up?" yelled someone. She was glad he did.

Finally she got her book, Bernard Hughes on English silversmiths. On certain utensils, she noticed scrollwork similar to that on Dad's piece. Unlike the Italians, who made their scrollwork an integral part of the form, British smiths seemed to ignore what they were working on and just layered their scrolls over whatever shape the saltcellar took. Realizing she had observed this, she wondered if she were becoming an art expert. She had never been an expert in anything before. Of course she wasn't. One observation did not an expert make, but it did an expert begin, until, of course, some expert told her otherwise.

Nestled under a green shaded light on a long wood table, she found an interesting segment on maker's marks. Every bit of English gold and silver had to have the maker's mark since King Edward established the London Assay office in 1377. The marks were lions, leopards, and things like that. But she would have remembered seeing an engraving like that at the base. She tried to remember if she had seen anything like that on Lucky when Dad showed it to her. He had turned it around several times because she was curious about it, wondering if it made some sort of noise or lit up. A lion or a leopard or any engraving like that she would have remembered at nine. Dad's cellar didn't have it. And then she turned a page, and they were staring at her, undeniable, blatant, the British saltcellars. Trunks of gold with scrolls. Several of them in the Tower of London on display, others belonging to royalty, and a scant few in private collections. Some had roofs over the salt bowls. Some had bells. But all of them stood massive, trunklike, heavily scrolled. She had found the home of Dad's cellar. Unmistakably England.

Suddenly, someone was standing over her.

"I'm sorry. We're closing," said the young man with *Grassi* on his shirt.

"Already? Is it three?"

"It's five forty-five."

"Oh," said Claire. "Well, what do you know? Almost six. Thank you. What time do you open?"

"Ten. Do you need some help?" asked Grassi. He wore eyeglasses and had a sweet face.

"Thank you, no," said Claire.

"Can I walk you to the exit? I'm leaving myself."

"Sure," said Claire. She gathered up her notes. It had been a wonderful day. It had been a day of days. She would have the whole evening to cherish what she had done. The big thing was not finding England. The big thing was taking that first step up toward the library. After that England was inevitable. After that, it was all inevitable. She was going to find that time and place where Dad's cellar was made and track down who had sold it where until that time and that place where she proved he came into possession of it honestly. For some reason the young man escorting her to the door thought she had said she would go out with him.

"Oh, thank you for asking. That's so kind," said Claire. "But no. No. I'm busy."

"What about tomorrow night?"

"I'm busy with work. I don't want to go out with you. That's not too harsh, is it? You don't think that's harsh?"

"Nah," said the young man. She had hurt him. She didn't want to hurt him. She wouldn't have hurt him. But then again, she didn't have time. Of course she had been too harsh. Was she becoming a New Yorker? Was she living a life where she didn't have time for people's feelings now?

Claire stopped the train of thought, right there. She wanted to share the triumph of her day. Dad would have loved to have heard of this day she had had for herself. Anyone who cared about her would have. She did. She wanted to scream "Hooray for me." Back home she made a mark on the wall covering the fourteenth and fifteenth centuries and tacked up a map of Europe on which she circled England. On the very first day, she was sure she had discovered the saltcellar's time and place.

But she did not know the ages she was going to have to explore before she would understand about the cellar her father had possessed for two-score years. Parts were far older than England and even the date ascribed to the birth of the Messiah. And it was newer too, as new as the autumn night, and the cold of the winter yet to come in other cities of the world.

Artie Modelstein was lying in bed with Trudy, watching a football game between his feet, feeling her comfortably asleep next to him, satisfied that they had, as she had said, "reconnected on significant levels again" when the phone rang.

Whether his skin could transmit messages he couldn't know. But Trudy was awake on Claire's voice.

"I'm in New York for good now, and I have established a base," came the twangy cheerleader voice so sure of its own energy that it expected the world to jump with it. "I want you to have my telephone number. I think we can best coordinate if we know what everyone is doing. I've discovered some absolutely exciting things."

"Look, it's eleven P.M."

"I'm sorry. What's a good time to get you?"

"At the office. Maybe ten . . . in the morning."

"Fine. Arthur, this is so exciting. I've located the country it was made in."

"Good, and I'll speak with you tomorrow, thank you," said Artie.

"Who was that?" asked Trudy.

"Business."

"That woman you befriended out of the kindness of the Arthur Modelstein heart?"

"She phoned me. I did not phone her. There is no guilt in owning a telephone," said Arthur Modelstein, innocent.

"She felt free to call."

"She's a crazy lady. She feels free to do anything. You want to meet her? You want to hear what I'm going to say to her tomorrow? You want to know what I'm going to say?"

"No, Artie. I trust you. I just don't want to trust you for the wrong reasons, that's all."

"What does that mean?" asked Artie.

"You know."

"For the nondestructive, nonmanipulative, nonentangling relationship that you asked for, Trudy, this is none of the above," said Artie.

"You still know what I mean," said Trudy.

He did. But he knew she couldn't nail him on it.

In the morning, he saw that she had finished his coffee and left a note saying he needed more and that the conversation they had started the night before was not finished.

At 10:00 A.M., to the second, Claire Andrews's phone call arrived and posed an immediate decision for the evening to Detective Modelstein. On the one hand, there was to be a confrontation with Trudy at his apartment that night, or, on the other hand, there was the beautiful young woman with the fresh summer smile and enchanting innocence and yet-to-be-explored blouse and body, talking about her place, a wall, which she was using to track down a historical piece, and a mattress.

"I just have a mattress in the place; otherwise, I would invite you up."

"That's all right," said Artie.

"There's no pots, pans, silverware."

"I'll bring pizza and wine."

"I owe you a dinner."

"I'll bring it," said Artie. He did not trust her with food. He trusted no one from America's heartland with food. She might bring a bologna and mayonnaise pizza for all he knew. He trusted only Italians, Greeks, and other Jews to eat well. Everyone else had suspect taste, including the blacks, who for Artie were absolutely interchangeable with southern whites. He had seen black detectives order breakfast. He had watched a blotch of butter melting in white paste. He had been told with a big grin that they were grits. Southern whites ate that way, too. Artie had not finished his breakfast but had settled later for a danish on the run.

And of course most of the Irish were the worst of all. He was always sure their mothers learned to cook by reading the back of Betty Crocker boxes.

He decided not to tell her the good news but save it for the evening. He was sure Geoffrey Battissen was going to crack. If ever he had anyone who was ready to make a deal, it was Battissen. He had been there twice: the first time, he was told to leave, and the second time was even better.

Geoffrey Battissen threatened to bring a lawsuit if Detective Modelstein ever returned to the Battissen Galleries. So that morning Artie returned and Battissen refused to see him, leaving a customer and running back to his office. His red-headed assistant, as though ordered, blocked the way. A loud click came from the back of the gallery. Battissen had locked his door.

To avoid Detective Modelstein by locking himself in his office was like trying to get rid of a fund appeal by sending money. It was the one thing that would give some kind of handle, because once Battissen refused to be questioned he could be arrested as a material witness. And from that Artie might be able to break him into turning on everyone else, if there were someone else. There at least had to be a buyer, or possibly the art dealer still had the cellar, this despite Feldman's curious warning or prophecy that great stones mysteriously never stayed with the small fries.

"Look," said Artie to the red-headed assistant who had been left to block him. "I'm going to give you one more chance. If he won't talk to me, I am going to arrest him as a material witness. Now I've got nothing against your boss. But I've got a complaint that could lead to a grand larceny conviction. If this lady he took the cellar from doesn't drop charges, we're going to be dealing lawyers, grand larceny, and some heavy jail time. Tell him he's in a new league. And if he wants to get out of this clean, tell him to make a deal with the lady from Ohio. Thirty grand won't do it. She wants her property back. Do you understand?"

"I don't know," said the assistant in a whisper appropriate to the refined atmosphere of the gallery. She smiled nervously and ran her tongue over her superglossed lips. Artie wondered if she were turned on by this.

"Jail," said Artie in a decibel that would have done justice to an elevated train. "Jail. Theft. Grand larceny. Criminal."

"All right. All right," said the assistant.

"I'm coming back tomorrow. No talk, arrest warrant. Jail."

"Yes. I heard. Thank you," said the assistant.

"I'm not talking about the forgeries around here. Jail."

"Yes. Please."

And for good measure, of course, Artie phoned from outside, getting Battissen on the line and delivering the threat again. Like a good poker player who knew when his bluff was working, Artie knew when someone was going to fold.

No matter what Feldman said, Artie didn't have to understand the process of great gems. He understood people. He would let the great stones take care of themselves. And he had put in too much of his day already on this cellar and the stones that he was almost certain were gone for good.

Before he went to dinner with the lovely lady from Ohio, he got a tip on a sure collar. An old friend of his, part of his familiar world, had opened up another jewelry store, this one on Canal Street. He was an Iranian immigrant, named Mordechai Baluzzian, and Artie had been told Baluzzian was acting as a fence again.

Not only was Baluzzian dealing hot goods, but he had the audacity to put in the front window a large pear-shaped diamond ring that was definitely hot goods.

There was the normal cry from Baluzzian of persecution, and the normal hint of a bribe, the latter annoying Artie.

"C'mon," Artie said, and the man just smiled and hinted at a larger bribe.

"I'll collar you for that, c'mon. This one-karat flawless pear-shaped

[103]

with the baguettes has got a report on it. It's steaming," said Artie, standing over a display rack of rings in the Canal Street jewelry store of Mordechai Baluzzian, who had more sale signs in his window than goods.

"I purchase it from the most legitimate of dealers. The most legitimate," said Baluzzian. He was a small dark man with delicate hands that seemed to do his weeping for him. He wore a three-piece gray-striped suit more appropriate for a boardroom than for this store on Canal Street.

"We'll run its gem prints," said Artie.

"I never saw the man before," said Baluzzian, kissing his fingers as though making a holy vow.

"C'mon, Mordechai. Why do you say these things?" said Artie.

"If I were an Ashkenazi, you would look the other way."

"Mordechai."

"A nice emerald for your wife. Take it."

"I'm gonna break your head."

"I know of worse that the Ashkenazi do."

"Good. Tell me. You know I work with information. You give me something good on them, then we're talking business, then we're talking about some reduced charges."

"How can I? They are such criminals, Arthur, no one knows how they do it. No one."

"I've nailed a Hasid," said Artie. "They're not saints."

"One. In all your years, one. And then some retail store. You have never touched a dealer. Never. Never one of your sanctified diamond dealers. If they had dark skins, Arthur, it would have been more than one."

There was some truth in what Baluzzian said, but not much. Granted, the Ashkenazi did not deal with the Iranian Jews, but neither would they ever deal with Artie either, who was an Ashkenazi also. It was a closed business, and the reason so little fraud was engendered among dealers was that the rabbinical courts did not believe in punishments of a few years, but in terms of banishment forever. This Baluzzian did not wish to know.

"Give me help. Give me information," said Artie before booking Mordechai Baluzzian, whose hostility toward Ashkenazi did not extend to his selection of lawyers. This Ashkenazi lawyer was now trying to make a case against Artie on grounds that arresting Mordechai Baluzzian for the fourth time might be construed as harassment and prejudice. Just before he went over to the address in Queens Claire had given him, Artie made one more phone call to the Battissen Galleries. It was four-thirty in the afternoon, and they had closed for the day, according to the answering service.

At Battissen's home, another answering service said he was not there. At both, Artie left a message that if Geoffrey Battissen did not get back to him by the morning he was going to have to swear out a warrant for his arrest as a material witness.

Then he picked up a bottle of Chianti and a large sausage pizza with peppers and onions and drove out to Queens. Claire lived in a high rise off Queens Boulevard and overlooking the Long Island Expressway.

Claire met him in a clean white suit and invited him into a spotless, furnitureless apartment. He had to put the pizza box on the stove top, and he poured the Chianti into a green coffee cup and a glass that apparently used to hold jelly. She had paper towels but no plates.

"I'm going to swear out an arrest warrant for Geoffrey Battissen tomorrow," said Artie. Claire clapped her hands and kissed him on the cheek. It felt good.

"Not for theft but material witness. I think he may have had help. It's too big a theft for someone like him. The word is he's a petty chiseler, but he is not a big-league thief."

"Oh Arthur, this is just wonderful," said Claire, drinking a toast of Chianti from the coffee cup. She had given the glass to him. She cradled the green cup like a flower and leaned against the stove. There was no place to sit.

Artie felt strangely proud, like a little boy showing off in the classroom where Claire's notebook belonged.

"You see, if he had just been cooperative to a degree we wouldn't have had anything. And I sense, you get a sixth sense about these things, that this is a man who is going to break. And when he breaks, he'll break all over his friends."

"Do you think there are others?" she asked.

"Well, the book on him is he's weak. And he's not in this league. I think you just may be getting a nice phone call from him. He's ready to do something, I know it. I smell it," said Artie.

She opened the pizza box, to the sausage and onions and peppers, and laid a still warm slice on a paper towel and offered it to Artie like a bouquet.

"I will never give up hope, you know. And neither should you."

"I guess maybe around you I can hope," said Artie. As soon as the slice left her hand, it dripped and he had to dodge the red splatter, getting the dripping cheese precariously into his mouth. There was no place to put it down. It had to be eaten safe or worn. Somehow, in a white suit, Claire Andrews spilled nothing and took no larger bite than she could chew easily.

"I guess you're used to winning against odds, huh?" asked Artie. He felt awkward. Lust was easier to deal with.

"I'm actually not even used to being on my own. I just do what I have to do, I guess. And it's working out, isn't it?"

Artie desperately looked for more towels to keep the olive oil from running down his thumb into his sleeve.

She talked about why she felt she had to do this, about her father's lucky piece, about how she had suddenly discovered that the people back in Carney didn't really think as highly of him now that he was dead.

"Everyone believed he was dealing in stolen property just because I couldn't get the receipt right away."

"I think you're going to have to get some proof," said Artie.

"I will," said Claire.

"Good, because it will help if you have to take Battissen to court."

He tried to get the conversation away from her father because as long as it stayed on that sadness, he was never going to get to that mattress in the bedroom.

"If I do dwell on Dad too much, will you stop me?"

"Sure," said Artie, who realized they were still talking about her father by agreeing not to bring him up again.

He wanted to ask if she were a virgin. He wanted to ask if she ever committed any acts she was ashamed of. He wanted to bathe her in the red wine, get her out of that unsullied white suit she had worn a full day in New York without soiling. He wanted to ask her if she would like to roll around in olive oil with him. He wondered if any other part of her body besides the upper part of her chest had freckles. Probably her shoulders. He wanted to offer her a solemn promise to kiss every one of her freckles, anywhere it might be. He thought she might even laugh at that. He would. Trudy would. One didn't ask about freckle kissing when one listened to sadness. One even felt bad for thinking about freckles when someone talked about a dead father, and caring, and fear, and taking life to herself for the first time. And being so honest about the damned thing.

One kept saying "uh huh," suspecting latent incestual impulses the way she kept talking about the man. But the more she talked about this place she could not return to the more he realized that even if Carney were not the dream town, it came close and this girl came closer.

Why did she have to be so damned innocent, with those eyes that looked at him so trustingly? That said to him she thought he was a wonderful person, like some knight-errant somewhere. Artie remembered courtly love from an English survey course in his first semester at City College, before he dropped out. He seemed to remember a lack of sex with that.

And this was not getting her out of those clothes and into bed. Dead fathers and a home she was not going back to were misty-day, walk-in-the-rain kind of conversations. He had to get into something new. Artie brought up the cellar. He could get off that subject easier than her father and her hometown.

"One good thing about Battissen is he's got an investment in his store. He's got something to lose. He's not some second-story bimbo on smack. We've got some leverage here."

"Of course," said Claire.

"Also, I haven't heard any sounds of them. So maybe this thing isn't broken down yet."

"Do stolen gems make sounds?" asked Claire.

"I mean people will hear rumors. So yeah, they make sounds. Somebody will say he's heard of a big red stone that he thinks is hot. And I'll hear of it." He did not tell her what Norman Feldman had said about the great stones being beyond the level of a New York City detective. With her in this kitchen, sharing the wine from make-do glasses, he felt there was no level beyond him.

"Are they your friends?" she asked.

"Some are in a way. Yeah. Some are. I just arrested a guy today I kind of like. It's crazy, but he's an immigrant and he doesn't understand America yet. When he does maybe he'll steal differently, but then maybe he won't at all, you know. Maybe his son won't."

"Do they tell you these things because they're your friends?"

"No. They tell me these things because it's in their interest to do so. Because I'll do them favors if I can, because they want to get even with someone, because an orderly market without criminals is better for everyone. Lots of reasons."

He felt her put a hand on his chest. He liked that. It was time for a move, but the move was to her living room. In a bare room, no furniture, not even a chair, she had marked up a wall and covered it with papers.

She stood before it with the exhilaration of an Olympic athlete hearing her record time over a loudspeaker. She had the same wild eyes as when she first signed the complaint against Battissen.

"This is it, Arthur," she said, making fists of her hands as though she had a discovery so exciting she didn't dare open them because it would fly away.

He was sure the bedroom was through one of the doors around this bare white-walled room with the cheap white window shades and no lamp.

"Nice," he said.

"This is the wall, Arthur."

"I see."

She opened her fists and gestured to marks at both ends of the wall.

She had cut off time, she said. Even before she had narrowed everything down to two simple, probable centuries, she had removed infinity from her calculations by simple logic. What did Arthur think of that?

"Yeah. Nice. Nice," said Artie, wondering where was her simple little school notebook with all the innocent hope.

More than that, she went on, she had pinpointed a place. The pinpoint was an entire country. It was circled by a ballpoint pen.

Four pieces of paper in a crude drawing represented her memory of Dad's cellar.

"It was three A.M. and I knew I wasn't going to remember the cellar any better than then, so I tore pages out of the very notebook I showed you that morning in front of your apartment and drew it as quickly as possible. So I wouldn't confuse myself. Or hinder myself."

She smiled. With that mess on the wall, she was now claiming conquest of time and space. And she was actually thrilled about it. With all her beauty, with all the nice things she had to offer, Artie couldn't accept this exhilaration at a messed-up wall. It was crazy. She was beautiful and sweet, and innocent, and crazy. And he had contributed to the madness. Conquering infinity?

"Wonderful, isn't it, when you think this is what we've done the first day," she said.

"Well, I just kind of do my job, you know. A dull sort of . . . dull . . . reality sort of thing. Time and space are for Einstein, you know."

"I'm not saying we have it now. But it's a beginning. Look where we were just a few days ago. Do you see, Arthur? Do you see? Be honest."

"Look, the edge I have on Battissen doesn't mean we're going to get anything back. In fact, I don't think we will, honestly. So he'll break and maybe he'll try to make some kind of deal. I maybe misled you with the excitement of the moment, you know. Instead of absolutely nothing, we have a little something now where we should have had nothing."

"But England. I know now it came from England. I didn't even know for sure it was a saltcellar until that thief told me. It is not hopeless. We are not nowhere."

"Look, I know you have problems at home with what people believe, but no one's perfect. And so to hell with them."

"What are you saying?" She cocked a suspicious brow.

"This is nice, but . . . I don't know."

"Don't you understand what I've done here? We're both working at this from different ends."

"I get paid for it."

"What does that mean?" she asked.

Artie could see anger in her eyes, a sense that he had somehow betrayed her.

"What does that mean?" she demanded.

"Miss Andrews, all the bag ladies you see don't sleep in alleys with their belongings in bags. Sometimes they are rich enough to wander through their lives in their own apartments."

"Is that your way of saying I'm crazy?"

"Does your mother bake pumpkin pies?"

"I don't know. Why did you bring that up?"

"Does she bake pumpkin pies?"

"I think Cissy, the cook, sometimes does. I'm not sure. What does that have to do with anything?"

"Then if you have this nice house with servants, what are you doing running around New York? What are you trying to prove?"

"I thought you listened to me. I thought you understood, Arthur. I thought in all the world you were the one person who could understand."

He saw her fist clenched, he saw just the promise of tears, he saw her turn her head away in anger.

"I am so disappointed in you, Arthur Modelstein. I am so disappointed. Why on earth did you come up here to say things like that?"

Artie was about to remain silent, feeling overwhelmed and somewhat guilty for things he was not even sure he had done. But the evening was already ruined, and his mind had already switched to Trudy as the lesser of two aggravations for the night. Whatever made him think there could have been peace with this woman?

"Can I ask you, Miss Andrews, what the hell is here in New York for you? What is here, lady? What's here?" said Artie.

Claire spun around, her face red, her blue eyes flashing. "I am here," she said.

They shook hands good night.

VIII

And if he gives way to fear, he is not of the company of true knights and veritable champions, who would sooner meet death in battle than fail to uphold the quarrel of their lord. —CHRÉTIEN DE TROYES
Le Conte du Graal, 1180

Geoffrey Battissen did not care. He had listened to too much logic from too many supposed experts, and he wouldn't be in this position now if he had listened to none of them. He didn't care that he was looking at little bags and boxes that had been the cellar, which had been taken apart supposedly in this very room that smelled so of foul eggs that he was forced to keep his handkerchief over his face to prevent his giving up lunch all over the place.

"We've got to give it back. I know we can make a deal," he said.

He was told that that was not only impossible but also silly.

"I have a business that has run quite well for twenty-two years. In that time, I have purchased a condominium on the East Side, provided for myself every summer on Fire Island, and lived a comfortable life. I was assured by you that this was beyond what any local police department would even be able to understand, much less be able to do anything about. I am facing what I was assured was impossible. An arrest warrant."

He was told that all of this would be moved to places no local police force could bother with. He was offered a hundred thousand dollars cash for now. He was told not to bother things. He had done his job. Let others do what they were supposed to.

"I don't think you understand what's happening to me. These people are hounding me out of my business. They are taking my life away from me, a life I have crafted for myself. I am not giving it up for some extra money. We can still make a deal, and I'm sorry. If they arrest me, I am going to make sure I will look after myself and that includes, if I have to, pointing directly to you."

Battissen nodded to the last large bag sitting on the work table in this foul room. He was told to open it. There was a piece of clay inside, pinkish clay. It looked like a modern ashtray or something from a child's ceramics class waiting for a glaze.

Geoffrey Battissen did not see it long. He didn't even sense the perfect infinite blackness that was upon him the moment the graver thrust perfectly up into his posterior cerebral lobe, making the rest of his body, including that part of the mind that saw and recognized what it saw, lifeless meat on its way to eternal decay. The stroke into his brain was executed with the smooth competence with which the cellar had been dismembered, and with just as much remorse. It was the second death in less than two weeks.

"Mr. Feldman. I'm so glad I could reach you. My name is Captain Harry Rawson and I'm deeply interested in purchasing a major ruby. I've been told you're a splendid source for that."

"Who?" came the voice over the transatlantic telephone.

"Rawson. We're the Rawsons of Hereford. I am in London and I shall be in New York within a day or two. I should like to discuss a major purchase with you."

"Who?"

"Would you care to speak with my banker for references, Mr. Feldman?"

"I don't know you."

The line went dead. Rawson had the operator reconnect them.

"Yes?" came the voice from New York.

"I do believe we were cut off, Mr. Feldman," said Rawson.

"No. We weren't," came the voice.

And the line went dead again.

Rawson made a connection again and this time the first thing he said was: "The British Museum said I should get in touch with you, that you were one of the few in the world who would deal in rubies of fifty carats or over, that were exceptional . . ."

The line went dead again. A shame, thought Rawson. He had been to a Bond Street jeweler who explained that at the size and quality of gems Captain Rawson was looking for, no jewelry store would be of much help. These great gems were so valuable they even transcended the laws of thievery, timeless in their value, powerful in their worth, and not so much an adornment as an event.

The British Museum said there were only three men in the world who would deal in a stone that size, and before Rawson had tried to conduct a conversation with Norman Feldman of New York, he had thought how convenient to have one of those ruby dealers in the very city where the Tilbury Cellar was last seen.

Detective Modelstein heard every morning from Claire Andrews precisely at 10:00 A.M., and precisely at ten he told her the same thing.

"Nothing."

He knew she wanted to talk more, because she tried to explain what she was doing. He didn't want to hear of it. As Feldman had predicted, Artie's normal channels of informants were of no use. There was not a hint of any of the stones moving in New York City. And he suspected that this Ohio lady might just phone him every morning at 10:00 A.M. for the rest of his NYPD career. He might even get used to it. However, that would be hard, considering that he would know every time that at the other end of the phone was a beautiful and intelligent human practicing her one streak of madness on him.

He was surprised that Battissen had not phoned to make a deal. For a man in over his head, he should have done something foolish. So Artie went through with the warrant as a material witness, but when he got to Battissen Galleries he found it locked and empty, and what could have been two days' mail lying pushed through the slot on to the other side of the door. Several yellow delivery slips showed packages were waiting.

Nor had Battissen, Artie found out, been home for two days either. With a partner, Artie got a search warrant for both gallery and apartment. The partner kept commenting how antiseptic Battissen's apartment looked. There was lots of glass furniture without dust or fingerprints. Even the refrigerator had neat olives and pickles. The only used thing in the place appeared to be two plastic straws in a black and pink china cup, which told Artie Battissen indulged in cocaine, which did not mean much considering many apartments on the Upper East Side had such paraphernalia.

It was not that Battissen's apartment was so neat that it looked unlived in. It looked never lived in, like a magazine advertisement for furniture. The bedroom had a wild zebraskin rug on the floor in front of a stark black platform bed. Everything was neat. Everything was put away. Battissen even had neat garbage. Bags to be thrown out were folded before being stuffed into a white plastic liner.

Artie yanked a burlap sack out of the garbage container and shook it out. Brown dust fell at his feet, probably the first mess this place had seen, he thought.

He let the sack fall full length. It was about three feet high and wide enough to contain a fat cylinder. He looked inside and then shifted the bag under the kitchen ceiling light, very carefully. But there it was. His eyes couldn't miss it, a glint flashing back at him. A speck of gold. Burlap would scratch gold, and when it scratched it took minute particles with it.

This bag in Geoffrey Battissen's garbage once held the big gold jeweled thing of a saltcellar belonging to the lady from Ohio. He had taken it and fled. That's what the pressure had done. The flight warranted grand larceny bulletins to other countries and a visit to Norman Feldman, this time at Feldman's apartment on the West Side. He brought a whipped cream cake and stuffed grape leaves.

Feldman's apartment was hardly better furnished than his office. There was a sofa that probably was worn and ugly the day Feldman purchased it, a cheap formica table surrounded by gaudy plastic-covered chairs that would have looked more natural on a lawn than in a dining room, and a black and white television set with a coat hanger for an antenna. He had a workroom he never let Artie enter, and this probably meant no one entered it.

Feldman lived in the apartment because he owned the entire building.

"You said an art dealer like Battissen wouldn't have anything to do with a major gem. Well I know he had possession of it in his apartment in a saltcellar. He's flown with it. He's in that league 'cause he's got it. Now what is the horseshit about having to be someone special to deal those stones?"

"I didn't say that," said Feldman. "You've got to listen. I'm not going to go through everything again. And I am going to tell you once. Major stones have a level they live at. They're sold at. They're bought at. A natural level. You don't think kings and queens and millionaires and dictators happen to stumble on these things in some garden somewhere, do you?"

Artie nodded. He never got insulted, and perhaps that was why he had become Feldman's one friend, for whatever that was worth. He accepted Feldman as actually being easy to work with because the man never wasted time on what others would call niceties, such as courtesy and politeness.

"Okay, understanding that, let me tell you that all major gems are found by poor people. Every one of them. Maybe because poor people work in the dirt, or look down a lot, or because there are just more of them. But they are always found by the poor, and they always end up with the rich, very rich. Look, it takes a lot of money to let it sit in one stone. And so even if Geoffrey Battissen did get hold of that ruby, he would not have it long. Doesn't belong with him."

"He's gone, you know. Not a sign of him. And he had this thing with the ruby in it, last reports."

"I guarantee something like the ruby you're describing will not stay with that person. It's not just money either. Can you imagine needing a gem?"

"You mean like a breath or something?"

"Right. With a great gem, people don't buy it because they think it will look pretty. They have to know the stone. They have to understand, and then they don't just want it. They need it. So forget some thieves."

"You're right. I haven't heard a whisper. Not a whisper of any of the stones and they were stolen in this city."

"Right. Stupid. I was telling you that. I'm not going to talk to you anymore. You're crazy. I've been telling you that. Forget it."

"There's this woman—"

"Why didn't you say you were talking about screwing? I knew you weren't talking stones. That I knew."

"It's not that."

"It's always that," said Feldman.

Artie ignored the comment. Feldman indulged in sex the way he dined, as a necessity, possibly a necessary biological burden. Artie tried to explain about someone who just might latch on to the stones despite Feldman's odds against it.

"Well she's kind of . . . she doesn't . . . she isn't bothered by reality. She's like . . . like a football coach. Rah rah. Nice, intelligent, lovely lady, and she's like a football coach. Who knows what she'll do? Do you know what football coaches are like?"

"I played for Colorado."

"You played for Colorado?"

"I played guard."

"What did you weigh?"

"A hundred and sixty pounds. Everyone was smaller then."

"Even then that was light. They don't have halfbacks that small nowadays," said Artie. He tried to imagine Feldman blocking someone. He couldn't.

"We had a good team. I wanted to play. I don't think coaches are crazy. That's the price you pay for the game you play."

"What I'm saying is maybe her enthusiasm and her money will get her to her property."

"Impossible."

"Why?"

"If you saw some colored guy with a red stone in his ring, would you think ruby? A big red stone."

"Course not."

"In that respect, everybody is alike. Nobody is going to talk to her."

"But she's got money. What, is her money no good?"

"If I went into General Motors to buy the place would they talk to me? No. They wouldn't because they don't know me. If Henry Ford calls up, they'll talk to him. There's a possibility. Forget that lady."

Artie had an idea. "Would you do me a favor?"

"No," said Feldman.

"You don't know what it is. How can you say no?"

"No."

"Would you tell this lady what you told me? It would make my life easier."

"So you can have more sex. You have enough already."

"Will you do it, asshole?" asked Artie.

"Okay," said Feldman.

"Why did you say yes?"

"I want to see who's bothering you like this."

"She may never stop bothering you."

"You let yourself be bothered," said Feldman.

Detective Modelstein had been surprised that Feldman had played football. But there were always surprises. Like how they had met. Artie was tailing some punks whom informants had set up. The big kids had already promised the informants, who were fences, good-sized colored stones. Their plan was to simply mug one of the carriers they knew near Forty-seventh Street.

They moved out of an alley at a sixty-two-year-old man, and they stopped moving well thereafter. One of them had his third rib cracked into his heart and the other's nose was shattered and the elderly man was trying to ram the shards into the mugger's brain with the heel of his hand when Artie and the other policeman stopped him. With some effort. The man was indignant at being stopped, indignant at being delayed in his evening to file complaints against the two muggers, who would only be released. The elderly man said something like this could never happen in an Arab country, and what was an added surprise was that the man who thought so highly of the Arabs was a Jew. It was Feldman.

Feldman, it turned out, had worked for the Office of Strategic

Services during World War II in Burma behind Japanese lines, ironically or perhaps most reasonably in the Mogok region of Burma, where the great rubies were mined. As much as he knew, Feldman was there first when the war broke out. Artie never knew more.

They ate the lavish whipped cream dessert quietly, absorbed in the decadent luxury of sugar and cream.

"You ever kill a man?" asked Artie.

"Why do you ask?"

"I've known you what, eight years? Sometimes I don't see you for a year on end. Sometimes twice in a week. I always find out something new about you."

"So why do you ask if I ever killed someone?"

"I dunno. OSS. Football. I'm wondering who you are."

"Someone who does things right," said Feldman, raising a finger.

Claire Andrews was stumped. She had exhausted much of the easy literature on cellars and now had been forced to visit art libraries in lower Manhattan looking for an English saltcellar encrusted with jewels. One art historian told her there was no such thing, that it broke form. Weeks before she might have even suspected Dad didn't really have a saltcellar. But her research had taught her something incredibly important. She had seen so many differing opinions on subjects that she no longer took someone's word as Bible. Her opinion counted. She could look at an art historian and insist upon seeing certain volumes, even when he assured her she would not find what she wanted. And when she didn't, she did not feel she had wasted her time. She had proved to herself another road did not have what she wanted.

It was not that she was calling other people liars or diminishing the value of information from others. Rather, in this dogged process, tempered by the draining repetition of going through files and checking notes, and having to unsort the repetitious tangles herself, she had gained a respect for her own judgment. It was a thing that had come about not by arrogance but by necessity.

This was not the research for a term paper where so many organized works hung around waiting for her to pick out chapters like convenient and ripe plums on well-worn paths. This was a search that had never to her knowledge been tried before. And the path she found was the path she had to make, from so many people referring to similar things in different ways, and so many contradicting each other. It was a path made by guesses and assumptions, and those demanded that a person make a judgment. She had to become her own authority even to proceed.

She had learned to trust herself because she had no choice. And so on a cold gray New York day, chewing on an eraser, and sorry that the dishes were done so she could not do them again, or anything again, anything she was sure would turn out right, Claire Andrews made a decision about her father's cellar. Since it was obviously British, and since no other British cellars hosted gems, therefore the gems had to mean something.

If she could accept that fact that she had just declared to herself as pivotal, then the route to the ownership of the cellar was the gems. They had to exist before the cellar existed and someone had to own them.

And so while Captain Harry Rawson of the Queen's Argyle Sutherlanders learned to use a jeweler's loupe from a Bond Street Jew, and Detective Modelstein tried to fathom the mysteries of great gems from the dealer Feldman, Claire Andrews went back to the New York Public Library and within two books taught herself what the British captain and New York detective had to be told by others.

Great gems went with great people, and as often as not they had their names, like the Amalfi emerald, or the Hope diamond. In book after book, Claire discovered gems were the historical perfume of the rich and powerful, and when empires collapsed and cities were sacked the gems fled and surfaced again with new people, sometimes with new names.

But the scent was always there. Because history was about the rich and the powerful. The gems went along with it.

It was an enormous discovery, she knew. She understood that no matter how forbiddingly awesome the search might be, it was now quite reasonably possible to find Dad's cellar. She was no longer working on faith alone.

She would have to change her research tactics. Book by book, page by page would never do. She had to organize on a computer. She probably would have to contact people overseas.

She was exhilarated and yet she was depressed. She desperately wanted to tell someone about it. She would have liked to have told her father as first choice. And second was that detective.

When she phoned him in the mornings, she wanted him to talk more about anything, but he was always so abrupt. She wanted a chance to explain to him again what she was doing. She was not some mental defective, but somebody doing something important. Most importantly, important to herself.

Then why did she need him to acknowledge it? Why did she need anyone but herself?

The furniture had come, but only a couch went into the living room, which stayed a workroom, the new computer going by the window overlooking the Queens street, and a new worktable set before what was now called the cellar wall.

Among her most treasured belongings, shipped inside her old bedroom dresser now in her new bedroom along with her bed, was Dad's picture. But she did not want to put it up in this apartment, not yet. It did not belong yet. It was not home enough yet, or something enough yet.

She had to tell someone about her success. She went through a list of people, even her minister back in Carney, but none of them seemed to be right. In what she knew was a mistake, in what almost every American woman beyond her twenty-first year would have known was a mistake, she phoned, for some reason to be buried later in self-recrimination when it was all over . . . Mother.

Mother was glad to hear from her. She even sounded interested in what Claire was doing, saying, surprisingly, "How nice." Several times she said, "That's nice." Or, "How nice."

Claire spoke for almost an hour. When she was done, her mother, without a pause, without a comment on all the research or anything Claire had been telling her, said: "You know the Johnsons will be going to New York for Thanksgiving. If you're not coming home, why not meet them for dinner. I'll get you their hotel."

"Is that it?" asked Claire, feeling the degradation and fury of another encounter with the force that refused to accept she was someone who could do something. Something important. Something she was sure no one else had done exactly in the world. Ever. Before. Special.

"Is there something more? You're not angry, are you? Is there something wrong?"

"No."

"Oh, gracious. There's something wrong. What is it now, Claire? You've got to tell me so I'll understand."

"I have been telling you, Mother. I have done something incredibly special."

"It's lovely, dear. I said so. I don't know how many times I said so. I said it was very lovely."

"I am not engaged in creating a bouquet for a flower show."

"Claire, you've got to be reasonable. What do you want me to say?"

"Nothing," snapped Claire and hung up. Why had she phoned? She felt small for being angry, and smaller for still needing Mother's understanding and approval. If there was one person in the world Claire should have known would not validate her efforts, it would have been her mother. Claire really knew that before the phone call; only now she felt bad for getting angry on top of it all.

She stared at the phone, wondering if she should call back, but she was twenty-eight years old. And she knew there was no redemption at the other end of the cord.

The next day she experienced a breakthrough that terrified her. The detective not only spoke to her civilly, but said that since one of the stones in the cellar she claimed may have been a large ruby, he had arranged for her that day to speak to the foremost expert on that gem in New York City, and perhaps the world.

"Norman Feldman himself. My god. Oh. I'm not ready. I don't know enough. I can't see him today. I've seen his name in books. That is Norman Feldman."

"I think he can explain your situation to you. Just meet me at his office in an hour."

"I can't make it in an hour. I just won't know nearly enough in an hour," said Claire. This wasn't some librarian or even some historian. This was a man whose name she had read in two books and a magazine article.

"You don't pin him down that easily. You may never get to see him again."

"I don't know enough."

"You'll never know enough for him," said the detective, unnerving her even more.

In desperation, she grabbed one book to read on her way from Queens into Manhattan. It had absolutely not one significant word she could use in speaking to Norman Feldman. So she wrote down a list of questions to ask on just the little she knew.

He's just like anyone else in the world, Claire. He is a human being with needs and fears like everyone else, she told herself. And of course she did not believe this. All the self-assurance that she had forged in the last two weeks seemed to melt at the prospect of meeting this man she had hoped some day in the future, in an educated future, to talk to. She thought of the incredible waste in seeing him now with only the questions she could fashion virtually off the top of her head.

"I'm really not ready," said Claire when she met Detective Modelstein outside the building.

"Just listen to what he has to say about a ruby that size."

"I only have an estimate, you know. I made a fast calculation on its size, and I would say it has to be over fifty carats," she said, following the tall detective into the building. He held open a door for her. She liked that. She liked his aftershave too. She wanted him to be a friend so she could have a friend on this occasion.

"Just listen to what he has to say about your situation."

"He won't think I'm stupid, will he?" asked Claire.

Why was Detective Modelstein smiling?

The office was not too bad. It was plain almost to the point of discomfort. And Feldman was a rather ordinary-looking gentleman with a face somewhat baggy and frowning, but he was not the overpowering sort she had feared. She looked to Arthur Modelstein for reassurance. There was that grin again.

"Mr. Feldman, my name is Claire Andrews, and my father, an honest man all his life, was killed in this city trying to—"

"Artie says you're looking for a large ruby," said Feldman.

"Yes," said Claire.

"Would you know a ruby if you saw it? Could you tell it from a police car bubble?"

"I believe there is no ruby as large as a police car bubble yet found, Mr. Feldman."

"Would you know it from a piece of red glass?"

"Not yet."

"Then what are you doing here?" asked Feldman.

"I . . . I . . . I tried to prepare more, but Arthur said it had to be eleven o'clock today. I'm not blaming him, I understand how important you are and—"

"You don't know a ruby from a Parcheesi piece and you're going to ask me questions? I'm doing this as a favor to Detective Modelstein. The least you could do is come up with an intelligent question. I might as well be talking to a wall. Did you come up here to gush over me?"

A flush seized Claire's cheeks. She fumbled with a pencil on an open page of her book. Artie stopped smiling. He had wanted her sent home, but not quite humiliated like this. With her bright yellow print dress and her notepads now falling off her lap, she looked, Artie thought, like a daisy being chomped by a bull. He looked to Feldman to ease off, but he doubted it would do any good, and was sure of it when Feldman didn't even respond. This was not strong Feldman or weak Feldman; this was Feldman, the man who could excoriate museum curators in print and never fear a libel suit because he was the authority, the man known to start a conversation with "shut up."

There was nothing anyone could do for this poor lady but let it all happen and then, he hoped, send her back to her home, where there was furniture in the room and maybe, maybe, a pumpkin pie in an oven on Halloween or something.

Hesitantly, getting all her pads back on her lap, Claire spoke: "I wanted to let you know how much I respected you. That I knew who you were."

"You don't know who I am," said Feldman. "Why do you say such stupid things? You don't know what you're doing. Nobody knows who anyone else is. How can you tell me you know who I am?"

"I'm sorry," said Claire.

"Do you even know who you are? Do you know? You come here without a question. Are you planning on selling gush? Rah rah. A cheerleader. This is the real world, girlie."

"Excuse me, sir. I do not like to be called girlie," said Claire. Artie had never seen a face so red. It could burn.

"Then go hire someone to kiss your ass. Get out of here. I don't have time for you."

"I have a question," said Claire, swallowing, trying very hard not to cry. She would rather bleed from her eyes than shed tears from them now.

"Wonderful. Shoot," said Feldman. Artie wanted her to take it back, but it was too late. It was too late for everything.

"Mr. Feldman," she said, glancing down at her notes, "how many dealers do you know who would handle a pigeon's blood ruby over fifty karats or so?"

Artie thought he saw a slight smile form at the ends of Feldman's perennially downturned lips.

Claire had a pencil poised to take down the answer. She stared at the page as though keeping her face safe from having to look at Feldman's withering stare.

Feldman did not answer.

Claire looked up. "Would you say there are five, seven, ten? Are there as many as ten?"

"What if I told you there were fifty?" asked Feldman, leaning back in his chair, pushing his hands into his pockets.

"I would find that surprising," said Claire.

"What if I told you anybody can deal a ruby, all they have to do is sell it. That makes them a dealer."

"Whom would they sell it to?"

"Someone who wants to buy it."

"And when they bought it, whom would they call to assure them of what they were really buying for two or three million dollars, or more?"

"Some experts, lots of experts."

"Really? Who? Who is an expert? I never saw one listed in a telephone directory. Who would be these experts on something smaller than an Easter egg that changes hands for many millions of dollars? Who would they be?"

Feldman smiled. Artie wondered why. Was Claire making a fool of herself? Feldman wouldn't smile at that. For Feldman people making fools of themselves was as common as weather.

"Could be a museum director. Lots of museums have gem collections. Smithsonian. Natural History here in New York, the Paris—"

"May I read you a quote from one museum director who is under severe scrutiny from his board, because of a comment you made when a member of that board asked your opinion—"

"Three," said Feldman. "Three dealers in a ruby that size is the answer you want?"

"They're like collectors, aren't they?"

"There are more collectors."

"How many?"

"Won't tell you."

"Why not?"

"I'm sure you know why," said Feldman. He was beaming.

"If a pigeon's blood ruby of fifty karats or more were for sale you would probably be contacted, wouldn't you?"

"If a person knew what he was doing, yes. Or two others, whom I also won't mention."

"If it were for sale in New York City, it would have to be you, wouldn't it?"

"No. It wouldn't have to be me."

"Why not?"

"Airplanes. Ever heard of them?"

"But that would mean crossing borders to get an appraisal of the stone."

"Try thinking, girlie."

Claire put down her pencil and folded her book over it.

"Mr. Feldman," she said, her voice quivering again, "I find it inconceivable, knowing who you are, that you would not be aware of a stone like the one I describe, practically from the moment it was for sale anywhere in the world."

"Not from the moment," said Feldman. He was beaming. Artie had never seen a beam in Feldman.

"In fact, I may venture," said Claire, her voice sharpening and rising so that Artie could see now the latest trembling was really a growing rage, "that you have already seen the ruby, and that if you haven't, you will, and that in all likelihood you may have to be involved in its sale."

"Not have to exactly," said Feldman. He was chuckling and looking to Artie.

"Then let me apprise you now in front of Detective Arthur Modelstein of the New York City Police Department that a large pigeon's blood ruby of over fifty karats with the engraving of Christ on it is stolen, and that I would appreciate any information you have on it and must warn you that if you have it in your possession or attempt to deal it, you are dealing in stolen merchandise."

[122]

Claire Andrews sat rigid, staring at Norman Feldman, who was absolutely aglow.

"You are one very clever lady. You know, Artie never thought to ask when he bothered me about that large ruby, how many would deal in something like that."

"Mr. Feldman, you may think you are above the law, but you're not."

"I'm not a thief, girlie. And I heard you. Now get out before you ask any more intelligent questions."

The phone rang. Norman Feldman took his hands out of his pockets and placed them on the desk. He was not smiling anymore.

Outside the office, waiting for the elevator, Claire began to tremble and then laugh, covering her mouth like a schoolgirl embarrassed.

"I can't believe I spoke to Norman Feldman the way I did. Oh, Arthur, I have so many exciting things to tell you. Everything is going so well." The strange smile had disappeared from Modelstein's face. He pushed the button to the elevator, a bit more furiously.

Inside, Norman Feldman had changed his mind. This lady was smart enough to get herself killed. He wondered whether he should tell Artie, and decided not to, because Artie would not know what to do and might get himself killed trying to save her.

IX

Thou art harder than stone, more bitter than wood, more barren and bare than the fig tree, how durst thou presume to venture where the Holy Grail abides.　　　　　—SIR THOMAS MALORY
　　　　　　　　　　　　　　　　　　　　Morte d'Arthur, ca. 1470

The cellar was gone and so was the thief.

"So you think he is in Brazil because there is no extradition treaty with America?" asked Rawson.

"I've notified our state department as such," said the American detective. He was the large sort, with a strong body that seemed to dominate his somewhat untidy desk. His suit was a bit flashy with a strangely colorless tie that seemed more an accommodation to official requirements than his taste.

He lacked a sense of formal respect. He asked his questions bluntly, and on those rare times he used the word "Mr." it was not so much a sign of respect as distance. He had also noticed Rawson's cut left hand and asked about it, commenting on how all those little marks must have been made by a strange tool. Rawson had explained it was gardening. But more important, Rawson realized, this detective was hiding something. And he was hostile.

"And you didn't arrest him when you had him here?" asked Rawson.

"I'm not accusing you of anything. I'm sure you had a good reason."

"I did not have enough evidence to arrest him. I had a complaint from the owner, whom he did a form of switch on."

Rawson watched the strong jaw set just a bit more when Detective Modelstein mentioned "owner." Was that the cause of the hostility?

All Rawson had done was to inform the detective of his claim on the cellar, showing a May 1945 complaint to Scotland Yard listing the cellar stolen from the Rawson family. It was something the Yard could swear to honestly. Intelligence had written up this complaint, correct even to the inks and type fonts of 1945, and then secreted it into Scotland Yard files, a far more effective way to validate ownership and time of loss than trusting the Scotland Yard sort with a secret.

But when this photocopy of the complaint and the gem list was presented, the American detective had put Rawson on the grill.

Where did Rawson hear about this? Why did he come now? What made Rawson think his family's cellar was the same as the one reported stolen?

"You know, it didn't even make the New York newspapers; how is it gonna make the London ones?" Detective Modelstein had asked. He had the sort of body that could loom over one. And he had been looming.

"Our family is in the trading business, and one of our local representatives picked it up and sent it on."

"From which paper?"

"Really not sure altogether. But I'll check it out for you if you wish, Detective Modelstein."

"That's all right. Now about these gem prints on the diamonds. Prints didn't come in till about the thirties, and to my knowledge diamonds stopped being polished in the seventeen hundreds. Do you want to explain that?"

"Quite. We made the prints on the diamonds and took the dimensions and estimated karat weight on the other stones when we moved the cellar at the outbreak of the Second World War. A bit of hysteria then. Thought the Jerries were going to invade."

"Because you thought it might be stolen and you wanted to be able to claim it if it was, even after it had been broken down," said the New York detective.

Detective Modelstein obviously knew his job. He talked with an easy familiarity about stones, even though he didn't show the proper deference common from the Yard. But he knew his city and he knew his criminals, and he was the sort, Rawson estimated, who would have made a splendid noncommissioned officer. One might not get as many snappy salutes, but things would get done well.

This office at One Police Plaza, despite its remorselessly barren rows of desks set around building pillars, had a sense of disorder, a sloppiness that would not have been tolerated in a British police station. Papers lay about on desks, notes were tacked up on walls, and there were no clear areas from which superiors could command. People came in and out freely. And yet Rawson's practiced eye could tell when people were getting things done. This office functioned. And Detective Modelstein functioned well within it.

The man had little doubt the cellar was not being sold in his area of the city. A good sign. He knew his beat. He knew the man who had stolen it, the nature of the man's business, in relationship to crime, of course. The detective had almost no idea of art itself. In brief, he knew what he had to know, and Rawson understood it would be better to have this man as an ally than an enemy because he additionally suspected, but did not know for sure yet, that this detective had well learned to do pretty much what he wanted within the rules. He could hurt one's cause. And he was angry about something concerning the other owner.

"Please let me explain," said Rawson. "I'm not here in competition with any other possible claimant. In fact, the other person might find me helpful, if nothing else."

The large shoulders shrugged.

"You say you own it. She says she owns. I don't know how it can't be competition," said Detective Modelstein.

"This cellar has been in our family for generations. I have to go after it. It does not make the most business sense in the world. Honestly, in my opinion, it didn't mean that much to the Rawsons when we had it, nor that much when we lost it. It just sat there. For centuries it sat there. If we get it back, it will sit again. But because we had it, because it was ours, I have to pursue this thing. Do you understand?"

The large detective shook his head. The dark eyes were open, unabashed, questioning. But he said nothing. He let it all lie on Rawson, using the silence to work for him. Rawson had to continue.

"If the other owner needs the money this would bring, I am not averse to making a financial settlement. This is not a strict business matter."

The detective thought a moment. Somehow there was something more here. The detective had large strong hands, and he moved them as though wrestling with an explanation. Rawson knew he had been judged as to how much he could be trusted. He gathered it was somewhat favorable but not too much.

"There's this lady. She is a basically decent person who's lived kind of a protected life. She comes from a small town. It's not like New York or London. It's kind of a decent place. I don't know if you're aware of that sort of town?"

"I gather, like our villages. Very close. Don't like strangers particularly. Don't change their ways."

"Well, I don't know about that. Maybe. I don't know. But her father maybe created some jealousy or something, and she loved him. This girl and her father were close. You could feel the closeness—it was that strong. They did so much together."

"In what way close?" asked Rawson, in a way that opened all manner of doors.

"Strictly father-daughter. If you ever met this lady, the one thing you might think is she is too nice, you know. I mean it. Well, he obviously didn't know what he was doing in trying to sell this jeweled cellar through some art dealer, and when he died in this accidental stabbing, a mugging of sorts, she took it on herself to sell it. And it was stolen from her and it got into the newspapers near her hometown, where people, according to this woman, began to think her father might be a crook. So because they're righteous people, she and her father, she takes it on herself now to prove absolutely and finally that he's innocent."

"Why would they think he is selling hot goods?" asked Rawson.

And here the detective paused, judging the man who was before him.

"I give you my word, I will do anything, even up to the cost of many hundreds of thousands of pounds, not to hurt this woman," Rawson added quickly.

"Why? Why do that?" asked the detective.

"Because I gather I would have you as an enemy if I hurt her, and I need you. Also, it is not in my self-interest to harm this woman in any way. I don't need publicity, and if it would make you feel more comfortable I would make a promise now not to contact anyone from the media who might embarrass her." It was a good promise, of course, because he wasn't going to do it anyhow. Rawson wanted this search to be as quiet as possible, with, of course, as few questions about this cellar as possible, to protect the great secret of England and Her Royal Highness.

Rawson had said the right thing. The detective opened up.

"He didn't have a receipt, and he kept it secret from everyone in that town but her that he ever owned it. And now, this," said the detective, holding up the list of specifications even to the diamond prints and the interior framework with the funny English words of "poorish bowl."

"Well, we just won't let this get out, will we? And I'll speak to the woman very carefully."

"She's very sensitive about this subject. Her father. The saltcellar. Outside of this one subject, she's really a fine person. I don't know her that well, but what I do know is fine. But you get her on this subject, and she gets strange. It's a horrible thing to see. A beautiful, intelligent, fine screwball. Crazy."

"I'll be very careful," said Rawson. He saw the detective shudder a bit.

"I'd like to be the one to tell her about this," said Detective Modelstein, holding up the specifications sheet. "I'm not looking forward to it, but I know her."

"Good idea. Meantime, you will get a list of these jewels out to the appropriate markets?"

"I'll notify local jewelers, but don't expect much on the stones. There hasn't been boo here on them."

"I wouldn't imagine the market would be with fences and such," said Rawson.

"You deal in stones?"

"No," said Rawson with a laugh. "But now you have their prints. And good luck. You know where to reach me in New York, and be assured there are many tens of thousands of pounds reward for any help my family might get. To police officers, too."

The detective shrugged. No bribe opening there.

Rawson wondered if the man wanted to shake hands. He didn't. But he did add as a good-bye: "Thanks for the thing on the lady. I appreciated it." That was his price.

Walking along the massive shopping street of Fifth Avenue with everything set so monumentally in concrete, Rawson wondered if the thief might save the poorish bowl and shuddered at the thought of the cellar being broken down in this city in particular. Because if it were, the thief, the only one who knew what England's Grail looked like since Elizabeth and her goldsmith, might have thrown it away.

The Holy Grail might hide forever in the staggeringly massive garbage heaps of New York. How to get at it then would be a greater challenge than Hercules cleaning out the Augean stables. Fortunately, there was always the Queen's purse, and the greed of the thief. Who knew that once tracked down trying to sell the gems, he wouldn't be most helpful in finding the poorish bowl, or at least in describing what it looked like?

Rawson settled into his suite at the Sherry Netherland, ordered himself a Scotch whiskey—one had to stress the word *Scotch* in America—and phoned the ruby dealer again. This time, Rawson did not introduce himself, but said: "Sultan Al Hadir." He knew the Hadirs dealt in major gems, and just possibly theirs was a name that could open this sealed door. It was just a frail chance.

"Yes," said Feldman, the first positive word so far.

"I had called before," said Rawson.

"I know the voice," said the dealer. "Why would he send you?"

"I was an aide to him for a while," said Rawson. Interesting that this dealer would know Hadir, when Jews were legally not even allowed to set foot in Banai.

Rawson could imagine a homeless Jew somewhere arriving in a land that proclaimed no Jews could live there and going right to the palace to make a deal, possibly even to arrange to live there.

He had wondered at times what it would be like to be a Jew in the middle ages, the rules of conduct, of entry into strange places, of being part of a place, and of knowing one might have to leave quite shortly. He had assumed that to be a Jew might well be a full-time occupation, like being an officer in Her Majesty's service, and that earning a living while in that state might have been some sort of second job.

Of course he did not get that sense from the detective whose name sounded Jewish and was somewhat dark. There didn't seem to be that inner strength to the man. Rather, it was all external in his bulk, in his official manner, like some tough sergeant in combat. Maybe even an officer who had been in service too long and had no real future but a pension. This, of course, in a somewhat crude American exterior. Maybe the detective felt at home in this country. After all, it was a nation of immigrants.

Rawson waited for Feldman to answer.

"I still don't know who you are."

"Does one have to have a recommendation, like a gentleman's club?"

"Don't bother me anymore with your silly lies. I know who sends whom on what," said Feldman, and the line went dead again, and even though Rawson dialed three more times, no one answered the phone.

Rawson drank his whiskey in the comfort of his suite and set the remnants of the British empire to finding a middle-aged homosexual art dealer who no longer apparently resided in New York City and could well be in Rio de Janeiro.

But through many inquiries in Rio and dozens through America and around the world, often very unofficially from one intelligence agent to another, Harry Rawson found out over the ensuing days that Geoffrey Battissen, fifty-three, partial to men in their twenties, had closed his art gallery of twenty-two years almost two weeks before and had not turned up in Brazil. Or Paris, or Singapore, or London, or many other cities around the world where someone who often told his friends he would never live in a small town again might flee. Rawson got the reports, looked at them once, and then shredded them several times and scattered the shreds on the sidewalks of New York City, where they would pass into the largest garbage heaps in the history of man.

When Artie got Claire's 10:00 A.M. phone call the day after Rawson had appeared at the Frauds floor, he regretted trying to save her the coldness of a stranger. Unfortunately, hearing her voice, he realized what he should have known, indeed did know, the day before. He was going to have to show her something that might rudely cut off her big adventure, showing she was chasing someone else's cellar and casting real questions on how her father came by it. It would get her home, of course. But Artie would be the one to have to share the despair and sadness. Still, he knew he could do it better than the Brit.

So he found himself phrasing the information in a strange way.

"Look, something has come up that I'd like to discuss with you sometime this week, maybe at the end of the month or something."

"Oh, I'd love to see you," said Claire. Her voice was dewdrop bright.

"Whenever it's convenient. I don't want to intrude on anything. Not a rush."

"Come on over now. I'd love to see you."

"Right now?"

"Absolutely," she said.

"As soon as I get rid of some work," he said.

"Wonderful," she said.

And so Artie proceeded to do what he had learned to do best in life: delay. He dawdled around the Frauds squad, finding paperwork, doing paperwork, discussing paperwork, being asked several times if he had anything important he really wanted to talk about.

A homicide detective came in and wanted to know if he had overpaid for his girlfriend's engagement ring. Artie put the loupe to his eye and saw that the almost two-karat stone lacked tinges of yellow and the clarity was good, not good enough for a blue-white though, not pure enough. It was a good commercial white diamond with inclusions that did not diminish the clarity.

"It's a good quality, probably first pique, as they say, and commercial white. Whatdya pay?"

"Two thousand."

"Was he a friend?"

"No."

"That's a very good price," said Artie.

"It's not hot," said Detective Sergeant Dennis McKiernan.

"I don't want to know where you got it," said Artie.

"A guy needed the money."

"You strip a stiff?"

"Hey—" said McKiernan.

"Anything under five for that stone is a nice price," said Artie, annoyed that he would be asked to appraise something that might be shady.

"Thanks," said McKiernan with a snarl.

The word got around Artie was in the office, and the jewelry started coming up for his appraisal. It was jewels of the middle class, small stones, baguettes, little things of very little value, set in gold or silver, and treasured by those who had them. The problem was telling them the dollar value of things they were emotionally attached to, the kind of jewelry most Americans bought, which wasn't worth nearly what they paid for it.

There was always the comment that he should have been a jeweler, and Artie answered that he often thought so himself. What he didn't say was that he liked the secure paycheck of the department too much. He planned on doing something like that when he retired, he would say.

It would be in that wonderful time never burdened with struggle and risk: the future. Unfortunately, he had trouble putting Claire in that wonderful time.

Thinking about this got Artie mad. Who was this person to come into New York City, attempt to sell hundreds of thousands of dollars or even millions of dollars worth of merchandise, and then make Artie feel guilty because he found out she was lying to herself, just like he told her? He had told her the sale was suspicious the first day.

Therefore, he should not feel the slightest qualms in saying he had told her so.

But he felt qualms. He had qualms in the armpits and under his eyelashes. He would rather go to the shooting range with the guns going off and the smell of powder and endure jerks happy with their substitute penises that could kill someone. That is what he would rather do than drive to Queens and tell Miss Andrews about the prior claim on the cellar that proved her father had bought stolen merchandise. He was loaded with qualms. He was qualm heavy. He was a qualm bomb. But there came a time during the day when even the master procrastinator could not delay leaving the office.

And so just at three in the afternoon, he finally found himself outside the door of her apartment, having been rung upstairs by her cheerful voice on the intercom. She was wearing a checkered shirt and blue jeans, and her hair for the first time was blown in loose strands that looked even more perfect. And worse, she was smiling, and she was glad to see him.

"It's furnished. I was going to invite you for dinner. I can cook. Some things. C'mon in."

"Yeah. Good," said Artie.

There was a dining-room set of wooden solidity, somehow a little too large and a little too fine for the clean, small apartment. The living room had a single couch, but everything else was devoted to office, including a personal computer and computer disk file nearby. The wall now looked like a museum display of history, with pictures of large trunks of gold clustered above the section of the historical line that read 1400 to 1600. There were also pictures of large colored stones cut out of books. None of them was engraved, so Artie knew they were not the ones in the cellar. He had the photocopies of the 1945 Scotland Yard report in his pocket.

"Arthur, I am so glad you came. This is so exciting. I've made contact with a researcher in Britain. There is no question but that this cellar is British. No question. Even though they never put major gems on their cellars, this is the British form. The lions. The scrollwork. They had fine, fine goldsmiths. And I am going to find out why our cellar has got jewels. It's so good to see you."

"Yeah. Good," said Artie.

She was so happy about what she was doing, Artie thought momentarily of not telling her at all. Let her run after this cellar that undoubtedly was in pieces now and the impossible proof that her father was innocent. She could have a very nice life chasing what wasn't there. She had the money. She had the time. She enjoyed it, and maybe she would get tired after a while. Who was Arthur C. Modelstein to declare this an insanity?

She talked ecstatically about her map of the world and her computer, which organized the colossal amount of data she was gathering. It made logic out of turmoil.

"That's always helpful," said Artie.

"You see, the one thing I learned was that the leads to our cellar are out there. But the information has to be organized. People don't refer to gems the same way. They will talk of a red stone and call it a ruby, indiscriminately so. Do you know the crown of England has a spinel, not a ruby? They didn't know the difference then. It's so exciting, Arthur. Now I have a taste of how exciting your work can be."

"I see you're kind of at home here now," said Artie.

"Arthur, it's not home, but it's where I belong. Boy am I glad to see you."

"Why?"

"I don't know. I just am. I am. You're a nice person. There aren't too many in the world. Do you want some coffee?"

"Coffee would be good," said Artie. He went into the small kitchen, where she had set up a pot of boiling water. Above it was a spice shelf, with spices ordered into groups. Some were for meats, some were for desserts, some were for vegetables. Claire explained that the ones closest to the other groups could be used for either.

Artie glanced around. There wasn't a stray envelope or newspaper lying around. Everything was in place. It was as though he had walked into a file drawer.

"You always this organized?"

Claire laughed. "Oh no. I just like things easier to deal with. I like them in place. I guess I'm really lazy. I hate having to look for things."

"That's organized," said Artie. He felt the British report burn in his jacket pocket. If he were an amateur shoplifter, that report would have been the hot goods he was trying to get out of the store. He felt a strong desire to pat it, to make sure it wouldn't fall out and expose itself so she would ask questions about it.

He drank the coffee. He got a small lesson in the organization of the world into time and space. He got a lecture on jewels that surprised him, how only in the last few hundred years were they considered a form of monetary exchange. She was now tracking the jewels. And it occurred to Artie that already she might know more than he.

"For most of man's history they were considered to have magical powers," said Claire, bubbling. "Did you know that?"

"Yeah, well, I kind of have to deal in today."

"But yesterday has to do with today. Nothing ever really ends. We just aren't usually aware of things, like jewels having meanings. It was more than just coincidence that Dad's cellar should have had so many stones. Cellars not only don't have gems in them, but when the middle ages put gems on something it meant something. Wasn't just showing off like maybe a rich lady would wear a diamond necklace. Do you know what I mean? Is your coffee all right?"

"Yeah," said Artie. He took the report out of his jacket pocket, the Scotland Yard statement, the gem prints, and everything that gave ownership to a British gentleman and his family.

"Claire," he said, "people don't always know other people, or circumstances. I've been in police work almost fourteen years now. If my own mother, aluva shalom, should be arrested for, say, dealing in a hijacked television, you know I wouldn't be shocked. My own mother."

"What does *aluva shalom* mean?"

"It means rest in peace. She's dead."

"Well, of course you would be shocked, because she's dead."

"Sure," said Artie.

"That was a joke, Arthur," said Claire. "I didn't mean to dishonor your mother's memory. I'm sorry. Is that why you're so glum?"

She sat on the room's one chair, with her back to a computer terminal. Artie was on the couch.

"Right," said Artie. She cradled her cup of coffee in her hands as though to use its warmth. She was so damned open. So happy. All the place needed was a log fire, and they could spend the afternoon talking about childhoods.

"Why couldn't you be a bitch?" said Artie.

Claire laughed. "Oh, I can be a real bitch. I can be the worst bitch you have ever seen. You don't know me that well."

"Bitches don't say that. Bitches say the world is a bitch. They don't say they are bitches. I know bitches."

"What are you really talking about, Arthur?" asked Claire.

"I saw another claimant to the cellar this morning," he said. He wanted to die on the couch, maybe crawl under one of the cushions. She just nodded. She was still happy and bright and just nodding. She was nodding when he handed her the photocopy of the 1945 Scotland Yard report, which included the gem list belonging to the Rawson family.

"A cellar very similar to the one you describe, to that drawing over there," said Artie, nodding at the wall, "was stolen from the London home of Lord Rawson on May 18, 1945. It's right here. And this is the list of the gems. That ruby with Christ's head was eighty-seven karats. The sapphire is one hundred and forty-two karats, and the engraving is that of Poseidon enthroned. The gem prints are there also for the diamonds. You had garnets and topazes and jade also. It's all here."

"Then you're not mad about what I said to your friend Norman Feldman?" asked Claire.

"Feldman? No."

"I'm so glad. You were so glum when we left his office. And you looked so angry when you came in. May I see the list of that man's cellar?"

"That's a Scotland Yard report on the theft."

"You've dealt with them before?"

"No."

"Okay. I just wanted to know who affirmed it. The claimant affirmed it, I take it."

"I don't think it's a phony," said Artie.

"It looks like a good list he's got. Could well be applicable to my father's cellar. Possibly."

"You don't think that's your father's cellar?" asked Artie. He couldn't believe her pleasant businesslike calm.

"I think somebody came to America and made a claim on Dad's cellar. I'd like to talk to him," she said.

"That's it? That's the whole thing? It?" yelled Artie. He felt his neck veins about to explode, pumping outrage into his head. He had been so miserable, and she was so calm and happy, like a lunatic babbling about daisies when someone told her the roof was collapsing around her head.

"Of course I'd like to talk to him. Information is the most powerful thing you can have, Arthur."

"If I thought something belonged to me and somebody came in with a prior claim to that thing, I would have doubts."

"Arthur, you jump to conclusions."

"Lady, I am a fucking New York City cop. You are a fucking . . . a fucking Ohio person."

"Arthur, please don't swear. It's not becoming."

Artie threw up his hands to the very heavens that had foisted this all upon him, the hopelessness of reaching this woman, the waste of bad feelings for this woman, the absolute impenetrability of this woman.

"Do you wish to discuss this with me?" she asked.

"No," said Artie. "I don't wish to discuss anything with you ever. I wish to say good-bye."

And he was gone. Without even a handshake. And she didn't know what she had done. What did he want her to do? She understood, of course, the implications of a previous claim. But if there was one thing she had learned it was that every bit of information was only that. Information. He had come in with some very good facts and was outraged that she did not immediately assume the interpretation he wished. And that interpretation was a lot more than Claire would make about her father without more facts, especially corroborating facts. She didn't know how Dad came into possession of the cellar, and neither did this Captain Harry Rawson of the Rawson family of Hereford.

She sighed. She wished Arthur had a bit of Bob Truet in him. Bob would listen to everything. Of course there wasn't such excitement in telling things to Bob. And when he understood them, she always had the feeling it went into that cloudy white space that was his soul.

She was alone again. She waited a few minutes on the chance that Arthur would return and then took the Scotland Yard list to her computer.

Strangely, there was no picture of the cellar, just the list, and yet, as she went down each gem, she knew the incredible probability they were the same. But still it was a probability.

What she decided to do with this absolutely wonderful list was to assume they were the same, without coming to conclusions about her father's ownership. She would deal with that later. And making that decision, she could now track the stones better. Because if there was one thing that remained the same through history, it was the size of a stone. And everyone weighed them, from a Roman siliqua equal to a karat, which was one-twenty-fourth of a Roman slidus, but four times as large as a Phoenician obol, or one-twentieth of a Persian drachm or one-third bigger than an ancient Arabian qurot. Everyone throughout history measured the size of gems.

Arthur had given her in that specific list the absolute perfect markers of identification. He had given her the certainty of stone. And she wanted to thank him. But he was so irrational about some things. He wouldn't listen.

And all day while she reorganized her search, she knew there was no one to tell, no one to share, only the loneliness of her success.

There were no new people in her life. She never socialized much anyhow, but in New York City no one said hello, no one seemed to care. There was no one to even argue with much except perhaps Detective Modelstein, who was too excitable even to argue. He had resorted to helpless swearing and running before she could get to know him. She understood that his initial sexual pass was almost form for him, even if he didn't understand it. He was more than just eating and fornicating, as his female acquaintance had claimed, and she was surprised that the woman didn't see it. This could only mean they weren't really that close, she believed.

Unfortunately, Arthur had developed such wonderful defenses against hope, as though he would have to pay for every one of them in crushed dreams, as though he clung to the dark side of the world for safety, lest his real good nature come into the light and he be destroyed for believing.

Was she naïve? He was a New York City detective. He certainly had seen the worst in the world.

And was she telling herself these things because she wanted to feel she had a friend in him, because she really had no friend in New York City?

Claire Andrews got mad and she got mad at herself. She could sit in her apartment thinking about not having a friend, thinking about Dad not being there, thinking about no one being there, or she could do something about it.

It was 9:00 P.M. when she went to a nearby Queens Boulevard department store that had a pet shop. Originally, she thought she might get a dog, but abandoned that when she realized it could only go outside on a leash and that it would spend most of its time inside an apartment. New York City was not a good place for dogs.

Cats could do well inside apartments. In fact, they liked nothing better than sleeping. She forced herself away from the friendly puppies back to the cages with the kittens. She really did want a dog. A dog could be a friend.

"I'll take a cat," she said.

"Which one?" asked the salesclerk.

She looked back to the dog cage. There was an absolutely perfect terrier bouncing around the cage, trying to get at her, trying to be her friend.

"Any one. Just put it in a box and give me kitty litter, and do you have food, cat food?"

"We have something that will last until you can get to a supermarket. They're cat snacks."

"Fine," said Claire. She paid for the cat with a charge card. If she had to give up a cat, that would not be nearly as hard as giving up a dog. She remembered when Rusty had been put to sleep. He was twelve, which was like eighty-four for a person, she was told, and Rusty had had a good life, and Rusty was in pain, and they were doing the right thing for Rusty. That's what Mother said.

Dad said it was always a bitch to lose a friend. And Mother had been horrified that he would use that language to their daughter, who was fourteen.

But those were kind words, somehow in ways she could not explain, the kindest words she could have heard. She went on a long walk with him that day, like many of the long walks they would take by the Miami River, but this one was more important. She asked him how many friends he had lost. And he said he had lost two friends in his life. One during the war and another, Billy Cassidy.

"But Billy used to drive you around. Go on errands for you."

"He was my friend."

"Why didn't you put him in some high job if he was your friend?"

"Because he didn't belong in one, Peanuts. The worst thing can happen to a person is being in the wrong job. Wonderful thing about this country, beats others all hollow, is that you're not born into your job."

It was spring and the Miami was strong, roiled muddy and eating away at the green banks that during the dry summer would grow back. The air was sweet with grass, which made it all the more painful that Rusty was not with them.

"Some people say you grow up when you have your first drink or your first sex, Peanuts. I think it's when you lose someone you love. It lets you know how precious the days are, every minute of them. It's bullshit, that stuff about they are in a better place. Just bullshit. They're done for. That's it. They're gone and it hurts like a sonuvabitch."

She was crying again, and he picked her up and held her, and they held each other and then walked some more along this river they all knew, and which if you ever went out of state no one had heard of. She didn't grow up that day. She grew up when Dad died, because she knew the world was never going to hurt her worse again.

The cat whined in the box all the way home, and when she let it out, she saw it was gray and white and so small and furry she wondered whether she would step on it. It went whining around the apartment and didn't want to be picked up. It was one of those absolutely awful compromises. This was not a friend. This was a furry ball that wanted its distance and required a litter box, water, and food. It examined the cat snacks briefly, rejected them, and then disappeared into the apartment on its own.

If nothing else, getting the cat was a good break, and Claire went back to work refreshed. She remembered seeing something about a large red stone that might have its Arab weight listed, some time around A.D. 900. It had been in a sword that was captured from Christians, and she was calculating the ruby's weight in qurots when a furry white and gray ball began playing with her pencil.

"Get out of here. You're a nuisance."

She pushed the rubber eraser at the fur. Her cat thought it was a game. He slapped at the pencil. She pushed again. The nuisance slapped again.

"All right, nuisance, I'll play," she said, and had a little delicate jousting match with her cat that now had a name, Nuisance. That night, as she was going to bed, she felt Nuisance crawl up on her stomach and start to purr. Both of them needed something warm.

She went to sleep not knowing that the New York City Department of Sanitation had discovered Geoffrey Battissen just outside Queens. He was in a green garbage bag that broke open when another layer of refuse was tractored into the miles-long pile.

X

Keep your body pure and unsullied before the Holy Grail and without
stain of lechery. —WALTER MAP

Queste del Saint Graal, 1225

For his anger at the homicide de-
tective and his insinuation that Detective Sergeant Dennis McKiernan
might have gotten a ring too cheaply for the sake of honest appearances,
Detective Arthur Modelstein paid dearly.

"He's got to have some next of kin," said Artie.

McKiernan, a wiry sort with a gaunt face that seemed to have an
antibody against warmth, informed Detective Modelstein that the de-
ceased had no relatives willing to identify the body, and therefore a
member of the NYPD known to have seen him last would be used to
ascertain the identity of Geoffrey Battissen.

"Aw, c'mon, Denny," Artie said to Detective Sergeant Dennis
McKiernan. "He's a got a secretary or assistant or something."

"At this time we are investigating as to that factual data," said
McKiernan.

"You're stickin' it up my ass because I thought you lifted that ring
off a stiff."

"By the way, I got the ring out of the diamond precinct," said
McKiernan, referring to the precinct that patrolled Forty-seventh Street

in undercover clothes so that no one would feel free to snatch the thousands of dollars worth of stones dealers routinely carried in their pockets. It was the safest street in New York and the dealers appreciated it.

McKiernan was saying he had gotten a dealer's deal.

"I'm sorry," said Artie. "I should have figured that. I should have known."

"C'mon, Artie. Are you a jeweler or a cop? We need you for the identification anyhow," said McKiernan, who when they got to the morgue showed all was still not forgiven.

"Ever seen a dead man's dick?" asked McKiernan, pulling out the metal drawer on which lay a very still, cool, rotting form. All Artie could think of was how obsessively neat Battissen had been in life, and how now it didn't matter that he stank not only from himself, but from the garbage dump in which he had been found. Fortunately, Battissen was dressed.

Artie nodded and turned away.

"That him?" asked McKiernan.

"Yeah," said Artie.

"You sure?"

"Yeah," said Artie.

"Look here," said McKiernan and turned the head to show a black blood clot behind the ear. A beard had grown around the fleshy face, and the eyes did not have a person behind them.

"I'm looking. I'm seeing. That's him," said Artie. McKiernan made a move as though to wipe off his hands on Artie's jacket, and Artie prepared to take McKiernan and clean off the morgue floor with his face. McKiernan had mistaken Artie's aversion to death for a general weakness. Artie was not weak.

He weighed two hundred and ten pounds, most of it still muscle, and if forced to fight he never failed to acquit himself well. He just did not have the meanness to want to fight or hurt someone. No matter how combative McKiernan was, Artie's strength and speed would have ended it all quickly.

"Just kidding, Artie," said McKiernan.

"Why lie, Denny?" said Modelstein bitterly.

Artie left the morgue quickly and went home to change his clothes and bring his suit right to the cleaners. The sweet stench of death, as every detective knew, stayed in the clothes. He wanted to get away from it, all death. Arthur Modelstein knew it would happen to him one day. He didn't like the idea of it, had never become quite reconciled to it, but hoped that since it had to happen it would occur while he was busy doing something else, sort of come up on him when he wasn't home.

Then he would be gone and he wouldn't know it had happened anyway, sort of a best conclusion to a bad situation.

In a way, he felt he had to warn Feldman and the girl, Feldman because Claire had all but proved he was probably going to be a traffic point in some way for the ruby, and Claire because now there was a second death involved. This meant her father's death might not have been accidental. And she might by extension be in some real and serious danger now.

"Norman, I want you to know there is now blood attached to that ruby. If you should deal in it, you will be an accessory after the fact."

"That's like telling a furrier minks suffered to make a pelt," said Feldman. "Wonderful warning." The pouch of a face was now drawn up in an exquisitely joyful grin.

"What's so funny? I'm talking about murder one. You can tell your friends in the big deal gem business that there is a murder charge associated with every stone in that cellar," said Artie.

Artie, standing beside the desk, dropped a copy of the Scotland Yard report Captain Rawson had given him. Feldman, his feet up on the desk between the many phones, with surprising agility, picked it up, glanced at it, took the paper clip holding the pages together off the document, opened his right drawer, dropped the clip into a white lacquered box the size of an English muffin, and handed the report back to Artie.

"There are laws in this city and this state and this country," said Artie. "Stolen gems. Accessory after the fact. You can go to jail. Anyone can go to jail."

"Go play with the Hassidim, will you?"

"What are you talking about?"

"I'm busy. Go ask that pretty lady. She'll figure it out."

At least, thought Artie, she might leave now that there was real danger. He wondered why he even cared anymore, but he did stop off at her place that evening. Was he still interested in her? He didn't really know, nor did he know in what way he might be interested in her. She was like some puppy he had gotten stuck with and was trying to find a right home for. Of course, he had never wanted to drape himself over a puppy.

He was not prepared for what he saw when she opened her apartment door, and it almost knocked him off his feet. Claire Andrews was dazzling. She wore a black sheath that clung to her body like glistening paint, revealing one bare white shoulder, setting off her fine blond features. Her hair was drawn back in a French braid, intertwined with pearls. She carried white gloves, and when she smiled, she shamed diamonds. Claire Andrews was going out for the evening.

"Is everything okay?" she asked, extending a hand.

"Sure," said Artie, realizing his mouth was open. What was he going to tell her—that he had always known she was beautiful, but he never knew she could be absolutely stunning?

"I came on police business," he said, and as he entered he saw that the gentleman with her in a perfect tuxedo was Harry Rawson, certainly born to evenings like this. He smoked a cigarette and looked as though he were posing for a men's magazine. Both of them did. They could run off together to rich-people land.

"I'm sorry to interrupt," said Artie.

"No, no. Please," said Claire.

"I see you two got together," said Artie, looking at the British captain.

"I phoned Captain Rawson. His London office told me he was at the Sherry Netherland. We share a common interest, as you know."

"Yeah. Sure. Reasonable," said Artie. The words were hard coming out, and he didn't know why he felt quite so embarrassed. What had he been protecting? At this moment he felt very much like the fool, and as quickly as possible he told them both about Battissen's death.

"How was he killed?" asked Rawson.

"Knife wound like . . . Claire's father."

"I hope this doesn't bother you, Miss Andrews, but may I ask Detective Modelstein more questions about these deaths?"

"It does, but do. Please," said Claire.

And so Artie told the elegant British captain that Homicide said Battissen had been killed with a thrust above the ear into the posterior cerebral lobe. And of her father's death Claire could elaborate.

"I got to leave, sorry. Thank you. By the way, Captain, Homicide is in charge of this case now. In America, life takes precedence over property. Good day, both."

"Are you all right, Arthur?" asked Claire.

"Sure," said Artie. The word was hard coming out. Somehow he felt betrayed, and her very concern was offensive. But what was he feeling betrayed about?

And even asking that question told him that night that this lady was not good for him. She had him talking to himself. It was a discomfort and a sense of ill being he had seen in others and learned to avoid. The operative word here was *avoid*. Applicable totally. And with ferocity he enjoyed Trudy and dinner that night at his place, cooking kosher hot dogs and telling Trudy several times how comfortable it was to be with her.

Less than two miles from Artie's Nineteenth Street apartment, Claire Andrews dined on salmon mousse, fillet of guinea hen with a wonderful

Haitian salad, and wine from a vineyard Captain Rawson personally assured her would never allow an intolerable year.

It was dinner in a way she had never known, with Captain Rawson explaining how certain dishes differed around the world. He was a gracious guide to fine dining without being overbearing, rather like an exceptional wine. She noticed he used the waiters effortlessly where her father would order them around. And the waiters seemed to appreciate someone who knew how to dine. And they were a beautiful couple, too. She sensed the restaurant was glad to have them there. She felt important in a way she had never known before, important just by being elegant. She wished she smoked because she knew she could do it so graciously now. She laughed at his dry humor.

He talked of England with the deprecating charm of the truly secure. He talked of Arab sheikdoms and the friends he had met and ways he had learned among them, and of sharing a blood red sun setting over scorched dry rocks like a mantle of the desert. He knew the streams of history and the absolutely fascinating rivulets that fed into them, so that for a man of his education and breeding the world was a tapestry of unending threads. And this tapestry he spread before Claire Andrews as the real feast of the evening.

"I suspect America may be unique among countries. You're a land of beginnings, and that is a wondrous thing. The rest of us on this planet live on platforms of the past. Tradition, custom, continuity, whatever we can get of it. It supports us, but really it keeps us down," said Captain Rawson. "I guess that's true of all supports, what?" It was not a question to be answered but to be enjoyed.

Captain Rawson allowed the good brandy to heat to the warmth of his hands in a snifter. One of them had been injured by many tiny little cuts that looked so painful. He had gotten them gardening and said only that they healed better in the air.

She wondered what sort of tool could do that sort of damage.

"If I knew what it was, do you think I would have made hamburger of my palm?" And that was so funny. What a beautiful answer. They laughed. The world was laughing with them.

It was all so elegant, people stealing glances at them, the maître d' sending over courtesy drinks, the scent of orchids about them in little silver vases, and the perfect darkness in the corners, with the food arriving in the white-gloved hands of courteous waiters.

It was absolutely a shame even to ruffle the mood, but when Captain Rawson brought up the cellar, Claire took out her notebook and pen from her ever-so-delicate silver purse.

"In your claim you didn't say whether your family purchased it or had it made. Which?" asked Claire.

"Why do you ask?" Rawson inhaled the aroma of the brandy.

"We're competing for ownership, aren't we? I have to prove my father innocent."

"Has it occurred to you that your father in all good conscience purchased it from someone who might have stolen it from the Rawsons?"

"That among many things, but it doesn't really get us to the bottom of things and I am not looking for a whitewash of my father. I know him to be an honest man, and the truth of all of this can only help. So please, if you would be so kind as to answer my questions. Did you buy it or have it made?" The pen poised over the notepad.

"Had it made," said Rawson. He stopped warming the brandy.

"Who was the goldsmith?"

"I don't know, my good woman. This was a few centuries ago."

"Well, you see it does matter, because my father's cellar to the best of my recollection had no maker's mark. Ever since King Edward established the London Assay Office in the fourteenth century, every piece of gold had to have a maker's mark. You can tell just by looking at it who did it."

"It's just possible it wasn't made in London," said Captain Rawson. His voice was steel. Claire did not let it bother her.

"If it was made in England, and if it was gold and did not have a maker's mark, it could be a capital offense at the time. Killing a peasant wasn't, but playing with gold was. Your laws."

"Perhaps it wasn't made in England. Perhaps my ancestors bought it in Italy."

"This is not an Italian cellar. They would not use this much gold. My father's cellar was a trunk of gold. It was English. You see, what we are discovering is that there are some possible discrepancies in your claim."

The captain laughed with warm tolerance. Claire continued.

"Moving on toward something more recent, why aren't you providing a picture of the cellar?"

"I doubt it is still in one piece."

"It certainly was in one piece in 1941 when the gem prints were made. Why not a photograph, then?"

"I don't know," said Rawson. He killed his cigarette in the ashtray with a crush of a thumb.

"Now, while you don't have any sort of picture of the cellar, besides modern gem parameters, I see here a 'poorish bowl.' What's that?"

"The interior, I believe. Waiter." Rawson leaned back, clicking his fingers loudly.

"Is something wrong, sir?" asked the waiter.

"No. All fine, thank you," he said.

"Because if anything is wrong . . ."

"It's fine. The check."

"I hope I haven't spoiled the dinner," said Claire.

"Not at all," said Rawson. He gulped the last of the brandy and drummed his fingers.

"Because if I have, I'm sorry. Would you let me pay for half of the dinner?"

"No. This is a business expense. As you know, I am only here to reclaim family property."

"I feel awful," said Claire. "This was a lovely dinner and I spoiled it." Of course she did not mention that she probably would not have gone out with him if he hadn't suggested it instead of a business meeting.

"You haven't spoiled a thing," he said graciously. In the cab back to her apartment, she went on about the poorish bowl, noting, too, the amazing number of jewels on the cellar. It was the use of these jewels, so different in form from other cellars, that posed what she considered the ultimate question.

Riding up in the lift to her flat, Rawson learned with horror that she had only acquired her research techniques over the last two weeks. She hadn't even known it was a cellar until the thief Battissen told her. She was new to all of this, and who knew how extraordinary she would be a month from now. Could a chance footnote in history lead this rapacious mind to tear away four centuries of British silence and discover, in ways Rawson could not fathom now, that this cellar indeed covered what Britain held as the Holy Grail?

It was cause for concern, but not panic. There were still four centuries, four centuries in which it was a kept secret. If he could not have unraveled it without that inscription in the Round Tower, then she certainly couldn't. Still, he was unnerved at how far she had come.

At the doorway he used all the power of the charm he knew he had in abundance to create an atmosphere of romance. He would seduce her and then with no more than a simple misdirection get her going into one of the infinite vast areas in which historians had lost their lifetimes.

He certainly had done worse for Crown and country in Banai. This would be far more effective than anything he had done there. He smiled down at the pretty face and lowered to her lips.

The red lips beneath whispered: "I was wondering, Captain, you never mentioned royal blood. Weren't saltcellars the province of the Crown usually?"

"No," said Rawson.

"Which of your relatives wrote 'poorish bowl,' and how did he know about it? It seems like sort of an odd thing for a family to pass down unless it was important."

"My good woman," said Rawson wearily, "they may have passed it down, but not to me. And I will make a deal with you. I will tell you whatever I find, and you tell me whatever you find."

"I can't promise that," said Claire.

"Why not?"

"I'm not sure our interests are the same," she said. She did not invite him into her apartment, and if she had, Rawson was not sure he would go. She said again she really did hate to spoil such a lovely dinner.

The real problem was in the New York City morgue, and Rawson prevailed on Detective Modelstein to give him access to the body of the slain art dealer.

"Okay with me. It's homicide anyhow," said Detective Modelstein.

Rawson detected a faint hint of frost. Was something going on between him and the woman? Still, that was minor. He had to make sure of what he had heard from the detective in her apartment. He wanted to see for himself the thrust into the posterior cerebral lobe.

"You know this guy?" asked a Detective Marino.

"No, I don't think so," said Rawson as the sheet came down over the death-darkened face already decomposing.

"Yes, or no?" asked Detective McKiernan.

"No," said Rawson, looking at neither of them. With a gloved hand, he lifted the head, until he saw the mark just under the hairline, a dark encrustation the size of a dime. The pathologist apparently had cleaned away part of the wound, and Rawson could see the weapon made a hole the diameter of a pencil.

It was a thin instrument, and the thrust was alarmingly impeccable. It was perhaps the cleanest death blow he had ever seen. The art dealer was dead in an instant. The person who delivered it was a far cry above any of the New York hoodlums with bombs and machine guns that Americans liked to consider professional killers.

The person who had done this to the corpse was far more dangerous than anyone Rawson had expected to find on this side of the Atlantic.

"You sure you don't know him. You looked like you knew him," said Detective McKiernan. "You sure as hell recognized something."

Rawson smiled and shook his head.

"Sorry, no," he said. He was sure none of these detectives even suspected what they were all up against.

XI

Not only would he yield no inch but his strength never failed nor
flagged.   —*High History of the Holy Grail,* ca. 1200

It was a joy. It was a blessing a
thousandfold, and Mordechai Baluzzian almost praised Allah in a Farsi
phrase so common in Tehran bazaars that Iranian Jews like him used
it, too.

The Ashkenazi had made a mistake, and not just any Ashkenazi,
but a dealer in diamonds, and not just any dealer in diamonds, but a
rabbi's son, and not just any rabbi's son, but the son of the leader of the
Linzer Hasidim himself.

Baluzzian, recently arrested by Detective Modelstein, now had something against that detective's beloved Ashkenazi, those prideful Jews who
would not share a market with their Iranian Jewish brothers, so arrogant
with honor of honesty, their famous "word" on their famous "street."
So much for their word and their street.

Cut diamonds of gem quality had come into New York for a sale,
but they were not being marketed on the street. "Why?" asked Baluzzian
and other Iranian dealers. They had to be stolen. But the asking price
was virtually that of the market. These were not prices of stolen merchandise. Why? The Iranians not being fools, and also never being
invited into the market for stones of this quality, four of which were

supposed to be blue-white flawless, took some reasonable precautions before making an offer.

They had people followed. And one of those people kept stopping off for visits at the house of the Ashkenazi rabbi's son, who was a dealer on the street.

Suddenly the good fortune in dealing such stones paled before the prospect of such delicious revenge. Now to be certain of their good fortune, Mordechai and two other Iranians made complicated offers of payments, on inspections, on sales—different prices for different deals. And before an answer could be given, always one of the negotiators stopped at the rabbi's son.

The answer was simple. The rabbi's son knew they were illegal in some respect and thought the Iranians would never discover that fact. This was evidence. Only one question remained.

How best to make the Ashkenazi pay? And the answer was public humiliation. Make them go into the courts and be tried in front of the world, in front of Gentiles no less. Show the Ashkenazi to be the basest of thieves so that they could never look down their noses again at Iranians who did business as they had always done it in the Tehran bazaar, living up to those codes a thousand years before America was even discovered.

What was needed was a public arrest. But could one trust the New York City Police to pursue justice against an Ashkenazi rabbi's son as it would against an Iranian?

"We are all talking about Detective Arthur Modelstein," said Mordechai Baluzzian. "I personally have never been able to do business with him."

Neither had the other two jewelers who formed this special little group, who had all known each other from the bazaar, where they had been merchants and their fathers had been merchants and their fathers before them, since centuries before Christ in the time of Cyrus the Great, whose name was still blessed around their dinner tables.

Could they trust Detective Modelstein? After all, he had never arrested a dealer on the street to their knowledge. He ate with the Ashkenazi dealers. Had he ever eaten with an Iranian jeweler? Had he come to their homes? Would he ever marry one of their daughters? Would he take their money and then laugh at them, letting the rabbi's son free?

"He doesn't take money," said Baluzzian, who in Farsi had called Detective Modelstein a pig's penis for refusing previous bribes.

"I don't trust that sort of policeman," said another jeweler.

"If we are not paying him, who is?" said the other.

Any reasonable man might have assumed it was those he did not arrest. But Mordechai understood, perhaps better than the others, that this was a country of unreason.

"Perhaps no one is paying him?" he ventured.

There was laughter, as though a child had spoken. But it was obligatory laughter, not with feeling. Because all of them had encountered so many in this country who could not be reasoned with, some who even would throw them in jail for offering favors, money, special deals for reasonable people.

Their problem was that while they were Jews and there were strict laws against any dishonesty, and while they had been Persians who also had strict laws against such dishonesty, and while they had lived in a Muslim land that also had strict laws against any dishonesty, they were also Bazarris, merchants of the bazaar. And that was the code they did business by and lived by.

Dishonesty was selling stolen goods to another merchant without telling him they were stolen. Dishonesty was a public official taking money for a service and not providing it. Dishonesty was cruelly harming another merchant by reporting his infractions to authorities.

This later dishonesty had been practiced by the Ashkenazi Jews of many sects, who, when these Iranians honestly came to them openly declaring goods as stolen, not only refused to deal with them, but turned and phoned the police, American police.

One might have thought the blacks would show more compassion, but they were as bad as all the rest. One even brought charges on attempted bribery. Of course, through the mercy of the courts and a good lawyer, and the blessings of the Almighty, the merchant was not convicted. But it did show the mentality of the police. And it was to such a policeman now that Mordechai Baluzzian was suggesting they bestow their valuable information.

"We will give him a gift such as the Ashkenazi will never match," said one of the others.

"No," said Baluzzian. "We will give him only the information for him to perform his duties."

"And what happens when they give him a pittance? They will get him for practically nothing," said another dealer.

"Why should he take something from them when he has taken nothing from us?" asked Baluzzian.

"Because they are his kind."

"Are the blacks their kind?" asked Baluzzian.

"They got to them first."

"I will have Detective Modelstein to dinner. I will present him what we know. I will let him know how valuable the prosecution of this crime would be to all of us."

"And you will let him name his price?"

"If he has one," said Mordechai Baluzzian.

"Of course he has one," said one merchant.

"He will bankrupt us," said another.

"I want to be there when the money changes hands."

"If any of us can pull this off with that pig's penis Detective Modelstein, it is you, Mordechai."

"I want you all to come to dinner," said Mordechai Baluzzian.

"Keep your daughter locked up if that detective is in the house. They are animals. What if he rapes your daughter in your house? It is your word against his, and he has a gun," said the man who had just listed as an injustice the lack of Ashkenazi interest in the same daughter.

And so Detective Modelstein, Frauds/Jewels, NYPD, was invited to a dinner in the home of Mordechai Baluzzian for a discussion of great import.

"I'd rather everything be out in the open," said Artie, who had received this invitation upon being asked to come down to Baluzzian's new store. The other one across the street had been closed down the week before because it had been proven to be selling necklaces from a shipment stolen at a Bayonne, New Jersey, pier.

"I am not offering you a bribe. I am offering you an arrest."

"Who, Mordechai?"

"Baruch Schnauer, son of Reb Schnauer."

"From the street?"

"The very one."

"Let's have dinner," said Artie. His stomach would regret it, but his job wouldn't.

There were countless little courses said to be the best of Persian food. There was lots of rice, and most of the dishes tasted as though they had incorrectly been thrown together from leftovers in the refrigerator, lemon and beef for one.

Artie knew enough to smile at each one and say how good it was. Unfortunately, this was a signal for a middle-aged woman to put more on his plate.

The conversation was of the world, of jewels in general, of life, of marriage, of good bargains, and of bad ones. Of the perfidy of human nature. Of the ultimate justice of God. Artie was glad they did not press him on whether he went to shul.

And then after dessert, a jelly with an exorbitantly sweet cream on top, Baluzzian gave Artie what he came for. There were six diamonds for sale off the street, each of twenty karats or more, four flawless blue-white.

"Might these stones be polished?" asked Artie.

"They could have been. One of the sellers is a Tel Aviv cutter."

"You didn't see them yet?"

"Not yet. They want an agreement and then they're ready to show. They want serious buyers. And being Ashkenazi they have the arrogance to ask almost a street price."

"I think I would know why," said Artie.

"You know of them?"

"I want to get Baruch Schnauer and I want to get the person he bought them from. And I am sure if I get him he will give me the man who sold them."

"You will not let him go?"

"I can't let him go. I think he's involved in a murder one."

Mordechai Baluzzian kissed his fingertips and blew the blessings heavenward in thanks at this unexpected gift.

It was fairly clear what was on Baruch Schnauer's mind. The rabbi's son knew there was something wrong with the stones; otherwise he would have traded them with people he knew and trusted. But the temptation of six diamonds, more than twenty karats each, four flawless blue-white, was too much.

Why? Because, Artie reasoned, he was sure he would never be caught. And why? Because the stones were polished in the ancient manner before cutting, before gem prints. He had succumbed to the greatest of all temptations, the lure that absolutely no one could ever catch him.

But if he would not be caught, why not deal them on Forty-seventh Street?

This question was asked by Detective McKiernan and his partner Sebastiano Marino of Homicide, who, because they were in charge of the Battissen death and were unknown to the street, were going to set up the buy. And Artie answered: "If this rabbi's son messes up with the jewelers downtown, it's still downtown, not Forty-seventh Street. There might be some embarrassment, and some legal action in a municipal court, and maybe some severe explaining to do all around. But if ever he messes up on the street, if he ever is found to break his word on a deal, much less sell stolen merchandise, then he faces the rabbinical court and their decision is something else entirely."

Artie's voice lowered. Marino and McKiernan leaned forward in the chairs of the Special Frauds section. They had heard of this court.

"This court doesn't have jails and it doesn't have policemen, but when they find a dealer guilty, he will not be invited to Antwerp, where the rough diamonds are sold every season. His word and therefore his business will be no good, not only here in New York, but in London,

[151]

Tel Aviv, Antwerp, wherever diamonds are traded. And not just for a year or two or ten, but forever."

McKiernan did not like it. He did not like busting a rabbi's son. He suggested Artie bust Cardinal O'Connor.

"There's blood on those stones. Those diamonds are evidence in your case. What a great collar for you," said Artie.

"How do you know it's the stones from the cellar?" asked Marino.

"I know," said Artie.

"How?" asked Marino. He was shorter and stockier than McKiernan, with a soft, somewhat gentle face, but with a shrewd quick mind. Unlike his partner, he did not waste toughness in minor personal interchanges. Artie knew him as someone who would be tough only when necessary.

"Do you know what a twenty-karat flawless diamond goes for? You're talking a few hundred thousand apiece," said Artie. "These things don't go marching around the world in sixes every day. They're from that saltcellar."

"But if it was pros who did this job on Battissen, and I guess on the lady, too, wouldn't they sell them one by one?"

"A pro would know there were no gem prints on a polished diamond," said Artie. "When diamonds were polished, they didn't have gem prints. Therefore, if a modern cutter cleaves them to light he is really for all practical purposes dealing in new and untraceable stones. So they would think. That's why they could come back to the same city they were stolen in."

Marino made a shrewd point.

"To a city where you put out word for six large diamonds?"

"I didn't put out the word on the diamonds because if you don't say you have the gem prints, that's as good as saying they're untraceable. Hey, it paid off," said Artie.

"I don't know," said McKiernan.

"A gem print is like a fingerprint. If you cut a finger it's still the same print. Same thing with diamonds. That's why they got 'em. If anything goes wrong, you can lay the collar on me. I'll stand for it. I've got my own pride in this. There are jewelers downtown who think I won't make a bust on this kid. I said I would."

"Okay. If they're not the same stones, it's your collar," said McKiernan.

"Don't take glass from this guy," said Artie.

"I'm a cop, not a jeweler," said McKiernan.

It was not that hard a buy to make. It just required an awful lot of cash. The agreed-upon price was four hundred and fifteen thousand dollars. A hundred thousand apiece for the flawless stones, and five thousand for the lesser dark Cape diamond, graded at third pique, and ten thousand dollars for the silver Cape, first pique.

They had to bring one hundred thousand dollars to see the stones, whereupon they would be allowed to take one of the flawless blue-whites with them after examining all of them and return with the remaining three hundred and fifteen thousand for the other stones.

Best of luck, Baruch Schnauer was the one who met them to take them to the buy. He wanted to be with the cash. McKiernan and Marino were not wired because they were undoubtedly going to be searched for guns, and if that happened they would be uncovered.

They were to be followed by a plainclothesman and an unmarked car. They were to make the buy. It was hoped that the tail would be outside the place of exchange, and when they came out, they would give the high sign for the bust to be made by the others, who would of course carry guns. There was little doubt there would be some armor with the stones. This was neither a protected store nor "the street." Everyone knew that if Artie were seen within blocks of this area, the quarry would scatter like quail.

The buy was in a second-rate hotel on the West Side, in the Seventies. The seller was a diamond cutter from Tel Aviv. Neither Schnauer nor the cutter resisted arrest.

In no way did the stones resemble the weights of the British claimant's list. They had been cut brilliant from the polished rounds. Artie maintained the Rawson-Andrews stones lost the weight when they were cut. But they were still the same stones. Unfortunately, there was also some difficulty matching the gem prints to the Rawson–Scotland Yard list. The evidence Artie had promised seemed to disappear that very night.

The rabbi's lawyer was at the Tombs before McKiernan and Marino could consult the Patrolmen's Benevolent Association on how to save their careers. Neither of them would listen to Artie explain that neither Schnauer nor the cutter, Avril Gotbaum, an Israeli citizen, had validation as to where they got the diamonds, and that that was unusual for established dealers and cutters.

Even Marino, normally easygoing and rational, was screaming. He accused Artie of being not only not a cop, but, as it turned out, not much of a jeweler either. There were hints that the police might be let off with some form of a mild complaint, if the charges were dropped and if an apology were delivered, and if other amends as yet to be stated were offered. Of course, the Schnauers' lawyer said this did not preclude a civil suit for harassment, emotional harm, and severe discredit to image and business.

Into this awesome flurry, Arthur Modelstein pressed charges against both the Israeli and Baruch Schnauer for dealing in stolen goods, despite an additional whispered threat from both Marino and McKiernan that somehow, some way, if Modelstein went through with this, they were going to get him in an alley somewhere and shoot off his dick.

Artie appeared before the judge, who set bail of over one hundred thousand dollars on each suspect and bound the case over to the grand jury.

Then Artie helped the district attorney's office prepare the case for the grand jury, even as Marino and McKiernan kept repeating they had nothing to do with the bust after a certain point; they were only interested in homicide, knew nothing about jewels, and had relied on Modelstein, a thing neither of them was prepared to do now or in the future.

"I know those are the stones," said Artie. "If I know anything in the world, I know they are. I know they're hot. They'd be on the damned street if they weren't."

"Unfortunately, we have to be able to prove it," said the assistant district attorney, not in the least unmindful of the influence of the Linzer Hasidim at City Hall. These policemen he had before him had arrested the son of the leader of that sect. The homicide detectives seemed to understand the predicament.

"I don't know why the lab said they didn't match," said Artie. "But they didn't say 'totally not match,' right?"

The assistant district attorney shook his head. This was not good enough by far. To go against the son of the leader of the Linzer Hasidim, he would have preferred enough evidence to have convicted Moses on his way down from Mount Sinai.

"Okay. That's because the prints were taken while the gems were still in this stolen object for which I have not one complaint, but two. Claire Andrews of Carney, Ohio, reported it stolen just weeks ago in this city. Captain H. R. Rawson of London reported it stolen in 1945, with the accompanying gem prints. Stolen and stolen. They're the diamonds from the saltcellar and they're hot."

"Would that hold up in court?" asked the assistant district attorney.

"Phone the lab and tell them. They'll verify it. A print in a setting is different from a print when a stone can be turned to show all its facets."

"Fuckin' jeweler we got here," said McKiernan. Artie refused to be cowed while the assistant district attorney phoned the lab. But those minutes of waiting were done while enduring glares from Marino and McKiernan that could melt skin.

Finally the district attorney looked to all three detectives and with the phone receiver still off the hook, said to Artie: "They say you're right."

Artie, familiar with sting operations, knew how to fake appearances. He just nodded, as though this were not a time to shout ecstatically, as though there had never been any question.

Marino gave him an apology in the form of a playful punch in the shoulder and congratulations. They had their case. McKiernan, educated by nuns, still had reservations about going up against anyone dressed in black.

Because there might be problems of defamation of character, the arraignment, the binding over to the grand jury, was done with no more fanfare than a traffic accident. No one went running to the press on this one. The Linzer Hasidim were still the Linzer Hasidim, and they voted in a bloc and they voted in every municipal election.

Nevertheless, Mordechai Baluzzian thought the New York City Police Department was more glorious than the immortals of the Persian kings. Their mothers' wombs should dance in joy for the blessed day they were conceived. Gifts were offered and declined.

Artie couldn't help laughing. He felt good. Baluzzian wanted to know if the Reb Schnauer himself had to come down to court to free his criminal son.

"No. I don't think so," said Artie. "But I told you we'd do it and we did it. And we don't need payoff. And any time you try to buy me off for something again, I'm gonna throw you in the slammer."

"Bless your name."

"Cause you understand now, this is the way we do things here," said Artie.

"I was the one who knew," said Baluzzian.

"If you do hear of some cop on the take, turn him in. We'll do the collar."

"USA," said Baluzzian.

"I hope you believe it."

"I always believed it. Now I know it," said Baluzzian with a delicate hand gesture signifying a precise but powerful point.

"Okay," said Artie, and it was one of those moments that he felt glorious to be who he was, as though he had justified a lifetime, as if a lifetime needed justification. It was as though firecrackers of joy were still going off inside him. However, he understood how dangerous it would be to enjoy this too much, to become addicted to this sort of feeling. Trying to repeat heroism, going out of one's way to repeat it, needing it again, could lead him into dangerous situations. This had been a bonus of life, and he was not going to look for it as a regular paycheck any more than a bribe. The danger in taking any questionable gift was not so much in the single gift itself but in getting used to it so as to need it. Artie had seen it happen to other policemen, and he had known early on he was only saving himself inestimable grief by being absolutely straight. It made life more serene.

Harry Rawson thought Detective Modelstein was splendid, absolutely splendid, fine police work, and he asked Artie if he might be his guest for a drink at his suite in the Sherry Netherland.

Artie, still willing to do a little more basking, agreed.

"They didn't think New York was a risk because they were sure stones cut like that were before gem prints, you know. And so they figured if they cut the stones, who could prove anything?" Artie explained at the suite, giving credit to the Rawson family gem prints. Artie couldn't help noticing the luxury of the place.

"A well-done to Detective Modelstein," said Rawson, holding up a glass of whiskey in a toast. Artie pointed out that they had forgotten the ice.

"You take whiskey with ice?" asked Rawson.

"It's like drinking it out of a bottle if you don't."

"What a strange way to look at it. You know ice numbs the soul of a good drink."

"I take it with ice," said Artie. It was an elegant suite, with heavy drapes to the ceiling, antique-like furniture, spacious high ceilings with ornamental moldings, and every moment Artie expected Claire Andrews to come out of the bedroom, half-dressed, to be surprised by Artie, and to be embarrassed. He was sure they had to have something going on.

When the ice came, both of them drank a toast. Rawson was in a smoking jacket and seemed to linger over the taste of the whiskey. Then he leaned forward, over the small glass table on which the whiskey and glasses and ice had been set.

"Tell me, Modelstein, how do you see it? The whole thing."

"You mean the theft of the cellar, the murder, the diamonds?"

"Yes. The overall picture."

"The cellar was broken up, of course. And this guy Battissen was never really a dealer at that level of stones. It was out of his league. He must have been killed within a day after he had the cellar."

"Level?"

"I am told the big stones are something else and are traded and sold by different kinds of people than I deal with."

"Exactly. That's who we're after. Good point."

"I dunno," said Artie, shrugging. It was more complicated than that. "These are people I know. Nothing special about them. The Schnauer kid. Gotbaum, the cutter from Tel Aviv. They're at the level I deal with. They aren't anything special."

"But you're after the ones who are special. The big cheeses. The killer."

"Someone killed Battissen. I don't think it was the Schnauer kid."

"Do you think the cutter did it to Battissen? Was the cutter in this country then? Who did it? Who are they? Where is the rest of it? That's what I believe you're after."

"Sure," said Artie. He did not like being led, especially when he knew where he was going.

"Not that you haven't been splendid so far."

The compliment was more patronizing than the advice.

"We're on this thing, Mr. Rawson. I think we'll find out that the cutter bought the stones from the killer, or someone the killer sold them to, and then brought the Schnauer kid into it as dealer because of the kid's New York connection. We're on it. People are going to go to jail."

Rawson put down his glass. He leaned forward, fixing Artie in a constant gaze.

"Actually, I am not interested in legally pummeling some poor rabbi's son. I think the poor man has suffered enough just by being implicated. The disgrace as you can imagine—"

"He broke the law, Mr. Rawson."

"Indeed, but I think we have the golden opportunity we are looking for. You seem to believe the cutter, this Gotbaum, is not our man. And, of course, the poor boy who undoubtedly spent most of his life in a yeshiva, as you, a Jew, must know, is not the big cheese we're after. We have them, and they have the big cheese. We're in a perfect position to trade. Don't you think?"

Artie shrugged.

"It's the key, Detective Modelstein. We've got to use it now."

"We'll certainly put pressure on them," said Artie.

"Good," said Rawson and asked for the names of the cutter and the rabbi's son as well as the names of the two homicide detectives.

Artie was not so innocent as not to smell an end run. Rawson wanted the rest of the cellar; Artie wanted the collar to stick on the Reb's son and the cutter. Rawson, Artie was sure, was willing to trade a simple little police arrest in New York City for information leading to the rest of the cellar. The diamonds were already recovered. He had no interest in justice being meted out to the two at hand. As owner of the cellar, he could refuse to press property charges. The case could go out the window.

"I can get you the exact names of the cutter and everyone back at the headquarters. Just give me a little time," said Artie.

"To do what?" asked Rawson.

"Get the names."

Rawson cocked an eyebrow and smiled.

"Race you, old boy," he said.

"For what?"

"For what you're going to do, and what I'm going to do."

"This isn't a game for me. I live here. I work here," said Artie.

"Not a game for me at all either. I just want you to know I am not sneaking around behind your back."

"You have a right to protect your property interests to the best of your ability."

"I never figured you for a cold bastard, Modelstein," said Rawson. He grinned broadly. Artie shrugged again and had a bit of difficulty looking him in the face. It was some great game to this man, like polo. Artie could see the Rawson type going into some hell pit in some distant land, explaining cheerily: "Because it was there, old boy."

Artie had always known this kind existed, but it was exceedingly unnerving to meet him face to face. He was sure Rawson would be useful in a war, but in peacetime a danger. He had avoided eye contact because he found himself liking this handsome, suave, wealthy British liability.

"You know where to reach me for any official help," said Artie, and then dashed off to get to Claire Andrews ahead of Rawson. Unless he had gotten to her already, unless they had an affair going already. He hoped he had one thing to work with. Rawson's involvement proved that at one time at least, the cellar had been stolen goods. And Claire Andrews working on the beatification of her father would have to be against that fact. Artie hated having to go to her for this, but he knew Mordechai Baluzzian would be there in some downtown store long after this lady left. And Baluzzian was part of his world.

Nuisance, as was his wont, chose to walk across Claire's computer keyboard just as she had come to a crucial decision on the cellars. In all the scattered references to cellars, she still had not discovered even a hint of jewel adornment. What had been a key isolating factor at the beginning was now a wall. There was no such thing so far as a cellar with those kinds of jewels. The Elizabethans just did not use them for that.

The conclusion might have been that this was not a cellar at all, even though it had that ugly British trunk shape to it, and Harry Rawson did say it was a cellar. Yet his claim, too, had something spurious about it.

Was it wishful thinking?

No, she thought, as Nuisance made a place for himself in her lap. On first examination, the Rawsons were not great lords. They were not Wellingtons or Kents. And nowhere in the ownership of cellars did she see any lesser personages in possession of these great British pieces.

But problems, she had found, were often solutions that hadn't been worked out completely yet. The gems made it an extraordinarily important piece. And something that important had to be associated with someone or something famous. The Rawsons were never more than knights, according to her English research. And that was the point, that was what she was writing down when Nuisance chose to walk across the keyboard, almost erasing her day's work.

"I hate you," she said. And then stopped herself from flinging him across the room and kissed his furry neck. He was better than a pet. A pet listened to directions. Nuisance had a mind of his own. She understood now what cat lovers understood. You were with another being who didn't need your approval.

With one hand, she made a new overall directory in her system. It was for history. She had come a long way since that day when she made a mark on the wall. She had made inquiries into sales of saltcellars over the last fifty years. She was sure her grandmother on her father's side had not owned it. She was a poor woman. So Dad must have bought it within the last fifty years.

There was no sales record, yet something else emerged. From the crude picture she sent them, not one goldsmith could identify the cellar.

At first she had thought it was because of her crude drawing, but they acknowledged that while her sketching was more than a bit rough, it was good enough to tell them they had never seen it either in presence, sketch, or photograph. And certainly if one had been sold or stolen in the last fifty years, they would have heard of it. Several times she mentioned spring of 1945, and several times she was told that that too was in the last fifty years.

So either the Rawsons for some reason of their own had kept their theft silent, or there was some question as to the validity of the Scotland Yard report.

In either case, she realized for the time being, the sale of the cellar itself was a dim path with diminishing rewards. Not much could be done there, barring some sudden revelation like a sales slip somewhere. She had enough control over her search now to understand she was making a major directional change. Now history alone was going to tell her about this jeweled thing that had belonged to her father.

She was also discovering many other things, the foremost being that she could live alone and in a strange city. If she hadn't been so distraught, and actually so desperate about things, she thought she might never have tried this. But trying it, she found she could do it, and other things as well.

She could make a fuss. She could pursue a course and not worry what everyone else would think of her. She was neither a McCafferty nor the daughter of Vern Andrews who had to act a certain way. She was in a city where no one had ever heard of either.

She had interests to pursue just as everyone else had interests to pursue, and she would let them take care of theirs because she was taking care of hers. No one else was going to do it for her. No one else was secretly seeking her father's favor or knew that she was a McCafferty. What she got, she earned. And if she didn't earn it, she wasn't going to get it.

None of this, of course, could replace people saying hello to her in the morning, or chats about flowers, or being asked how she felt, or caring about how someone else felt. There had to be at least two hundred other people in this apartment building, and she didn't know any of them. She knew they had friends because she saw people visiting. But being next door to someone did not mean knowing them. It meant a cursory politeness, at most.

People made their friends not by place in this city but in some other way. Work. Sex. Or something she had yet to find.

"If it weren't for you, Nuisance, I would be lonely to despair," she said. But she was lonely. It was just that with Nuisance, she wasn't alone being lonely.

Arthur Modelstein phoned that afternoon as she was preparing dinner, and she was delighted to hear from him. Something had come up concerning the cellar and he wanted to talk to her.

"You've got to let me make you dinner," she said.

"Okay. But look, have you made any decisions today on the cellar?"

"I make decisions every time I sit down at that computer."

"Have you spoken to Harry Rawson today?"

"Yes."

"May I ask what he said? This is important."

"He said he wanted to talk to me."

"Anything else?"

"Not yet."

"You're wonderful. Look, let me talk to you before he does. You should hear the whole story."

"Arthur, you must think I am some compulsive little girl who can be swayed by the first person she talks to."

"Well, I'm not sure what kind of relationship you have with him. You see?"

"No, I don't."

"Well, you weren't exactly dressed for ditch-digging the last time I saw you both."

Why were men like that? Why was this detective like that? Didn't anyone wait for evidence? Why did they assume things?

"Oh, no. Not Harry Rawson. It was more a business dinner if anything."

"Oh," came the detective's voice in a high pitch. He sounded

[160]

honestly happy and surprised about that. "Well, good. Look, I'm coming over. I want you to hear me out."

"Would you like pastrami? I can make you pastrami."

"What?"

"It's a Jewish dish."

"You don't make pastrami. You buy it. At a delicatessen. What do you eat in Ohio?"

"I don't know. Creamed chicken. Tuna casserole. Roasts. Vegetables. Food."

"Buy some pastrami. I'll bring dessert."

"I can cook. I make spaghetti."

"I didn't say you couldn't."

"I'm glad to hear from you again, Arthur."

"Yeah. Well, good. Okay. Coming over."

Artie was not sure how to broach the request. He was sure that he had a touchy woman on his hands and that any hint that she might not be capable of something or was naïve in some way could set her off.

So, carefully, so as not to seem as though he was talking down to her, he began with police procedures and how the law was a strange thing and often people made deals that went wrong.

He laid out a fact.

"We recovered the diamonds in an arrest."

"Wonderful," said Claire. She was at the stove making dinner. Artie sat at the kitchen table. The vinyl tablecloth still had the creases from its packaged folding.

"We know that because the prints matched close enough to Captain Rawson's list." There. It was out.

And it didn't bother her.

"It only proves the gem prints match. It doesn't prove anything more to me."

"Good," said Artie.

He felt relieved that he had gotten through that point because the prints did prove the diamonds were Rawson's in 1945 and certainly did damage to Claire's claim on the cellar. Of course, a civil court still had to work that out, but until it did, Claire's criminal complaint was still valid. And that was what Artie needed.

"Will you insist upon seeing proof that it belonged to his family?" she asked. "I don't see anything so far that would indicate he actually owned it other than a report of theft. The Rawsons don't have a bill of sale either. I've been doing a lot of thinking about that, Arthur."

She pointed with a fork she was using to stir spaghetti. She cooked while Artie sat at the kitchen table and tried to drink a Seagram's Seven and ginger ale. It was a popular cocktail in Ohio.

He was seeing Claire in what might be considered her work clothes, faded jeans and a checkered shirt—like the ones she had worn before. The fork stirred the boiling spaghetti and then went back to pointing out the problem of the ownership of the cellar. She hadn't gotten his drift yet. She went on about the cellar, and Artie nodded as though she made a world of sense.

"Do you think I should have newspapers of that period examined?" she asked. "British ones. I haven't really done my British research as I should. I've been locked in America. The answer is in Britain and I know it. Your diamonds taught me something. No matter how bleak something looks, all the facts are not in, Arthur, until they are in. Don't you think?"

Finally Artie had to say it. Flat out, he had to beg.

"I need your help," he said.

"What on earth for?" said Claire. She poured the boiling spaghetti into a colander and then ran cold water over it briefly before she divided the portions and covered them with a canned sauce she had heated. Then she set one plate before Arthur and one before herself, brought out some grated parmesan cheese, and there she had it. Dinner. What was so hard about cooking?

Salad would have been nice, she noted, but she had not had time.

"Try your spaghetti."

"In a minute," he said. "There are going to be people, Rawson in particular, who are going to suggest to you, as a claimant, which you are, a legal claimant, that you should drop charges against the dealers in the diamonds. They'll say this is the only way to get to what they will say are the real thieves."

"That sounds like a reasonable approach."

"I'm going to ask you to continue to press charges and not pull this case out from underneath me."

"Why?"

"Because I'm going to get these guys without trading off."

"That sounds reasonable also."

"There's something more going on here. You don't know immigrants. My grandparents came over from Russia."

"I thought *Fiddler on the Roof* was beautiful," said Claire.

"Yeah. It was a nice play. Nice movie. That's not what I'm talking about. In these foreign lands, a cop was always someone who was in truth just another piece of shit. Cops would rob people if they could, and they were just another bunch of crooks who could be bought off. I'm not saying there aren't cops on the take here. But if they are, they're breaking the law and not upholding tradition. Do you know what I mean?"

"I think I do," said Claire.

"I'm a cop. My grandparents were immigrants. There are new immigrants here who don't trust cops. They've tried to bribe me, like routine. It's their way from the old country. So I've ignored that generally, even though it's technically a criminal offense. These people for the first time came to me with information that helped me arrest these two on the diamonds. If we should let these two go, these new immigrants are not going to understand we are after bigger fish. They are going to believe we were reached, that we sided with those who were here before, and business here is business as usual like in their old world."

Claire nodded. Artie continued.

"By not making what would seem like a reasonable deal to us, we are saying to these people, Hey, this is America. You know? I know you think I'm jaded, and when I told you to take that deal a couple of weeks ago, you thought I lacked some moral fiber or something. I was just telling you what I thought was best for you."

"I know that now, Arthur."

"But I am proud of being NYPD. You know. Yes, NYPD. We're all right. I want these immigrants to know it, too. I want them to know an American policeman. Do you understand? Someday their kids will know this is a different country. And this arrest in a way will help. It's important to me."

Artie saw a thin line of moisture rim Claire's bright blue eyes.

"That's beautiful, Arthur. Of course I will not let the charges drop."

"There may be pressure on you," said Artie.

"What can they do?" said Claire. "Reasonably, what can they do to me?"

Nuisance jumped up on her lap, and she cradled him, keeping him away from the spaghetti.

Artie looked at this sweet young woman loving the furry little ball and wondered what he had let her in for. There were two dead already, and he really knew of no good way to get to the rest of the cellar without making Rawson's kind of deal. He ate his spaghetti and listened to her talk about the course of history and nothing so grand as that cellar coming into the historical stream without a ripple.

"You see, what I'm doing now is looking for the splash," she said.

He did not once tell her she was crazy. On the other hand, he did not kiss her good night either.

XII

His aggressors' blades splintered and rebounded as if they had been hacking at an anvil, and they flailed away till their swords were shattered and they were weary and sore from their efforts and still they had not wounded him to the extent of drawing blood.

—ROBERT DE BORRON
Joseph d'Arimathie

CLASSIFICATION: Maximum Security, for H. R. Rawson only
SOURCE: Classified
AUTHORIZATION: Classified
SUBJECT: Avril Gotbaum, 47, Israeli citizen

Gotbaum, born Jaffa. Served Israeli Army reserve until 42 years of age when heart condition made him ineligible for service. Became a diamond cutter in 1968, through uncle. Father of Uri and Rachel. Respected member of diamond community. No apparent weaknesses, like extramarital affairs or drugs. No criminal record. Major interests: soccer and his family, but doctor warned him against attending matches because of the hysteria in Israeli stadiums. No information available on contact for recent diamond purchases for last two weeks, but estimates are it was some respected dealer in some way, because one would not know of Gotbaum without being in the business.

Exceptionally difficult working in Israel because of current tensions, therefore response to complete request impossible.

Harry Rawson knew a word job when he saw one. The service was riddled with them. One got an assignment, did what was safe and easy, and then verbalized. What he had not gotten was what he wanted. And that was everywhere Avril Gotbaum, the cutter who had been arrested with Schnauer, had been for the last two weeks and every person he had talked to. He did not need a common recap of the diamond industry and neighbor gossip. His response was brief. It was three words: "Comply original request."

It was written down on the back of Sherry Netherland stationery, as an executive from a British trading firm waited for it. The executive would not know what was in the envelope as he did not know what was in the envelope he delivered to this suite. It could have been trading information. He would give it to someone else at the firm and go about his business for the day.

The trading executive had once tried to start a conversation with Mr. Rawson in the hotel suite under the assumption that the man was important and that it would not hurt to get to know him. He had been put off with a simple word: "Please."

Now Mr. Rawson told him to leave with the ostensibly polite words "Thank you." But the way he handed the envelope to the executive was a dismissal.

Harry Rawson understood that good things as well as bad things happened by accident and that one who could survive the bad things and take advantage of the good things usually won.

There was a precious link now to the remnants of the cellar, and there was the charge of theft, which might be traded away for information. But just in case, and just because the world did not operate in an orderly manner, he had pressed for some information on a contact with Gotbaum. These things always helped when trading for information, especially if the man suspected you might already know much of it anyhow, such as the list of contacts.

He had hoped to have it in hand before he saw Mr. Gotbaum, just as he had hoped to have Claire Andrews in hand before he got to Mr. Gotbaum. Unfortunately, she had been quite cold.

"He broke the law, and I am not willing to negotiate, Mr. Rawson. And I am afraid that has to be final."

"I'm sure you're aware you don't really have much of a claim. All the proof comes from my gem prints."

"We can let a court decide that."

"Miss Andrews, are you acting this way because you just don't know what the world is like and have no idea how courts will decide?"

"I'm not the one who is unwilling to go to a court," she had said.

"Miss Andrews, are you interested in vindicating your father, catching the thieves, and recovering financial reward, or in poking me in the eye like some nasty little girl?"

There had been a long silence at the other end of the telephone.

"Are you going to answer me?" Rawson had asked.

"I don't like to be talked to that way, by you or by anyone, Mr. Rawson."

"That isn't an answer to my question."

"Mr. Rawson, even in New York City there is a right and a wrong."

"Catching a murderer is more right than catching someone dealing in stolen goods," Rawson had replied.

"I have faith that the New York City Police Department will get them all. Deals do not have to be made."

"And who assured you of that?"

"Detective Modelstein."

"Did it ever occur to you that he is in the jewelry squad and that he would naturally be more interested in jewelry arrests than homicide arrests?"

"Not for one minute, Mr. Rawson."

"These people have a world to themselves and neither you nor I are part of it. We're outsiders."

"What do you mean by that?"

"It may come as a great shock to you, Miss Andrews, in this great melting pot of a country, but I daresay you are not part of the jewelry squad or a Linzer Hasidim, nor would I imagine they would be part of Carney, Ohio. Everyone has his own interests."

"I trust the people I trust, Captain Rawson. Don't think you can take advantage of me because I'm vulnerable."

"You are hardly that, Miss Andrews. You certainly don't have to prove anything to me along those lines," Rawson had said.

"I neither know nor care whether you really mean that," Miss Andrews had said.

Gotbaum was more reasonable. He was unshaven and talking in Hebrew. He lay on his bed in an undershirt and gesticulated with a piece of pastry he was eating. First, he motioned Rawson to sit down, then he made a point with the pastry to the person on the other end of the line. His voice rose and lowered. Rawson picked up a couple of Arab words that had filtered into Gotbaum's speech.

Roughly translated, the words dealt with a sea of grief, something that may or may not be maneuvered through, and the wherewithal was in the room with him now. Rawson did not let on he had made out the rough contents of the conversation in Arabic.

"All right," said Gotbaum. "You say you're the owner, Mr. Rawson. Fine. What do you want?"

"I want to let you know that I personally have nothing against you. As a matter of fact, you may have been taken in by the same person who stole my property to begin with."

"Innocent, you mean," said Gotbaum. He took another bite out of the pastry.

"Yes, how would you know they were stolen? What I am saying is that our interests do not necessarily diverge. You were in all innocence betrayed by someone who sold you stolen goods. I was robbed. I think the guilty person should pay, not you."

Gotbaum finished the pastry and wiped his hands on the bedsheet.

"Mr. Rawson, this is all horseshit. I am guilty as sin. I didn't think there'd be gem prints on a polished diamond. I thought that I was dealing with artifacts and that I could get away with it. Our angel of a rabbi's son, Baruch Schnauer, thought so, too, or he wouldn't have set this thing up in a hotel room like this."

"You don't sound like you are confessing," said Rawson.

"I'm not. I just don't have time for games. You talk like you're in some Arab tent where everyone waltzes around everyone else's feelings. Look, that's not a bad way to do business. I don't do business like that. It wastes time. If I want friendly company, I got friendly company. And that's not you. So I'll tell you what I told our blessed little Baruch Schnauer, whose father has influence in this city. You get me off, I'll get him off."

The Israeli was right. Bluntness to the point of rudeness or, more importantly, ignoring questions of politeness certainly did speed things up.

"I want the person who sold you the diamonds."

"How do you know I'm not the thief?"

"Because the thief brings them to a diamond merchant. That's the logical course of events."

"You got a point. Look, I really have no desire to hand up this person. But I have less of a desire to do time in an American jail or pay a fine. And even less to be an outcast in this business that the good Reb Schnauer could arrange with one rabbinical decree. But it's going to cost me to hand up this person, in ways I won't tell you."

"You want money as well?"

"Fifty thousand dollars."

"Not a penny," said Rawson.

"I got lawyer costs, everything. Phone bills to Tel Aviv."

"Five thousand," said Rawson. It was not the money of course.

He understood bargaining. If he gave in too quickly or easily, the price might balloon. And still it would not be the price, but the deal, and very possibly a threatening inquiry into why he would be willing to pay so much. So Rawson bargained to save time and protect the royal secret.

"A little more than airfare, please. Do you know what I'm losing on this? I should get something from the stones," said Gotbaum.

"Were you selling them on consignment?"

"This is all shit for me. It's just the degree of it now and what I can escape with."

"Ten, when I get everything I want. Who sold you the diamonds?"

"First, the charges get dropped. From the other owner, too. My lawyer told me about her. Says she's got to drop charges, too, until your and her ownership are settled. I need you both."

"The thief may get away," said Rawson.

"Then hurry," said Gotbaum. He was making another call.

CLASSIFICATION: Maximum Security, for H. R. Rawson only
SOURCE: Classified
AUTHORIZATION: Classified
SUBJECT: Baruch Schnauer, 23

U.S. citizen. Member of the Linzer Hasidim sect, orthodox Jews, traditionally led by his family line, founded in Linzer, Poland, 1770. Part of sect moved to New York, other to London, in 1880s. Extremely tight-knit group, but able to determine the son may be somewhat less than the father, in eyes of community. But an attack on son considered an attack on father. Father member of rabbinical board that settles disputes in diamond district. Linzer sect a small power in New York City itself. Influence with mayor and local congressman. Sect votes as a bloc. Settles own legal disputes among themselves. Great disgrace that crime should be judged by outside authorities.

The meeting in the home of Reb Schnauer was more formal and sedate than with the cutter. He was an old man with a long white beard, and an assistant with a longer black beard seemed to hover around his desk. The study was dark but for a small muted yellow light from a single lamp. Books filled the room from floor to ceiling on three sides, almost blocking out the shaded window. Not all the books were in Hebrew, and one of them Rawson recognized as Gibbon's *Decline and Fall of the Roman Empire*.

"So, you are the owner of the six diamonds, Mr. Rawson. This is what I am told. Gem prints are not things that lie. Of course you will understand that my son's lawyers must examine everything as though the claims are false."

"Rabbi, I share with you the grief that has come to your son. It is an unfortunate thing of great magnitude, and I have not come here to press a claim. I perhaps most of all am aware your son could have acted in complete innocence."

"The courts judge guilt, and He who knows all decides innocence," said Reb Schnauer.

"I seek the person who sold the stones to Avril Gotbaum, who weighed upon your son to sell this property."

The rabbi raised his hands as though surrendering. But Rawson saw that his head was shaking also. He did not want to know any more information about this matter.

The assistant motioned for Rawson to get up. Rawson felt the surprisingly strong and rude grip of the assistant guide him from the room. The rabbi had his hands now over his ears, and his head was bowed so that the white beard lay on the desk.

"It's horrible, horrible," whispered the assistant. "I'm so glad you came. We are doing everything. The Reb is stricken by this. Seven generations, seven. And this. The name Schnauer in the world is more pure than flawless. A stone should be as pure. And now this. But we are not fools and we are not helpless."

The study was behind them now, and the assistant talked pointedly.

"You are willing to drop the charges, I take it?"

"I have nothing against that good man," said Rawson, nodding to the study. "But there is a problem of—"

"Claire Andrews and Detective Modelstein," interrupted the assistant. He had very black eyes. Rawson had not seen eyes that black since the Arabian desert. Somewhere in the house someone was cooking something heavily laden with beef fat, not fried, rather a mellow boiling smell.

"Yes, I think the detective influenced her."

"We know Artie. He can be handled. What do you know about the woman?"

"I don't know, not too much. She's from your midlands I guess. I've tried to reason with her," Rawson added in a polite whisper.

The assistant made the common symbol of money, thumb pressing against inside of forefinger.

"No, she has no price in this thing. She's not after money in this, trust me. I felt her out during a dinner," said Rawson.

"All right. All right, there are other ways. The rabbi must be kept out of this, you understand. He is a sacred man. A learned man. I am sure you understand our needs, and we yours. After that, everything else is details."

"Of course," said Rawson. He wondered whether knowledge was considered as hereditary as divine right to rule. It seemed that there was nothing man wouldn't try to pass down to his heirs.

He was sent to a law office in the Twin Towers in downtown New York City, with expensive paintings and subdued furniture, all set under track lighting. The rabbi's son was there with three lawyers. He was as pale as his father, but there seemed to be more tension than dignity. He was more than ready to make a deal, but unlike the cutter, he was not open about it.

"I am looking for the man who stole this piece the diamonds were in," said Rawson. He noticed several Harvard degrees framed along the walls.

"What about your claim to the diamonds?" asked one of the lawyers.

Baruch Schnauer quieted his own lawyer with a hand. He had taken off his black jacket and was wearing a white shirt with suspenders and prayer shawl sticking out from underneath the shirt, and, of course, a black yarmulke covered his head. But he lacked his father's dignity. He spoke quickly, almost without thought.

"Let the diamonds rot. You are willing to drop any charges, but there is another supposed owner who will not. What is her claim?" asked the rabbi's son.

"It's complicated and emotional," said Rawson.

"Is it valid?"

"She doesn't have proof she ever bought it, and I have proof it was stolen from my family."

"She doesn't have gonished then. But, okay, I think we can all work something out. Gotbaum is a liar. A liar. And he is sitting there in his hotel room, waiting for me to get his slimy ass off the hook. All right, we'll do it. Everyone will deal. You'll drop charges because he'll give you what you want, and the lady will go along because we'll give her whatever she wants. Okay?"

Baruch Schnauer looked around the corner office with the view of New York Harbor. He checked with everyone.

"We're just left with the details of what everyone is going to do now that we know everyone here is on the same side, right?" he asked.

"They do have to be worked out, though," said one lawyer.

"Yes, work them out. Work them out. I should have known. Six stones, did I need more warning than six? The son of the seventh son, needing more than six."

Outside the inner office, Rawson stopped by a secretary and inquired what was the significance of six stones, or the number six. She didn't know, but a passing lawyer asked if this came from the situation with the rabbi's son.

Rawson told him it did.

"Numbers in Jewish tradition are symbolic. Seven stands for perfection. The closest thing to it is six, which is absolute evil, hence the devil being represented by six-six-six."

"And those numbers mean something to Baruch Schnauer?" asked Rawson.

"Now they do," said the lawyer, who had business elsewhere. On the fly, he called out that ages and years in the Old Testament were almost all symbolic and not literal.

Which left Harry Rawson wondering what the Old Testament meant by saying the earth was created in six days. He was sure the same rabbis who dwelled on numbers had worked that one out, but he was not sure what conclusion they might have come to about it.

Artie Modelstein knew pressure when he felt it, and he never resisted. He handled police superiors the way he handled his mother and his older sister, and sometimes his father. Although he could reason with his father. This could not be said of the Modelstein women or Inspector Burke.

Inspector Burke was cold reason coated with political understanding and a sense of where Artie stood in the NYPD. He never once openly mentioned punishment or reward, but for twenty minutes he talked about nothing else.

To all of this Artie nodded, and at the end, he repeated some of the key phrases given him by the inspector. Apparently the inspector had gone to the same school as Artie's mother because he said at the end: "Are you jerking me off, Modelstein? Because you know where jerkoffs end. They end up in Homicide."

Inspector Burke apparently had gotten the word from McKiernan about Artie's reactions to a dead body in the morgue. He also could have gotten similar stories from a half-dozen other policemen.

"I will serve where I am sent," said Artie. "I have no reason not to feel I am part of the department, and my loyalties are with protecting the citizens of New York. What does seem a bit unnerving is why you would think I wouldn't do my job."

"You will talk to this woman who is causing so much trouble for us and for the city. And I mean the city, right at the top."

"Sure," said Artie.

"Do you have some emotional involvement with this woman?"

"I'm going with someone at this time, sir."

"I didn't ask that," said the inspector.

Artie made all the promises Inspector Burke could have wanted and then asked what more he could do. Burke said to keep them and was told what Artie told so many people so many times: Artie would do his best. Then Artie went about his own business.

He did call Claire Andrews, and he intended to visit her so that he could say he spoke to her. He was not, however, going to tell her to withdraw charges against the cutter and Baruch Schnauer.

He phoned her immediately. She was not in and had one of those answering systems that said she couldn't get to the phone right now, which did not mean she was hovering nearby. Break-ins knew that those messages were as good as the phone ringing with no one picking it up.

Artie worked the street and then moved downtown to Mordechai Baluzzian's new store. Baluzzian, who had blessed him for arresting the Ashkenazi dealer, now cursed him.

"What have I done to deserve this?" asked Artie.

Baluzzian dashed behind the counter and came out with a pile of newspapers. A woman behind the counter began yelling at Artie, and Baluzzian yelled at her. Artie assumed that was how married Iranians talked to each other.

Baluzzian dropped the papers on the counter and with a dramatic wave of the hand indicated that Artie should look at the papers. In the papers, he would find what he had done wrong.

"There's a lot of papers there, Mordechai. What's wrong?"

"Find it?"

"What?"

"Aha," said Mordechai Baluzzian and opened the first page of the *New York Post*. Then he turned the next page of the *New York Post*, and the next, and each time he allowed a triumphant "Aha."

"I don't see anything," said Artie.

"Yes," screamed Baluzzian, hitting Artie's chest with the back of his hand. "Nothing. Where is the shame? Where is the disgrace? Where is the headline that says the great rabbi's son, the pure Ashkenazi, is a thief? Where in this Ashkenazi paper are those words of shame?"

"I think this paper is owned by an Australian," said Artie.

"If an Iranian were charged with dealing in stolen goods, then there would be such a headline as the world had never seen before."

"Mordechai, they didn't carry more than a sentence on even a murder connected with this thing. And some papers didn't carry that. It just wasn't a big enough story for them. Look, you've been charged three times with possession. Two times it didn't make the papers at all. This is a very big city."

"I am not the son of the respected Reb Schnauer."

"You're right, Mordechai. It is a story the papers should have gotten."

"Then phone them. They will listen to you. You are one of them. You are a detective."

"We have press officers and things like that," said Artie. He was not about to make a phone call after Inspector Burke's warning. Although the moment the press found out about the rabbi's son, he was sure it would be a story, and a big one if anyone ever helped the reporter connect the death of an art dealer with the cellar. All the pieces were there. They just had not come up at the right time to the right reporter.

Artie suggested that Mordechai Baluzzian call the papers.

"They don't listen to me."

"They will listen to anybody with a tip."

"I have called maybe twenty times in one week once, telling them what vermin the dealers on the street are. But, you see, they are in the pay of the dealers. If they are not related to them. Everyone works for the dealers."

"They got you down as a crank," said Artie. "You should have waited till you really had someone. But don't come to me, Mordechai. I am not in the news business. I'm in the arrest business. And I arrested the Schnauer kid. All right?"

"He may never see a day in jail," said Baluzzian.

"Have you?" said Artie.

Baluzzian tugged at Artie's sleeve and pressed something hard into his palm, about the size of a medium jelly bean. Artie opened his hand. It was a blue stone, roughly over two karats.

He pushed it back into Baluzzian's hand.

"Stop that shit," said Artie.

"It's a gift from a friend," said Baluzzian. "Please."

"I'm gonna nail that kid because he dealt stolen," said Artie. "And I promised you and I still promise you. So stop it. It just hasn't hit the papers yet."

Baluzzian looked like a hurt little boy. His features, normally blown up in rage or contorted in some sort of exaggerated pleading, now collapsed into silence.

His brown eyes lingered on Artie's for a moment, and then softly, he said, "Let us hope."

"It'll be there. Okay?" said Artie.

Outside, Artie phoned Claire again, and then on the possibility that she really was occupied and could not come to the phone, he drove to her apartment house. He rang the downstairs buzzer and she did not answer.

So she wasn't there. Probably. He would have felt better if this were a more modern building, but it had the old kind of door buzzers without a camera, and all anyone would have to do is keep ringing apartments until one of them buzzed him in as a delivery.

Artie drove back to his office with the squad radio on, listening for anything to do with blondes. He knew what he had done. He had dragged her a bit deeper into this, when she could have avoided it. He told himself she was in it already, and now instead of some useless venture, she was actually helping. Therefore, what he had done was good. Therefore, he realized, he was now able to lie to himself as well as to her. It was never as safe and sure as he had made out.

Claire Andrews had spent a frustrating day with jewelers. She could have told herself she had learned another place not to look. She had hoped to augment the immensely disorganized histories of jewels with a face-to-face explanation from people who made their living selling them. The historical problem with jewels was that at different times they meant different things, and it was most confusing. In some references, they were supposed to have miraculous powers; in others, they represented a symbol of power itself; in others an ornament of conquest; and in modern times structural analysis and cash.

They were historical, medicative, protective, mystical, religious, and celebratory. And she had yet to see even a hint of any cellar so jeweled as Dad's. Therefore, the jewels meant something; and therefore, she had to know what jewels meant at least in the 1300 to 1500 period, and probably longer.

So Claire had finally come up with the idea that the persons who might be able to give her a perspective on the big picture were jewelers. Unfortunately, they might have been dealing in shoe leather for all they knew about the vast rich history of gems, the superstitions of gems. In the lower end, it was layaway plans. In the upper, it was necklaces, but never was it what the world used to think of them.

Jewelers knew prices. They knew the formation of stones that would get those prices, and that was all they knew. They talked with her because they all believed they might sell her something. When she pressed one on the meanings of stones, if he knew anything about gems having power in themselves, he said he had a theory.

"Everywhere the Hope diamond went it caused trouble. Now America has got it. A gift to the Smithsonian as a national treasure and from that day to this, the whole country has gone to pot."

"Do you believe a diamond can do that?"

"Look at what's happened."

"Are there lots of people who believe that?"

"That's mine. I figured it out myself."

"So you are not aware of superstitions regarding stones."

"Not a superstition. It's a fact."

By the time she got home, she was glad to see Nuisance. In fact, she was always glad to see Nuisance. He was there and he was warm and furry, and sometimes when she needed to pet him, he wouldn't move. And so she listened to her messages as she cradled him in her lap, something she could give love to.

Bob Truet phoned. Some strange people from out of state had tried to reach people in Carney to find out about her. Of course, they probably got nothing, Carney being Carney. It was good to hear his voice until he began talking about romantic involvement again.

There were two messages from Arthur, and when she phoned back his office, she was told he was gone. She wondered if he had a good life, and wondered if he were ever lonely and assumed not. With his dark good looks and normally easy manner, she was sure he had plenty of women, not just the one who had entered his apartment that first night—with a key.

There was a strange message from someone who knew her from Ohio State. He left two phone numbers. The first was his office, the second his home, and she wondered whether she should bother phoning an office at six-thirty at night. But he was there, and glad to hear from her. His name was Dale Roberts, and he remembered her as a Chi Omega at State. He was working for a law firm here in New York and had seen her name come up in a case.

"You know, you walked into a can of worms like you couldn't even imagine. I figured anyone from State ought to help someone else from State."

"I don't understand," said Claire. She had discovered this was the best statement to make. At first, she used it tentatively, as an admission of weakness. But it had worked so well, she now moved it into place with precision. It forced the other person to add details.

"There's something happening in the city that, because it's New York City, is doing damage that none of us could ever imagine."

"I still don't understand."

"Could I explain to you in person?"

"Possibly, but what are we talking about?"

"This diamond incident that may relate to a claim of stolen property of yours."

"Yes?"

"I'd like to explain some background."

"I'm here."

"It's complicated. It really is. I would like to take you to dinner and go over the nuances of this. I think, Claire, that you, like me, once you understand what's happening to these people, will see a whole new world

[175]

we just were never exposed to at State. I don't expect you to understand. I didn't at first."

Why did she believe Dale Roberts was handsome? Why did she believe he would have to be handsome? Why did she believe that Dale Roberts never really knew her at Ohio State and would boyishly confess that at dinner if she were to go to dinner? Why did she resent him? Because of all the above.

"I'm rather busy," she said. "I'm afraid you are going to have to try to explain this to me on the phone."

The explanation could have been a brochure produced by a public relations firm for a factory, except it referred to the Schnauers, their centuries of service to the Jewish community, the tradition of their rabbis, seven generations, each leading this little band from the ghettoes of Europe to the safety of Bensonhurst, Brooklyn. What these people had was the respect and trust of their peers throughout the diamond industry. Because of one unsuspecting act, the son of this revered rabbi was now facing a criminal action.

"It doesn't matter whether the courts find him innocent or guilty. Seven generations of wisdom and knowledge are immediately tainted because of one criminal charge that is going to be thrown out anyhow."

The phone felt clammy. She resented this man.

"You want me to withdraw claims so that the charges can be dropped," she said.

"I want you to understand what's happening."

"Do you represent this family?"

"Excuse me if I didn't make it clear. Yes, my firm represents the Schnauers."

"And you were chosen as the Wasp to deal with the Wasp?"

"We don't operate like that. I volunteered because I knew you couldn't possibly understand what this meant coming from the same kind of town I did, where a minister is a minister, and he is not wrapped up in an industry and centuries-old lineage."

"But you would like me to drop the charges?"

"Can I ask you why you are pressing them?"

"Because it's the right thing to do."

"Do you think you will have any remote claim on the stones, or that cellar?"

So they already had Harry Rawson, Claire realized. And she was certain of it when he offered partial payment of the value of the diamonds on behalf of Mr. Rawson.

"That's interesting," she said.

"Think about it," he said.

"That's not what's interesting. Why is he offering this?"

"Because he wants to get the rest of his property, and he can't do it until he can find out who unloaded these diamonds in the first place."

"I prefer to trust the New York police to recover everything. Thank you."

"That is astoundingly innocent," said Dale Roberts, and the warm rolling sounds of home seemed to have vanished. He had been pumping up his midwest accent for her. It was still there, but it was not the home boy in the big city anymore. It was someone who belonged here. She hoped she would never get like that.

"Look, Claire, I don't think you have much of a claim to the jewels. Now I am part of the team defending the Schnauers. Understand that. But if Mr. Rawson gives you a partial claim to those stones, then he really acknowledges a certain legitimacy to your claim that you have never had before."

"Do you represent Mr. Rawson, too?"

"No," said Dale Roberts.

"But he has empowered you to make the offer."

"He has let it be known that this is what he would give," said Roberts.

"Thank you," said Claire.

She made spaghetti for herself and opened a can of tuna with egg for Nuisance. She had found that when Nuisance was eating, he was not bothering her.

This gave her time to think more clearly about Harry Rawson as she looked at the pictures of the large British saltcellars. If one of them were melted down, would a British lord chase the gold? No. The symbol of the heritage would be gone. All they would be chasing was value.

Of course, this cellar did have value. There were the diamonds found already, and the topazes, the jade, and the large sapphire and great ruby.

Would he settle for some of the gems, or was it one gem that was more valuable than all the rest and he wasn't sharing that information with Claire? Or was he the sort of man who would strike a deal thinking most of something was better than nothing of something? Obviously, she was standing in the way of something he wanted.

But was it the stones? Would the remnants of the Rawson cellar be worth something as an element of a heritage?

Maybe. She didn't know. She didn't know England. The puzzles about Harry Rawson pointed once again to that island called Great Britain.

She walked into the living room and looked at her map. If she hadn't done so already, she would have marked that island in pen. She felt like adding another circle anyway. She didn't.

Harry Rawson knew something that could prove her father innocent. She was sure. There was something about that cellar that he had not told her.

She was tempted to trade that for withdrawing a claim of stolen property and somehow let the legal manipulations free the rabbi's son.

But she had promised Arthur to press charges. And that promise was right in so many ways. This rightness was why she was pursuing all this in the first place. She would find what she needed the right way. And knowing this reminded her that her father could not have been a criminal, because where else would she get such integrity but from him? This very feeling made her sense her reward was only beginning.

She went to sleep that night with Nuisance curled up in his place against her breast. She could feel him purring.

The next day, when she returned from the library after a day of slogging through book indexes on the history of England looking for the name Rawson and not finding it connected to anything she wanted, she noticed that Nuisance did not come whining to the door when she entered. She ran into the living room and bedroom to check the windows. This wasn't Carney, where a cat could come and go. She was horrified of what might happen to him on the street. One kept a cat in the house to keep it alive. To make sure of it. And that was why she had kept the windows open no more than a crack, ever.

But they were not open.

"Nuisance," she called, knowing this would mean nothing to him. He didn't answer to his name. Maybe he was hiding. Sometimes he would sleep under the blankets, sometimes under the radiator, any place that it was warm. And anxiety in her voice meant nothing. Nuisance followed Nuisance's plans for Nuisance's benefit. Like the time he had run through her spaghetti.

But when Nuisance did not appear even when she was typing something crucial into the computer, such as a note on a list of things to do, namely check Rawson's name in *Burke's Peerage*, a listing of all the lords of England that might give her some clue to his reasons for things, she became worried.

And she did the last-resort thing for Nuisance, what always made him come. She turned on the can opener. And still he didn't come out from hiding.

Perhaps he had gotten wise to the sound of the can opener without a can? She tried it with tuna and egg combination. She even put it in a dish and called out that she was serving food.

And still no satisfied little patting feet of Nuisance, no little self-satisfied ball of gray and white fur.

Then she began to check every hole and crevice and space in the apartment. And when she reached the bathroom and pulled open the shower curtain, she screamed.

Hanging from the shower nozzle was a ball of gray and white fur, its tongue sticking out, its neck twisted by a hangman's noose.

Someone had strangled Nuisance.

"No," she screamed, and ran for the phone to call Detective Modelstein. This time she got him.

"Who would do something like that? Why would anyone do something like that? Who could do something like that?" she sobbed.

The detective told her to stay there and do nothing. He knew exactly why.

XIII

Rectitude is so robust and sovereign a virtue that it maintains all things in true perspective: it is undeviating and renders unto each his true desserts and what is rightly his. —WALTER MAP
Queste del Saint Graal, 1225

Claire lay Nuisance on sheets of newspaper, and when she folded it over him she said, "There, there baby," thankful to him for being in her life if only briefly. Because while he was there she had not been alone.

She was not going to get another pet because she felt that with all her losses, her father and now Nuisance, she wasn't going to let the world get at a love of hers again. But even as she thought this, she knew it was not true. And it had nothing to do with getting another pet.

She realized a great truth in her pain. She was going to love again, and she was probably going to suffer for it again. But in accepting that, at that moment, she understood that the world could never make her stop. It could only bury her.

All the confidence she had expressed, and sometimes believed, and sometimes forced herself to believe when she doubted, now was hers.

She put the body wrapped in newspapers in a shoe box and waited for Arthur.

He came in ashen-faced and berating himself.

"Hey, Claire, I made an awful mistake," he said. "You're in an awful position here. I should've known better. I should've known."

"A crazy brutal man killed a cat," she said. Why was he so upset? He didn't love Nuisance.

"Hey, it means if they can get your cat, they can get you. So don't make trouble. The problem is they're not crazy. This isn't crazy at all. I wish it were. I didn't know they'd do this."

"Who are they, Arthur?" she asked. She made him sit down at the kitchen table. She decided not to show him the open shoe box.

"The people who have been coming at you other ways. First, they try nice; then, they try pressure; then, they try this. I didn't think they'd go this far. You couldn't figure them for this."

He seemed to have difficulty moving his body and his hands. Claire wanted to comfort him. He was a brave man and he didn't know it. She was sure of that. And a decent man. She was sure of that, too. He was also cute, but she would never tell him that because he undoubtedly didn't think of himself like that, this tough, worldly New York cop. He would only get even more excited.

"What do we do now, Arthur?"

"They've shown they can get to you. They've shown they're willing to break into your apartment and kill. They've raised the stakes too high. Much too high."

"Would you like some coffee?"

"Not now. Claire, did you hear me? The stakes are too high now. They cajole, they promise you, they threaten, they even lean on you a bit, and just before they kill you, they give you a last chance. There is no other step here they're gonna take but killing you."

"I'm not so sure, Arthur. I am going to make some coffee for myself."

"What do you mean you're not sure?"

"I want some more facts. I don't want to cave in to wild fear. I'd like some more information."

"All right. I think they're gonna kill you. And this whole thing isn't worth it."

"Can your department offer me protection?"

Artie nodded.

"And how effective is it?"

He was startled by her shrewdness.

"Probably could save you," said Artie. "Maybe not. Do you really understand what happened here?"

"I received a threat from someone who would murder cats," said Claire.

Arthur's hands tried to explain what he seemed unable to. They opened helplessly, almost begging.

"Look, the kind of people who sneak into apartments and kill pets are the same people who put bullets into people's faces. And the people who hire them to kill animals are very good bets to hire them to do likewise to you. Did the message get through? Do you understand? This is not a tour of New York City you are taking, hearing about the sights. They killed your kitty so you wouldn't think they were doing some cheap shot over the phone."

"Killing a cat and killing a human being are two different things, Arthur. For one, I believe killing a human being incurs a charge of murder. And we know something else from their killing Nuisance," she said, boiling some water.

"Yeah, what is that?" snarled Artie.

"They chose not to kill me."

"What is that? What is that meshugas I'm hearing? Somebody breaks into your apartment, kills your pet, and you've figured out they haven't killed you yet, and therefore we should all plant daisies in the sunshine. Lady, get out of this game. Give them what they want. The price is too high."

"It's too high here also, Arthur. Someone killed my father. I don't know for certain it was some random mugging that got out of hand. I don't know that. My father is dead. Now someone has murdered what I consider a friend of mine. You may just think of Nuisance as a pet. But for me he was a friend. And they violated his life, and they are not going to get away with it. They have crossed any possible line of compromise."

"And when they kill you?"

"You yourself said your department probably could protect me. I've met you, Arthur. I trust you. This is something they shall not get away with. You were right when you told me not to make some sort of deal with them, and you're still right."

"You're ready to die for this, then? You know, dead. I want you to know exactly what we are talking about, because this is dead or alive time."

"I don't think it is that. I think they've gone to a lot of trouble not to kill me. I don't think it is in their interests to kill me for whatever their reasons. That is the way I see it."

"And who are you?"

"I'm Claire Andrews, Arthur. You should get to know me sometime. Do you want coffee?"

"Was that the coffee you served me the other night?"

"Yes."

"No."

"It wasn't that bad," she said.

"From your experience in these matters, you deduce they're not going to kill you. Is that what I'm hearing?"

"You heard," said Claire.

"All right. I'll get some people over here."

"You look extremely angry, Arthur."

"I am fucking outraged!" yelled Artie. He wanted to break chairs, scream down walls.

"Is it because I am taking over decision-making you think should be reserved for the New York Police Department?"

"Look, you want to get even. Get even smart. Trust me. I know what I'm doing. Give them what they want. I promise you they won't get away with it. I'll get them. I plant a hot stone in some package Baruch Schnauer is dealing, and then I'll come in airtight. Five years from now. I'll set him up against another rabbi. It'll come hard and perfect, and he won't get away. He won't get away with it, and everyone will remember this incident and they'll say he was always a crook. Please don't put your life on the line."

"And your friend Mordechai Baluzzian?"

"That can be dealt with. Dead is no deal."

"I don't think that situation with the Iranian Jews is a matter of a deal, Arthur. I'm sorry. I have to be firm on this."

There was a silence as deep as all despair from Detective Arthur Modelstein. He did not take the coffee and he did not encourage conversation. He made sure a squad car got posted in front of her building and a patrolman rotated for round-the-clock duty stood at her door, and only then he left and drove alone, murderously angry, to the Bensonhurst section of Brooklyn. There, violating the laws of America, the State of New York and the City of New York, he forced his way into the very home of the Reb Schnauer, and in the living room thereof, before many of the rabbi's followers, who were horrified, did Arthur lay before the rabbi the iniquity of his son.

Neither followers' cries nor raised hands ceased the fire of damnation that poured from the mouth of this detective. He bore witness that the son quite obviously saw great profit and little chance of blame and had crossed that line separating honest men from dishonest, the good from the bad, the acceptable from the outcast.

And more, the son took the life of an animal from an innocent girl who only sought to testify honestly before the law, trying to force false witness in a court. This did Arthur Modelstein proclaim before the great rabbi himself, as many around them declared how the detective should be punished. And Arthur yelled back to the most delicate and learned ears of the renowned rabbi of the Linzer Hasidim, the seventh rabbi of the line.

"Murderers!"

Many tried to push him from the presence of Reb Schnauer and were succeeding. But the aged hands of the rabbi did not cover his ears this time—they covered his eyes in shame. And he ordered his followers to leave the good man alone, repeating the threats of damnation for him who interfered with the work of good men, of which this detective was one.

Seven generations spoke through the mouth of Reb Schnauer when he said with great pain: "Bring me my son. And do not let him gather his toadying followers, or his smart lawyers. But let him come himself, as my son and a man, alone."

And to the intruder whom everyone knew, he said: "Since when do you enter a house like this without a covering for your head, Artie?" For everyone on the street knew Detective Modelstein.

"Sorry, Rabbi," said Artie. Reb Schnauer raised a hand to indicate this should not be apologized for.

When the son came, he was given a choice as harsh as the stone deserts of Sinai. Either he renounced his ways and confessed his sins to the law and to the rabbinical council, or he would no longer be the rabbi's son.

When Artie saw the boy fall to his knees, weeping and begging forgiveness, all the anger went and he felt ashamed to witness another man's disgrace. He asked to leave and was told he should not.

The old man embraced the boy, kissing his cheeks.

"Come," said the seventh rabbi of the family from Linz, "we will share our shame together. We have done an injustice to this girl, and we must make it right."

And he quoted the Talmud that there is no shame in the shame that comes from correcting an injustice, for real judgment is not in the eyes of men or nations but in Him alone, the only eyes that mattered. "Artie, take us to her," said Reb Schnauer. "We may frighten her so many of us all at once."

"How many of you are coming?" asked Artie.

"As many as must hear my son apologize and make amends to the woman."

Only when Claire Andrews heard Artie's voice on the house intercom did she press the enter button. She was not prepared for the crowd that filled her apartment. Men in black, wearing their hats indoors, all with beards, pushed and angled and squeezed their way into her one-bedroom, living room, tiny kitchen apartment. Those who could not get in stood at the door.

She thought for a moment that if they kept the door open, Nuisance would get out. Then she realized this was not a danger anymore, and that hurt.

"This is Reb Schnauer," said Artie. "He is the leader of the Linzer Hasidim. Rabbi, this is Claire Andrews."

An old man with eyes as dark as caverns of wisdom and beard immaculate white lowered his head and raised it in a nod.

"This is my son Baruch, who before his brethren wishes to tell you something."

A young very pale man whom Claire thought might have been handsome if he were not so obsessed with looking like everyone else in wide-brimmed black hat and black coat and hair wildly all over his face and head stepped forward.

"I am Baruch Schnauer. I tried to deal in your stones, although I did not know they were yours. But I should have been suspicious. I employed people to get you to withdraw your claims and the charges. I am sorry. I apologize and wish to make amends."

"You can't bring back my cat, Nuisance," said Claire.

"What?" said Baruch Schnauer, looking to Detective Modelstein.

"Your guys strangled her pet as a warning," said Artie.

"I never ordered that. I never threatened her life. Never, Father," said Baruch to the old man.

"Can you account for the actions of those you hired?"

"No, Father."

"Then you killed her cat. And if we had not stopped this now, you would have killed her. The guilt of the hired man and of the master are one."

"Can I pay you? Can I make recompense?" said the son.

"I don't want your money," said Claire.

"What can we give?" asked the father.

"Actually," said Claire, "I do need help. I am looking for something, and I need help. My father owned a saltcellar of great value. A saltcellar is a valuable . . ."

"We know what a saltcellar is, my child," said Reb Schnauer. "Was it Italian, French, German, English?"

"English, I believe. It was a trunk of a thing."

"That would be English," said the rabbi. There was a murmuring in a guttural language behind the rabbi, and Artie explained that everyone was being informed as to the discussion, some even what a saltcellar was. The language was Yiddish, some of which Artie understood.

Artie also asked Claire if she really wanted to go into this thing now with these people.

"Of course I do."

"They're kind of very practical on things. If you have a favor coming from the Reb Schnauer it's a valuable thing. I mean it's like a few thousand people out there all owe you something. What I'm saying is maybe you'll want to think a bit about it."

"I know what I want, Arthur. I would think you should know this by now, more than anyone."

"They're very practical people in some ways. They might not understand this . . . project you're on."

Even though Artie was talking in a hushed and private voice the Reb Schnauer heard him.

"For someone who has spent so little time in studying Talmud, if any time at all, you seem to understand us very well, Artie. Of diamonds, you know a bit." The meaning was clear. Artie did not know what he was talking about.

Artie shrugged and opened his hands, indicating he was bowing out from the business of the Reb Schnauer and the lady from Ohio. He opened his hands for the lady from Carney, Ohio, and the Reb Schnauer, seventh on the line of the rabbis of the Linzer Hasidim, to enjoy themselves. He wasn't leaving. He wanted to watch this. The pretty little blond lady with her Ohio State rah rah would be like a kazoo in a funeral parlor. Even as he watched the Linzer Hasidim crowd in on her to better hear the story, he had to hold back a chuckle. The very intensity of their faces made the whole thing more laughable as she started to explain about Carney, Ohio, a place undoubtedly as strange to them as Mars or Tibet. Where was this Carney, Ohio, and what was it like? were the questions asked by these men who knew a few square blocks in Brooklyn and one street in midtown Manhattan. A few of them knew a building in Antwerp or London in which diamonds were exchanged. Outside of that their faces were continuously buried in holy writ.

After a few answers, everyone seemed to comprehend Carney, Ohio, a small American town in which everyone knew everyone else, and the father starting as a poor man, becoming rich, and marrying a rich woman. There were those in the town who resented his success, and when he died it came to light that he was selling something very valuable that some said was stolen. Many people believed this slander because of the nature of the object, the cellar, and how he was selling it. Claire wanted to prove his legal ownership of the cellar, and to do this, among other things, she was looking at its history.

This cellar had many jewels, of which the six good diamonds were a part.

There was a murmuring and several discussions. Baruch Schnauer talked rapidly in Yiddish to his father. Artie could only make out a couple of words.

"They were polished, my son says. This is an old style for a diamond."

"And there were six of them. I believe that there had to be mention of them in history. But I don't know where to look. I don't know where to begin. Gems meant different things in different times and there isn't a jeweler I know who seems to understand this," said Claire.

"They were matched, did you know that?" asked Baruch Schnauer.

"No, I didn't."

"Yes, not well matched, two of them had flaws. But I think in the time they were matched, they would have looked identical to those doing the matching," said the son of the rabbi.

"Does that mean something?" asked Claire.

"To a Jew, yes, but a Jew would never match six, not an Orthodox Jew."

"Why is that, Rabbi?" asked Claire.

"Six to us means evil."

"Jesus Christ," mumbled Artie, but no one was listening to him.

"It was a warning I didn't listen to," said Baruch Schnauer, the son of the rabbi.

"The message you didn't listen to was in the Talmud. Thou Shalt Not Steal, Thou Shalt Not Lie, Thou Shalt Not Bear False Witness, Thou Shalt Not Covet," said Rabbi Schnauer, his voice rising, his hand trembling, because it was apparent even to Artie that the boy's biggest sorrow was not that he had sinned, but that he had gotten caught.

"This day we have both lost something," said the rabbi to Claire and took her hands in his and gave her a blessing, as he did for the soul of her father, and for all those who loved her. He asked that her way be made safe, that her journey be fruitful, and that her righteousness be her shield and her convictions be her sword.

He told her that they would assist her in her search and that he already thought he remembered a reference to matched large diamonds, but not in a place that one would expect to find a mention of stones.

What Claire should know was that diamonds were not always a thing for trading or marriages. There was a time when people actually believed they held wisdom.

Eight days later, one more because they would not give her something on the sixth day and still another because they would not bestow it on the Sabbath, the Linzer Hasidim gave to Claire Andrews, daughter of Vern, of the little American town of Carney, Ohio, the fragments of scholars who referred to the Seven Eyes of Seville.

There were three wood boxes, some of them containing rare manuscripts, some photocopies of manuscripts. It was all for her. She felt a bit awkward in her dungarees, receiving such a gift from these formal black-coated men. But they had not really announced themselves. She offered them tea, but they refused, thanking her.

They repeated what the Reb Schnauer had told them.

"If these are the same diamonds, then the greatest of all commentaries on them comes from Rambam, the great Maimonides, when he says there is no wisdom in a stone, for it is not the property of objects to be wise. He says the only value in a diamond or any other gem is what man places on it. Otherwise it is no different from the pebble underfoot. A stone can no more make a person wise than it can make him good. A stone has no will of its own, much less power to act on it."

"And it was in Seville, not England, that these stones were seen?"

"There is no mention of England. Unfortunately, we cannot be sure what happened to these diamonds, or even if they are the same. They did not use our measurements then," said one man, who appeared to be the leader in the absence of the rabbi.

"What measurements did they use?"

"All great learning in Spain at that time used Arabic. The references are in qurots, and we can't be sure how accurate they are. Maimonides wrote a very humorous commentary asking if a one-qurot diamond made a person somewhat bright and a ten-qurot diamond made him a genius."

"Could you show me where in these writings the qurots are mentioned?" asked Claire. She finished drying her hands from the sink and booted up her computer.

"We cannot verify the weights."

"I wondered that, too, but I've found that weights are business, and when it comes to business and numbers, there is more accuracy than, excuse me, even in the scriptures," said Claire. The screen came up black with flashing green, and she got into her weights directory.

"No, this is not so," said the leader. "Numbers in scripture mean different things. Some are exact and some are symbolic. Except the size of things. In Israel there are archeologists who are anathema to the A-m-ghty who believe no scriptures find the measures of stones and places to be exact."

"So we can trust measurements. They are exact," said Claire, glancing back. The men buzzed among themselves. There was general nodding.

"Just read me the weights," she said, and there was more discussion. And then the weights came in qurots from one reference to another, all from Spain and from North Africa. None was from any source they knew in England.

There was also another problem.

"In the Seville coda, it is said a Jew owned the diamonds. It is so unlikely he would ever break up seven to make six. A Jew would not do that," said the leader.

"Well, let's see," said Claire. "And thank the Reb Schnauer."

That night she compared the numbers on her screen from the manuscripts to the Rawson gem list. A modern karat was exactly one-third bigger than an Arabian qurot. Claire had never been good at math and she hadn't bothered to buy a math program for her computer, which she probably couldn't use well anyhow, she reasoned. By hand, she copied the Rawson numbers from the screen in pencil and then multiplied each by one-third and then took the third and added it to each of the six gems. Then, saying a little prayer, she looked back up at the screen where there were the seven qurot weights for the seven stones.

"Oh my," she gasped, holding a hand over her mouth. "Oh my, oh my, oh my."

Five of the six matched to the first decimal, and the sixth matched to the second. Her eyes went up and down from pad to screen, from screen to pad. She now even knew the size of the missing stone.

"I found them. I found the diamonds. I found you. I found you. I found you," she screamed, blowing kisses at the screen.

She jumped up and danced around the bare floor, her arms raised in victory. There should have been a stadium of people cheering for her here, but it didn't matter. For sure, she had broken through the centuries. And if she could do it once, she could do it twice. She could do it for the sapphire and the ruby and probably for every mystery of the entire cellar.

What a breath of victory. What a triumph. What a sense of awe that history should be speaking to her from her IBM PC. She had done something and knew something now that no one else in the world knew. The diamonds were the same. Six or seven. No matter if a Jew owned them or not. She had found them to be the same.

The Hasidim had translated most of the manuscripts into English, and she made out that the family that had owned the diamonds was called de Cota. And they were quite powerful in Spain for a while.

She made herself a cup of cocoa and, careful not to spill any on some of the old manuscripts, glanced between them and the translations.

The jewels were an oddity on that sort of saltcellar in the first place. Maybe the jewels were a message about the cellar? But what was the message? Would a Jew sell off the matched perfection of seven to make the ultimate evil of six? Wouldn't he sell off two instead of just one, to avoid that symbolism?

She blew on the cocoa and looked at her separate date chart for the diamonds, references in the 1100s on the Christian calendar and the last in 1288 by a Talmudic scholar comparing the belief in diamonds as having wisdom to worshipping an idol. Wisdom was a property of man and was holy; the diamonds themselves were worth only what men declared they were worth. The diamonds were less than animals because animals could give sustenance to people, but the Seven Eyes of Seville in themselves could not feed one person one meal, much less tell him the meanings of the Almighty or the ways of man.

Claire sipped the cocoa. The last time the diamonds had been seven was at the beginning of the Spanish Inquisition, a brutal and successful effort to remove any Jews or Moslems from Spain. Could that have anything to do with seven becoming six?

By the time Claire finished the cocoa, she realized she didn't know why Jews thought the numbers had meanings. It was a good question, and she knew where to get the best answer if she wanted to understand something.

Riding to Bensonhurst in the back of a taxi the next morning, wearing the lightest possible makeup, no jewelry, and her most conservative black dress, Claire understood how much she looked forward to each day now with this work at hand. She had been forced into it by circumstances more numbing than she wished to think about, but now that she was in it, she was glad. Where else would she meet someone like the wise Reb Schnauer and the Linzer Hasidim? She wondered what it would be like to spend a life studying like these men she had gotten to know in their brief chaperoned encounters. Of course, as far as she knew the Linzer women never studied like the men.

She saw them for the first time on her visit to the Reb Schnauer, all wearing bandanas of a sort, even the little girls, all of them staring at what Claire knew was the strange woman who studied with the men. Herself.

A woman led her to his dark study with books stacked up to the ceiling. The door was left open slightly so that others could listen to his words if they wished.

Reb Schnauer sat in an easy chair, his frail white hands resting on his lap. Claire sat across the room on a metal foldout chair. She felt herself closing her knees tight and making sure her dress covered them.

"Why, Rabbi," she asked, "is six evil and seven good?"

There were many explanations, he said. But they all came from the book she called Genesis, where in six days the Almighty created the world and on the Seventh He rested. So too on the Seventh, the Sabbath, should man rest and give this day to God.

"Six is the world without the Sabbath. Six is man without God. Six is man alone."

"And that?" asked Claire Andrews.

"Is a definition of hell," said Reb Schnauer, and she heard muttering from outside the door and she realized people were listening in.

"Then, if the removal of one stone was a deliberate message and if it were a Jew sending it, he would be saying this thing he put it on was either hell or without God."

"Of course, what is the difference?" asked Reb Schnauer.

"That's an awfully expensive message," said Claire.

"It is the ones that are not listened to that are expensive," said the Reb Schnauer. And there was sadness in his eyes and his voice, and Claire wanted to hug him, but she knew she would probably be violating some of their laws if she did. Only the men seemed to hug each other among these people.

That day, the rabbinical court had decreed that never again would the son of Reb Schnauer be allowed to trade in the commerce of diamonds. Because of his dishonesty, his word and his goods would no longer be accepted among these Jews around the world.

And in a New York court, he had pleaded guilty to a felony charge of being an accessory after the fact, naming Avril Gotbaum of Tel Aviv as his source for the stolen gems.

Back at her apartment, Claire got a phone call from Detective Modelstein with his thanks.

"Good for you. We won," said Detective Modelstein.

"What did we win?" asked Claire, still feeling the weight of sadness from the old rabbi.

"Reb Schnauer's kid pleaded guilty today, naming Gotbaum. We got him. We're the only ones who can keep him from jail, and this only if he talks. Two months ago when you came into Frauds I would have given you no chance at recovery. None. I think we're going to get these guys. I think we're gonna do it. Isn't that wonderful?"

"No," said Claire, thinking about the man who had lost a son.

"We are gonna get the people who killed your cat."

"Well, that's good, I guess."

"What's the matter with you? I can't figure you out."

"Reb Schnauer lost a son today."

"The kid was a crook."

"Oh Arthur, I so wish you were better than that," said Claire, and she asked that the conversation end there, because she felt tears coming to her voice.

XIV

Avril Gotbaum didn't care if the phones were tapped. He was already going to jail. He spoke loud enough into the phone so anyone within fifty feet on either side of a wall could hear him. He wasn't looking for discretion anymore. He wanted penetration.

"Gonna be no problem, right? I'll tell you no problem. All I got is you to trade now. The little momser Schnauer handed me up. These detectives are all over me. There's a homicide with this one. You didn't tell me that at the beginning."

"Don't do this to yourself," came the voice.

Gotbaum laughed and rolled out of the New York hotel bed still holding the receiver. He wiped the cake crumbs off his undershirt and looked in empty packs by his bed for another cigarette. His large stomach stretched his white rumpled undershorts, the elastic band cutting little red welts into his hairy girth.

Gotbaum looked up to the ceiling as he talked.

"Myself? Do to myself? My big New York protection has just pleaded guilty. Gone. All I can do is cop a plea and give them you for a trade in sentence."

"You don't want to do that."

"I am not hearing very good reasons."

"The only proof they have is that you are identified as having supplied the diamonds. They have to prove you knew the stones were stolen."

"They can do that, asshole," said Gotbaum.

"How?"

"They can get a half-dozen people to testify that the way I sold them was suspicious."

"They still have to prove it. They still have to convict you. With fifty thousand dollars you could get a very good defense."

"I think I could get that just for giving someone your name."

"That's not smart."

"You're going to have to show me why. Avril Gotbaum is hereby officially and totally for sale. I'm in a hotel with a hooker in every other room, and the only difference between Avril Gotbaum and the ladies is price and where I'll let you stick it in me."

"Wait."

"You better have a nice package for me."

"I have the cash you need."

"We're talking about my life," said Gotbaum. He got two other offers that afternoon. And his line never varied, even to the New York City policeman from Frauds/Jewels.

"Hey," said the tall muscular detective with the gun hidden under his armpit, "I'm the only one who can keep you out of jail."

"I hear the way they work it in America is I am not guilty until convicted," said Gotbaum to New York City detective Arthur Modelstein.

"With a rabbi's son as a witness against you, I'm not too much worried about conviction. You're ours for when I want you. On the other hand, have you ever thought about dying? There's at least one certain death with this thing, and maybe two."

"I've been through four wars. I'm an Israeli. I can take care of myself."

"Good, then you'll enjoy our jails," said Detective Modelstein.

Captain Rawson came later. There was a slightly more difficult situation for him. Before, he had something to trade for information on the man who had sold Gotbaum the polished stones. That went out the window when some lady from America's hinterlands couldn't be convinced to withhold charges. As the British captain explained, it was her steadfastness that finally broke the rabbi's son, and so now the political influence Gotbaum might have counted on was, if anything, turned against him.

"But there are things we can still do," said Captain Rawson.

"I'll tell you what I'm tellin' everyone. Whoever brings Avril Gotbaum the best package will get Avril Gotbaum."

"I have no desire to see you in jail, and I really am not competing with the police department of this city," the captain said. He had that very British way about him. He could look dressed for high tea climbing out of a sewer at midnight. "I understand that now only the police can offer you some kind of deal on jail."

"You got it."

"What I propose is to not interfere with them in the least. They want what I want. The name of your source of the diamonds. The difference is I will pay just to get that information earlier. You'll still have it. You can still trade it off for a reduced sentence. And you'll have the cash bonus from me to boot. What could be better than that?"

"I'll see. There's still more bargaining out there."

"Obviously, it's the man who sold you the diamonds."

"See. You know the score."

"Then do me a favor, old boy, would you get yourself protection please? There was a killing that alarmed me considerably. It was perhaps the most professional thing I've ever seen. A perfect clean stroke into the cerebral lobe. Victim must have dropped as though someone turned out a light. These are not people to play with. I want you alive to tell the courts where you got the diamonds from."

"I don't panic into deals," said Gotbaum.

The British captain sighed. "Then at least let me stay with you until you testify or hire someone to be with you at least. I do believe there is a very dangerous killer involved with what those diamonds came from."

"What is it with you Brits about professional killers. Killing is killing. The whole world does it. I've done it. I can take care of myself. You want to sweeten the pot, we'll talk. Otherwise our business is done."

Gotbaum nodded to the door and ordered cigarettes and a sandwich from room service. He wasn't supposed to smoke and he wasn't supposed to overeat, and right now he didn't care. A heart attack could be a relief in this situation.

At 3:00 A.M. he phoned home to Tel Aviv, where it was 8:00 in the morning. He told his wife everything was going to be all right, but she was worried. There had been people asking questions about him in the neighborhood, she said. A friend had a premonition. She, too, never liked the idea of six when she heard that was the number of the stones he was selling.

"You would have thought a rabbi's son would know such a thing, no?"

"It's going to be all right. Tell everyone I'll be home soon."

About 4:00 A.M. there was a knock so light Avril thought it was one of the prostitutes working the hotel. He put on his pants and thought it was funny that for a prostitute he was going to dress.

When he opened the door, a hand came through throwing him back into the room, and before he could get a knee up into a groin or belly, he found himself rolled on his stomach, his eyes to the floor and tape viciously pulled around his mouth so he could not speak.

He felt his arm was breaking, as he was forced to his feet, using his head as a balance to get up. His body was slammed down into a chair, and he couldn't believe he was being thrown around like this by someone so much lighter.

He felt his shirt cut open very carefully and very precisely. He heard the explanation of why this was being done, also softly. But the explanation explained nothing. This had no purpose. Nothing had purpose.

Avril felt the prick of the knife on his chest. Certainly it wouldn't go farther; certainly the lesson had been learned; certainly the tape would come off and they would talk again as they had talked before.

Avril felt a horizontal cut across his chest, no wider than a stick of gum. He felt warmth dribble down his stomach. It was his own blood. All right, he knew. He understood. He didn't need more demonstrating. Take off the tape and he would say so. He would do anything, tell anything, explain anything, promise anything. Make the pain stop and Avril Gotbaum was his. Gotbaum yelled it into the tape and his own voice slammed back into his throat.

Another cut came, vertical, down from the horizontal, and then another cut, making the top of a square on Avril's chest, and while that hurt, it was nothing compared to when the man took the leaf of skin between his fingers, and pulled down sharply.

KINGDOM OF TOLEDO, 1059

It had yet to be polished, but it was as long as a forefinger and as wide as a peasant's thumb and would have made an unfortunate sixth if the merchant were foolish enough to have it polished now in the Christian city of Toledo, when, with just a little bit of discreet care, he could have the diamond worked in a Muslim city and then do it only when he had one more to make seven. It looked like hardened mud, but when a fine craftsman took it to wheel and cloth it would hold purity and clarity as no other stone. It was the water stone, the diamond, the stone of wisdom, which Emmanuel did not believe. He felt no smarter for owning six instead of five, and certainly his father became no less wise when he gave Emmanuel three.

People believed these things about stones, the way they believed in candles and omens, because life was just too powerful and frightening without them. He had known at an early age that the great and terrifying things of life were always beyond the absolute control of man. What one did was to perceive them as best as one could and then make what adjustments one could, and that was the most of it. Knowing this had made Emmanuel, a Jew, at twenty-six, advisor to His Most Catholic Majesty, the King of Toledo, an exalted post he viewed with more caution than pride. To be a Jew meant one had enemies. To be the court Jew meant one had more enemies, even among some Jews. But even to be a human being meant one had enemies, so one might as well ride a good horse through the trials of life as trudge behind it like a slave.

This day he could not bargain as hard for the rough diamond because he was needed at the palace. They had captured a Muslim officer from Cordoba and were prepared to burn him and sell off his woman for a slave, but before they did so, they wanted to torture information from him. They had people who could work iron and tongs, but there was no one like Emmanuel for talking to Muslims. And this after all was not only a Muslim officer but the commander of the walls of Cordoba. Perhaps Emmanuel could glean the secrets of the walls and make possible the capture of the richest prize in the Iberian peninsula.

The knight who had captured the officer, a crude man of more muscle and anger than judgment, was eager to do the burning.

"And did you ask him what he was doing away from the walls of Cordoba?"

"He had committed a crime. He had the arrogance to ask to speak to the king. I told him the king did not speak to Muslims, much less criminals. I have the right to burn him myself. He is my capture."

Emmanuel found the Muslim officer sitting proudly on a crude wooden stool in a coarse stone room with a heavy lock. A dark-skinned young woman sat beside him on the floor, covering her face with her hands. The officer's clothes were as fine as Emmanuel's, much finer than the Spanish knight's, yet his hands showed they were familiar with the sword. Emmanuel's hands were pale with delicate blue veins, hands that had touched neither sword nor plow. The Muslim had to know what was in store for him, yet he showed no fear.

At the officer's feet was an uneaten meal and a flagon of untouched wine. There were dark clotted blood marks on his forehead where he had been struck.

"Would your woman like chador?" asked Emmanuel in Arabic.

The Muslim, a fine-featured man with elegant bearing and an obvious sense of himself, nodded.

"Would you like food you can eat and drink that is not proscribed?" asked Emmanuel.

"For my woman, thank you."

"What makes you leave Cordoba?" said Emmanuel.

"I have come to speak to your king, not his servants."

"I am afraid you must speak to me first," said Emmanuel.

"How does your king rule without speaking to people?" asked the Muslim. Emmanuel smiled. It was an extremely logical question. Unfortunately, this was not Cordoba, where the Hajib, or chamberlain, held open court like the desert Arabs where anyone could bring a matter of dispute before him. Of Cordoba Emmanuel knew that it was so wealthy even streets were lit at night, and its grand mosque was such a thing of awesome beauty and size it could both swallow and shame the finest churches in all the Christian kingdoms. And there was something else about Cordoba the merchant Emmanuel knew from his trading. The Hajib, off on a pilgrimage to Mecca, was due back shortly. He had landed at Cadiz, and already his stately entourage was at Alhama. And the woman at the officer's side was quite beautiful and young.

"Our king speaks through people, even Jews," said Emmanuel.

"Don't they burn Jews?"

"And Muslims, and on occasion Christians," said Emmanuel. "They are going to burn you."

"That is stupid," said the officer without fear, but his woman gasped.

"Granted, but stupidity has never been an affliction dreaded by rulers. Wise or stupid, His Majesty will not speak to you, but will speak to me. Can you give me something to tell him?"

"I could, but your knight who felt that blows were a way to talk to people took a gift I had brought for your king."

"Ah. I felt he was a bit quick for burning even for so brave a knight."

"It is what we call 'lesson.' It was the property of the Muslims of Cordoba."

"What does it look like?"

"It is a vessel covered with silver and has a Christian saint in a stone of the sea on it."

"And he took it from you?"

"After he beat me, yes. One of his blows fell on it, and he wanted to see what hurt his hand."

The chador arrived, and Emmanuel made sure the food that came was from his own kitchen, one in which pork had never been cooked. To the Toledan knight, Emmanuel was quite cautious and discreet. The last thing he would do would be to accuse him of stealing. So he said,

"His Majesty wishes to thank you for capturing the silver vessel for him."

"It's my prize by right of capture," said the knight.

"And so the king will adjudicate once he sees it," said Emmanuel.

"You're not going to believe the word of a Muslim, are you?"

"I am just the king's servant," said Emmanuel, "but I will most assuredly stress how you gave it to me immediately for the king's judgment."

"It is a powerful stone and goodly silver, Jew. See that it gets to Our Lord," said the knight.

It was a funny bowl, in design one Emmanuel had never seen, and he had seen old vessels from Rome and Greece, even from Africa, and from the wild Hunnish nations to the northeast. It was definitely not an Arab bowl. It lacked the grace and sophistication of their craftsmen.

It was a lump of clay with a dark splotch of lacquer at the bottom, encased in silver, with a large engraved sapphire set into it. He couldn't imagine why the Arabs would call it a lesson. More importantly, he couldn't imagine why the commander of the walls of Cordoba, which had so much treasure, would take this alone.

His woman was eating, but the officer, whose name, like so many Muslims, was Muhammed, still refused to eat, even though Emmanuel had made sure they ate off silver. His silver. With Muhammed's permission, he asked if he could move the woman to another room so they could talk more freely.

"I would be most appreciative of that," said Muhammed.

And when it was done, when the woman, whose name was Jihan, had been assured she would not be disrobed or raped, Emmanuel sat down on a crude wooden chair across from the stone bench of this cell of a room, and asked, "So what brings you to us barbarians, Muhammed?"

Muhammed nodded to the strange bowl.

"This brings you?" Emmanuel held up the bowl before Muhammed's eyes.

"It is a gift for your king. It is a Christian treasure."

Emmanuel turned the bowl in his hands. "I am sorry to say I think not," he said.

"But that is a Christian saint in the blue stone. Your king worships such images."

"Not this," said Emmanuel.

"You lie," said Muhammed.

"What for?" asked Emmanuel.

"That is a great Christian treasure. We captured it from your masters generations back. We know that. We use it to show what Christians worship."

"Not this," said Emmanuel.

"How could you know such a thing?" asked Muhammed, and Emmanuel detected the first loss of composure. Muhammed's voice rattled with anger, and his black eyes seemed to steam contempt. Obviously Muhammed had been counting on a grand reception for this thing.

"See this spear with the three prongs," said Emanuel. "This is the pagan god of the sea, Neptune for the Romans or Poseidon for the Greeks, but nothing for the Christians."

"It is a Christian thing. We know it. That is the bowl Christ used last."

"At the Last Supper?"

"I think. I don't know Christian things. They said last. A most valuable relic. More than the skull of Peter. Christ drank from it, and it was important in your ceremonies. Omar himself captured it when he took Jerusalem."

"Omar the Great?"

"The one."

Now Emmanuel's voice cracked, and his eyes widened.

"Why did you call it the lesson?"

"Because it proved how foolish Christianity was in worshiping the drinking utensils of a prophet instead of Allah, Himself. That was the lesson, and why we kept it."

"Never repeat that to anyone, or what this is. I may be able to save your life, as well as my own. It may gladden your heart, but that knight who struck you will probably die."

"It is a great relic then?"

"If I told you, you would have to die. Do you understand that, Muhammed?"

"It makes no sense," said Muhammed.

"Never again, Arab, speak to me of sense and religion."

Emmanuel, the Jew, did not return for many hours. And Muhammed did not know how close to death he had come in that time. Emmanuel begged for an immediate private meeting with the king at any cost, and before he spoke, he set the bowl before His Majesty and said quite simply, in a tone belying his tension, that there was good evidence that this might be the chalice of all chalices, the cup of the last covenant of Christ, the Holy Grail. And then he said nothing else.

He did not have to say they now had in their possession the most valuable relic in all Christendom, that for which songs were written among the Franks and the Germans and the Britons.

More valuable than pieces of the true cross, of which His Majesty had three. More valuable than the straw from the manger of Christ, which His Majesty kept in an alabaster box, more powerful than the finger of St. Paul, enshrined in the great cathedral. This was the cup of the new covenant, that which said on the seder night of the Last Supper that there would be a new religion, a new faith coming from the old. This was what true Christian knights sought, and what everyone knew could conquer the world once it was found.

The king held it in his hands and turned it around several times.

"It is Christianity itself," said the king.

"No, that it is not, Your Majesty, but if it is what it might be, then it is the Grail itself."

"And we should build a great cathedral for it, greater than the mosque in Cordoba. We will show our power."

"And what about the power of Cordoba?" asked Emmanuel. He knew this was dangerous ground, even though the king had agreed to see him in his most private of rooms, the one without windows and with only one door. The walls were bare but for a wood crucifix, and only the inlaid ivory table might distinguish this from the cell in which the Muslim waited.

"It will die; it will become like Toledo is now, a Christian city. It will be ours," said the king.

But Emmanuel pointed out to His Majesty that Cordoba had lost the Grail, that its power was not enough to keep it. Neither its walls nor its magnificent warriors could keep this relic, and Cordoba certainly was much more powerful than Toledo or many Toledos.

"Be straight, Jew," said His Majesty.

"If it is the Grail, and if it has these powers bestowed on its owner, certainly they are not the powers to be free of theft."

"You have made that clear even to your lord," said His Majesty.

Emmanuel smiled. The king could be astute.

"This was only stolen because this Muslim thought that it was the Grail and that it would be valuable to any Christian king. Who would not trade a ship of gold for this, and if they were to trade a ship of gold, why not pay a quarter-ship of gold for the army to take it?"

"You are saying we are not strong enough to hold it now."

"Not against those who would want it, Your Majesty."

"I will not give it up."

"Of course not. If it has the powers it is supposed to have, there will be a day you can, if you wish, display it in any one of your many cities. Of course, great power did not help Cordoba keep it."

"Out with it now," said His Majesty, pointing a finger to Emmanuel, the Jew who dressed like a grand señor, and had access to this highest council, whom men talked about behind his back, and whose very brilliance stirred jealousy in the base minds of those who could not understand that brilliance.

"It should be hidden not in some walled chamber that can be broken into, or behind some locked door to which some thief may manufacture a key, or even behind guards whose loyalty just once in a hundred years has to waver. But put it there before the people with a reason to protect it heavily but not so much a reason that the most powerful would try to steal it."

"How?"

"A gold chalice. You have a right to protect a gold chalice with a jewel, the king's chalice, for the king's mass. These are not left on street corners, but rather quite reasonably most protected."

"And we silence the Muslim who brought it. We must. It is not an unfairness I like, but it is my crown and it is my kingdom, and he knows what we have. And damn you, Jew. He's a Muslim."

Emmanuel knew the king meant an execution, and to argue for justice, a cause the king often respected, would be useless in a matter of survival. For what justice was there ever in war, when the town that lost gave up its women for rape, its children for slavery, and all fighting men for death. And the king did delight in his wars as did all the Christian kings of the Iberian peninsula. But Emmanuel, who knew that to kill a Muslim would not be that far a step from killing a Jew, even the court Jew, had expected this, and said: "Our Muslim already knows to keep his tongue. His life depends on it. It is the tongues that will ask why we kill him and his woman that worry me. They will ask, was he the one who brought the gift? And was it not shortly thereafter that His Majesty had himself made a large gold chalice?"

"He brought a woman?"

"It is undoubtedly why he left Cordoba. The Hajib is returning soon, and the Hajib, an old man, had many young women in his harem. I would venture this one was one of his. The Muslim is handsome, the woman is beautiful, and the Hajib is coming home."

"Did he say that?"

"Need we ask?" said Emmanuel, and the king laughed. Of course, there was the problem of the knight who knew about a bowl and had tried to keep it for himself. That knight would be the only one whose voice could, unfortunately, not be trusted.

"Jew, you have me killing my good Christian knights and letting Muslims live content in my kingdom."

"Not me, Your Majesty, but your wisdom," said Emmanuel, who did not need to mention he had to keep his own tongue about the Grail because the first whisper of it in the streets of Toledo would mean his head.

Emmanuel was right about the Muslim's motives. But he was not right in his estimate of the peculiarity of the relic, that it was just another physical thing men put foolish hope in. He watched with horror as, in the following year, Christian kings found the weaknesses in Muslim defenses and took Valencia, Murcia, Andalusia, Aragon, and Saragossa, and in every city, the people were given a choice: accept Christ or die.

And Emmanuel, the Jew, knew that if they did this to the Muslims, certainly there would be the day they would do this to the Jews. He told his son the great secret of the king's chalice. And that son told his son, and on the day Seville itself fell to the Christians, there were the first rumblings of what would be the Inquisition. It was a day in which the great family Cota, descendants of Emmanuel of Toledo, celebrated. For they had purchased in this city, now under the Spanish king, the seventh diamond now polished clear, said to hold all the wisdom in the world, although the great Maimonides had proven along with other rabbis that this was foolishness.

But the very fact that he and others had mentioned the Seven Eyes of Seville made them even more fashionable to own. And if there was one thing the family Cota was in this new and powerful Spanish Empire, it was fashionable.

They were not that serious about their Judaism like the poor often were. They would say, to much laughter, we are serious Spaniards who happen to be Jews.

The Inquisition soon reminded them that they were either Spaniards or Jews. And the Cotas could not bring themselves to leave Spain as so many did. And they found to their surprise that pressed under these circumstances, the thing in them that was Jewish became not some accident of birth, but a purpose. The water of their Christian baptism seemed to light a fire in their secret Judaism, one the family Cota had not known for generations.

They thought the Inquisition would pass like other waves of irrationality. It did not pass. With whips and fire and prongs that tore human flesh, it pressed itself on the spirit of Spain, on the enlightenment that had once been Spain, and on the eldest member of the Cota family in particular, the one who had been passed the secret of the king's chalice.

He had eaten pork freely before and liked its taste. But when he had to eat pork, when others watched to see if it were enjoyable to him, when he had to eat pork when he normally would not eat pork because Christians were watching, then it became meat rancid to the soul.

And taking a wafer in his mouth and supposedly eating God, while understandable, even admirable, when others did it by faith, became abomination when done to show even the peasantry that he was a weekly communicant.

What religion, he wondered, as he now in secret places on his vast estates studied the laws of Moses, the Mishna, the Talmud, the Torah, what faith could possibly be built on a sword that forced a man to lie?

What faith could be satisfied to build itself in great houses instead of human hearts? What had been respect, even admiration for another's faith now burned as contempt, partly for himself. For he could have at any moment risked his life and his family and fled to some Muslim land where there was greater tolerance. He could have gone to the fires, as some did for whom lying had become a greater burden than life.

Instead he vented all his burning contempt with sweet words of devotion, giving for placement in the great chalice in the Cathedral of Toledo, which his father had told him contained the Christian Grail, six well-polished diamonds, having smashed one with a hammer so there would never be seven again.

NEW YORK CITY, THE PRESENT

When the six stones arrived at New York County Court in New York City, they were considered a sign of neither ultimate evil nor wisdom. They were cash valued at one hundred seventy-five thousand dollars apiece and listed first as Exhibit A in a conspiracy to sell stolen goods and then as Exhibit A in the torture death of Avril Gotbaum of Tel Aviv, who had been awaiting trial on the original conspiracy charge.

The skin above his nipple had been cut in a strip and, according to the coroner's office, was being pulled down slowly when his heart gave out, causing death.

In a small Queens apartment, a young American woman, whose only previous accomplishment of note had been to win best flower at the Garden Club of Carney, broke the code of the Spanish Marano that had survived undetected for four hundred years.

She did it with a pad, a pencil, a telephone, and a mind that had been awakened to its powers. The last time the diamonds had been noted was in the possession of a Spanish family named de Cota, shortly after the Inquisition, this from a Spanish court record that she had consulted in her search for continuing mention of the stones.

Given that they ended up in a British saltcellar, was it therefore possible they had been brought to Britain and bought by someone for the cellar?

Claire did two things. The Linzer Hasidim had a community in London, a major diamond center, that looked for records of the diamonds there. In neither religious nor business records was there a mention of either six or seven diamonds in a group of roughly the twenty-karat size.

They also without as much assurance told her there was no Jewish family that they knew of named de Cota, and yet in the history of the

Jews of England, Claire found a de Cota, settling with other Spanish Jews, but this one quite late, in the time of Elizabeth I. Like descriptions, names changed from country to country and now de Cota's descendants were named Coater.

It was no great feat to find one in a London telephone directory.

"Yes, yes, we did have an ancestor named de Cota." The woman's voice was British as a cold shower.

Claire felt a tingle at having found her. It was as though she had walked the very lines of the centuries on her wall. She gripped the phone tightly and made sure the ballpoint pen was working by scratching first on the pad and then, when it didn't give ink, on her blue jeans. That got it to work.

She could taste the victory and was almost afraid to press on.

"Were there any family records of diamonds?"

"If there were," said the woman, "they certainly didn't come to me. I believe he arrived penniless. He was a Marano, you know. He was a Jew."

"You're not?"

"The Coaters have been Anglican for generations. I have a brother-in-law who is Jewish. I'm an Anglican, not a very good one perhaps, but what is a good Anglican?"

"Is there anyone who might remember a family tradition or stories about de Cota?"

"I've told you everything we know. Is there some claim on diamonds? It would be an absolutely splendid windfall."

"Not since the fifteenth century in Spain," said Claire.

"I do know this. He was supposed to be deucedly grateful for sanctuary. That probably doesn't help at all, does it?"

"Yes, as a matter of fact, it may," said Claire to Maude Coater of Kensington Square, London.

If England gave de Cota sanctuary, would he give a gift of six diamonds to his protector? Why not five? Why not, most of all, the seven?

No, de Cota was a Marano. He lived his Jewish life in secret, possibly in great hate. Was it possible, therefore, that being unable to speak out, he spoke to those fellow Jews of the world in their language of numbers? He made six of the seven diamonds, which said "not of God."

And since there was no mention of these diamonds after the fourteen-hundreds in Spain, was it possible that they weren't hidden but put on something in Spain itself, put on not as the Seven Eyes of Seville, which would be noted, but put on as six?

Put on what?

Something that a Jew should be aware was "not of God," that made its way to England with a Duke de Cota and became, for some reason, a saltcellar. She stopped doodling on her pad and, on the map of the world on her research wall, made a strong blue line from Spain to England, the path of that thing that was for a Marano "not of God." Could it be Christian? Maybe, thought Claire, getting herself a Coke from the refrigerator.

XV

He trusted more in His help and succour than in his sword, for he saw most plainly that no prowess achieved with this world's arms would suffice to save him unless Our Lord came to his aid.

—CHRÉTIEN DE TROYES
Le Conte du Graal, 1180

At 4:32 A.M. Harry Rawson got a phone call. It was a British voice and the caller did not tell him who he was.

"Rawson?"

"Yes."

"You're in a red flag warning. Feldman, Norman, is a red flag."

"Thank you," said Rawson and hung up. He had made a few of these calls himself. It could mean many things. The ruby dealer could be working for some government, even the United States. He could be aligned with some terrorist organization, something that would make him a danger to be around. Was Feldman the professional killer?

Rawson would have to find out exactly. But this was enough for now and was well appreciated.

He debated turning on the light or going back to sleep. He was not bothered by the warning. That just meant things were working well.

He was bothered by the Grail itself, this "poorish bowl" he was hunting, supposed to be the great remnant of an empire, an empire that imploded itself back on the island that had given birth to it so that Great Britain itself had all the problems of its old colonies and none of the grandeur of ruling them anymore.

He could have said to Sir Anthony, come to New York, named after the Duke of York, and see the judge and jury system in Kings County, working with the idea that a man was innocent until proven guilty; and then go up to the Bronx, where Spanish and Yiddish and Latvian and Lithuanian and Polish and Italian and languages he couldn't even name were spoken. And hear them all learning the English tongue upon roads called Kingsbridge. That was the living empire.

It was not the repossession of a poorish bowl.

England as they knew it was over. The staid, sturdy populace had now degenerated, like the people of ancient Rome, to vicious rioters at public games. The British craftsman was now a joke even on television, where some contractors trying to demolish a building failed, to the amusement of the American announcers. England could not have defeated even Argentina alone without the American assistance that helped to guide their ships across waters Britain once ruled. That empire was done for, and only the parades were left back home.

Harry Rawson neither turned on the light nor went back to sleep, but went to the windows and looked out at the predawn lights of New York City. Runnymede was here. The Magna Carta was here. The idea, the most important idea, that a policeman was here to protect the citizenry and not rule them was so very British. He wondered whether Detective Modelstein understood that. He could tell him. Modelstein would probably think it was some sort of arrogance.

Central Park glittered in random lights before him. Parks were British. They were all over London. Nothing quite this big though. Central Park was an American interpretation.

There will always be an England, he thought, even if we sink into the sea. But he wasn't doing all this for England. He was doing this because he was English.

He wondered if non-Englishmen could ever understand that. He didn't care, really, he thought. Never did. He had once cared about other things, but he was young then. This life took the young out of him, the way ammonia could bleach fresh grass.

He had seen death and suffering in so many ways in Banai. A head cut off, a hand cut off for stealing, tortures. But even more ruinous to the spirit was the deceit and treachery so common it had to be assumed by everyone, including one's own countrymen. That was where his young Rawson had gone since Sandhurst.

The problem for Captain Harry Rawson, assigned Argyle Sutherlanders, was that in the thirty-fifth year of his life he had learned in little painful ways to believe in nothing. And he was the man England had sent to search for the Holy Grail.

While Rawson was having breakfast in his suite, the reason for the red flag became apparent with the delivery of a sealed typewritten report. Norman Feldman, sixty-seven, of New York City, was an especially dangerous killer, this first determined in Burma, where Feldman adapted to local customs including indigenous tortures. Therefore, the decision had been made to cancel surveillance until such time as the proper authorities wished to sanction hazard duty.

The source of this information, Rawson found out later in the day, was an ex-CIA official who lived in Darien, Connecticut, just north of New York City. Rawson also found out, as he suspected, that there was a question of whether surveillance had been terminated for reasons of hazard or because his people had already lost Feldman twice in New York City. He had left the country without their finding out until he had returned a week before. To which country he had gone Rawson's Intelligence support did not have the foggiest.

Infuriated, Rawson drove up to Darien, Connecticut, to do the background himself. He was going to find out what the red flag meant exactly. The source for the information was Feldman's OSS superior in Burma during World War II. Access to that source was through the former British commander of the Singapore battalion, who was a friend of Feldman's OSS superior. This was all old-boy friendship.

The OSS commander had become a CIA section chief for Burma-Thailand after the war and then retired to the New England village of Darien and a modest house with a suitably modest lawn. He lived amid the loot from his career in the Far East, with jade vases, bamboo furniture, and Thai paintings of pagodas and dancing women.

He said he was more than happy to help a friend of the former British commander of the Singapore battalion. His name was Brewster, and he wanted to make the assistance into a boozy afternoon of reminiscences and a discussion of world affairs among like-minded men.

Rawson knew almost instantly that Brewster was typical of the dross so prevalent in the American intelligence system and State Department, a result of America suddenly finding itself the new world power in 1945 with no more preparation than an exhausting war. The sort America got were usually those who couldn't find work outside. Unlike Britain, they did not get the best of their people. They got those who needed livelihoods and were in it because they couldn't do as well for themselves elsewhere.

As was common with most like that, they felt compelled to anoint every action with the absolving word *professional.*

"Frankly, I was glad when Feldman refused to stay on. I'm not against doing what you have to do. I'm a professional. But Feldman was a psychopathic killer. Psychopathic," said Brewster.

"Why do you say that?" asked Rawson.

"A professional will get in, do the job, and get out. Clean, fast. No mess. You understand?"

"I'm afraid I don't," said Rawson.

"You're not with MI 5?"

"God no," laughed Rawson. "Captain, Royal Argyle Sutherlanders, retired. I'm a businessman, and I needed some background on this man in New York. You say there are some problems with him?"

"I wouldn't have anything to do with that man I didn't have to," said Brewster, drawing himself up to the moment. "He once had someone killed by a death of the thousand cuts. Have you ever seen that? The person is a bloody pulp at the end."

"Feldman was a sadist?"

"Not especially. Man was a Japanese informer. Feldman had it done in the damned square of a village."

"Sounds horrid. Did he do that a lot?"

"How many times does he have to do it?"

"Of course I'm not a professional, but that does sound decidedly effective. Was he considered dangerous with his hands? Did you ever see or hear of him personally killing anyone with a knife or something like that? I'll tell you why," said Rawson with a little laugh. "I don't know if business is important enough to get near him."

"I couldn't tell you. Never knew what he was doing. Wouldn't tell you his sources. Wouldn't tell you how he did things. Wasn't professional. One time, we even had to threaten to shoot him. We told him the next time he went back into the jungles he might not return."

"And that brought him around?"

"No. The man was impossible to deal with. He laughed. He never quite took us seriously. We had to use him. He had the whole Mogok region of Burma wired for us. We could do anything there. We knew when the Japanese literally moved one truck a mile in any direction. We knew when they came, and went, and where they were going. We could stop their movements too and they wouldn't even know it. They would think they had trouble with their lazy Burmese coolies, but it was Feldman bribing someone or doing something. We never quite knew. We called him the obnoxious necessity."

"Did you attempt to kill him?"

"Oh, no. We just tried to get him in line. I was more than a little bit disappointed when, despite my protestations, he was offered a permanent position at the end of the war. And I was damned relieved when he didn't take it."

"Where did he get his training?"

"Trained with your Asia people as a matter of fact," said Brewster.

"Oh, I see," said Rawson. "What I'm trying to find out is, is the man still the sort one should avoid? Would you have any idea how many of these horrible killings he performed and, more importantly, might he still do them?"

"I just know of that one. What sort of business is Feldman in nowadays?"

"He buys and sells precious gems."

"Really?" said Brewster. "Is he successful?"

"I believe so," said Rawson.

"He did pop up a lot in the Far East after the war. Around Burma. Probably set himself up while working for us. Psychopathic killer. Never would have made a good professional."

"Just out of curiosity, what is a professional killing?"

"Clean. You go in. You put the man away. You go out. Nobody knows you were in. Nobody knows you were there. All they know is that someone has been offed. Maybe they wouldn't even find the body. That is a professional hit."

"Well, it all sounds brutal, you know," said Rawson, thanking Mr. Brewster for his help, promising to forward the gratitude to the former commander of the Singapore battalion.

Brewster had told him in so many ways that Feldman was really capable of anything, from calculated torture to that dangerous professional stroke into the cerebral lobe of the art dealer. Feldman could have learned that himself or picked it up from the Singapore chaps or just about anywhere a highly competent professional worked.

Feldman had understood as the sultan of Banai did that punishment was already too late for the one to be punished; rather, its real worth was in the eyes of the onlookers.

The horrible display in a village square probably helped Feldman reduce the number of people he had to kill. It might have been the only one he dispatched during the whole war. One of the reasons that there was so little crime in the Gulf states was that executions were public and cruel. They were meant to intimidate.

More importantly, Feldman had shown himself to be competent, and therefore following him to see if he were dealing the remnants of the cellar would require more caution. The man had to lust for that Christ's head ruby.

If a British agent saw the cellar in a bank vault, then perhaps Feldman did too. Perhaps Feldman had set everything up along the way. And then, perhaps he hadn't. The question was, would Feldman throw away a poorish bowl? Maybe. He certainly would keep the ruby. Would he be reasonable about selling the bowl? Probably. Would he keep his mouth shut afterward? Maybe.

As he drove down the Connecticut Turnpike on the right side of the road, despite the cold rain on leafless limbs of early December in southern New England, despite the green grass and occasional streams, Harry Rawson felt he was in some way back in the Gulf. There was death, suspicious people, moves that had to be held back until one knew where the pieces were, and the feeling that if one waited, one could lose the whole thing. Every day, garbage piled up in the dumps of the world where someone might have thrown the poorish bowl.

Artie Modelstein did not need McKiernan's description of the gruesome autopsy to know Claire Andrews was in trouble. But he listened to the awful details anyhow, saying to McKiernan, "Okay, Denny. I heard. I heard. Okay."

And McKiernan got the last scrap of vengeance for being stranded for a while on a political limb before the rabbi's son pleaded guilty. He described the tear in the flesh, and where it had been cut, and how it had been torn, and the way the tape had dug into the hands of Avril Gotbaum, who could not scream because his mouth was sealed.

"Okay, Denny. Okay," said Artie. They were sitting across Artie's not-too-neat desk in Frauds/Jewels.

"I thought you wanted to know," said McKiernan.

"I wanted to know about who killed the cutter. I wanted to know why. I didn't have to specifically know how."

"That's part of it," said McKiernan.

"All right. All right. What happened outside the actual death. Any priors on anyone that looks like he did this?"

"Do you want me to tell you or are you going to keep saying okay, okay, and then look like you're gonna puke?" asked McKiernan.

"Okay," said Artie. He looked away from McKiernan to the floor. He didn't even want to hear the word *puke.* He thought that if he recognized the taste of lunch in his mouth the rest was going to come up. He took a sip from a glass of water and breathed deeply.

"The guy got in and out so clean you wouldn't believe it. It was beautiful, Artie. Nothin'. Not a print. Nothin'. Not a sound."

"What was he doing?"

"Could be a warning," said McKiernan.

"Of course it's a warning. The question is who was he warning? It's enough of a warning for me," said Artie.

"A nosebleed is a warning for you, Artie," said McKiernan.

"Hey, c'mon," said Artie. "Some people are bothered by some things, and others by others. Don't rag my ass 'cause you shit in your pants when you thought the collar was going to come back on us. Enough is enough."

"He's right," said Marino. "He stood up for that collar when everyone else was running away from it."

McKiernan, who still believed that the measure of a man was his lack of response to death and that judicial respect for the powers that be was wisdom and not cowardice, reluctantly continued. "The tape gag could have been there just to stop the sounds of the screaming. Guy could have taken off the gag if the victim nodded that he was going to talk. So it could have been torture for information."

"Was it?" asked Artie.

"We don't know," said Marino. "Battissen was killed clean, one shot, good night. I'm not sayin' this to rag you, so don't give me that look."

"Not on purpose," said Artie.

"The girl's father was stabbed many times, wildly. The art dealer was done in by one clean stroke into the brain. The Israeli guy was carefully being tortured when his heart gave out. Three different kinds of killing, three different signatures. Are we dealing with three, are we dealing with two, are we dealing with one killer? I do not know, Artie."

"So it's a dangerous situation, right?" asked Artie.

"Officially no. We can't make it officially dangerous, otherwise we'd have to authorize protection all over the place. But realistically I'm thinking it could be any one next. Who knows what's going on?"

"But look, it's only people who had that thing or pieces of it," Artie pointed out.

"That cutter didn't have shit when he died. The stones were in evidence," said McKiernan.

Marino had another thought.

"I think the whole thing is cursed. You know they have those things in England. That guy Rawson, who's supposed to own it, or may own it, or whose family owned it, is from England. They have ghosts there. All the time. Place is loaded with 'em."

"So how can we get someone in to protect the lady?" asked Artie.

"You got a problem there, Artie. Her protection was for the people who threatened her with the dead cat. That one's been solved. The rabbi's kid copped a plea. We can't authorize protection because we suspect a curse," said Marino.

"I think that big jeweled piece is as much a killer as a pound of pure coke, and worse. Yeah worse," said McKiernan.

"There's a guy who deals big stones, I mean big stones," said Artie, "who says with gems that valuable there are no laws. No right or wrong.

When the guy was found in the dump I went to this guy's office and said there's blood on jewels now. Do you know what he did?"

McKiernan and Marino shook their heads. A squad captain stopped at a nearby desk to listen. Everyone could hear small conversations at a distance.

"He laughed," said Artie, raising his hands. "He just laughed at me. Like I was telling you you are now in a police station, he was laughing at my thinking killing mattered."

"Why'd he do that?" asked McKiernan.

"Because they all have blood on them, I think. I don't know," said Artie.

"Still not enough to get round-the-clock protection for the lady," said Marino.

"There's gonna be more death. Those were just the diamonds," said Artie.

"You want out?" asked Marino.

"You're damned right I want out. But first, I want this lady from Ohio out."

"You doing her?" asked Marino.

"I want her out of the city," said Artie.

"She had nice legs. I like legs like that. They feel good around your ears," said McKiernan with a big laugh. Artie didn't bother to answer.

So they all agreed that Miss Andrews should be apprised of the danger inherent in her search, but that only Marino and McKiernan would do it, because, as Detective Modelstein averred strongly, "She doesn't listen to anything I say anymore."

This was done the next afternoon. Inviting Miss Andrews to come down to Homicide, detectives McKiernan and Marino did advise Miss Andrews of dangers inherent in the situation, which had apparently gotten out of control because of a killer or killers operating outside of known modus operandi.

They regretted they could not guarantee her safety. They did not know where the killer or killers would strike again, and for her own safety they thought a reasonable response would be returning . . . for a while . . . to her domicile in Carney, Ohio.

They talked to her for half an hour explaining the different manners of death, including that of her father. And according to plan, they were very specific, even providing photographs to demonstrate the results of what killers could do in New York City.

Artie was waiting for them at Frauds/Jewels. They came in whistling and making circles with their forefingers near their temples.

"What she say?" asked Artie.

[213]

"Don't mean shit to her. Nothing. I showed her pictures that almost made me puke. Nothing," said McKiernan.

"Whaddya mean nothin'?"

"She fucking took notes. She wrote stuff down on a pad," said Marino. "You tell her about an eyeball rotting in a garbage bag and she don't blink. She writes." Marino sat down on Artie's desk. He shook his head. He was a handsome man, in his early thirties, with a noble face that could have come from marble fitting a name like Sebastiano Vincenzo Marino. But now he only looked confused and somewhat disgusted.

"And then?" asked Artie.

"She thanked us. Like we had fuckin' invited her to a party. Thank you. Whoo whee. Thank you for this lovely afternoon, you nice gentlemen," said McKiernan, imitating the singsong voice of a woman. McKiernan had the pinched expression of someone who constantly kept something unpleasant in his mouth. He kept his hands in his pockets as though waiting to be challenged.

"She still doesn't understand," said Artie.

"She understood everything," said Marino. "She didn't give a shit. She said she wasn't gonna run until she had something real to run from. She called me superstitious. Hey. I don't mind. But I'll tell you something, Modelstein. I wouldn't screw her with your dick. That is cold weather there."

"No. She's a decent kid," said Artie.

"The only picture she winced at was her father lying in the alley," said McKiernan.

"You showed her her father's homicide scene?" yelled Artie.

"Hey, you wanted her sent home," said McKiernan.

"But her father lying in that alley among the garbage?" said Artie.

"You wanted her apprised," said McKiernan.

"In the alley," said Artie, slumping in the chair.

"We apprised her," said McKiernan.

Detective Modelstein signed out that evening doing what he had become a policeman not to do. He carried work with him like a cloud. He had seen this in businessmen and so many of the worriers of the world. It was a thing he had worked all his life not to be. His father was a worrier. His father died young. But his father had told him, once, in a very beautiful time, that he envied his son, that his generation had to worry because they were all afraid of not making it, but Artie didn't. He liked the way Artie took the world, and he whispered one Saturday when other men were taking their sons to synagogue and Dad had taken him to a show at the Roxy: "Never lose it, and never tell your mother I said that."

And Artie hadn't lost it, despite his mother, despite his older sister. It had been a good life. Ordinarily on this Monday night he would get a six-pack of beer and a pizza with sausage, onions, and extra cheese, while pro football players battered each other on television, and be grateful he was not out on the field with them but pleasantly clogging his arteries while relaxing his mind.

This Monday night, however, he let the beer sit and found he wasn't tasting the pizza, and he was filled with anger at himself and with great foreboding.

Perhaps if McKiernan and Marino hadn't shown Claire Andrews her father's death scene, him sprawled in the refuse of an alley. Perhaps if Artie had not been the one behind them trying to frighten her home, perhaps if she hadn't been so relentlessly innocent, or if the Linzer Hasidim, which made the upper councils of the Mafia appear like an equal opportunity employer, had not chosen to embrace her insanity, he might not have thought about her that night. And then do what he knew he had to do.

He phoned the Carney police and asked to speak to whoever was in charge, informing them that this was an unofficial call. He wanted the name of a close friend of Claire Andrews. He was bucked up to the chief of police, who gave him the name of the publisher of the town's newspaper. Artie was alarmed at this, but the chief, Frank Broyles, speaking as one policeman to another policeman, said their newspaper was not the same as those in New York.

"There's no competition. Everyone gets along with everyone else, except if there is something really big. We had a couple of wise guys here from New York City a few years ago. They didn't last. Our newspapers are not like your newspapers. And besides, Bob Truet is sweet on Claire. Everyone thought they were going to get married before Vern got killed in your city."

"Good," said Artie and got Truet's telephone number. Artie was relieved that Bob Truet had all the urgency of a lover. It was obvious he was not acting like a newspaperman.

"I would definitely say, Mr. Truet, that she is in danger and she will not listen to us. Her apartment has been broken into. A pet killed as a warning. At least two men associated with this thing have been murdered, one horribly. She needs help."

"Of course. What can I do?"

"Tell her to come home. Reason with her. We're strangers. We can't reach her."

"Claire could always be stubborn."

"What about you?"

"She'll never listen to me. She never did."

[215]

"Is there anyone she trusts or listens to?"

"Only her father, and quite frankly, I am not sure even he had influence over her. Claire was always a very quiet girl, but very firm in her convictions."

"Firm enough to stop an ice pick with her ear? Hey, I don't think you people know what's goin' on here. This ain't some rich little bitch sayin' no to the county fair or something. They'll break out her brains laughing."

"I am aware of the problem, Detective Modelstein. I am more perplexed than you are. She had always been loath to go places herself, so I don't really know what's happened to her. I have phoned a few times and the conversations have died on the wire."

"You ain't gonna have a love life, buddy, with a corpse, so you better do something about finding someone to talk to her."

"I resent your tone, Detective Modelstein, and the insinuation that we are having an affair. We are close friends, unless she told you something different. Did she?"

"No. Your police chief gave me your name. She never mentioned you," said Artie, angry with himself that he had been probing for that. He was, after all, trying to get rid of this lady.

"Oh, well. I'm sorry to hear that. But it's no surprise. It was a one-way relationship. I loved Claire and I still do."

"I'm sorry to hear that," said Artie, who for no rational reason wasn't. Her minister was mentioned as a possible person to come to New York to reason with Claire. Also a girlfriend, but that woman had ceased to be close when the friend got married.

"What about her mother?" asked Artie.

"My God, never. Not Lenore McCafferty. No. No McCafferty. You would never send a McCafferty to Claire."

"I think she mentioned something about that the first night she came back to New York."

"It's important to Claire, I believe, that she feels people don't look down on her, don't treat her as a juvenile but let her exercise her opinion."

"Are we talking about Claire Andrews?" asked Artie.

It turned out to be the last resort. Her minister arrived on a Tuesday morning at Kennedy Airport looking worried and got more worried when he saw Artie with the .38 under his coat jacket.

They drove into New York on the Long Island Expressway, and Artie had his doubts almost immediately. The man was in his sixties, but a worn sixties, not with the sort of joyous enthusiasm ministers on television seemed to have.

"I'm not sure what I can tell her," said Reverend McAdow. He talked about Claire as a young girl, about how she had lived in the shadow of her parents, how she had so much to offer.

"You do understand you're supposed to get her out of here because she's gonna get killed?" asked Artie.

"I understand that; I just don't know that I can do it," said Reverend McAdow. "She's not a crazy person. She's very rational and very intelligent."

"Okay, work that, then. Work rational."

"I had planned to. That's the only way to reach her."

Artie did not press the minister more, because that was the most hopeful thing he had heard so far. He left Reverend McAdow off at Claire's apartment.

He heard her little squeal of joy when Reverend McAdow announced himself at the buzzer below. Things were looking better all the time. The message was going to be for Claire to come home for Christmas. There were colored holiday lights all over New York now, and she had to be thinking about that.

Artie drove to his own apartment to wait for the minister's call. He did not watch television. He did not eat. He did not do anything but reason fitfully with himself. He asked himself if he was doing this because he was sexually interested in Claire, professionally interested in averting a killing, emotionally acting like the good guy, or guilty because in a way he had gotten her kitten killed and she was broken up about it.

There was only one conclusion he could draw. And that was that if he went in any deeper with this lady, he was going to have more afternoons of grief like this one. Reverend McAdow phoned from Claire's apartment, inviting Artie to dinner.

"We've had a long talk, Detective Modelstein, and I think you should come over and hear Claire out," said Reverend McAdow.

Artie could not believe what he heard at Claire's apartment, with both of them sitting near a Christmas tree set up in the living room next to the long table with stacks of reports underneath that marked-up wall.

"When word got about as to the way Vern Andrews was trying to sell some valuable property, many people in town believed it was acquired under less than honorable conditions. Carney is a good town, and they are good people. But perhaps too many of us are too suspicious."

Artie cocked an eyebrow. Not enough of you, he thought.

Reverend McAdow continued: "I don't know what Claire will find, and I think she senses that also, without admitting it to herself. But this is a thing she must pursue for herself. At this time, she can't return to Carney. She belongs here doing what she must do. I think I love this young lady and I have known her all her life. And I am glad that I can bring some comfort of home in this Christmas season."

Reverend McAdow looked up at Claire and smiled. They shared a warmth. She grasped his hand and held it like a treasure.

"Yeah, well, I can see her getting lonely at Christmas and maybe wanting to go home. My God, if she left now, she might miss her own hit," said Artie. He felt his clenched fist tremble. He thought he would bite out his own eyeeteeth.

"If you could let her explain . . ."

"Explain what? You're supposed to explain. You're her minister. You're the one who's supposed to explain. What did you two talk about?"

"Arthur, please don't close your mind," said Claire. "Would you listen to Reverend McAdow. You brought him."

"What listen? You were supposed to listen. He's your minister."

"It's important to Claire that you understand she is not playing some reckless game," said the Reverend McAdow.

"How do you know? What's happened here? What's going on? You don't know what's a game and what isn't a game," said Artie, looking at the minister, betrayed.

"Please don't let emotion overcome your logic, Detective Modelstein," said Reverend McAdow.

"Logic? We got three dead already, including her father, Saint Vern Andrews."

"Arthur, that was uncalled for," said Claire.

"You won't mind much longer—you're gonna be dead," said Artie.

"Detective Modelstein, there are things people have to do to grow."

"What is it with you people out there? Death is not a growth experience, Reverend. You people talk some language I don't know."

Artie fumed, stamping to go, listening to Reverend McAdow explain all sorts of things about personal growth, the challenge of the world, a person's need to mean something, to do what was right.

And all the while Artie thought of how Claire wouldn't be noticed dying in New York. He understood people got killed in Carney, Ohio, also, but she wouldn't be alone there, and she would matter there if anything happened to her. A person should at least matter if she died. And he couldn't explain that to these two, who were now babbling about her research. The man who was supposed to get her home alive was now her cheering section. And she was really so pretty. And Artie didn't want to be the one to have to identify what was left of her.

They asked him what he thought now and he spoke to the minister.

"You just be the one to come out and identify the body, Reverend," said Artie, and wished them both a very Merry Christmas, and went out, sad and furious and helpless, into a joyous season of the year.

New York City was Christmas lights and panhandlers and phony Santa Clauses in front of pots, and Artie did his Christmas shopping early. At a hardware store near Canal Street he got a dead-bolt lock and what was called a "police lock," a large steel bar that fit against the door and set into the floor, so that it would take a tractor to push open an entrance.

Then off Houston Street he flagged down a squad car pair he knew he could trust.

"I need a tulip that works good," he said.

A tulip was that weapon an officer could place in the hands of someone he had shot, claiming self-defense. They were not as common as they used to be, mainly because more questions were asked now even if the corpse had a weapon in his hand. A tulip could not be traced to the officer. They had to be found in special ways.

"A hundred bucks, Artie," said the shotgun rider.

"Okay, now."

"You got a stiff waiting for it?" laughed the shotgun.

"No. I just need it now. And nothing bigger than a thirty-eight."

The shotgun blew air out of his mouth.

"You gotta have it now?" he asked.

"Now."

"Get in the back," said the shotgun. "What's those bars and stuff? You breaking in some place?"

"Locks," said Artie. They cruised around the perimeter of China-town.

"Okay, there," said the shotgun, nodding to four teenagers in glossy jackets. "They're packing. Pick it up for nothing. Our gift. Merry Christmas."

"I don't want to muscle for it," said Artie.

"You want it now. They're now. We'll back you up," said the shotgun and switched on the alarm. Artie was out of the door, wondering why he was doing this insane thing even as he did it.

"Police," he yelled, closing in on the first large teenager and throwing him into a wall. The others raised their hands and froze.

"Lean and spread," ordered Artie, propping the young men against the wall like bags of flour, forcing them to steady themselves with their hands in front, frisking them as he went along. He got a switchblade, an ice pick, and three pieces of hardware. He snapped the blades of the knives, dropping them in the street. He cradled the handguns against his belly.

"Hey, they're just kids. Don't charge 'em," yelled the shotgun. It was part of the act.

"Get out of here," said Artie.

"Hey, I want my piece, man," said one of the teenagers, and his friend boxed him on the side of the head.

"You own it," yelled the shotgun. "Hop in and file a claim."

The teenagers scuffled away, turning to make obscene gestures as they went. Artie brought the guns back to the squad car, where the shotgun examined them. He took the shells out of a small revolver and test-fired it to see if the hammer functioned.

"This probably works best, Artie. Hey, you were pretty good out there. I never knew you could move that fast."

"He was All-City linebacker," said the driver. "Went to Texas. Had a scholarship and everything. Papers called him one of the best pro prospects ever to come out of Clinton. He just quit and came home."

"They were crazy down there," said Artie.

"You could have played pro ball?" asked the shotgun, passing Artie a little automatic with a nod that it was functional.

"Who knows. Those guys don't walk right for the rest of their lives. They're crazy, too," said Artie. "I'm gonna retire with my whole body unharmed."

"You coulda been somebody, Artie," said the driver.

"I am somebody," laughed Artie. "I'm me."

He said the next time he needed a tulip he would wait.

"You're never gonna need a tulip, Artie. You're never gonna fire your gun," said the driver.

Artie could have told the driver he was right, but then he would have to explain why he wanted the weapon.

They returned him to his car on Houston Street, and he got to Queens before 8:00 P.M. Reverend McAdow was gone.

"This is a police lock. It rams a bar against your door. Use it," he said, dropping the bar loudly against the wall. "It installs. When you go out, leave something just inside the door that will be moved if anyone enters. If it is moved, do not enter your apartment. Do not, under any circumstances let anyone tie you up. You listening?"

Claire nodded. She was wearing an apron and a white and red checkered blouse and looked very much like a homebody. She had been doing the dishes.

"If they say they are going to kill you if you won't let them tie you up, you're gonna die anyhow if they do it. Just makes it easier for them."

Claire nodded.

"Don't rely on the security of this building. It's so loose, just treat it as though you had no protection."

Claire nodded.

"Now you can ruin my career and send me to jail if you let anyone know I am giving you this," said Artie. He waited for her to nod.

"Nod," he said.

She did with a little jerk of her head, her very blue eyes still locked on his, trusting. Good. She was listening.

He tugged her into the living room, and she followed. Standing in front of the Christmas tree, he took the pistol out of his pocket.

"This is illegal as hell. It's not registered, I'm sure. If by any chance anyone should get in here, use this. Do you know how to fire a gun?"

She nodded. Artie took her hands and put the gun sideways into them. He closed her hands around the handle.

"I'll get you a lawyer if you have to use it. If you tell anyone I gave this to you, I'm through."

"I never would."

"I'm just repeating so you'll remember, not so you'll keep your word. Keeping your word is not your problem, lady. You set?"

Artie saw moisture collect on her lower lids. When she nodded a tear came down her cheek.

"This is the most beautiful Christmas gift I've ever had, Arthur. What can I do for you?"

"There is something I would like, but I don't know if you would give it to me."

"Try asking," said Claire. The tears were coming heavy now.

"Go home."

"I can't do that."

"Then I don't want to know from you forever, lady. Good-bye."

"Arthur," sobbed Claire, "may I kiss you?"

"No," said Artie. And on the way out he said softly, just before he shut the door behind himself, "Watch your ass, all right?"

XVI

So I pass hostel, hall, and grange; by bridge and by ford, by park and
pale, until I find the Holy Grail.　　　　—ALFRED, LORD TENNYSON
　　　　　　　　　　　　　　　　　　　　The Holy Grail, 1869

I t was not the sort of stone Jardines
of Paris got every year, and the director general of the fashionable jewelry
salon on Square Vendôme understood Jardines was not equipped to sell
such a gem.

Yet there was a greatness about it, not only its size, one hundred
forty-two karats, but its character, deep blue, almost purple, rare for
sapphires, and its obvious antiquity because of the engraving of Poseidon
enthroned.

The question was not whether Jardines could make a profit but
whether it could avoid a loss. The entire management understood what
a single-karat sapphire, dark blue, or a ten-karat sapphire would roughly
sell for. One could price an emerald necklace and diamond necklace
because one simply added up the cost of the stones, all under ten karats
each, and then gloriously marked them up for the craftsmanship, the
ambience of the store, and the prestige of having bought at one of the
most elegant jewelers in the Parisian square of jewelers.

But a one hundred forty-two–karat dark blue sapphire was not worth
one hundred forty-two times a single-karat stone. It was worth just about

anything. And people who might pay three hundred thousand dollars for a necklace, or two million dollars for a home, or two million dollars for some business venture would not necessarily pay the one million for a single colored stone. Or two million. Or maybe not even five hundred thousand.

There were just so many people who understood their worth, and, of those who did, undoubtedly not all of them were buying that season. Assuming the director general of Jardines of Paris knew who they were in the first place.

Understanding all these reasons, why Jardines should not deal in a one hundred forty-two–karat engraved, velvet-blue sapphire, the director general made the takeaway offer at five hundred thousand dollars and asked for proof of ownership.

The seller held the magnificent gem in the palm of his hand and said, "It is mine."

Then he took the hand of the director general and placed it over the stone. The hand closed on it.

"Now it is yours."

"Of course," said the director general, who naturally understood European laws of ownership and also understood that the magnificent engraved sapphire could well have been from some archeological dig, or that the seller represented a president or dictator who was selling off his traveling insurance. There were many things, and none of them mattered when he looked into the heart of the sapphire and knew it was his.

He had bought it for the same reason that plagued so many buyers of great stones. He had to have it. Even selling it again, the very process of passing it to another for a great sum, excited the senses like having a woman for the first time. The second time was pleasurable, too, in some ways more so, because one could understand better the woman herself, but the first time was the adventure. It exceeded itself.

Even on the days he did not go to the basement vault and take the Poseidon sapphire, as he now called it, to the top floor to view it under the skylight, he enjoyed it. Knowing it was there was the enjoyment. He would wake up at night to go to the bathroom, and the man relieving himself was the owner of the Poseidon sapphire, as was the man who went back to sleep and woke up knowing the Poseidon was his.

It added greatness to his life. One day Jardines would not be there. France might not even be there, but the Poseidon would go on and survive everything they knew, including even the language. And others would know what he knew now, the worth of a great gem.

Before he owned it, he could not have imagined how thrilling it would be.

Of course, it had been purchased to sell and that problem now loomed large. A half million dollars American had been tied up, and that calculated at a thousand dollars a week for every week they kept it without selling.

The markup would have to include that. But what was the markup on a hundred forty-two–karat sapphire? He could look around Square Vendôme and see how Bulgari and Cartier were pricing ten-karat gems, but nothing in a night-blue sapphire at a hundred forty-two karats. Museums bought those sorts of stones, and should the price be what a museum last paid for something this size?

The director general of Jardines knew enough that he knew that this was not going to be like selling a necklace, even one that might go for more money because of the number of jewels. He remembered a customer had once referred to "significant sapphires," meaning neither Jardines nor any other store in Square Vendôme had one of them. At the time, having to hold up the prestige of Jardines, he did not press her to explain herself, but chose to ignore it.

She was the first one he called and she still doubted Jardines could have one. She was a British subject who was still wintering in Paris. In fact, if he remembered correctly, Lady Constance Jennings had not returned to England for many years because of some social slight she had suffered decades before and never forgiven.

With more than a little satisfaction, he told her it was a hundred and forty-two karats.

"It certainly has size. Who else has seen it?" she asked.

"You are the first, madam," said the director general, wishing he could ask "which others?" She knew who else would buy it, but he could never let her know he didn't.

As was customary, he had personally greeted Lady Jennings at the entrance to the store and had brought her to the upper office with the skylight and served her champagne and a light snack. As was not customary, he left her. Ordinarily, some other executive would bring whatever was to be shown. But for the Poseidon, the director general went himself.

On returning, he could see the contempt in her pinched British face for his daring to abandon her. What was it about British women that let them flower so beautifully when young and collapse beyond redemption when they became fifty-five, as though someone had thrown a switch and these poor women had to live with a Beirut of a face till death? Perhaps he was thinking these things because he was frightened. He had determined to ask for one point two million dollars and possibly not settle for less. He hoped he could bluff it out. But as soon as he opened its little white, satin-lined case and saw the Poseidon and knew he was about to lose it, all his doubts left.

Lady Jennings didn't even bother to hide her feelings.

"Yes," she said as she took the Poseidon out of the box with an ungloved hand. "Oh, yes," she said, holding it to the light, and turning it, ever so slowly, continuing, "Oh, yes, oh, yes, oh, yes." It was like a soft groan.

"Oh, yes. Yes. Yes. Oh, yes," she said, turning the Poseidon in her fingers and then letting it drop into her palm to feel its substance. "Yes."

She let it sit before her a few moments on the white felt pad, laughing at it, smiling at the director general of Jardines, even taking a sip of champagne. Their eyes met, and he knew they were doing this together. They had found each other.

"I will give you three hundred thousand dollars," she said.

The price would have been a strong loss, of course. He merely smiled tolerantly, and she understood for the first time that she was dealing with someone who should be selling it.

"Yes, well, I guess we know who we are," she said. "The Poseidon certainly belongs here. What are you asking?"

"One and a half million dollars American."

"My solicitor and jeweler will be here tomorrow."

The director general did not see her again. The solicitor bargained him to one point two million dollars, and the jeweler weighed the gem, examined it, declared it valid, and then at the appointed hour the solicitor reappeared bearing a certified bank check and took possession of the Poseidon. The director general gave it up like a general at the end of a glorious career, with both sadness and pride. He was told it would be worn as a pendant. Only when the transfer was consummated was the rest of the staff told. One did not announce the time and place of transfer of something as valuable as the Poseidon.

For this he shut the store late in the afternoon, calling all sales personnel and management into the main office of Jardines.

"At eleven-thirty A.M. Jardines sold a single sapphire of a hundred forty-two karats for one point two million dollars," he announced. Everyone knew it was the Poseidon.

There was polite applause, a light wine was served, and everyone was asked to be discreet, while no one other than the director general's partners were told to whom it had been sold. Word, of course, would get out. But Jardines would not only still be considered discreet, but also enjoy the prestige of having sold it. Even when it was gone, the director general felt a lingering excitement that made other business difficult to concentrate on. That night, when the director general's kidneys called, the man who relieved himself knew he no longer owned the Poseidon. It was the first thing he knew when he got out of bed.

Lady Jennings had the sapphire set in silver and diamonds and hurriedly organized a party to show it off. She did not want to wear it to someone else's party because she felt it should have its own. Didn't her secretary think so? Her secretary, of course, did. Lady Jennings did not like noise, she did not like the bother, and the party was set for February even though almost no one was in Paris then.

"Get warm bodies, I don't care. I want to wear it. I'm getting old. I want to wear it before I die," she told her secretary.

As it turned out, she paid dearly for filling the guest list with virtually anyone who was in the city. A nosy British consular official, who came from the right family and should have known better, went beyond bounds in asking her about her new necklace. Where had she bought it? When had she bought it? Did she have the Poseidon engraved? And how many karats was it?

"Young man, do I ask you what your finances are?" she finally had to say, and that ruined the evening. Lady Jennings did not like having to be impolite. She did not like noise. She did not like rude people, even if she had made the mistake of inviting him. But that wasn't the end of the bother. Some more people, people she didn't even know, were pressing her to allow Jardines to reveal from whom it had purchased the sapphire.

This her solicitor had told her, mentioning that it might somehow be of concern to her nation because it was the British Embassy that was asking. Jardines would not reveal the source of the sapphire unless she gave permission to do so.

"What national interest could it be?" she asked. She didn't want to hear anything more about it. She didn't want her solicitor to mention it again to her, and she wanted peace. If she wanted turmoil and insult she would have remained in London.

It was up to the solicitor to explain to the gentleman from the embassy that Lady Jennings had left London thirty years before and refused to return because of a slight from the Crown. The caller asked if the Crown might do something to make things right.

"Not now, not with Lady Jennings. Dreadfully sorry," said the solicitor, who didn't even know what the slight was because no one dared bring it up in Lady Jennings's presence. It was a safe assumption it had to do with some party she was not invited to, or invited to but offended at in some way, or some other social insignificance her wealth gave her the leisure and opportunity to stoke into a lifelong offense.

Harry Rawson got all the information in classified bits and classified pieces and told everyone to stand down. They had spotted the sapphire in Paris. He knew the stones could move internationally, and just because the sapphire turned up in Paris didn't mean the thief was still there. He wondered if a bribe might work on Jardines of Paris, but the bribe itself would attract attention if it didn't work, and it probably wouldn't. Already too many people had been asking too many questions.

He would let it lie quiet and move himself, probably against Lady Jennings who was a bit doughty and might do anything, even give her permission for Jardines to let him get to whoever sold the sapphire. For this he could use someone out front, someone reasonably legitimately interested in the stone, preferably not British. Already the sapphire had too much of Britain after it.

> CLASSIFICATION: Maximum Security, for H. R. Rawson only.
> SOURCE: Classified
> AUTHORIZATION: Classified
> SUBJECT: Arthur C. Modelstein, 34, USA Citizen.
>
> Modelstein, 34, son of Ira and Miriam Modelstein, of the Grand Concourse, Bronx, both deceased. Modelstein, a twelve-year veteran of the New York City Police Department, known as a competent officer. Scored upper 10 percent on entrance examination, but has never shown any leadership qualities or desire for promotion. This lack of drive evident throughout his life, according to multiple sources, including family, two older sisters who refer to their brother's life as a waste. He has no known scandals connected with his career. Considered honest, intelligent, and prone more to comfort than to duty. Do not offer a bribe. An active heterosexual. No drinking or gambling problems. Might prove difficult to deal with. Not known as a team player, nor especially desirable in violent situations.

There couldn't have been a clearer choice. The New York Giants were playing on Monday night football, and going after reports of the sapphire would put Artie right back into the grief of that saltcellar. He had not listened for homicides of blondes on his police radio for a week now. He liked it like that. He even liked Trudy better.

Captain Rawson was shocked.

"You don't want to go to Paris? How can you say that if you've never been to Paris?"

"Easy," said Artie.

"Have you ever dined in Paris, really dined? There are restaurants in Paris in which you begin at eight in the evening and don't stop until after midnight, with different wines and sauces and centuries of perfection just to entertain your palate. Beef that cuts with a fork in pastry that can virtually sing, Detective."

"And how do the symphonies taste?" asked Artie.

"If I were a poet I could describe the food. And the hotels. Paris lures people who spend lifetimes fathoming how to satisfy your needs."

"Not my needs."

"It's a city of thousand-dollar-a-night courtesans," said Rawson.

What impressed Artie so much was that this man in tweeds and oxford shirt of impeccable grooming could make a hooker sound like a poem, a meal like an adventure, and sleeping in a room like a form of heaven on earth. If Artie had described the same things, they would have sounded like some violation of a city ordinance. And he was smiling.

"What do you say? My firm will be happy to pick up the tab. We have taxes, too, in Britain, and if I don't spend it they will get it. Or the shareholders will get it. Or someone else will get it."

"You can't go over yourself and make the claim on that sapphire?"

"Of course I could. But if there is a policeman out in front, they will be at least more cooperative. Have you ever dealt with the French?"

"No. I don't think so."

"Then come and see."

"I dunno."

A detective passing by Artie's desk had been listening with half an ear and now offered advice: "Take it, asshole."

"Paperwork," said Artie.

"I'll do it for you, asshole. Paris," said the detective.

"They may not approve," said Artie.

"And then again, they may," said the other detective.

They did. And Artie had to phone Claire Andrews to tell her the Poseidon sapphire had turned up in Paris. She was, as he had expected, still in New York, and even more cheery than ever. She had sent him a Chanukah card with a thank-you again for the best Christmas gift she got from anyone, ending it with a smiling-face drawing instead of a period. He had thrown it right into the trash.

"I can't believe it's you, Arthur. It's so good to hear from you." She was bubbling.

"The Poseidon sapphire has turned up in Paris. It was sold through a jewelry store." Artie doodled on an NYPD memo he should have filed. His desk at Frauds was littered with them.

"Well, that's nice. That's very nice. How are you?"

"I'm fine. I told you I would phone if there was any information," said Artie. Why did he feel sucked into this thing again? It was just an official phone call made from an official office to an official complainant. It was all so surprisingly awkward.

"Yes, thank you. How are you?" she asked.

"Good. I appreciate your not phoning the squad room every day."

"You said you'd phone if there was any information."

"I did."

"Yes, I hear."

"Well, that's it, then."

"Yes. I guess. Oh, how did it turn up? Who tried to sell it? And what's its disposition?"

"I'm going to Paris to find out. I'll let you know when I get there."

"Please do. And see the Louvre. You must see the Louvre. I went there with my father two years ago. You must see the Louvre. It really shouldn't be all business, you know."

"I'll phone when I have information." And that was Claire Andrews still in New York, making him feel not too good about what he wasn't even sure now. There were benefits. Norman Feldman had been proven wrong.

To Feldman, Artie said good-bye in person at his midtown office.

"You are wrong, Norman my friend. We found the sapphire. A hundred and forty-two karats worth. A major gem, no?"

"You found it?" asked Feldman. His feet rose to the desk as he leaned far back in his hard oak chair. The shoes obviously had been resoled several times. The tops were cracked.

"It turned up in Paris."

"Just like that?"

"Just like that, sold through a jewelry store, which you said couldn't happen."

"Just like that it turned up?" asked Feldman. "The good Jewish boy from the Bronx in the New York Police Department found it? You found it?"

"Yes. It was reported to me."

"Does it interest you who reported it to you and how he reported it to you and why he reported it to you?"

"You've been proven wrong. Get off my back."

"You came here. I didn't go to you, Artie."

"Well, you were wrong. We're getting back the sapphire."

For the third time he saw Feldman laugh.

"What are you laughing about?"

"Never ceases to amaze me. You still don't know what you're doing."

"What's so funny?"

"You're going to get it back, huh?"

"Damned right. It's stolen property."

"If I bet, and I never do, I would bet a building against you. You don't know what you're doing. You don't know anything outside of New York, and so far you have only managed not to get yourself killed. I think it will stay that way, because you're lucky and stupid."

[229]

"I'm bringing back that sapphire and putting it in your face."

"No, you're not. Get out of here. I'm busy."

They didn't just fly to Paris, they took a Concorde, supersonic luxury on which champagne was served. The seats were a bit tight, but the flight was short and Harry Rawson was a boon traveling companion. As they saw the curve of the earth from the great heights of the Concorde, Rawson described man as being a traveling creature and said that what traveling did was replace myths with information sometimes even more extraordinary. Traveling was the end of fairy tales, he pointed out. Dragons and maidens died with the steamship.

Artie, matching Rawson champagne for champagne, disagreed. He had once arrested someone who happened to believe the world was flat. This in the age of space travel and photographs of a round blue globe. Not only that, the man subscribed to a magazine put out by some flat-earth society. The point being here that no fact could ever overcome what someone wanted to believe.

"I mean there is a subscription list out there of people who believe all the space photographs are lies," said Artie.

"And what if we were to take that fellow up here with us, Artie, and he could see the curve down there?"

"He'd wonder if we drugged him. I do believe, Harry, the last thing a person will give up in his life is a lie."

They were on their fourth glass and it was "Artie" and "Harry," and by the time the Concorde landed they were flying and had a brilliant reason for not coordinating with the French police right away.

"Because they are French," said Rawson loudly and with conviction at the baggage bays of Orly airport.

"And always will be," said Modelstein.

In the morning Harry had things organized, while Artie tried to shield his eyes from the harsh French sun as the silverware had to be set on a damned little marble table where, every time someone put down a fork, it rang.

They had an elegant suite sharing a sitting room in the Hotel Crillon on Place de la Concorde, but Rawson had insisted out of some maniacal compulsion that they eat breakfast out, lest they lounge away the morning. Artie realized that even though they had dined extensively the night before, and wined even more extensively, they really hadn't missed anything by not coordinating with the French police immediately. Rawson had done it at crack of dawn and then had chosen to eat in this place with sun and marble tables and people talking and shutting doors and slapping newspapers on leather seats.

"You see, the problem, Artie, is that we are dealing with powers.

Jardines is a French institution. They are proud of it. Our saying that Jardines deals in stolen gems is an insult to France. They're very nationalistic here, especially the police. It is not like America, where the law is the law is the law."

"Shh," said Artie.

"You're a bit up against it, aren't you?"

Artie nodded gently.

"Good upchuck, coffee, and a brandy get you right."

Rawson had said the magic word, and he found out in French where the water closet was and directed Artie in English toward its door. When Artie came back, he had improved immensely, to where he was only feeling awful.

Rawson had thick, black, sweet coffee for him and a glass of brandy. This improved Artie to feeling under the weather.

"Don't you get bothered by this?" asked Artie.

"Certainly. I feel wretched."

"You don't look wretched."

"Doesn't do any good."

"Does lots of good."

"How?"

"Tells the world to leave you alone or else."

"Sounds like it would encourage bother," said Rawson.

"Let's hit the French police first," said Artie.

"Don't think it will help."

"Let's see," said Artie, and when he got up from the table he found he could move and pretty much breathe in his painful fog.

The French police were cooperative and pleasant and totally unhelpful. In modern offices with desks like draftsmen's boards and maps with lights in them, they asked more questions than they answered.

Yes, they were aware of the report from Scotland Yard; Captain Rawson had given it to them. But that theft was in 1945. What proof was there that Jardines had knowingly bought stolen property? And what proof was there that it was stolen?

Artie repeated all the felony details, including the killings. The French inspector and his aides were sympathetic.

"But you see our problem is one of ownership. You have not proven that Jardines purchased stolen property."

"But it's here," said Artie. "It was stolen in New York in autumn, stolen before that in London. A hundred and forty-two–karat blue sapphire, Poseidon enthroned. I mean, how many hundred forty-two–karat velvet-blue sapphires with Poseidon on them are there? I'll tell you how many: one is how many. I doubt there is a second hundred and forty-two–karat velvet-blue in the world. So it is either this gentleman's property, or the lady's property, but it is definitely not Jardines's property." Artie was yelling. He didn't care if it made his eyeballs ache.

"I understand, but you see many people can claim ownership to things. Who owns a province taken by one French lord from another French lord in the year 900 A.D.? The descendants of the originally robbed? Whom did he rob it from? And what rights does one have to a famous painting stolen and restolen, sold and resold and stolen again. There has to be some reason to this, do you understand?"

"How about murder?" said Artie.

"Do you believe Jardines is an accomplice to murder, monsieur?"

"They are an accessory after the fact."

"Then we would have to prove they planned the theft and the murder."

"It's stolen. The sapphire is stolen," yelled Artie pounding the table.

"I hear you, monsieur, and I agree. It is stolen. I would say the gem has been stolen several times you are not aware of. The question is, who owns it now?"

"Not Jardines and not Lady . . . Lady . . ."

"Jennings," offered Rawson. He watched Artie grow red in the face and use his bulk to dominate the room. He could see that when aroused this gentle bear of a man might not be so gentle.

The French inspector, a man of somewhat worn clothes and worn enthusiasm for life, and perhaps worn sympathies from so many years in the Paris district, nevertheless backed away from the force of the New York detective.

Rawson thought Modelstein might actually punch someone.

But the truth was, and no one could get away from it: Jardines legally bought and sold the stone because they were not aware it was stolen. This was not only French law, it was European law. Artie looked to Rawson, who nodded confirmation.

"That sucks," said Artie. "I could steal that sapphire, sell it to someone who is unsuspecting, and without changing it that person could even wear it out in the street free and clear?"

"It happens. As you can imagine, Detective Modelstein, we have very good safes and our jewels are rarely out of them."

Artie exhaled and collapsed like a bag in the seat.

"We have nothing then? No claim?" he asked weakly.

"I'm sorry, no. Not unless Jardines wishes to cooperate. We have asked them to do so, on your behalf."

"Thank you," said Artie.

Rawson only smiled. Outside, he had one word for what went on. "The French."

It really didn't explain much to Artie, who had always assumed there were situations like this around the world because they appeared in New York, too. The point of life was to avoid them. If Harry hadn't paid for the trip and the rooms, Artie might have had one more drink and returned to New York City. But he liked this Englishman, even though he could look so fresh after a blizzard of wine. He could even feel sorry for him, not having anything else to do with his life but chase down a family treasure. He had made it sound sad the night before when Artie asked what he did for a living.

"I was in Her Majesty's Royal Argyle Sutherlanders, which gives me the right to this tie and a right to call myself captain, and mostly now I look for things to do, like this, tracking down our family cellar. It was a blessing, I tell you. It isn't going to mean a damned thing, Modelstein, whether I get it or not. Not a damn thing."

"Then why are you bothering?"

"For the same reason people play polo to win. The score doesn't mean anything really, but there are those who will kill themselves to win. And in the end what has anyone won?"

Even in the morning without champagne, it was as sad as it was the night before.

Jardines had them wait in a small, airless room on the second floor of the building for over an hour.

"The French are so obvious in their rudeness," said Harry. "We, on the other hand, are at least civilized enough to let the recipient of our rudeness believe, if he wishes, that he has not been insulted. That is the difference between us and them. Shades of meanness. You Americans, on the other hand, don't have meanness as a national character."

"I never met national characters. We have mean characters."

"Of course. One shouldn't generalize about people. I imagine at Balaclava there were those who reasoned why."

"Is that the Charge of the Light Brigade where everyone got themselves killed and Tennyson wrote a poem about it?"

"Exactly, and that was considered noble and laudatory, whereas today it would be grounds for some government investigation. Even the quality of goodness changes from age to age, like what is stolen in America and what is stolen here in Europe."

"I have a headache," said Artie.

"I can't believe you don't have thoughts about goodness."

"I do, but it requires talking," said Artie. Rawson laughed. In a little while, Artie said that perceptions of goodness might change but goodness never changed, and Rawson wanted to walk down the ages of the Platonic ideal, the absolute goodness of the laws of God among the

Jews, and God being above goodness or evil among the Muslims, and God being goodness Himself among the Christians, and the Hindus not believing in any of it. Good or evil. Things were what they were.

"I'm sorry I said anything," said Artie. And Rawson laughed again. He had big teeth, thought Artie.

The assistant to the director general finally saw Rawson and Modelstein and informed them that purchases by customers were never discussed with anyone without the customer's consent.

"You had to keep us waiting an hour and a half for that?"

The assistant to the director general apologized with a smile. He also regretted that he could not tell them who had purchased it either. Artie was about to tell the smug little man in the smug dark suit, and the very small office, that they already knew, but he caught Rawson's eyes, and something told him to mention nothing.

Outside, Rawson explained why he didn't want Artie to press on back in Jardines.

"We just might have an opportunity to force Jardines to reveal who sold the sapphire to them, if you're willing to go a bit beyond police bounds. I know how these people operate."

"Tally ho," said Artie in the elegant square with pedimented façades of glamorous perfumers and bankers and jewelry stores, Van Cleef and Arpels, Boucheron, Schiaparelli, Guerlain, Rothschild, and Jardines. "No's on the right of us, no's on the left of us, charged the two."

"You would have made a splendid fighting general."

"I hate bodies," said Artie.

"You'd get used to them."

"I never want to get used to them."

"But you do. Everyone does," said Rawson, swinging his umbrella before them like a gonfalon high, "especially someone who agrees to do something before he even knows what it is."

"I sort of got carried away with everything," said Artie.

XVII

He must outshine all other knights in virtue even as the sun's light
pales the stars.   —WALTER MAP
                                        Queste del Saint Graal, 1225

"I'm not leaving," said Artie, bang-
ing loudly on the brass knocker of the French townhouse. "I'm an American policeman and I am not leaving."

The butler opened the door again.

"Lady Jennings will not see you, sir, so I would most strongly suggest
that you leave."

"I'm not leaving. You want to arrest me, go do it. Right now. Let's
have this thing out in court now. I want that bitch in court now. I want
everyone to know you're dealing in dead men's jewels. There's blood on
that stone. I'm a New York cop."

Artie yelled until his own ears hurt. He saw the butler blink and
back into the safety of the large house. Artie followed into a large
reception room, yelling even louder: "I got two dead bodies stinking up
New York, and you assholes are hiding behind your money. I want to
see that bitch."

The butler attempted physically to move Artie back toward the
door, and when he felt the force of just one hand resisting his entire
body, he gave up and ran for help.

In the meantime, Artie continued to yell: "I want to see Lady Jennings. I want that bitch down here now. I want to look at her face. I want her to tell me she's not going to help. I want her to tell me murder is all right. I want her here. I want to know how she can wear that damned stone with blood on it. Let her tell me. Let her tell me. Now! Now! Where the hell are you?"

The butler came running back with a large gardener, a chauffeur, two curious maids, and a prim woman in her early thirties wearing a heavy suit fit for a matron.

The woman warned Artie that if he did not leave now, they were going to have to use force.

Artie dared them to kill him like the two people in New York.

The gardener, who fancied himself skilled at karate, grabbed Artie's right hand and using his own body for leverage, tried to hurl Artie's bulk over his shoulder. He ended up looking as though he passionately wanted to make love to Artie's muscled arm. Artie shook him off like loose relish on a sleeve. The stuffy younger woman took over.

"We're going to have to phone the constabulary."

"Phone," yelled Artie. "I want you to phone. I want Lady Jennings in court. I want her in court every day and every way. I got two dead bodies in New York, and that bitch sits here like she's above it all. She's part of this thing, and she's gonna get some of this all over her too. That's it. She's in it. She's in it, like death."

"Do you have to shout?" asked the woman.

"I'm mad. I'm mad as hell. You're not getting away with this."

"With what? Please don't shout."

"Am I shouting?"

"Yes."

"Then I'm shouting. We got two bodies in New York City and that bitch won't even make a phone call. She's not out of this thing."

"Please stop. I can hear you. Perhaps I can help."

"No, you can't."

"I am Lady Jennings's secretary. If you want something from Lady Jennings, you must go through me."

"I want to get her in court," yelled Artie.

"May I ask why?"

"All she's got to do is phone Jardines and tell them to tell us where they bought that sapphire, and I can get on after the killers. But she's hiding that."

"It's not that Lady Jennings wishes murderers to go free. Lady Jennings is a very private person—everyone knows that."

"Death is private. We got dead bodies," yelled Artie. "Who the hell is Lady Jennings to be private? She's coming into court. I'm gonna have every New York City newspaper on her doorstep for life. For fucking life."

Artie waved his hands, looming over the secretary. But she refused to move back even though her eyes were tearing from his volume and menace.

"I will speak to Lady Jennings if you refrain from your language and shouting."

Artie nodded agreement, but did not want to appear too docile; and he did not want to let any of them know how truly embarrassed he felt to be doing this. He faked anger as he waited. It had seemed almost harmless when Rawson had suggested it, definitely noble, two searchers against the jaded justice of Europe.

Unfortunately, once he was inside the house, he was in this thing, and there was no way to get out of it.

The secretary returned with an agreement. If Detective Modelstein would absolutely promise not to drag in the name of Lady Jennings or pursue Lady Jennings in any way or manner, but leave this house once and for all, Lady Jennings would authorize Jardines to reveal the name of its source for the Jennings sapphire, as it was now called.

"Okay," said Artie gruffly, when he really wanted to say thank you, when he really wanted to apologize.

"Now, may we ask you to leave," said the secretary.

Back at the elegant Hotel Crillon, Rawson was practically dancing. He had chilled Dom Perignon already waiting, and a snack of Scottish smoked salmon, caviar, and crackers Artie thought were too small.

"I knew you could do it," said Rawson.

"Yeah, it worked."

"Why so glum?" said Rawson, engineering a full glass of the fine champagne over to Artie, who sniffed it and put it down with a shudder, remembering his poor mouth of the morning.

"They only wanted to be left alone."

"That's why it worked."

"Yeah, but what did they do? What crime did Lady Jennings do?"

"I can't believe a New York City policeman hasn't leaned on people, so to speak, who were never guilty of a crime."

"That's different. I don't ever remember roughing anyone up, and that's what I did even though I never hit anyone, someone who only wanted to be left alone. I mean she was an old lady and she stayed in her room, and I never saw her and here I was like an animal bellowing."

"That's what worked, Artie," said Rawson. "It's all shit, Artie. Nations just wrap flags around it. Ever smell a body that's been dead a week?"

"Yeah. And I will never get used to it, and I don't want to get used to it, and I don't want to get used to seeing decent women afraid of me."

"To Sir Arthur of the pure heart."

"What's pure?" asked Artie, and he ate some crackers and wondered how Rawson knew Lady Jennings would break.

Jardines phoned and asked that they come to the store. Rawson advised Artie not to look triumphant when they got the information, but to let the British handle it.

"Thank you ever so much," Harry told the assistant to the director general of Jardines as they received the name of Werner Gruenwald, a Geneva businessman. This time they had not been kept waiting.

Outside the white-framed windows of Jardines, with the diamond jewelry and the diamond-encrusted watches and an emerald necklace lolling off a dark velvet stand, Rawson distracted Artie from his glancing at the windows by announcing: "Touché. We have been revenged. I got him."

"What revenge? What did we get?"

"I insulted him to the core, and he was fuming," said Rawson, twirling his tightly rolled black umbrella like a batonist.

"What insult?"

"You must understand the French. He was fuming. Our very politeness, our civility, cut him to the bone."

"You really like that, Harry? Are you serious?"

"Of course," said Rawson.

"You're crazy, you know."

"Mad as hatters, all of us."

"There's no *all* to anybody," said Artie.

"Did they teach you that in your Bronx schools so a polyglot nation could get along with itself?"

"How did you know I went to Bronx schools?"

"May I safely assume you did not go to Harrow or Eton?"

"Do they teach that stuff in Harrow and Eton?"

"They don't teach it, we breathe it. The French are the French."

A flock of white-hatted nuns guided children across a street.

"Do you think those nuns are the same as those thousand-dollar whores you talked about?"

"The nuns are French nuns. The whores are French whores. They forever in their souls are French: saints, chevaliers, and pleasers of the body."

"Do you really believe that?"

"Not quite," said Rawson, breathing in the Paris winter and exhaling in a large puff of white mist, "but often enough it's true. Don't tell me you would think of a black coming at you in an alley the same way you would think of a white?"

"How did you know I went to Bronx schools?"

"You said so last night, along with recounting your first experience with sex."

"And how was that?"

"If I remember correctly, you said it was an acquired taste but an inherent need. I thought that was most profound."

Artie nodded. His first time had been not so much a disappointment, but he had wondered if this was what everyone was so excited about. Afterward, it became both pleasure and necessity.

"How did you know Lady Jennings would break?"

"She is English, Artie. We're all mad underneath, and the nobility the maddest of them all. Communists, fascists, butterfly chasers in the Amazon, breeders of shrimp and shrew, horse racers, pederasts, and Lady Jennings, recluse, notorious for a thirty-year-old slight by the Crown. I didn't know it would work, Artie. As I said, I thought it had a good chance."

"It worked," said Artie with sadness that seemed at home in the gray French street with the leafless trees, and dark buildings, and wide boulevards and desperate little cars that seemed as though they would run over any living thing.

Werner Gruenwald spoke English with a German accent, repeated too often that he was a businessman of varied interests, and incessantly fussed with his eyes. He was either giving himself drops, or cleaning his pink glasses, or commenting on the importance of sight. He was fond of little health lectures in that regard. Gruenwald was Swiss.

Artie sat back and let Harry carry the ball. He would flash his badge if necessary. This would have no more legal force than it did in Paris, but might add some psychological note of authority to the proceedings.

It was a messy, small office with one telephone, no secretary, and a small window so high in the wall one got a view of the sky and not the streets of Geneva. It had been a shorter hop from Paris to Geneva than the flight from New York to Cleveland, and this gave Artie a sense of how small Europe was, how small the countries were. Harry had pointed out that the Continent, as Europe was called, as though it was the only continent in the world, was still terribly tribal, although no one wanted to admit it, and that many of the little square patches underneath them had once been kingdoms, with the lords little more than gang leaders.

"I would love to help you, gentlemen, but I am a businessman. And what sort of businessman would reveal a confidence?"

"Was it a confidence?" asked Harry. "I didn't know that."

"Oh, yes, yes."

"Jardines didn't know that; they gave us your name. I am sure they wouldn't have done that if they knew this was all confidential," said Rawson.

"Everything is confidential that is not public. Of course, that is how business is done. I am a businessman. I have varied interests."

"Being a businessman, you sell things," said Rawson.

"Of course," said Gruenwald. He took off his pink eyeglasses and squinted.

"I'd like to buy the identity of the person who sold you the Jennings sapphire," Harry said. Artie was surprised at how easily Rawson called it the "Jennings," acknowledging perhaps morally in some small way that the woman had absolute right and title to it. It was the second most valuable gem on the cellar. Artie wondered if all the major gems got their names this way, by someone along the way announcing title. Maybe it had happened many times. And maybe it would happen many more times.

Gruenwald did not answer the question right away. He was putting drops in his eyes again. He wiped the liquid off his puffy cheeks with a tissue and left the tissue on the desk. He returned the pink glasses to his stubby nose and responded.

"One hundred thousand pounds," he said.

"Preposterous," said Rawson. "I want his name, not his family estate."

"How funny. Humor in business is always a good thing. A good thing. Next to health it is the most important thing in life, yes?"

Gruenwald rested his chubby hands in front of him, on the small unoccupied triangle of his plastic-covered desk. If this was the wonderful world of major gems that Artie was not supposed to understand, he was disappointed with Feldman. He would bet the man was a petty crook, and yet look at Feldman's office. It was so bare it looked abandoned. So who knew?

Gruenwald made a counteroffer of fifty thousand pounds and refused to budge from it, but promised to get back to Rawson within a day. Rawson gave him the number of the Hotel Crillon and their room. As a special treat, Rawson announced that he had arranged for Artie to experience a thousand-dollar-a-night courtesan, under the theory that just because they were doing business on the Continent did not mean they had to suffer under the worst campaign conditions. Artie could understand that philosophy.

"Well, what do you think of Mr. Gruenwald?" This from Rawson on the short flight back to Paris.

"He'd sell anything. Right now, he's conducting an auction on that

[240]

seller's identity. Too bad everybody is so damned blasé about stolen merchandise here or we could get a tap on his phone."

"Do you think he's phoning the seller right away?"

"As soon as he made sure we weren't listening in at the office door," said Artie.

"I think so, too," said Rawson.

"So what are you after, Harry? You're not after the diamonds, because you were ready to trade rights to them away, according to Miss Andrews. You're not after the sapphire, I suspect, because you acknowledged it as the Jennings, so what are you after? I mean pieces of this thing are coming off, and you let 'em go. So the cellar doesn't exist anymore, we know that. You're not getting the gold because it's more liquid than a dollar bill—I mean I can spend that gold anywhere in the world—so what are you after, Harry?"

"Very good question, and quite astute."

"Not astute. Jesus, it's obvious. You gonna kill the guy who stole it or something?"

"Not at all, Artie. I am after whatever I can get of it, from the great ruby to the poorish bowl."

"And what if you get nothing?"

"A thousand-dollar lady of the night and the Hotel Crillon along the way is not nothing. This is not hard duty."

"You could do that sitting in London," said Artie.

"I suppose. But I'm not, Artie. I am of that mad British race, shrew and shrimp breeders, butterfly chasers, mountain climbers, and the glorious ninnies who gave us Balaclava."

Harry arranged the thousand-dollar ladies of the night through the concierge of the hotel, who welcomed him back, leading Artie to believe Harry had been here before. What puzzled him was why a man so suave, so well-tailored, so good-looking, would use a hooker.

At the suite, Artie phoned Feldman in New York City. It would be shortly before noon there. When it rang, he wondered who was in Feldman's office, or if Feldman was out. He also wondered if Feldman had given people he wanted to talk to a special ringing code, like two rings and hang up. Then again, maybe Feldman never answered the office phone during certain months. Anything was possible with him.

He asked the operator to keep trying and went back out into the parlor section of the shared suite to eat what Harry had ordered. The man knew how to travel. There was a light port wine with stuffed sweets and little meaty snacks in puff pastry, and Harry promised an extraordinary meal to go along with the ladies of the night.

The room had more elegant charm than Artie had ever seen in

homes, delicate furniture carefully gilded, lamps that looked like treasures, long dark velvet drapes with tassels, and soft chairs and sofas with sumptuous glistening fabrics. Artie asked how much it cost. When he found out it was more than the ladies per night, he whistled. He could get used to this. If he could afford this, he would never chase anything. He might not leave it ever, he told Harry Rawson.

The phone rang, and Artie took it in the parlor. The operator had Feldman on the line.

"Norm, we got to a sapphire dealer in Geneva," he said.

"So why are you calling me?"

"To get some information on him. I got this far, you got to admit, I'm doing something right."

"I don't know how far you got."

"Ever heard of Werner Gruenwald?"

"No."

"Is it possible he could be dealing large sapphires and you wouldn't have heard of him?"

"Doubtful. What did he sell it for?"

"Why do you ask that?"

"Because that is the only intelligent question you could have asked him," said Feldman. "I could tell you for certain a lot of things from the price."

"He sold it to Jardines. Ever heard of them?"

"Of course. He's a crook, and he doesn't deal in the market I told you about."

"How do you know?"

"Because he sold it for too little, and probably so did they."

"How do you know?"

"Because you have to know what you have to pay the right price for it. Does Jardines still have it?"

"Why?"

"Because I can get a price off them."

"They sold it."

"To whom?"

"A Lady Jennings."

"Good-bye bargain," said Feldman.

"You know her?"

"Yes."

"Maybe the ruby will turn up with her."

"Never. She's sapphires. She's got the eight hundred–karat James."

"I understand what you mean about recovering stolen property here now."

"You don't understand salt, Artie, or you wouldn't be running after those things. Good-bye."

Harry was watching as Artie hung up.

"I couldn't help overhearing and I didn't try to. Was that Norman Feldman of New York you were talking to?"

"Yeah."

"How did you get to meet him? He was the first person I tried to get in touch with because of the great ruby. He wouldn't even speak to me."

"I dunno. I always seemed to be able to talk to Feldman, from my first day in Jewels. I just went up there and he explained things to me. I learned quick . . . on most things."

"Why do you think he wouldn't speak to me?"

"Because, like God, Norman Feldman moves in mysterious ways. He gives money away like crazy. Will fight for the right time to sell a gem, fight his wife on a divorce settlement, then give over a million dollars to their kid, and not speak to the kid." Artie was smiling.

"You like him, don't you?"

"I do."

"Do you think he's dangerous?"

"I never thought about it. Do you?"

"Just wondered. Lot of death, you know. Claire's father, the art dealer, the Israeli," Rawson poured himself another port. Artie declined a refill. "Wondering what your homicide people thought of it."

"What do you think of it?"

"I think it adds the spice of death to the whole thing, don't you?" said Rawson.

"Harry, do you really think of death as a flavoring?" asked Artie. He didn't like the wine, and he would prefer a Coke if he could get it, or beer, or Scotch. He and this British aristocrat had gotten close as only two drunks could, with all the intensity of cellophane flaming and just as quickly, cold and gone. And yet during the workdays Artie learned to respect him, and to like him, a strange liking without the easy warmth he usually felt with friends. Perhaps it was because Rawson was English and rich, which were two alien things to Artie. He couldn't sense where the man was.

They talked about training and the police academy and Sandhurst, and they switched to the devil champagne while waiting for the thousand-dollar ladies. Rawson was a thinker. Before the first bottle of champagne was done, and while he was on his cyclical theory of history, Artie had a question, apropos of historical eras coming and going.

"Did you get anywhere with Claire Andrews?"

"God no."

"She said you didn't."

"You thought she lied?"

"No. I just wanted to know."

"I like courtesans, Artie. They are cleaner. There is no fraud unless you want to pay for fraud. Nobody is feigning closeness, and when they leave, they leave no emotional baggage. Your street whore, Artie, is the only clean screw in the world. And they are always pleasant."

"Pleasant is fraud," said Artie. "Why didn't you get it on with Claire?"

"I just told you. She is also a very difficult person."

"I think . . . I hope she'll be all right."

"She will always be all right, old man. The world will pick up our bodies off ash heaps, friend, while the Claire Andrewses of the world breakfast with orchids on the table."

"I think she's crazy. I think, maybe."

"Are you sweet on her?"

"If I were not a grown-up, rational human being, I could let myself go that way."

"Phone her."

"I'll phone her in New York. I'm a little bit high."

"Phone her now. I'll pay for it."

"She's a competing claim to you."

"Competition makes it interesting. Phone her."

"What for?"

"You have information on the sapphire. Phone her. Take the Dom Perignon with you. Go into your bedroom, and phone Claire Andrews, mid-American virgin, Sir Arthur."

"I feel strange using your money to give her information, not that I wouldn't give it to her anyway once I got back to New York. We're dealing with legal claims here."

"Claims, Artie," intoned Rawson, grandly waving his glass without spilling. "Haven't you learned anything about claims from the Jennings sapphire? A claim is a matter of public opinion of the moment. Get out of here. Phone the damsel Claire."

"I'm not getting involved," said Artie, taking one of the bottles and his glass as he got up from the very soft chair.

"Don't worry, our ladies will be here to rescue you from any involvement with the infinitely superior love for cash. Your reward for a job well done."

Perhaps it was the champagne, perhaps a fatigue he felt from traveling in strange cities where he couldn't relax, but Artie found himself just talking away with Claire about everything. They hardly mentioned the sapphire or European rights claims. They talked about Carney, Ohio, and the Bronx, and Europe, and New York City. She was surprised to find out that for Artie as a boy a trip to Manhattan was like her going to Columbus or Toledo.

Missing Christmas had been hard for Claire, and she had almost wavered and gone home, but it was easier to be without Dad in a strange place. Artie understood. He had lost both parents within a month of each other, and the first holidays without them were the hardest. Because holidays and families seemed to mean the same thing. It was an emptiness he had felt. They were stronger that first holiday in not being there, than they were when they were alive. If that didn't sound crazy? he said. She didn't think it did at all. Claire asked if he were drinking and he said champagne. He acknowledged how difficult life must be for her in New York and said he never expected her to stay at first.

Rawson came into the room to say the ladies were there, and Artie said he would be out in a minute.

"Are those dates?"

"Kind of," said Artie.

"Did you meet them in Paris?"

"Not yet," said Artie.

"Oh, a blind date."

"Yeah, I dunno how Europeans do these things," said Artie. "Harry's doing this thing, and I'm going along with him. But it looks as though your sapphire or Harry's is real. The real thing. Quite a stone. Not a fraud."

There was silence across the Atlantic.

"Some stones can be faked. They'll do anything for money, cut a sapphire top and put it over glass. You couldn't tell unless you looked at the sides," said Artie.

"Does he know a lot of women in Paris?"

Artie wanted to answer "the best women money can buy," but found himself promising to show Claire how to use a jeweler's loupe to look at stones when he got back to New York.

She said she would like that. And he thought, even as he said that, What have I offered?

An attractive woman in her late teens, more a girl than a woman, entered the room with a full bottle of champagne and a lascivious smile. The champagne in one hand and the glass in the other went behind her to her sides, leaving herself as the offering.

Artie held up a finger indicating one minute and signaled she should leave the champagne. He heard laughter outside before she shut the door.

When he was through talking to Claire, he went out into the parlor, and there was Harry Rawson, sitting in a silk bathrobe, smoking a mellow cigar, a glass of brandy in his lap and a table with three dirty plates and food in all manner of disarray.

"They're gone. And it was wonderful. A thousand-dollar whore, Artie, is lust raised to a level of perfection that men can only dream about. It makes ordinary fornication the bangers and mash of life."

"She looked young."

"Only in body, but the mind was that of a thousand-year-old courtesan with all tricks and devices to drive you mad."

"I don't believe you," said Artie.

"You'll never know, will you?" said Rawson. "And it bloody well serves you right."

XVIII

For had you all the riches of the world at your disposal, you would have given them away without a qualm for the love of your Maker.

—SIR THOMAS MALORY
Morte d'Arthur, ca. 1470

"I'm sorry," said Gruenwald to the afternoon guest in his Geneva office. "But the price has gone up. I have added expenses." Gruenwald carefully opened his eye-drop bottle and squeezed in a half dropper full of pink medicine, which he released first into his right eye, closing it until the sting had gone, and then into his left, wiping each eye carefully and gently with sighs of relief.

A businessman had to understand necessary costs, Gruenwald knew. He had to understand that if one traded cars, or razor blades, or tankers of oil, one provided oneself with the necessary insurance.

For trading a name, there had to be proper insurance also. But there was no underwriter who could guarantee safety of life, and that was the insurance Werner Gruenwald needed. And that cost.

Gruenwald hired the best strong-arm people in Europe, the Marseilles French. He had done some business with them before and was delighted to find out that they had added an absolutely brilliant wrinkle. A simple electronic beeper would stay with Gruenwald at all times. The bodyguard would not, for the simple reason that bodyguards clinging to their employers were more likely to be fellow targets. When Gruenwald buzzed, the bodyguard, who always hovered around like a scout, would come in and, if Gruenwald wanted, kill the attacker, or if Gruenwald needed some form of payment just let the man know. Gruenwald was not for killing.

The bodyguard was a six-foot barrel of a brute of a man, with a face that had registered many blows, and enough muscle to crack through a three-inch wide board with a lead pipe as though it were a sword. His name was Pierre. He was illiterate but obedient. He was perfect insurance.

So, knowing Pierre was nearby, Gruenwald contentedly dabbed the medicine from his eyes and said flat out that everyone was going to have to bear Gruenwald's insurance cost.

Gruenwald was still smiling when he felt the blow before he saw his guest had made a move. It stunned him, sending him back in his rolling chair, seeing stars amid the softening sting of the medicine. He tried to scream, but his mouth was covered. Something oily. His mouth was being wrapped in tape even as his body was thrown up hard against the wall. And then like a sack bouncing off a truck, he was pulled downward by hands. He tried to get both hands to his jacket and the beeper device. One hand was held, hard, being taped now to the chair. His spine was numb where it had hit something hard. He had been pulled down to the chair. Bounced up, silenced, then bounced down again, all with eyes stinging from the first blow. The right hand was into the pocket. Gruenwald kicked out to get some free space. He felt the beeper. He pressed. He pressed the case. He pressed the button. He pressed its seams, and its label and both sides. He heard it squeal. The same squeal Pierre had demonstrated. He held onto the button, squeezing for his life, so that call was constant, so strong he heard it in front of him.

The wrist went down to the arm of the chair, taped there unmoving. But that hand did not surrender the device. That hand kept pressing the button. Pierre's caller was so close now. In a moment it would be over. The guest would be crushed, and Gruenwald would be freed.

And then the squealing sound of constant beeps stopped. They stopped because the guest had turned it off, and he showed Werner Gruenwald he had the receiver. Slowly, the guest went to the door, closed it, and from Gruenwald's own pocket took out a cigar, lighting it slowly.

He did not look angry. He did not look pleased. He could have been staring at a case of emeralds with a loupe for all the passion he showed. Then, making sure the tip of the cigar had a full red ember, he put it close to Gruenwald's right eye and began to talk softly. To Gruenwald it sounded like madness. There were questions, there were threats.

Of course the price had changed. As soon as the man untaped his mouth Gruenwald would tell him everything at the bargain rate of nothing. That was when the burning cigar went right into his eye.

Arthur was supposed to be back in New York City with Captain Rawson and he hadn't phoned. He hadn't phoned for two days since he should have been home, and Claire was almost certain it was what she had done that night, when they enjoyed that beautiful conversation from Paris.

It was like a warm bath in another human being, very comforting, very desirable and very familiar. In this polar cap world, Arthur Modelstein, for that two-hour phone conversation from Paris about nothing really, was the warm respite of joy. She had never talked that long on the phone with anyone and when she had gotten off her ear was stinging from the receiver.

And then Claire, with her mind that could look at five sides to a four-sided square, began thinking about those women, those French blind dates that Captain Rawson had arranged. She wondered if they were in the room with Arthur while she was talking to him and feeling all those good things about him? Were they doing things with him or to him, while she was feeling all those good things and thinking good thoughts about him. Was Arthur so skilled at that sort of thing that he could talk warmly to her and receive other things from others.

More importantly, at that moment while she was alone in her apartment in Queens with a bowl of cold soup and a computer trying to get some organization on the massive diversity of different civilizations toward their gems, with a computer screen in her face, Arthur might have right that very moment been doing something maximally intimate with one of those women.

He was the sort who had many women, and before she had thought it through, she was on the phone dialing him in Paris, not caring that it was the wee hours over there. Possibly even enjoying it. After all, she was only calling to thank him for his concern. After all, she wasn't supposed to know things about being in the saddle while trying to answer a phone. He thought of her as the sweet, virginal, midwest innocent, so why should she know of such things? If he were having difficulty talking, why she would just press onward with her sweet-as-cornflower conversation. At worst, she would find he did not have a woman there. And what was she doing phoning Paris, France, to find out whether a New York City detective of thirty-four years of age was alone or not?

He was on the phone before she could hang up. He was groggy, drunk, sleepy, but saying she shouldn't apologize for calling because whether she knew it or not she had a nice voice even though she came from Ohio, and places like that way out there where they talked like that and couldn't help it, if she knew what he meant.

"I do," said Claire, as cool and uninviting as windowsill water. And that was it. Two days before, and he hadn't phoned and was probably now with his hundred and one other women. And all Claire had was what she had when she made the stupid, childish phone call: her screen with the gem weightings and chart for that one hundred and forty-two–karat sapphire.

The problem with the sapphire was that it was the most mystical gem of all. Some superstition held that even the Ten Commandments were written on sapphire, but that was impossible. Sapphires never came that big. On the other hand, there was a penchant for calling almost any dark stone a sapphire.

In one generation, the sapphire might be used superstitiously to corroborate fidelity of a spouse (it was supposed to change colors if the marriage partner cheated, but only the female, which had led Claire to surmise that most legends were created by men), or in another for a bishop's ring because the sapphire indicated holiness, or in another for good luck on the sea, hence the Poseidon engraving on the cellar's sapphire. And worse, because of the heavy mysticism and multiplicity of stones masquerading as sapphires, few were weighted and even fewer were sapphires.

It was confusion on a grand scale, and she realized she had to do something, so arbitrarily she divided the world into Asia, Middle East, and Europe. And then divided those into time periods and phoned the history department of Columbia University and asked to speak to professors of European, Greco-Roman, Near East, and Asian history.

"All at once, or will you take them separately?" asked a secretary.

Claire found herself starting to apologize. She had always been an apologizer back in Carney. It seemed to make life go easier, even if she didn't do something. She was always ready to take blame and get on with things. But now, she just didn't have time.

"I am going to pay one hundred dollars an hour. And I do consider it important, and please convey this information to the professors, please." Claire's voice was ice-pick sharp and just as unyielding.

And it was like a miracle. The secretary started apologizing, and Claire cut her off, saying it wasn't necessary.

A weak winter sun did little to warm the cold stone and concrete walks of the city campus of Columbia University when Claire arrived the next day. She had never told her parents, but one of the reasons she had declined going to Radcliffe, in addition to its being so far away from home, was that it was an Ivy League school. And that frightened her. A small town in Ohio mattered so little there.

In a small, somewhat untidy office, Professor Hadrian Vitas of Classical History (Greco-Roman), a handsome young man in his early thirties, in a too-stuffy tweed suit with a vest, gave Claire a strong lecture on how the things that lasted were things of the mind, plays, poetry, speeches. He seemed most interested in a gold pen he kept tapping on a very thin red book, which was Cicero's *Orations*. A stale pipe that smelled more like sulphur than tobacco lay in a large ashtray, its bowl opening toward Claire.

"Time has a wonderful way of weeding out the trivial, Miss Andrews. And whereas I am impressed by your generous offer of one hundred dollars an hour just to talk to me, I am afraid I can't undo what time has done. A sapphire with Poseidon engraved on it just doesn't stand out for me," said Professor Vitas.

"It would be one hundred and twenty-nine siliqua," said Claire.

Vitas twirled the pen on top of the book. He seemed interested in that.

"Translated from karats. It would be one hundred and forty-two today. That's a very large sapphire," said Claire. "They did believe in the classical era that sapphires could make them safe at sea."

"Yes, but why do you think there should be some reference to it?" Professor Vitas allowed a weak smile, apparently of immense tolerance. He checked the pen for the smoothness of its opening mechanism. And he sighed.

Claire spoke to his high forehead.

"Because one hundred and forty-two karats is a very large stone, and only important people would own such a major gem. So really there should be some mention somewhere in the ancient world of this Poseidon sapphire." She felt a hostile edge to her voice.

Professor Vitas took the cap off his pen and replaced it.

"Miss Andrews, a sapphire might be important to someone today, it might even have been important to someone then, but commercialism isn't quite my field." He looked at her. Finally.

"If there were commercial recordings, I wouldn't be bothering with you," snapped Claire. "As much as you may look down on businessmen, they got their weights right. Most of the ancient records, the ones that are found preserved, are of business. And they're accurate. It's your religious leaders, poets, and politicians who have to be washed of bullshit before you can trust a fraction of what they say." On *politicians* she nodded to the small volume of Cicero, who had delivered his orations in the

[251]

Roman Senate. And then she added bluntly, "Why did you agree to see me? I told your secretary the topic I was interested in before we met. I outlined it clearly."

Professor Vitas lowered the pen and looked at Claire with the amusement of a biologist discovering an odd sort of fly.

"I wanted to see who would pay one hundred dollars an hour to talk about classical history. Now I have. Let me take you to lunch with that fee?" He was grinning.

Claire wanted to throw something at that condescending grin, and then in a bolt of insight, she realized Professor Vitas was insecure. An Ivy League professor in his own office on an Ivy League campus was insecure. And why not? Why shouldn't he be?

And in that moment Claire realized she could hurt him. But she also didn't want to go out with him or nurse him along for the rest of the day. So she explained carefully that she was in search of the meaning of gems on a saltcellar her family had once owned, because she had been stymied in identifying its recent history with only a drawing. History was in a way her last resort, but not really the worst resort because famous people, as she had said before, were the owners of these sorts of stones, and they were the stuff of history. She was so clear about her own place and direction, she didn't even have to address any emotional rejection to him. It was clean. It was clear, and quickly Professor Vitas, perhaps insecure because he was so young in this prestigious position, jotted down many references to large blue stones, the most probable regarding her sapphire occurring at the great sea battle where Octavius, soon to be known as the emperor Augustus, defeated Marc Antony, of Cleopatra fame.

Unfortunately, there was no indication of any other special meaning of the sapphire, or more specifically where it had gone after that battle.

Professor Vitas was sorry he couldn't help more, but he did have one last question. Why didn't Claire use graduate students for her research instead of a full professor. She could get them for twenty dollars an hour, or possibly even less.

"I've used graduate students as researchers. They would take a week looking up what you just knew off the top of your head in forty minutes. I'm paying a full professor a hundred dollars an hour because it's cheaper."

Claire spent less than an hour with each professor, and with each professor she came prepared, and she became known around all the history departments as the sapphire lady. But of all the myriad of references that came up for a sapphire that size, none seemed definite. She saw one large sapphire, probably the Poseidon, transfer from Asia to the west with the conquests of Alexander. She saw several references in

Byzantium, the eastern Christian half of a declining Roman empire, which had been built on a fallen brief Greek empire, which had been built on a fallen Persian empire, which had at one time straddled two worlds, the easternmost region of which was probably where the big blue stone was discovered.

But after A.D. 1000, no one could find even an improbable mention of a big blue stone with Poseidon engraved on it, not in karats or obols or drachms. It seemed to have been swallowed up like the six diamonds centuries later during the Spanish Inquisition.

And then a Pakistani graduate student at Columbia phoned her asking if she were still purchasing research about a large sapphire in the ancient world.

"I have heard you were, so therefore, madame, I have made bold to ask if you wished further data on the very stone you sought?" His name was Ahmed and his voice had a singsong quality to it.

Claire contained a sigh.

"I'm sorry, but I have all the researchers I need. Thank you."

"Oh, that is no problem, but I do have a reference already in an Islamic text."

That was just about the second thing Claire didn't need. A religious text. She had been fortunate with Maimonides, who had led her to the even more exact Spanish references, but since then, she had come to believe that holy men were too much of another world to help her accurately in this one.

But Ahmed was so polite, she thought she might at a twenty-dollar-an-hour fee give him one chance, more out of charity than anything else.

"All right, read it to me," she said.

"It is about measures of things, and what something weighs, and does weight really make something more important in the measure of things."

"Most certainly does when you need accuracy," said Claire.

"I am sorry. I am referring to the religious text, what the mullahs deemed of value in their hierarchy of values."

"Go ahead," said Claire.

"Though this exceeds one hundred qurots, it is less than nothing because it weighs against the soul. It is an abomination."

"How many qurots?"

"A qurot is an Arabic weight. It's not the same as a karat. I'm not sure of the exact difference."

"I am. Is it one hundred and six qurots."

"More than one hundred and five, they say, because the language flows better in Arabic with more than one hundred and five. It is poetic, too."

"Why is it an abomination?" asked Claire, her body electrified, her lower lip precarious between her teeth, praying for the answer she hoped might come.

"Because there is an engraving on the sapphire. You may not be aware, but engravings, any likenesses of people are an abomination to a Muslim."

"I most certainly am," said Claire. "Bring the text right over. I'm in Queens."

Claire ended up paying Ahmed one hundred dollars for twenty minutes of his time and felt she had even at that almost cheated him. His text referred to the general Omar's conquest of Jerusalem from the Christians and a sapphire that, because it was an abomination, presented a problem to Omar the Great. His solution, according to the text, was to make it part of "the lesson."

And this abomination weighed more than one hundred and five qurots. Claire Andrews had found her sapphire at the first Muslim conquest of Jerusalem because a mullah had thought it an important example as to the measure of things, which was a way of saying the worth of things.

Claire Andrews had found it. When Ahmed left her apartment, having dutifully translated the entire text for her while she typed it into her computer, Claire waited until he was well down the hall to let out an Ohio State cheer that would have set off a stadium. She had found it. She had found the Poseidon sapphire for absolute sure.

"Give me an 'O.' "

ZASKAR REGION, 600 B.C.

It was big. Bigger than the eyes of Shiva in the great temple of the valleys beneath the Kashmir. And the boy had seen it. He had gone with his father to dig into the hard white rock looking for such blue stones as befit the eyes of the gods, and it was he, not his father, who saw the first spot of darkness. And it was he, not his father, who cautioned that it might be big and that the digging should begin far around. Four iron picks were broken taking it out, but such a stone as that, a melon of a stone, a cat's head of a stone, a man's fist of a stone, was worth a hundred picks. It could be a god itself, such was its size. It was far too big to be sold in the village, because only poor things were sold in the village. In the village one sold a fingernail of a stone, a shard of a stone, a pebble of a stone, but never a stone such as this, so blue and so big. One could only imagine what it would look like when it was cut from the marble host rock, cleaned, and polished. It would have the power to bring down the night sky itself, and everyone agreed it should be sold in a city, for a village would not have the price worthy of such a stone.

But in the city, where there were priests who could cure the worst of ills, and scales that miraculously measured weights the same every time and every season, there was not one person who could properly cut and polish such a blue stone of almost sixty-eight obols. For something that grand one needed craftsmen in a larger city farther to the west.

Yet none of the villagers who had accompanied the father and the son to the city, an assurance of safety such a stone demanded, could afford the great trek to the west, so it was sold to a man rich enough and strong enough to make the journey, not, of course, for anywhere near its true price. But the great blue stone was, after all, too big for such a villager to protect on such a long journey.

And so, like all great gems it left the hands of the poor never to return, and like all great gems it made its way to the level of society that could own it. And so great was the sapphire, not only in size but in the intensity of its blue, that learned men understood it had the power to protect the wearer at night because it held the night in the mystery of its soul.

And so that was the new measure when it passed from the Persian emperor to the new Greek conqueror whose wise men understood what every seafarer knew, that sapphires protected one on the journey across the waters. And fittingly, the sea god Poseidon enthroned was carved onto it before it went from Greek to Roman, to kings and emperors and wealthy men, even to a pirate briefly before he was crucified on the mast of his ship, returning the stone to the rulers of the world.

By the year 634 of a new God, Poseidon did not pose as great a pagan threat in Christian Damascus as it did in Constantinople, where Byzantine emperor Heraclitus demanded the Monophysite bishop appear before him to answer charges of heresy.

And he pointed to that great sapphire in the bishop's mitre as just the sort of abomination Christianity was being punished for.

"Even now, Islam is threatening not only your Damascus, Bishop, but Christian Egypt and Jerusalem of our Christ. Why now is that possible for such as Islam to challenge our great armies?"

The Monophysite, who this day before the emperor wore his mitre with the Poseidon sapphire, a thing he was in no way ashamed of, understood the crucial word left out of Emperor Heraclitus' lament. The armies of Islam were Arab. And it was omitted on purpose because the Monophysites were Arab. How could Arabs defeat armies of eastern Rome?

The Monophysite answered: "Our Lord Jesus suffered. And we suffer in His name."

"We are being told something. Why did Christianity take over Rome? Why, because the gods were false gods, and now we have elevated the false gods again, the gods of superstition, the defeated ones. Poseidon is not worshipped except in your churches, Bishop, your churches closest to the advance of those desert pagans."

The emperor was coming close to that word he had avoided. The bishop answered again: "All things are made by Him, so too the holy power of this blue sapphire, radiating its holiness upon all those who see it."

"Poseidon is a false god."

"God certainly made such a wondrous and mystical sapphire."

"Get that abomination off your head, Arab," said Emperor Heraclitus, signaling a guard to sweep the abomination from his sight. Almost like cuffing a stable slave, a guard knocked the mitre from the bishop's head to the mosaic floor before the emperor.

The bishop said nothing. Nothing could assuage this indignity. He did not even answer the ensuing commands to clean out heretics from Damascus, meaning the removal of Monophysites from religious posts. He retrieved his mitre himself, not even letting servants bend to the task, and repeated every word upon his return to Damascus.

There was a clear choice. Either the Monophysites stay with the Christian West and suffer the same degradation as that visited upon their bishop, or see what their brother Arabs might offer in the way of religious tolerance. The facts turned out to be too good to be true. In the Moslems' own writings, they guaranteed the right of Christians and Jews to practice their own faiths according to their own ways as people of the Book. They did not care whether Poseidon was on a sacred stone or if a Christian thought a stone itself had power. Christians had that right. And not only were Christian rights written in one Koran shown to them by the Moslem general, Omar, but in every Koran they examined to make sure this was not some trick.

Only one question remained: What gift to seal this alliance would they give Omar? It should be a relic, but all the great relics were in Jerusalem except for the cup of the covenant, held in the great Cathedral of Damascus. Yet this was just a plain clay cup with no grandeur, certainly not a worthy gift for the great Omar. There was only one solution, add another token of probable value, and that was the great Poseidon sapphire from the bishop's mitre.

Omar looked upon the gift not in measure of the stone, because the graven image for him as a Muslim made it unacceptable. Even if the sapphire were as big as a mountain, it would be worthless because of the image. It was set into silver that held a clay bowl that the prophet Christ had used. But how could he refuse a gift, especially one that came with two entire Monophysite legions that had once secured the eastern wall of the Christian empire? The answer was he could not. But it troubled him, and he knew another solution would have to be found, but first he had wars to fight.

Blessings came immediately with the two legions at the crucial battle of Yarmuk, when a sudden sandstorm blinded the opposing Christian armies and a great slaughter ensued. It was only a short time before Damascus fell to Islam as well as Jerusalem.

For Jersualem he allowed the Christian patriarch Sephronius to remove all his relics to the west, for who wanted them in the city from which Mohammed rode to heaven? This left Omar with the abomination of the graven image. Some of his captains pointed out that the sapphire was an awesome hundred and six qurots, but Omar answered only that its weight would weigh against him on the judgment day.

Yet it was a gift and he could not discard it. What to do with a graven image that would weigh more than a hundred and six qurots against him? And then it came to him in the laughter of a woman. For she thought how funny that anyone would worship a drinking bowl. And with that he knew. The one hundred and six–qurot stone would go down in his conquest of Jerusalem as "the lesson" that showed that while Christianity, like Judaism, contained some truths, here was an example of something so silly as to show, of course, it was not the one whole perfect truth like Islam. And Omar took the graven-imaged stone that would have weighed against him on judgment day and had it put on that bowl now called "the lesson." What once would have weighed against him because it was an abomination of a graven image now on judgment day would weigh for him in the scales of justice because he was using it not for its image but for its furtherance of Islam.

The sapphire was not used separately as an adornment again until the Paris party of Lady Constance Jennings, whereupon it was not called either an abomination or a lesson, but the "Jennings," and after the party promptly stored away in a safe where it would stay for all but seven nights out of the year, European property rights being what they were in the twentieth century.

Werner Gruenwald, businessman, of Geneva, Switzerland, one of the last to deal the great blue stone found in the marble of Kashmir, who had weighed it solely in dollars and francs as he measured all things, had not once during that morning cleaned his pink protective lenses or put drops into his eyes. His hands were still and cold and taped by his wrists to his chair, his eyes having been burned out of his head. A petty French criminal lay in an adjoining office, a lead pipe stuck in his belt, face down with a small bloody spot in the back of his head. Apparently the pipe had been some sort of weapon, but was useless, police surmised. As the forensic doctors assigned to the Swiss constabulary explained, the man had been felled instantly with a perfect mortal knife wound into the posterior cerebral lobe. It was so clean and precise, it could have been performed without any technical shame in an operating room.

And Claire Andrews meanwhile drew a large circle around Jerusalem and made an arrow from that city to Seville, which led to London.

Stepping back from her wall, she was certain now that she was looking for something that attracted great jewel adornments. More than that, this thing was thought foolish by Muslims and without God by a Jew in the Spanish Inquisition.

Probably a Christian thing, she thought, going into the small kitchen to open a Cherry Coke. Then she returned to the wall, where her eyes followed the line from Jerusalem, to Seville, to England. In England, this thing probably became the saltcellar, just like raw materials from other parts of the world became an American car when manufactured in America.

But why? And what was it? And why specifically would it be rejected by both Jew and Muslim alike? Because of the graven images on the stone? Both faiths felt that way about images. The rejection was too strong for just images. It was, after all, at one time worth breaking up a perfect set of seven diamonds.

What was history telling her? There was something larger here.

She wanted to phone Arthur to share her discovery. But she had already made that absolutely wrong phone call to Paris and that was why she hadn't heard from him for a week now.

XIX

Alas miserable wretch that I am. I have been vile and wicked beyond measure to let myself be brought so swiftly to the brink of losing what is irredeemable, namely virginity, which cannot be recovered since it is lost but once. —WALTER MAP
Quest del Saint Graal, 1225

Even before he knew about the Swiss businessman's death, Artie was haunted by how the jewels had moved. It was only by accident that they had found them. There were too many signs of a professional at work, no matter what the great ruby dealer of New York kept repeating about amateurs.

The rabbi's son had made a correct commercial if not moral judgment. Baruch Schnauer had been seduced by the greatest temptation of all, a certainty that he would not be caught. The diamonds should have moved with no problems in New York City. What knowledgeable dealer would think diamonds so old they were polished would have registered gem prints? And if it had not been for Harry Rawson's business contacts abroad, no one would have even known that the sapphire had been sold in Paris.

So if it weren't for accidents, most connected to Rawson, it would have been a very successful robbery. And Artie thought about that.

Whenever an important theft occurred, some major painting, a piece of statuary, anything worth millions, it was a safe bet that it had been fenced before it was stolen. The difficult part in a major theft was not in breaking through locks. That was technical. Every detective knew that the damnedest things could be broken into. There was no lock people put up that wasn't breakable, from the pyramids to the electronics at the Metropolitan Museum of Art. Most of the intricate defenses now-adays were figured out by crooks before they were on sale to the public.

In a major theft, it was the fence who was important, not the burglar. He was just the laborer of larceny. The person who could move the goods was important. He had to be the professional. And who could move a sapphire and a ruby like the ones in the saltcellar? Artie did not like to think about that.

And then Harry Rawson phoned him with the news that Werner Gruenwald was dead, that he had been tortured and that the body of a thug was found in an adjacent office.

"Thought you'd get the news through some police network."

"No," said Artie.

"This is private information I'm giving you for your good. Look, you may not be aware of it, but the thug was killed with the same sort of blow that did in old Geoffrey Battissen."

"Yeah, my friends tell me it was kind of surgical."

"It was probably the most professional killing that occurred in your city in the last decade."

"I wouldn't say that, Harry. We got some real good contract killers here."

"Artie, my friend, bullets are accidents launched in the hope of creating death. The posterior cerebral lobe with an instrument is death. I won't argue with your New York chauvinism. For your own good, please do watch out for yourself."

"How is it for my good?"

"So you'll protect yourself."

"From whom?"

"Well now, Artie. You'd probably know that better than I, wouldn't you?"

"Maybe."

"Your friend, the ruby dealer."

"Yeah?"

"He's a dangerous man."

"What d'you mean *dangerous*?"

"You don't know your friend's war record?"

"And you do? How come?"

"Artie, I am in a business that allows me access to information. I suppose I would be a lot better off if I kept my mouth shut."

"Are you telling me to back off this whole thing?"

"I'm telling you in your own vernacular to watch your ass."

"And what about your ass?"

"I'm an Englishman. Rudimentary common sense is alien to my nature."

"Feldman's strange, but he's all right."

"Artie, I know you. You are a drinking buddy, old boy. You're too shrewd not to know what's going on."

"So why are you telling me this?"

"Artie, you are amazingly circular when you don't want to go somewhere," said Rawson. He suggested drinks next time he was in New York City. He knew places in New York City, too. Artie should keep in touch in case anything turned up in New York City, like the ruby for instance. The ruby was another way of saying Feldman. Artie didn't want to believe what he knew had to be possible. He wanted to believe that Feldman would only kill in self-defense or for his country, and not for a great, great ruby. Artie didn't care how great a ruby was, or what Europeans thought about legitimate ownership. Stealing was stealing and murder was murder, and eighty-seven karats of anything didn't change it. Not even for someone Artie respected so much.

And so, doing even his minimal duty, Artie did have to phone Feldman to talk to him about what was going on and to ask him his whereabouts lately. But Feldman did not answer his phone and Artie went over to his Forty-eighth Street office, and he wasn't in. Feldman wasn't in the next day either, nor twice the following day. And just how safe was Claire Andrews?

Trudy said she had never seen Artie take work home from the office, and if he were going to worry about things, why remain a policeman?

Artie answered he did not think it appropriate to discuss work in her bed.

"Discuss it? It's in bed with us." She grabbed a hand of his and put it on her bare breast.

"Here I am, Artie. Do you want to pay attention to me? Here I am."

Dutifully, Artie fondled her breast, and she slapped his hand away.

"Get out of here. And I don't want to see you again."

"What's wrong? What did I do?"

"You're always the victim, Artie. You never do anything wrong, and you are always the victim. Don't shrug."

"What? What on earth, what!"

"I told you what. You're not here."

"I'm here."

"The hell you are. C'mon, Artie. I'm not your family. I'm not your police captain who you can say yes yes to. I'm Trudy. Remember me? I pay attention to you. I give you my body and my self. You've got to be here for me."

"What can I tell you?" he said, controlling any shrug that would have been perfect for this situation. But she had taken it away from him, like a zone defense could take away a long pass. And so, shrugless, all he could do was talk.

Trudy turned away in contempt and held out his underwear and pants. He knew enough that the moment he put them on it was all over.

"There's been some killings that have worried me, Trudy. More killings than I've seen in anything so far."

"It's not the dead bodies, Artie. It's that woman."

"What woman?"

"The blond sweetheart from Duluth."

"I don't know anyone from Duluth."

"Wherever," said Trudy.

"I know who you mean. I have not phoned that woman since I returned from France, precisely because I do not wish to get involved. That is how much you know about what is going on. I don't want to go near her. I don't want to go within a hundred miles of her. That is what she means to me."

But this evening, Trudy was not even buying the truth.

"I am a woman who has been second fiddle in seven, count them, seven relationships in a row. That is all I have in my life, and Artie, I am not taking it anymore. As I told you at the beginning, I am not taking it anymore. Put on your pants and go."

Artie did not take the pants. Trudy dropped them on the floor. Thus convinced she was serious, Artie dressed and tried to say good-bye. But Trudy had shut herself in the bathroom and was crying. It really was over.

"I'm sorry," said Artie.

"It's not your fault. Get out of here," she yelled back.

"I wouldn't hurt you for the world. You know I like you."

"Will you get out of here? Just get out of here. Get out of here so I can get started on my eighth straight second-fiddle relationship."

Artie left quickly, sensing if he stayed she might start asking why he thought he could get away with treating her like this, why all men in her life treated her like that, and the truth was she had all but told him from the outset that they were there just to enjoy each other, nothing serious, and every time he treated her that way she was hurt.

Nevertheless, he felt bad, ashamed, wanting to make things right, wanting to stop Trudy from crying, wanting to give her just the man that would make her happy. And he was wise enough to know it was not Arthur Modelstein. In fact, he was fairly sure Trudy met the right man every day and passed him by in favor of the Arthur Modelsteins of the world.

Perhaps the British gentleman was right. Hookers were the answer. They were the clean relationships. But he didn't believe that. And he felt sorry for Harry Rawson. Of course, why should he feel sorry for Harry? He saw the way he lived.

Artie went home that night and watched television and did not call Claire Andrews. He spent the night not calling her and realized that Trudy was a very smart woman because that was what he had been doing since he came back from Paris.

If the breakup with Trudy had been uncomfortable, anything with Claire Andrews was going to be five times worse. Everything was worse with that lady. The fact of that two-hour phone call was not lost on him. What did they talk about? They talked about nothing. Little things. Funny things. Not so funny things. Nothing. They had talked about nothing while he ignored a thousand-dollar-a-night courtesan, a fact he would never tell anyone in the department.

Claire was a person wise men avoided. She was the stuff for which beachheads were stormed, on which empires were built, from which discoveries against all manner of obstacles were made.

She was oblivious to danger and odds. This was not someone to be entangled with. She was not his kind. Trudy was his kind. Trudy understood the world was not a safe and good place. Trudy was the one he should get entangled with if he wanted to be entangled. Reliable, only moderately bitchy, and usually deceivable on important matters.

Of course, he had already paid the price for leaving Trudy. He was a thousand times better off not even saying hello again to Claire. That Paris phone conversation was enough warning for anyone. Two hours going by like a warm chuckle. Dangerous.

"You have done well, Arthur," he said into his bathroom mirror, "to have kept your distance. What you need now is another affair, a total physical, nonemotional, just body affair. Opposite Miss Andrews."

And he agreed with himself. And then phoned Claire Andrews as he had always known he would.

"I just got back from Paris," he lied. Why did he say that? That was a stupid, stupid thing to say.

"And you called me right away?" Her voice was happy. She was actually happy on the other end of the phone that he had called her right away.

"No," he said, "I've been back for days."

"Oh."

"I didn't think it was a good thing what happened when we talked in Paris. It got out of hand."

"We had a good talk," said Claire. "I enjoyed it."

"That's the problem."

"I hardly see where it's a problem." The voice was soft but it was cold.

"Lady—"

"Don't call me lady, Arthur. Don't play the tough New York City cop with me. I am a rational adult. I am not some innocent. Most of the people in this city came from somewhere else. Your grandparents came from someplace else. I'm sorry. I'm sorry I said that."

"What? Said what?"

"About coming from someplace else."

"They did. Russia. What're you sorry about?"

"We're different," said Claire.

"Right," said Artie, and immediately both of them understood they weren't sure how the other meant that.

"I think you should know and understand that I am a rational person, and I don't think you understand that."

"No, I don't."

"That's insulting, Arthur. Insulting to anyone from anywhere."

"If I told you that you are sitting on dynamite, and that you should get off, would you say I'm insulting?"

"If you thought I was too irrational to get off, yes, it would be insulting."

"There's two more bodies with this thing. One of them had the sapphire and sold it to that Paris jewelry store I told you about. The other was found nearby with a blow behind the ear, just like that art dealer Battissen who cheated you. Just like it."

"Yes?" said Claire calmly.

"Yes!" screamed Artie. "Yes! What is this yes? Dynamite. Dynamite. Dynamite."

"Arthur, who is being irrational? You're hysterical."

"Dynamite," he said more softly.

"Do you want to expand on that? Arthur, I am trying to be as calm as I can. I am trying to reason with you. Will you let me reason with you? Who was killed? Why was he killed? Under what circumstances was he killed?"

"You are sitting there on dynamite. That is irrational. You can die like anyone else in this world, you know?"

"Is it going off tonight?"

"It may."

"But it probably won't, will it? We don't know why these people are being killed, do we? There's more we don't know than there is we do know, isn't that so?"

"Hey, Claire, people are dying. All right? Enough to know? Okay? Enough for you? Is that enough?"

There was silence. Artie wanted to throw the receiver through the wall.

"I'm listening," said Artie.

"You won't like the answer."

"You're probably right. What is it? Not enough for you, right?"

"Arthur, no one looking for these gems has been killed. Everyone who has died has possessed them. I don't possess them. If Captain Rawson were killed, then I would have something logical to fear. But he is alive, isn't he?"

"What is this, the Carney, Ohio, homicide squad?"

"Arthur!"

"Yes."

"Let's sit down, and go over this, and hear me out."

"All right. I'll be right over."

"It's eleven o'clock. Come over for dinner tomorrow."

"I don't want to make it so social," said Artie.

"Bedtime isn't social, but supper is?"

"That's not what I had in mind," said Artie with a skilled and practiced righteousness, tempered perfectly with a hint of hurt. "That's not what I had in mind at all."

"I'm sorry," said Claire and was forgiven.

The next evening she had a splendid dinner prepared for him, from appetizer to dessert, but confessed that she had gone to a gourmet shop and bought it all, from the ducks with wild rice stuffing to the exotic soup, everything except the coffee, to which she added a powdered substitute cream. They ate at the kitchen table on a new linen cloth Claire had purchased. She wore an apron over a dark blue dress, set off by her lovely body and a tasteful strand of pearls. Artie had bought wine and a new very expensive casual sweater for the evening.

When he asked her why she would end such a wonderful meal with a substitute creamer, she said she knew Artie could not eat a milk product with a meat product.

"I'm not kosher," said Artie.

"Reb Schnauer didn't think you would be."

"You talk to him?"

"He's very helpful when he can be. Do you know I'm a righteous gentile?"

"No. What does that mean?"

"Reb Schnauer really is right about you, Arthur. You should know that. Were you Bar Mitzvahed?"

"Yeah," said Artie with a snap of anger. Who was she to ask him that?

"A righteous gentile is one who lives up to the laws of God as well as the best Jew, without, of course, the lifelong training of an orthodox Jew. I guess it would be a form of our sainthood. I think that's wonderful, don't you?"

"No."

"Why not?"

"Saints don't mind getting killed."

"Well, I'm not a saint, Arthur. I happen to be quite rational, and it bothers me not a little bit that you don't understand this. And I'd like to explain how I handle risk and what I am doing here. All I want is a fair hearing from you."

"What does it matter what I think? If you worry about what everyone thinks, you're going to go crazy."

"It matters to me what you think, Arthur. Come into the living room, please."

She got up from the table and led him into that partial living room that was mostly research center, with a wall full of papers and markings, and a long table underneath with enough file folders to occupy a major office inventing the atomic bomb. There was a big map of the world with colored lines crisscrossing it.

Artie had taken his coffee. She nodded to a chair. He sat down. She stood in front of a computer terminal. It was going to be a lecture.

"First, as to the danger. I'm as big a coward as the next person, Arthur. If I felt there was real danger, danger directed at me, not just danger out there somewhere happening to others, I would be the first to run."

Ordinarily, Artie would handle lectures by nodding and letting his mind drift off. But this point he could not let go by.

"What is this 'others' business? It's 'others' until it happens to you and then the next victim can think you're the others it happens to. There are random killings everywhere. New York, Geneva. That Swiss businessman got his eyes burned out of his head. The diamond cutter died while having his skin torn off. And there are two men who died so slick, it scares an officer in the British army. What makes you think you're not next? I mean somebody got in here to kill your cat."

"Torture is not random killing, Arthur, no matter how horrible. The tragedy of Nuisance's death was a very rational threat. I would gather that the weight of evidence would have to show we are dealing with a rational killer or killers here, from Dad on. My father's death seemed more accidental, a hysterical stabbing."

"Since when are you an expert on homicide?"

"I've got to be my own expert, and I'm always willing to listen to other opinions and evaluate them. The tortures weigh inordinately on the side of rationality, even more methodical than the single thrust into the head that killed Battissen and that other person found near the body of the Swiss businessman."

"I don't want to talk about this, Claire. I had a great meal. After a great meal is getting to know people time, not this . . . stuff. Awful stuff. Let's just call the deaths insane. I've seen lots of insanity that, take my word for it, caused just as many horrors as planning."

"Oh, I'm sure insanity causes many horrors, but you have to judge things by probabilities. By weights," said Claire.

And then Artie made the mistake of asking her to explain this weight business, and he could see her eyes suddenly sparkle as she turned to the wall, revealing a great discovery like the secret sunset she had just found someone else to share it with. "When I began I had a blank wall," she said. And she talked about facts and their reliability and unreliability. She talked about great gems and pointed out their paths around the world and time along her map. She talked about researchers and dead ends, and going on. And she talked about faith. Faith was going on when there was no hope.

And then she explained the whole wall. There was only one time that she had had no hope and that was her first night alone here, her first night alone. And the wall was bare. The hardest thing she had to do was start from nowhere that night.

"The rest really isn't that much," she said, amazing Artie with her knowledge of history and gems and how she weighed facts and made calculated decisions to pursue one course or another in a myriad of lies, partial truths, and entire lost civilizations.

Claire Andrews from Carney, Ohio, who didn't have a place to stay her first night in New York, had organized the world.

Artie had a question that had been bothering him: "A friend of mine says that great gems have blood on them and that laws don't apply to them. What does he mean?"

"Mr. Feldman?"

"Yeah."

"In history, people's lives weren't worth much unless they were nobility of some sort. People were considered property, and not that valuable property. The nobility were different. And they were the people who owned the great gems. But even they were usually slaughtered when they lost a war, and their gems as well as the land went over to the new conquerors. The common people were considered not even worth mentioning. When they make a mistake in history, you can have the numbers of people vary by tens of thousands from one report to another. But a gem, when they do mention gems other than poetically or mystically, won't weigh different by even an ounce. So much for human life."

"And today?"

"It depends which country, but in most of the countries of the world the people who own the great gems are the ones who make the laws. It's only recently, in the last few hundred years, that there are some places where the laws are meant to protect the people and not the rulers. So the fact that there might have been a murder associated with, say, the eighty-seven-karat pigeon's blood ruby just wouldn't mean anything. Only the ruby itself would mean something. I think that's what he means, Arthur."

"Yeah," said Artie. It made sense. "So somebody is after that ruby pretty bad, huh?"

"Probably, and yet I look at my map, and I look at my stones and at the histories researchers have waded through for me, and all I can say, Arthur, is only maybe they're after that ruby."

"What else?"

"Maybe an abomination that is a lesson or a thing that is not of God."

"That I really don't understand," said Artie.

"References that are associated with this thing along the way that I have not puzzled out yet."

"I'm still worried about you and the killings," said Artie.

"When Harry Rawson gets killed, then I am going to worry with you."

"You don't like him, do you?" asked Artie.

"He certainly is not the best influence on you," said Claire. "I've never seen you drink heavily before. I heard you drinking your champagne when you talked to me in Paris. You were probably too drunk to do anything after our talk."

"Are you asking?"

"It's none of my business. I enjoyed our conversation. I enjoyed it very much, Arthur."

"So did I," said Artie. He felt almost embarrassed. Something had happened between them, and he had felt it was such a private thing that even discussing what they shared was exposing it. But it was received the same way it was sent, and they were quiet together in the research room of her apartment.

Artie did not know where to put down his coffee without leaving a ring on some papers. She took it from him, and he breathed the scents of her body close to him, her perfume and herself, and he rose from the chair, and very softly he kissed her, a gentle touching of the lips. But it was too exciting for just a kiss. And he saw fear in her eyes.

"I think I had better go home," said Arthur.

"Do you have to?" asked Claire. Her eyes were so wide, so innocent.

"Yeah. It's all clean, you know. We had dinner, and everything's okay, and it's all right. You have your life here. No damage. It's good." Artie nodded.

"I don't think damage is the worst thing that can happen to a life. I think unuse of a life is the worst thing that can happen, Arthur." She was still so close to him, looking up to him.

"Good night," he said, and his voice was low, and he looked so strong and protective, so handsome in his acceptance of things, that Claire wanted to grab him and kiss hard that sweet and open face. But she didn't. She smiled, and now she shrugged. She didn't want him to go, but she knew all of this was too awkward to continue.

"Good night. I think this is best," she said.

"I think it's horseshit," said Artie.

"Horseshit is best," said Claire. She walked him to the door.

And just before he left, he seemed to have some change of mind in some way.

"I'll see you tomorrow night. Okay? We'll go out."

"Fine. Wonderful," she said, but she wondered what was wrong. She was sure this darkly good-looking hunk of man who knew his way around, who had testimony to that from the woman who had the key to his apartment that first night, would make some sort of overture. After all, there was that half-hearted overture that first night.

She waited for him to return and then dramatically make some sort of pass. She would receive it with a playful laugh and then ask him softly to wait. But she did not see him until the next night, when he joked and generally played through dinner, telling her his impressions of Paris and confessing that he did not get to see the Louvre. She was dying to ask who the women were in the Paris hotel room. He went off about the sapphire, and she mentioned that a lawyer she had hired to pursue the ownership matter had told her that Lady Jennings was not French but British.

"There's such a difference between French and English women, isn't there?" she added.

"I wouldn't know," said Artie.

"You've never known English women, I guess."

"I went with an English secretary for a while."

"They're different from the French."

"I don't know."

"Were your friends in Paris American?"

"No. They were French. You know, the thing about Japanese food is you end up eating stuff you would never think you would eat." They were in a Benihana restaurant on Third Avenue.

"Speaking of sushi, Arthur, who were they?"

"Thousand-dollar-a-night prostitutes." He put down his chopsticks and stared her right in the eye.

"You're lying."

"No. They were Rawson's. He wanted me to try one."

If Claire disliked Rawson before, she hated him now. But when Arthur did not add to the explanation, she knew he knew what she was trying to find out. So she didn't hide it.

"What happened?"

"Nothing. I was talking to you."

"Too bad," she laughed lightly. "I was wondering what a thousand-dollar-a-night woman would be like." What a liar she was. Of course she did wonder, but the wonder didn't come near the joy that he was speaking to her instead of going to bed with them. She felt glorious. She felt beautiful. She felt wanted.

They went out on the weekend, walking down through Greenwich Village, coming back not to his place but to hers again, and just hanging around and talking. She confessed she felt like a weak person at times, overwhelmed at times, and wanted to know honestly if Arthur found her a bit on the mousy side. She watched his eyes like a hawk.

"No. If anything, you're a bit too tough. Analytical. You've got a mind like a computer."

"So you think I'm without life?"

"No. I think you're nice."

"Nice?"

"Yeah. Very nice."

"You wouldn't give up a thousand-dollar-a-night prostitute for nice. Nice isn't what people give up thousand-dollar-a-night people for," said Claire. She wanted more. She was going to have to work on being more relaxed and casual. For five meetings it went on like this, sharing, playing, questioning, wondering when Arthur would make a move, wondering if she wanted him after all this time, wondering what it would be like, wondering if he was as sexual as he appeared, wondering if she had absolutely no sex appeal, wondering if she should meet him half-naked sometime, wondering if she should touch him between his legs and start things, wondering if he had some hidden problem, letting her active mind spin her beyond any reasonable course of action with so many variables. The problem was she didn't know where she stood. There were no weights at all. No probables or improbables. No forests or trees, just lots of wood burying her.

And all the turmoil of questions ended with a very warm kiss one Monday night that went on a bit longer, snuggling in his arms on her couch in her living room.

What had she done? Where were they going? She did not know, but all she knew was that when he said, "Let's go to your bedroom," she said yes.

And they did not go right away, but kissed, and touched each other, with his hands caressing her so wonderfully everywhere, right on the couch, so that by the time they reluctantly left that place for the bed, she was wanting him without any question. Her useless mind was waiting somewhere inactive to collect the results.

Claire was delighted to find out he was gentle and caring and strong. The world did not shake, and neither did her body scream out with exotic uncontrollable passion, making her some sort of limp rag. She enjoyed it. She trusted him, and she enjoyed it very much, and she wanted to do it some more, and when they were lying in each other's arms, she was happy. She wanted more of this and she wanted more of him.

Artie was astonished at the joy.

"Are you happy?" she asked.

Where is this going? he thought, with a sense of looming, severe entanglement.

"Are you happy?" she asked again.

"Sure," he said.

"I'm very happy. I didn't think I would be. But I am now," she said.

"I am happy," he said. And he meant it. And why not? What was there to be unhappy about, wondered Detective Modelstein, except someone who had his eyes burned out, and someone else who died while his skin was being stripped, and two others who got sure perfect stabs into the brain.

They went out for a midnight snack at a nearby delicatessen, and she asked him what he wanted for breakfast, and he told her rolls, and she ordered two, and he ordered four more with cream cheese, to go.

In the morning, Claire was the Claire Andrews he knew before they had gone to bed, but he should have expected that. She got a phone call at 6:00 A.M. from Great Britain, and she bounced out of bed, saying she would take the call at her work station. He knew she was excited because he heard her say, "Wonderful. No wonder we didn't find it before. No wonder."

Artie pulled the blankets over his head. He did not have to be awake for another hour so he did not listen. And even if he didn't have to be up for another hour, he still might not have listened. He had made an accommodation with her research. She would do it, and he would stay out of it.

But Claire had taken this accommodation for support. She woke him at 6:07, when he had fifty-three more minutes to sleep. She had to share an important event with him. She was going to put something down on her map in black ink. Artie remembered that the line around the world from Jerusalem to England was in black ink. So it wasn't one of the stones. It was the mystery thing, the abomination, or whatever she was talking about. He knew he couldn't tell her how much more important sleep was to him at this moment, not when she was so excited.

He was in his undershorts and Claire wore a T-shirt with a giant print daisy through which he could see her wonderful body, and he put an arm around her waist as she leaned over the table to write on the map. She bounced into him coming back, grinning. Not even 7:00 A.M. and the bright blue eyes and yellow hair were bouncing. She was hugging him and grinning. So he had to look.

Just west of London, in block letters so big they extended into the English Channel, she had written:

TILBURY

"Dad's cellar was called the Tilbury, and it was made in 1588 for Queen Elizabeth the First, celebrating her victory over the Armada, and you will never guess how I found this out. It's wonderful, Arthur. It's wonderful. It's absolutely wonderful. I've given it an almost positive on my scale of reliability."

"You want me to heat the rolls from last night?" asked Artie.

XX

For just as folly and error fled at His advent and truth stood revealed, even so has Our Lord Chosen you from among all knights to ride abroad through many lands to put an end to the hazards that afflict them and make their meaning and their causes plain.

—WALTER MAP
Queste del Saint Graal, 1225

"Arthur, it's so exciting. I know what that black writer must have felt like when he found his ancestral home generations after slavery. Arthur, it's so wonderful, it's chilling it's so exciting."

Artie did not mention rolls again. He did not get dressed right away, but as was called for he listened while Claire explained. Her hands moved. She clacketed facts like a machine gun and then explained the facts. She was so excited he didn't even dare ask if she wanted coffee while she talked. She had barred his way back to bed or into the kitchen with her enthusiasm that labeled any lack of interest a form of betrayal. Artie knew well the ground he stood on.

"I sent my drawings out to two researchers in England. I wanted to know about this saltcellar. I asked them to research through this picture, so they went looking through catalogues. Then, like I did here, they looked for saltcellars. They looked at books of saltcellars, histories of goldsmiths, and nothing. They said there was no evidence of any jeweled saltcellar. This is important because when you find out how I found out, you'll laugh."

Artie nodded. She filled a daisy T-shirt deliciously, not packed like a cannoli but with lots of tantalizing points and rounds. Artie would have to remember to ask a question when she was done. She was gorgeous in the morning.

"When you track things through history, you see the same thing referred to in different ways and different things referred to in the same way. It can be confusing, but it teaches you things. Like in the Bible, Jonah was swallowed by a great fish. Well, that certainly doesn't explain what it is, although for centuries people thought they meant a whale. But it never said that. And now they think it's a grouper because a whale doesn't have that kind of gullet."

"I don't follow," said Artie. Even at noon he couldn't have followed, a noon with coffee and lots of daylight, with the newspaper read and the mind awake.

"Right," said Claire, beaming. "Because I haven't told you what I did and what I found. I took a chance and got a researcher who had never seen my picture. I didn't even mention the word *cellar*, although the work is obviously British, couldn't be more British if it had the Union Jack chiseled into it. Magnificent scrollwork, grotesque form, God Save the Queen." Her darling blue eyes rose upward on that. Artie was supposed to understand that.

"I described the jewels and the jade lions. I described the amount of gold, and I did not use the name *saltcellar* at all. I mentioned history. Where in history might he find it? I wasn't looking for sales slips from London goldsmiths, mind you."

Artie minded.

"Perhaps I mentioned the word *triumph*, I don't know. But I talked of its grandeur, a grand piece. I talked of royalty. And do you know where he found this cellar?"

Artie shook his head.

"In his uncle's out-of-date schoolbook, in a patriotic passage that would be ridiculous in a British schoolroom today. A schoolbook. To commemorate the victory over the Armada, Queen Elizabeth," said Claire, turning to her green and white computer screen, "did have constructed to a weight of fifty pounds a triumphant gold piece with jade lions rampant—our lions—ennobled with the large Christ's head in a ruby— our ruby—and large sapphire, and diamonds, and lapis lazuli—those little black spots there in my hand-drawn picture—and topaz. I don't remember the topaz, but your friend Rawson's list has them."

"So what do you get? I mean regarding your father."

"Regarding my father, I'm not sure. But I'd like to know how the Rawsons have claim. I understand European laws regarding ownership are different from ours. But I want to find out. For better or for worse I want to find out. Do you think I'm right?" She waited on Artie's words, glancing quickly from her drawing on the wall back to her computer.

Finally Artie asked, "Do you care?"

"Yes. I'm asking." Claire stared drill holes through his eyes.

"It's not my father and it's not my property. In any way."

"Do you think I'm right?" she asked, demanding an answer, impatient and a bit angry that Arthur would even consider attempting to waffle on something he knew was so important to her.

"I see what you're doing here. I didn't understand before, just how much you've done and what you've learned. What you've learned is wonderful."

"Do you think I'm right?"

"You're learning a lot. You really are," said Artie, raising his hands as though trying to contain an upcoming assault, his eyebrows arched high with innocence.

"Answer me. This is important, Arthur," said Claire.

And he knew not only that he had to answer, but that it was going to be something he was going to have to live with, so it had to be fairly close to the truth if not the truth itself.

"You are right if you're not endangering your life, spending money you don't have, wasting your good mind, and because you have room for me, too."

"I think that's yes, Arthur. I think that's yes." For some reason tears rimmed her eyes.

"Yeah. If all those things are so, it's yes," said Artie, and he was allowed to shower as she explained that the researcher now had so much more to work on. He had the Tilbury Cellar, as it was called. They only knew now that it had been locked up at Windsor from 1588 to the printing of the schoolbook. Rawson's claim had to be total balderdash. Total.

"Are we going to see each other tonight?" asked Artie.

"I was planning on it. Did you think we weren't?" asked Claire.

"No. I thought were were. I hoped we were."

Neither of them mentioned what was happening. Artie went to Feldman's apartment house that day and informed the superintendent he was looking for him and also slipped a note under Feldman's door.

Claire and Artie spent that night together and the next and the one after that, and five days later, when they didn't spend a night together both of them missed each other, and Claire suggested he not only come over but bring his toothbrush and a few shirts, just so that he would have them at her place in case.

He said that would be a big step and he wasn't sure of it, and then he showed up with two suitcases and never slept again in his apartment that month, and they both knew without ever saying it that they were living together. Claire thought quite a bit about what it meant, and Artie avoided thinking about it at all. She finally had to tell him it was ridiculous for him to pay so much for an apartment that he wasn't using, and he said he couldn't get out of the lease. As it turned out, he had never read the lease, and Claire got it broken with one phone call. Artie put up fierce resistance to save his furniture, most of which he had never liked, and Claire was able to reason him out of everything but his television set, which she thought he watched too much, and an old chair that he refused to have recovered.

"No. Not the chair. Not a daisy, not a peony, not a silk or burlap. I want the gray covering on the gray cushions the way they stay. That's it. It," boomed Artie setting the chair in front of the television, which occupied a small corner of the living room opposite the computer screen.

She suggested a new gray cover. There were many nice things that could be done with gray. He said the last thing he wanted was another gray cover. He hated gray.

"You're being illogical, Arthur."

"It's my chair. It. Mine. Closed. No talk."

"May I put a little something over the cover?" asked Claire.

"No."

The chair, as it became known, never the lounging chair or just a chair, was the one point that seemed to collect all of Arthur's stubbornness, leaving the rest of his life free of contention. Claire could see the virtues and comfort in his easygoing way, and he was learning to appreciate how thorough she was and how, like most perfectionists, she was unable to take a compliment lying down.

He told her once, during some problem she was having getting information from Windsor Castle about the Tilbury Cellar, that she was perhaps the most fantastic all-around person he had ever met. She answered that she had learned to research and question only because she had to do it. If what she had done was not fantastic, what was? he asked.

"Cooking a seven-course dinner," she answered.

Why didn't it seem surprising that she would pick the one thing she couldn't do well as her yardstick for perfection?

There were sensational times of love that ended in deliriously pleasurable exhaustion, and there were some not-so-sensational times of love, but it was always nice in some way. Sunday mornings, not getting out of bed, reaching for a cup, and then touching, and then just getting carried away from kisses that started out as acknowledgment of happiness and transformed their bodies into passion. Their bodies learned to say things their minds only suspected. And there were flowers, and holding hands, and going places, and going absolutely nowhere and doing nothing in better ways than either of them had ever done the most wondrous things before.

Then one night, just before he went to sleep, Artie said to Claire what he had never said to a woman since he was seventeen, when he used to give it out like Crackerjack rings as another device to score. But this he said as a man and he had been thinking about it for more than a week now. It was a most dangerous thing.

It was a response to one of Claire's constant questions.

"How do you think of me specifically?" she had asked, reading an article in a psychology magazine, with a pencil poised over some list of questions.

"I love you," said Artie. He heard the magazine drop. He pretended it was a chance remark and kept his eyes closed. Finally she asked, "Have you had many women?"

"I haven't loved many."

"How many have you loved?"

"Loved?" asked Artie. He knew he was in dangerous territory, but he answered fairly truthfully anyhow. "Just you."

"You've only slept with me? I can't believe that."

It was getting more dangerous than he had planned.

"You asked love, Claire."

"I understood that. Now I am asking how many you've slept with."

"Because I told you I love you and you're the only one I love, is that why we have to move into an area of possible contention?" He kept his eyes closed, but it was a ridiculous defense.

"I know you love me, Arthur. I was curious about other women."

"I've slept with others. All right? And they don't matter."

"How many?"

"I dunno. They aren't important. You are. There's only one number that's important to me. And that's the right one."

"Roughly how many?" she asked.

"Who counts? Sick people count."

"A thousand?"

"No. Of course not."

"Five hundred?"

"What is it with you and numbers?" The eyes were open and he was sitting up in bed. Her magazine was on her lap and she was staring directly down at him. It was the clear curious eye of a biologist examining what was beneath her.

"Five hundred. You've slept with five hundred women."

"Thirty, maybe. Maybe thirty."

Claire Andrews pushed herself to the other side of the bed. She did the pushing off Artie's chest.

"You've slept with thirty women?" she asked, her voice ringing with horror.

"I didn't know you at the time," said Artie. His chest hurt.

"Thirty women, Arthur. That's terrible."

"No, it's not. If I go out and sleep with someone else now, that's terrible," said Artie, offering fidelity, something he had not openly promised before.

"What does someone think of sex when he sleeps with thirty women?"

"You want to know the truth. I'll tell you the truth. Wonderful. I thought wonderful."

"Do you think of yourself as promiscuous, Arthur?"

"No."

"I think that's promiscuous. Thirty women."

She pondered that a moment and went out to get a glass of water for both of them. She wondered what things he had done with thirty women. She wondered if that were thirty women in total, or thirty serious or relatively serious women in total. She wondered if that meant he was unstable.

What she really wondered was whether she was thirty-one between thirty and thirty-two, and how thirty-one fared against the field, and hated the idea of a field, until he did the absolutely right thing when she returned with the water.

He kissed her and told her he would at that moment have given up having the experience of all the other thirty if he had known she was going to come along.

He did not ask her about her number of times, but she wanted to tell him. There had been someone else, but he was not nice, and he was not a good lover. For someone who had had thirty women, Arthur was too interested in how he stacked up against that one. And Claire told him truthfully that the other had no meaning, other than being a very unpleasant first and second time.

"Do you love me? You didn't say, you know?"

"When I'm absolutely sure, Arthur, I'll tell you. I've given it an awful lot of thought."

"That I'm sure, Claire. You give everything an awful lot of thought."

"Do you think I think too much?"

"No."

"Do you mean that?"

"No."

She wanted at that moment to tell him she loved him. But did she? It was a very good question, and it didn't let her sleep. He was not the kind of person she expected to fall in love with. But what kind did she expect? He certainly didn't share as much with her as Bob Truet could.

Arthur was from a different place. He thought of a pumpkin as something exotic and of baklava as a snack. She watched him doze off. She didn't want to lose him. Was that love? Was it ownership she felt? Was it pure sexual pleasure she felt? Was it an end to loneliness she felt?

Was it love?

She put on her bathrobe and went out into her living room. She wished her father was here to talk about it with her. Poor Dad, she thought, as she looked at her drawing of the cellar made so long ago. He had tried to sell it whole apparently. If anything, that was a proof of innocence. What confluence of wealth and desire for such different stones would come together to buy a monster like that? If Dad were dishonest, then he would have broken down the cellar.

His ignorance could be a proof of his moral innocence, if not of the legality of his owning the cellar.

What was bothering her?

Arthur was not the man she had pictured as falling in love with. Arthur was not like Dad. But he certainly had everything she needed, and wanted, things she didn't know she wanted until he gave them to her, like the comforting touches, like listening to her, and being proud of her, and thinking she was wonderful.

Bob Truet thought she was wonderful. But it was not the same. Why was it not the same?

Deep into the darkest hours of morning, Claire came up with the answer to that question and many others. She went into the bedroom, kissed Arthur on the lips, and said, "I love you."

"Love you, too," he said and rolled over, going back to sleep. She was tempted to wake him up and make him be aware of this wonderful thing she had acknowledged. But that was not the way to deal with Arthur. He did not respond well to absolutes, and he did like his sleep. As much as she wanted certainty in this relationship above all, she knew only the days together would let them know for certain where they were going. The rest was hope, and all the questioning and all the analysis could not change it.

She was in the most wonderful thing of her life and it was beyond organizing into categories.

The next day, her latest researcher in England came up with some disquieting news. The Tilbury Cellar, according to Windsor Castle, was still there; it had never left.

"Are you sure?" asked Claire.

"There was an article in May of 1945 about schoolchildren prevailing upon the Crown not to sell off the Tilbury or any Crown jewels to help pay what everyone knew would be a monstrous war debt. Course none of us knew at the time, the debt would be the British Empire."

"And they didn't sell it. Are you sure?"

"Absolutely. Still there. I have some more information if you want it. The cellar was called the Tilbury because Tilbury was where it was fashioned by Simon Sedgewick of London."

"And what was his maker's mark?" asked Claire.

"On this special cellar there was no maker's mark. It was taken right from Tilbury Field and, in honor of the victory and the sturdy British seamen, never allowed to be used for salt."

"Never used for salt?" asked Claire. That was Dad's. Somehow, that royal cellar might have been sold off secretly and he just as secretly bought it.

"Never," said the researcher.

"Send me a picture of the Tilbury," said Claire.

" 'Fraid they just don't do that."

"Why not? I can buy pictures of the Crown jewels. What's so special about the Tilbury?"

"It's not done. I asked."

"Why isn't it done?"

"Lots of royal possessions are not photographed."

"Offer them money."

"It's royal."

"That means you can't get it, right?"

"Yes."

"Do you know for certain a picture has never been made? Could you tell me that?"

"No, I couldn't."

"All right. This is what I would like you to do. I want you to check out the artists of England from 1588 onward and any foreign references to the valuables of Elizabeth. Don't read everything right away. Just go looking for the forest, so to speak."

"Quite a forest."

"It always seems formidable at first, but once you get the forest, you understand better how to go through it."

"Well . . ."

"I know it seems awesome now, but it works. Once you have the size of it, you'll see what can be discarded in simple quick decisions. Believe me, it works. I know. How good are you on foreign langauges?"

"I speak five."

"European?"

"Yes."

"Good. There was a time of tremendous intrigue between the Continent and England. On the foreign stuff, sort of let yourself follow Britain's interests at the time. Who were they considering alliances with and things like that."

"What would that do?"

"If somebody wants to woo someone, they invite them to dinner, so to speak. Who knows what they would show to or confide in about with someone they want as an ally. They might share things they wouldn't with their closest court members. More importantly, a foreigner writing about England would notice things your own native British historians and diarists might not. It's a way to go. And look for visits to Windsor especially. Okay?" she said. And added, "Am I overloading you?"

"It's a bit."

"Phone me in two days and let me know how you're doing. I can get you help. In the meanwhile, ship me everything you have so far on the Tilbury."

She wrote down the date and the assignment in the researcher's file and then added a list of more questions she would ask Harry Rawson if she made contact again. Somehow Arthur seemed to be able to reach him and she never could. And why did Arthur like him? She started to add this question to the Modelstein file, when suddenly she erased every reference to Arthur's name, leaving only questions for the police. Arthur was not part of this file. He was part of her life.

Two days later her researcher called; he had struck paydirt. There was a Count Desini of Bologna, an ally of Queen Elizabeth I in her struggle with the Roman Catholic Church. Bologna contested papal lands at that time, and although the Desinis were staunch Catholics, they had a friendly interest in English survival, especially after it defeated the Armada.

Count Orofino Desini had visited Elizabeth at Greenwich and at Windsor and had described both in diaries, including "many strange and wondrous objects." There were no diaries available in Britain, but the descendants still lived in Bologna and were generally friendly to anyone wishing to promote the Desini name. But the best news was that the count fancied himself an artist and sketched many things, particularly the unusual.

"You stay there. You've done beautifully. I'll phone the family," said Claire. "Wonderful."

"And if they don't speak English?" asked the researcher.

"I'll work out something. Thanks," said Claire.

She waited until morning to dial Bologna, and with a translator she had hired for the occasion, she made a search by phone for the Desini residences. She did not need the translator when she reached a niece of the Contessa Desini. Yes, as one of the most important families on the Continent, said the niece, the Desinis most certainly did archive their history.

The niece knew of the Count Orofino Desini's diaries.

"He was, madame, possibly a consort of the queen herself, although being a gentleman he did not mention that in his diaries."

"I am interested in any mention of a large gold piece. It could be referred to as a saltcellar. It was heavily jeweled. Gold."

"A relic?"

"No. An English piece. Big. Gold. A ruby. A sapphire. Diamonds. Jade. Lapis lazuli. Topaz chips and such."

"The Count Orofino?"

"Yes."

"Are you with a magazine?"

"No. I am researching a big gold piece."

"For a book? You will include us in a book?"

"I may write a book, yes," said Claire, which was not altogether a lie, but not altogether the truth either. Because she also might become a professional golfer, and so far she didn't really care for the game.

"I will look," said the niece.

"He would have seen it at Windsor. It was called the Tilbury Cellar, though I am not sure it would have been called that then."

"Good. I will phone you back. The Count Orofino was greatly responsible for the development of Bologna. Did you know that?"

"No, I didn't. I'm sure that's important."

"To us, yes. Cheers."

"Ciao," said Claire. Why was the woman using a British form of farewell? Why did Claire use Italian?

Before 10:00 A.M., Claire found out that there was another record of the cellar made at Tilbury, viewed and sketched by Count Orofino Desini. But regrettably, the family did not allow copies to be made. These were private papers, and if Claire Andrews wished to read them, the Desinis would be more than happy to provide her a room in one of their residences for such. But a picture, no. And photocopy, definitely not. Photocopying cooked delicate old parchment with its harsh light, reverting it back to the unstretched shape of its original sheepskin.

And unfortunately, there were few words to read over the telephone. The count had decided to leave the world and posterity not words, but a physical sketch of the cellar.

"I'll be right over," said Claire to the lady in Bologna, Italy. When Artie asked what she wanted to do this weekend, she said she already had it planned for both of them.

XXI

And indeed, it is true, as the story of the Holy Grail testifies, that
none ever saw him weary from the labors of his calling.
                                        —WALTER MAP
                                 Queste del Saint Graal, 1225

Just before he left for Italy with
Claire, Artie got the strangest phone call from Feldman. The first strange
thing was that he phoned at all. Artie had been trying unsuccessfully to
reach him for weeks. The second was that he gave a direct warning.

"Watch yourself. You have no idea where you're going or what
you're doing."

"Get your ruby yet, old man?" asked Artie.

"Artie, do you know who everyone is?"

"By everyone you mean who?"

"You don't know who. You don't know what. You go running after
your cock like it's the Grand Concourse in the Bronx."

Artie signaled that he wanted the call traced and simultaneously
pressed the switch that taped the conversation. He was in Frauds/Jewels.

"You said we'd never find those gems. Well, we found them in New
York. We found them in Paris. You know Paris, don't you?"

"I know you have no idea why that dead man even got the sapphire.

I'm trying to tell you, schmuck. This is different and dangerous. All I can do is warn you."

"What are you warning me about, old man?"

"Lady Jennings got the sapphire at a good price."

"You know her? She speaks to you?" asked Artie.

"Young man, she does. She does not speak to Werner Gruenwald, and she does not speak to Dr. Peter Martins."

"What's this with Dr. Peter Martins?" asked Artie. Dr. Martins had been one of the prizes longed for by Frauds/Jewels for years. It wasn't the protection of his society friends that saved him; this former surgeon was always just slick enough to be beyond even being charged with anything. Yet Artie knew the man was a fence, even if his customers were in some kind of blue book. Since the first day of chasing the cellar, this was the only name he had recognized.

"Dr. Martins is one of your people. He's a gonif, Artie, and he was one of those buying the cellar from your girlie's daddy, selling inside a bank vault. All those gems inside a damned bank vault."

"Her father was a businessman. He wasn't a thief. No," said Artie.

"What's this 'no.' He was selling the cellar from a bank vault to anyone for fast cash."

"How do you know?"

"I love you, asshole," said Feldman and hung up. Love? Artie was still trying to figure that out when he was told that the trace had Feldman in his office, but when Artie went up to Feldman's business place, Feldman was not there, and no one had seen him there for weeks. Which, of course, was wrong. Feldman did move in mysterious ways, ways outside of Artie's knowledge. Was Harry Rawson right about the blow into the head? Was it something that special? Dr. Martins, a surgeon, could have delivered that blow. And what did Feldman mean about love? Artie liked him. He knew he was possibly the only one who liked him. But they would go years without talking. Perhaps, thought Artie, in a life so bereft of human contact, Feldman mistook friendship for love. A cracker could look like a banquet to the starving. The more he knew about Feldman, the less Artie realized he had ever known him. Was he lying? Why bother to lie about that?

And the killings?

And there was Claire's father.

Artie went direct to the International Bank branch on Madison Avenue, where Claire had said her father had stored the cellar in New York. He had the access sign-in card pulled for evidence and dusted for fingerprints, along with comparisons of handwriting, specifically for Dr. Peter Martins. But Artie didn't need prints or handwriting analysis to tell him what he really didn't want to know about Vern Andrews. There were fifteen names. Vern Andrews had been selling the cellar from the vault. And ten of the fifteen names were James Smith, of which one checked out absolutely to Dr. Peter Martins, a known dealer in stolen gems on whom somebody someday was going to make a good first-time collar.

Vern Andrews had gotten this large safety deposit box on short notice because his lawyer was a director of the Carney National Bank, which did business with International. The lawyer was named Comstock, and he acted very lawyerly over the phone, until Artie told him bluntly there was no way he was ever going to charge a dead man with selling hot goods. This was for the benefit of Vern's daughter Claire.

"Claire will not believe her father was anything but a saint. Now, of course, I would never admit to assisting someone selling hot goods. I didn't know what the safety deposit box was for," said Comstock.

"I'm not looking for you either," said Artie. "Look, you wouldn't just happen to have anything that might prove his ownership?"

There was laughter from Carney, Ohio. Of course not. Every James Smith on that access card knew it was stolen. And so did Artie before he asked the question. And so, of course, did the man who wouldn't trust the police or jewelry establishments for protection, Vern Andrews.

Comstock went on: "I've known Vern and his family for years, and I respected Vern. But Vern would cut any corner he could. Just about everyone in Carney knows this except Claire. Is she all right?"

"Yeah. She's okay."

"Why are you calling now?"

"Just checking out some names."

"Anything new happen regarding that cellar?" asked the lawyer.

"No," said Artie. So the story hadn't gotten to Carney, interestingly enough. But then why should the guilty plea of a rabbi's son and the torture death of a cutter over diamonds be important to Carney, Ohio, any more than a murder in Geneva would be news in New York City. The fact was, none of the newspapers had yet to connect them all.

"Let me know if anything turns up, and whatever you do for Claire Andrews will be appreciated here, and let me tell you we know how to express our appreciation concretely."

For a flash of a moment, Artie wondered whether Carney, Ohio, might be more like Mordechai Baluzzian's Tehran than New York. But only for a flash.

So Artie knew what Claire didn't want to believe was so, and not for one moment did he consider telling her about her father. In fact, he even resented the lawyer revealing that Andrews cut corners. Was Claire right when she contended that now that this once powerful man was dead, the envy came out in little slices of venom? The lawyer didn't have to tell him about Vern Andrews and corners. Of course, it was Claire who was the only one who didn't know, Claire the rational, Claire the conqueror of infinity and the wearing years of history, Claire the indomitable, Claire the lovely, Claire the sweet, Claire of the Cherry Cokes and frozen dinners and laughter, sweet and honest Claire. Your daddy was a crook.

On the plane over to Italy, Claire sensed something was wrong and when she asked, and Artie answered that he loved her, she took it as an admission. And of course pressed on until she got an answer. So Artie came up with one.

"I was worried about Feldman. He phoned a couple of days before we left," said Artie. They were going to spend a weekend in Bologna and he was going to enjoy it, although the tourist class seats in the back of the plane were already pinching and they weren't twenty minutes out of Kennedy. "He said because Lady Jennings got a good price on the sapphire, something was wrong with the people who sold it. I didn't quite follow."

Claire put down her notes on her plaid skirt. She didn't even have to think about it.

"What he means by Lady Jennings getting a good price is that anyone she bought it from had to be selling it at the wrong price, and the one who sold it originally, the Swiss businessman, had to have sold it for the worst price of all. Which meant he wasn't part of that business."

"So what's wrong with that?" asked Artie.

"For us, nothing. Although it could mean strange people were dealing in it. Crooks. Killers. People like that," said Claire.

"Oh," said Artie. She was so sharp and she didn't make the connection with her father.

"Arthur, when we get back, could you reach Captain Rawson for me?"

"Can I stay out of it?"

"What do you mean by that?" asked Claire.

"I'm in this too much. You know, it's your search and Homicide's problem, and you have a claim and Harry has a claim, and that's for lawyers. I love you, Claire, and I don't mix love well with work."

"I still don't follow, Arthur. Is something else wrong?"

"No," said Artie and scrunched himself into a comfortable position in the tight seat and then went comfortably asleep to the droning rhythm of the jet engines crossing the Atlantic.

Claire hated that in him. It was not that he could leave a problem by feigning sleep. She knew he really was asleep. He had done this before. She had awakened him before. It was like starting an argument with someone just getting out of bed. On the other hand, Claire would wrench every straw and fiber of a problem into orderly rows if it took till dawn. They were so different, she thought, loving his dark beautiful face asleep against the window, his arms folded over his chest, his mouth open, snoring. She got a blanket from the overhead bin and covered him. She would get him on this later.

Artie awoke over the Atlantic for dinner.

Claire, who had been trying to establish the British situation in 1588 for some explanation of the strange security procedures regarding that strangely jeweled cellar, said, "Why are you denying me help in my search?"

"What?" asked Artie.

"For some reason, you want out now. I asked you to phone someone you have access to, Captain Rawson. I want to set up a meeting with him. I have some very interesting questions."

"All right. I'll phone when we get back," said Artie, arranging his tray, noting they did not serve champagne on this economy flight as they did on the Concorde. "Do you want salt?"

"I have it on my tray. You know what I mean," said Claire.

"We're going to enjoy ourselves in Italy, aren't we?"

"As much as we can, of course. You know what I mean."

"The Concorde had great champagne."

"You know what I mean," said Claire. She knew he could not sleep while he ate.

"You want me to be as committed to this thing of yours as you are, and I'm not. I'm sorry."

"Committed, but not as committed, of course," said Claire.

"I'm committed to you, Claire Andrews," said Artie. He wore an open-necked shirt that hinted at the large dark-haired chest he knew Claire liked to feel she owned. He kissed her on the cheek. The cheek did not move. The fork in Claire Andrews's hand did not move. Nor did the very rigid spine.

Artie went back to his appetizer, a warm creamy shrimp dish. He ate for a while, until Claire's fork landed on his plate quite sharply.

"No," he said. "I am along for the ride because you're taking it. I'm sorry. That's who I am."

"I'm sorry, too," said Claire.

"Does that mean something?" asked Artie.

"It means I'm sorry, but I'll have to work out the rest. You know I have to think things through. But I suspect it just means I'm sorry, that's all. I would have thought that by now you would have shared some of my enthusiasm."

"I am more in love with you than with anyone or anything in my life. Ever," said Artie, and fixed his stare on her eyes. They refused to meet his.

"All right," she said.

"Not all right," he said angrily.

"Wonderful," she said, and turned to see him waiting for her and they kissed long and hard on the plane, and then they laughed together and ate their meal.

It was a night flight to Bologna, and while Artie slept through it, Claire worked. He didn't even awake for the landing and only when Claire nudged him did he look around for where he was.

Claire was fresh as a white sunrise beach.

"How do you do it?" asked Artie, when they were waiting for their luggage, and he had unsuccessfully tried to fall asleep while leaning against a post.

"The trick is you don't go to sleep. That's how you get tired. Sleep makes you tired. That's how I studied for exams. I'd stay up all night and go right in while I was fresh."

Claire, the sleepless. Even her plaid skirt remained pressed, and her light blue silk blouse, with the sweater tied around her neck, made it seem as though she was just up for the day, instead of having worked through the night into another time zone.

Artie had kept his sports jacket in the luggage just to make sure it stayed fresh. He got a cab for them, and instead of going to their hotel, as he wished with the fervor of the sleep deprived, they met the Contessa in her home for breakfast.

Signora Desini wore black, with an elegant strand of white pearls, and served them little cakes with sharp bitter coffee on her stone veranda. A butler was there to bring things. It was an intimate, pleasant little repast with a magnificent city laid out before them from this old villa that had once been a castle. Claire, so recently of Carney, Ohio, supposedly the wallflower, looked as though she had been born to breakfast with the nobility. Artie nodded politely, then dozed. Claire talked politics, four hundred-year-old politics.

Signora Desini stressed that during Count Orofino's time there were problems in England, deep religious problems, where politics and faith were one, and leaving the Church of Rome was only a small, small part spiritual. This all was to prepare them for viewing the diary of the count.

It was kept in a room of its own in an air-controlled case, which had to be unlocked by inserting a brass key into a stainless steel tube at the side. There was a slight hiss with the air rushing in as Signora Desini turned the key. She lifted the heavy glass lid over the case and removed a leather-bound volume a good foot thick, its wavy yellow parchment pages pressed down by centuries.

"Moisture is the enemy of parchment," said Signora Desini and put the book onto a black wood table, on which light from tall, thin leaded glass windows shone pale and white in the cold stone room of the Desini archives.

She opened the book for Claire, proudly, like a hostess showing off her favorite room and letting the guest enter first to get the full impact of its beauty.

Claire touched the yellowed page tentatively. Signora Desini beamed. Artie sat down on a chair, excusing himself for sitting while the ladies stood.

"I'm almost afraid to look," said Claire.

"The truth can be wonderful, too, sometimes," said Signora Desini.

Claire turned the pages very carefully, seeing the count's sketches and writing, in the fine black ink of an artist's pen. The soft stretch of old parchment in leather binding played against the silence encapsuled underneath the dark vaulted ceiling. The odor of old candle wax wafted into the walls over centuries came back again on this warm breezeless day among the silent stones.

Claire turned the pages. Everyone could hear the book creak.

"This is Latin," said Claire.

"The only language for the educated then."

"Queen Elizabeth spoke six languages fluently," said Claire. She was whispering. In this room, one did not have to talk loudly. Claire imagined orders being given for a thousand plots against a thousand friends and allies in this room, each whispering in some other castle of a thousand other plots against the Desinis.

She imagined great works of art being commissioned and people dying young of diseases they could not cure. Of superstition and genius, of Michelangelo, Da Vinci, and of Cellini and the delicate work of art that was his saltcellar.

And she turned the pages until on reaching one she sat down gasping.

There in the fine pen strokes of an Italian count dead for centuries was the cellar she had seen in Dad's basement back in Carney. That was lucky. The polished diamonds as round little tubes at the base. The great ruby with Christ's head implanted on a thick bosom of gold. The jade lions even more graceful than she remembered—perhaps the count's innate sense of art overcoming his need for accuracy. And the Poseidon sapphire, Poseidon so well drawn and called, of course, in this manuscript, Neptuno, the Roman version being Neptune. She put a photocopy of her crude drawing from memory next to it. Considering the years, the ages, it was recognizable enough.

"Yes," said Claire. "Arthur, look."

Artie leaned over from his chair.

"That's it. That's the Tilbury. That's Dad's. They're the same," she said.

He nodded. He was thinking hotel. If she had shown him a mushroom next to a wildebeest, he would have nodded. He thought of soft, warm Italian beds, with sheets and pillows, and lots of sleep, perhaps waking up to some very special kind of breakfast.

"What do you think, Arthur?"

"Good. Very good," said Artie. "That's it. We got it. Let's go."

"Signora, could you tell me what the count says? I don't know Latin."

"He says this is the great jeweled gold piece of Elizabeth, without form, without purpose, but which she showed him as a sign of her nation's power. He proposed to her a question about the form of power, that without purpose and direction, which Bologna could help provide, power could be formless, and her answer was typically English, that power didn't need form or Bologna at too high a price."

"What was the price?"

"He doesn't say."

"Does he say anything else about the Tilbury Cellar, the power perhaps?"

"That it was called Tilbury and crafted there, within the smell of the sea that had protected the pride of England."

"Was he insulted?"

"I sense that. We were an older house than the Tudors, after all."

"Is there any mention of the reasons for the jewels?"

Signora Desini said she was sorry, but no. They were difficult times, and he would put nothing in paper that he did not expect someone to steal a look at. There were even greater Desinis than Count Orofino, the Desinis being one of the exceptional families of Europe, older than the Hapsburgs, did Claire know?

When Claire and Artie drove down from the hill from which the Desinis had ruled almost since the cross became a symbol of worship and not execution, Artie said, even as his body dozed, "She's married to that family."

"Is that what you thought?" asked Claire.

"Sure. What'd you think?"

"I was thinking, why sleep in a hotel when you can sleep on a plane to Britain?"

"No," said Artie.

"We know it's the Tilbury. We know we've seen it. We know for certain that there can't be three similar cellars with the same stones, the same placement even. Therefore, my father's cellar was originally called the Tilbury. What happened to it and why, I want to find out. We've never been so close, Arthur."

"The hotel," said Artie, who wondered how Claire could sidestep Rawson's claim so easily. He knew she had to have some kind of an answer and he didn't want to hear it. He wanted a bed, sheeted, pillowed, and fluffed and warmed from his body, possibly even hers also.

"What if you were in the army, and you were close to winning the major battle—would you go to sleep?"

"I understood those things about the army and warfare, Claire, when I chose to be a policeman instead of a paratrooper, or whatever."

"I'm surprised you even became a policeman."

"I have yet to be apprised of the moment I vowed to give up sleep for an NYPD badge."

"It's so important, Arthur."

"So am I."

"Of course you are," said Claire and kissed him, and then snuggled into him and then asked exactly how much sleep he was going to need before he felt rested.

They were delayed getting to the hotel by a procession for St. Julian. Artie slept as Claire watched, the music from the little band providing more cacophony than rhythm. She could feel the excitement of the townspeople. On the platform borne on the shoulders of men dressed in black came a gold foot with jewels.

"What's that?"

"Da foota Blesseda Sainta Julian," said the driver.

"Not his *real* foot? His real *foot*?"

"Si. Da foota. Julian, he giva da foota to his people. You wanta baby, pretty lady? Touch da foota." The driver turned around, explaining with his hand. Claire had read about relics of pieces of saints' bodies, but she had never seen one before. The driver kept explaining how powerful it was. Perhaps because he repeated it so much, Claire started to feel that maybe the remnant of the saint's body in the gold and jewels actually could do things. Of course, it couldn't. This fervent Catholicism was so different from her Presbyterian faith.

She told the driver to follow the procession. It ended at a church. The people sang and clapped their way in. She didn't know whether she could trust the driver or the people, so she took Arthur's wallet and passport from his jacket and told the driver to tell Arthur she had them if he woke up.

She made her way into the rear of the church. The gold-encased foot now rested on its platform before the altar. She wondered what Christ would do if he saw people in his name worshiping a gold-encased foot. They went up one by one and touched the gold foot, kissed it. Some touched and kissed their hands.

Claire could not imagine her Catholic friends doing such a thing. She had been to a Catholic mass at Ohio State, and she could not remotely imagine the intelligent, highly rational priest at the Newman Center involved in anything like this.

It was scary. It was so pagan. She was glad she was Presbyterian. She would rather follow Reb Schnauer and cut off her hair, and even take a subordinate role as a woman, than worship the gold-encased foot of a corpse. How crude. How frightening that people would do it. She found herself moved forward in the line shuffling ahead. People were saying things to the foot up front. She was going to be put in front of that thing. What could she do?

Would she laugh out loud at these poor people? She didn't want to insult them. But it was so funny. Asking the foot of a dead person to help them. What would Arthur say? If Julian were so powerful, why was he dead? Arthur would say that. She hoped she wouldn't laugh.

She would be polite. She would nod politely, not to the foot, but to the priest. Perhaps she would say thank you. What would she do if someone tried to press her hand to the foot in mistaken sympathy for her, as though she were ignorant. Would she firmly but politely not allow her hand to touch it? Why was she so bothered when she had seen people do worse? Because she was in it. She was very much in it, now, moving up to the gold-encased foot.

For a moment she thought she would turn her head away, but that would be acceding to some sort of supernatural power. It was only a piece of a dead person, which would have been buried had it been in Carney.

Thus thinking, she allowed herself to be moved amid the incensed air, along the nave of the church to the front, where a woman bowed and kissed the gold encasing the shape of a foot, leaving Claire in front of it, pure glistening gold with baguette cut emeralds and small beads of cabochon sapphires, about two karats each, implanted in the base beneath it. In that casing were bones centuries old from a man canonized by his church, one who, it was proved, had done some sort of miracle. A priest stood beside the foot wiping off with white linen where the woman had just kissed that worn big toe.

Everyone had touched it.

Help me find the answers, Claire begged in thought, as she bent down kissing the toe.

She couldn't help herself. She was just drawn to its power. Like any superstitious peasant. It had been there. Visible. Touchable. Kissable. And thank God, no one had seen her do it. Arthur was still asleep in the car when she returned.

"Itsa' powaful," said the driver.

"Yes," said Claire.

He went on about the strength of St. Julian's foot, how it made Bologna great, greater than Naples, Milan. What did they have, he asked, in the way of powerful relics? He answered his own question in clear English.

"They gotta shit. Who they got? Saint Gennaro? He's shit." It was like someone going down a baseball lineup.

Arthur slept eight hours and ate two meals and wanted to see more of Bologna before they left. Claire said they could come back on a longer vacation sometime. She almost said honeymoon. Did she want to marry him?

Artie ate again on the plane to London. He asked why Claire didn't suffer jet lag.

"I do. I just don't let it get to me," she said to him.

In London, the only available room was in the Brittania Hotel, expensive, but with a good desk and telephone service. They got an official custodian at Windsor Castle, who explained that while they might visit those rooms open to the public, the Tilbury vault was not one of them.

"Well, I don't believe it's there," Artie heard her say as he lay on the bed, watching her lean over the desk. She had the white-handled telephone pressed to her ear and she was writing down things.

He stripped to his shorts and T-shirt and put his hands behind his head. When he thought she was looking at him, he waved and smiled broadly.

She ignored him.

"I can prove to you it's not there," she said into the phone.

There was another pause. Artie took off his shorts and waved those. She ignored him.

"Well, how do you know, if you haven't seen it? Yes, I would like to talk to him."

Artie stood up in bed, nude from the waist down.

Claire turned away to the wall. "All I am asking is to speak to someone who has seen it, that's all. I want nothing else. Yes. I will wait."

Artie took off his T-shirt and threw it at Claire's head. She caught it, put it on the desk, and folded it with one hand as she talked.

"I didn't think you had. Yes, I would. I would be most happy to speak to him. Absolutely . . . ," said Claire. She held out Artie's folded shirt for him to take.

"These people are such jerks. I do believe now that something worth millions could well be lost. No one has seen it. No one has seen it. And they say it's there. How do they know it's there, right?"

"Look at me," said Artie.

"Here's your shirt," said Claire.

"Hey, look at me."

"Arthur, please. Later."

He waited with the shirt in his hand, an arm's reach from her and she didn't even know he was there. She was on the phone again, now calling people fools directly. Artie made out that she was talking to someone in the British government.

"Listen, I know I saw the Tilbury Cellar in New York City. Now what's going on here? What kind of a shell game are you playing? You're damned right I'm calling you a liar, and she's a damned liar, too."

Claire slammed down the phone and cried. Finally, she looked at Artie.

"They're such damned liars and idiots. And she is the worst liar of them all. It is so frustrating. I am run around and around and around. Arthur, believe me, if there is one big liar in the world it's her. She's behind it. I'm sure. To hell with all of them."

"Who's she?"

"The Queen. I couldn't even get past some damn clerks."

"Of England?"

"They didn't even bother to lie well, Arthur. That's what's so frustrating. I catch them in lies, and they just repeat them."

Artie put on the shirt, and he put on the pants, and gently he eased Claire away from the telephone to a couch. She started to talk and he put a finger to her lips.

"You've been up for two days, dear," he said softly. "Even super Saint Claire Andrews has to rest. I know you will consider a need to sleep like the rest of us a sign of special moral weakness in yourself. But the human body needs it. Even yours."

He held her in his arms even as she talked away, but when he felt her hair against his face, he knew she had finally succumbed. He carried her into bed, where she slumbered half a day, and when she woke up they made love in the big soft bed with all of England outside, quite chill, and quite distant from their beautiful room and beautiful lives.

She moved her cheek along his and whispered, "Why would they lie?"

Artie got out of bed and got dressed and pointing a finger at her head, said, "Enough."

"Arthur, we're so close to the answers. My father died over this. I'm so close to the meaning of the Tilbury. How many cellars in the world would have those stones, identical, let alone being placed identically?"

"That doesn't matter. Not when we're making love."

"We were finished."

"I wasn't."

Artie turned from her and went outside for a walk in a cold March rain in a leafless park outside the hotel. He walked the dark paths under dripping dead-limbed trees, fuming, and when he got back to their room, Claire was dressed. She looked so adorable and fresh, and he couldn't stay mad long, not when she was laughing.

Fortunately, she did not review every last detail of her phone calls around Britain at that moment, but took him sightseeing. To the Tower of London no less.

It was not a tower but a sprawling dark stone fort where the British had mangled various members of the populace who, now that they weren't a danger to Crown and country, were considered heroes of history.

Claire squeezed his arm as the Beefeater guide led them with a little group along the paths of the fort interior. For her, she said, it was like going home. She had read so much about England at the time the Tilbury was made, according to the scant information they let out.

"You know Elizabeth wouldn't stay here," said Claire.

"Who?" asked Artie.

"Elizabeth the First. She was confined here for a while before she was Queen. This used to be a royal residence, but her mother was beheaded here so she never used it for a royal residence. She did her torturing here. In those days it was a common punishment. Today, torture's only used by some governments to get information."

The dark stone walls, the walks, the ravens, the rooms where royalty had stayed and royalty had killed were all so close about her now. Like a great hunter she could get the scent of the quarry. It was so close and so far from that 3:00 A.M. alone with a blank wall in her Queens apartment. Those first marks had led her here. She had found this place and the time in infinity.

At the building with the Crown jewels, she paused before a display of royal saltcellars behind glass. If one put jewels into the massive cylinders of ornate gold, one would have the Tilbury. There was the very same feel to them. She squeezed Arthur's arm tighter. It was here. Every reason for it was right here. Near here. Somewhere here. Moving crowds pushed them on to where the crown of England was on display too, heavily jeweled, with that central red stone that later ages showed was not a ruby. She watched Arthur. She wondered if he were estimating the price of something like that for one of his jeweler friends.

"What do you think it's worth?" she asked.

He cocked his head. "The way they use gold and jewels is different from anything I've seen. Those jewels in the crown represent power. Lots of fanfare. Knights and ladies, all that stuff. It's a crown. Not a bracelet or earrings."

"You're right. But it reminds me of something I saw in Bologna. A sense of holiness in the way people used jewels. I mean this crown and those cellars are different. And the people who made them knew they were different. And don't get mad at me, but my father's cellar, the Tilbury, reminds me more of the crown than those saltcellars."

"I was thinking that, too," said Artie. "From your sketch."

She hugged his arm.

In the building displaying English armor, Artie became depressed when he saw deadly crossbows, polished swords, and a wall of lances, hundreds of them.

"Killing. That's what it was. I should've known. The crown was window dressing. This is what it was. Killing. Harry Rawson was right. It's a bloody history. Knights and ladies and jousts. Horseshit. They killed with these things."

"Didn't you know that?" asked Claire.

"I knew it. But when you see all this machinery polished and ready, you know it was gang warfare, and the toughest gang was the King's. This place ruins England for me."

England got better for Artie when they walked along the Thames, past Waterloo Bridge, along the Victoria Embankment, looking at the steady opaque flow of the mud-dead river and the new boats moving quietly. Here was the sense of propriety that he liked, an order and a politeness in which, if a person minded his own business and did not pick fights, he could get along quite nicely without any of that lance and spear mayhem back in the Tower.

His hand found hers, and they walked languidly without a destination, feeling the dampness, sharing the newness of things in this country, and the oldness, and the differences and the similarities, and it seemed so soon that they were on the Westminster Bridge and Big Ben was behind them, and Artie stopped and took Claire in his arms and kissed her with all the love he had. He said he would like to spend a month here sometime, and she agreed, and neither of them mentioned honeymoon.

"Arthur, since we're here, I would like to proceed with something, and I'd like your help. It's just one thing. Please."

Artie didn't want to ask what. He was silent. Stately cars passed them without the honk and din of New York traffic.

"The statement from Scotland Yard that you gave me, the photocopy—"

"Yeah?"

"Could you as a New York City policeman go to Scotland Yard and ask to see the original and see if the paper is suitably aged, get a feel to see if it's new as I suspect. It may not be. The British could have faked that report, I suspect, from what I know of the Tilbury. I think I understand Captain Rawson's place in all this. I think he is working for some sort of fraud very possibly by the Crown of England. While you're doing that, I will travel to Windsor."

"You'll go there and do what?"

"I am going to sit there until they show me the Tilbury. Make them arrest me or something. I think that just might force them to open up. I wouldn't do this, Arthur, if we weren't so damned close. Damned close."

"Close to what? What are you looking for?" asked Artie.

"What's behind this all."

"Why?"

"You know how I feel about my father."

"You're not going to prove him innocent, Claire, because he wasn't."

"Arthur!"

She stepped back from him, her feet planted on the bridge, her face tightening in anger.

"Yeah, he wasn't storing that cellar in the vault; he was selling it," said Artie.

"So?"

"To a bunch of crooks. Everyone knew it was hot. They didn't use their right names. And one of them was a major gem thief."

"That's their problem. Dad had financial problems that required discretion. That is why he would sell it from a vault."

"You mean to say he didn't know Tiffany's was discreet. Cartier's was discreet. Bulgari was discreet. Hey, he wasn't a yokel. He knew. Those places are where men buy jewelry for their mistresses—they are the most discreet. He sold it in a damned vault because he couldn't ask the police to give him protection. That's why he sold it from a vault."

"How do you know he sold it from there?" asked Claire.

"I saw the damned names in the damned vault registry. He signed in. Crooks signed in. They all signed in the damned registry for the damned vault. That's how they did it. That's what he was doing."

"Why didn't you tell me before you thought Dad was . . ." She paused. "A crook."

"Because I intended to live with you before."

"You're leaving."

"Lady, there's no place for me next to your obsession."

"You agreed it was rational."

"Yeah. You rationally care more about this insanity than you do about me. I saw that here. This is going to hurt me a long, long time. I didn't want to tell you about your father. I didn't want to hurt you. I thought maybe it would shock you."

"Arthur, don't go," she said.

"You can keep me. I think you could keep me forever," said Artie, and he kissed her once on the cheek and walked away. He heard her run up behind him and felt her near.

Artie could not look at her. He was not strong enough to do that. He sensed she was crying, and he could not look into her eyes.

It was a long wide bridge, and the clock high above them boomed away. Claire didn't speak until it had stopped.

"Arthur. If my father were a crook, why wouldn't he break down the cellar into its jewels so that he could sell it? Any criminal would know that."

"Because he was a wiseass. How many times did you tell me how he was a self-made man, and people resented him, and he did things his own way. He trusted himself. That's what you said. He said trust yourself. Do it your way and win, I believe, is what he used to say. So he came from Ohio and he tried to unload that cellar in secret. A wiseass would do that. Good-bye." He had said it all. She had not stopped him saying it. And he left.

"You're not facing right. You're going away from our hotel."

"I'll find it," said Artie.

"I'll take you," said Claire.

"You know, it doesn't take a genius to figure out Captain Rawson is about the Queen's business, and that lady, no matter how gracious she might be, sits where she sits because of those things that stuck into people back there. You're going up against a whole country. And countries tend to win, even against you."

"I'm not going to Windsor, Arthur," said Claire.

"Why not?"

"Because I'm going with you. I'm not losing you, Arthur."

"You're not," he said.

If nothing else, she felt he should admit there was a royal subterfuge going on here. Great Britain was at least as guilty of something as her father, but she knew that in Arthur's mood he didn't want to hear about intrigue as anything but something to avoid. She was not certain what she would do. All she knew was that she was not going to let herself lose Arthur at this moment. And probably never.

Harry Rawson arrived in London in time to hear an impassioned plea before tea that he should do something, anything to stop Claire Andrews. Now. Here in London if she were still here. Back in New York when she arrived. Suborn, bribe, blackmail, kill, maim, anything. But now. She had to be stopped now.

Sir Anthony accused Captain Rawson of negligence, of using Crown funds for his own pleasure, of dallying while England had entrusted him with its most sacred mission.

"This woman will expose us all, every one of us from Elizabeth the First to you and me! How could you let her get this far? Your orders were specific. It was even more important to England, to the survival of what is left of us, that it never, under any circumstances, be known that we had that object for the span of our greatness."

Sir Anthony hit the carved wood mantle of the fireplace in the rear parlor of his Belgravia townhouse. Rawson sat in the stuffed damask-covered chair and crossed a leg.

"How far has she gotten?" he asked.

"To telling some people the Tilbury isn't in Windsor. To saying we're liars. She knows it was the Tilbury."

"Which means?"

"If she's gotten this far, she can go the rest. She'll have it, Captain Rawson."

Harry Rawson held out his left hand. Only a few dark reddish stripes indicated that he had ever stopped a blade trying to catch pieces of heathstone in the bowels of Windsor's Round Tower.

"My hand has healed. I daresay, even with the best of stonemasons, that little inscription will not be put back all that clearly. The link is gone." Rawson opened and closed his left hand several times. The palm bore only a few faint reddish traces of what had once been scars. "Healed. Gone."

"Captain, precautions were taken so that no one outside of the royals themselves would even know precisely what the Tilbury looked like. I never did. I only knew it was a gold saltcellar with gems. A 'glory' so to speak. Neither its shape nor its exact form did I know. Even the different jewelers who measured the stones when the Tilbury was moved from Windsor for the duration never saw the whole cellar. For centuries, our sovereigns thought the secret was safe. Now this woman tracked down a sketch we knew nothing about secreted in an Italian castle. She will know."

"Indeed, she is impressive, Sir Anthony. My sympathies are with her boyfriend. I would hate to wake up with a hangover next to her hearing that midwest twang question me on the previous night's whereabouts."

"She knows it's the Tilbury. She knows I am lying. And she damned well may break the secret of Elizabeth the First, and that, Captain, is a disaster."

"Just what do you propose? You mentioned several options. I suppose you have one in mind?"

"Is that all you can say? You swore here, you took an oath to defend the sanctity of the Crown, to return it . . . damnit, to return our Grail to Her Majesty's possession, to preserve at all costs this great secret of our island race."

"I not only took the oath, Sir Anthony, I meant it. But you are going to have to accept that there is a great leap between British peculiarity over a saltcellar and possession of the Holy Grail itself. That is a thing of King Arthur and the Round Table, Celtic legends in Ireland, providence and chivalry, Wagner, von Eschenbach, *Morte d'Arthur*, Tennyson. It is our great European myth of the great chase won by virtue and holiness."

"I am talking about the cup Christ used at the Last Supper, Captain Rawson."

"And that is even farther removed. That is Jerusalem. That is Semitic. What Jew or Muslim reveres dinnerware?"

"What are you talking about, Captain? Out with it now."

"The cup Christ used at the Last Supper is probably among the other clay shards that make up the rubble layers upon which that city was built."

"I beg your pardon, Captain."

"Relics were a thing of later Christianity. Certainly Christ's Jewish followers who abandoned him to the Romans were not about to save the damned drinking cup if they wouldn't save him."

"You could have told me that before you began, Captain. It would have been good to know."

"What makes you think it would make a difference, Sir Anthony? This is the most important thing in my life. It doesn't matter if I am chasing the Grail or one of the multitude of frauds so prevalent in Europe. It does not need to have been used by that Jesus in Jerusalem. It only has to be the one Her Majesty orders me to get. It is her orders that are sacred, Sir Anthony. And that means so are yours."

"Then stop that American—woman."

"So that you won't be embarrassed? Don't be ridiculous. I didn't swear to protect the Crown's silly cover story about the Tilbury. I swore to protect the Crown, to protect England's secret, to protect England.

Once we have it back, no one can say we are doomed without it. Of course, they won't even know we have it back," said Rawson. He waited for an answer.

Sir Anthony trembled. His dark gray suit hung on him as though carved, a rigid man in a rigid suit angry at a world of change.

"You're close to it, then?" asked Sir Anthony.

"Very," said Rawson.

XXII

Long suffering is like the emerald whose color never varies. For no temptation of whatever magnitude can overpower long suffering which always gleams with a green and constant light.

—WALTER MAP
Queste del Saint Graal, 1225

In the north light, finally in the north light, the great pigeon's blood ruby showed its magnificent red strength, eighty-seven karats of it. The coloring held power throughout, even at the peculiar angles chosen for carving. The ruby among all stones was usually cut wrong to include as much stone as possible. This one was no exception, but its last lapidaries probably lived after A.D. 300 because the dominant and therefore most recent strokes carved the face of Jesus Christ, this over some other image, carved with another instrument, probably of a previous god.

Still, even through the shameful marks, this great ruby showed its passion. Norman Feldman looked into its soul through the jeweler's loupe. The almost imperceptible chrome inclusions were the absolute final proof that this was natural ruby and not some synthetic. No matter how science had advanced, it could not produce synthetic imperfections, not like these, which made the ruby parade as it turned in the light, and in those imperfections and the size and purity of color of the rest of the stone lived its greatness.

"This one has the smell of new death. Too many bodies," said Norman Feldman. "Everyone's been acting like an idiot. Well, at least you haven't destroyed it. So far. It would have been a shame."

Dr. Peter Martins, trained as a surgeon, and now dealing jewels across borders that would change a lot sooner than any of the gems, noticed two things. First, Feldman had not asked him about the killings. It was as though they didn't exist until he implied he didn't want the ruby because of them. Secondly and more importantly, the ruby dealer did not push the stone back across his desk, but held it, turning it over and over, never taking his eyes away from its insides.

"So you're here. You can't move the stones. I knew you'd panic. You knew how to steal, but you didn't know what you were stealing."

Dr. Martins slapped his kidskin gloves on his left wrist and crossed his legs. The ruby dealer was still examining the gem.

Feldman went on: "Everybody gets into the act, and nobody knows what he's doing. Everyone's been a fool. That art dealer person, for trusting you. The Roman who did this engraving, for desecrating this stone on one surface. Vern Andrews, who came from Ohio and knew it all. And some very smart people to boot. Fools, but you're looking at the biggest fool of them all. I'll deal it."

Dr. Martins reached across the clean desk of Feldman's office.

"I can't leave it with you," he said.

"How can I deal it then?"

"I'll stay near you."

Norman Feldman gave up the stone, careful to place it securely in the center of Dr. Martins's palm. Even a fall to a wooden desk could damage a ruby, especially one of an extraordinary eighty-seven karats.

Feldman shook his head, with a little smile. He was not going to let that man near him without watching him. He was not going to go to sleep with that man within a walking block.

"I can't let you take it away. This is not a business with sales receipts," said Dr. Martins.

"Why did you sell the sapphire to that Swiss businessman, if you want to call him that? I was curious why someone would do something like that. I knew it was you when I figured out the price. You think of yourself as a dealer in gems. I don't know why you gave up surgery."

"You have to love surgery, and I have my contacts, and my sources, and I do quite well in gems."

"Selling a velvet-blue one hundred and forty–karat sapphire without inclusions for a low six figures is not doing well."

"I've never dealt in stones this big; that's why I'm here."

"You don't know who to sell it to."

"I understood it was a low price to that Swiss businessman, but I had my reasons. If there weren't other pressing problems, I never would have dealt with him. I'm not that big a fool."

"Sell your ruby then. Get out of my office."

"What is it worth?"

"Ah," said Feldman, "not forty times what a two-karat ruby would sell for. This one you have to figure out its time in the world, and who is out there in the world. Not a number you could come up with."

"Could I buy an appraisal?"

"Sure," said Feldman. "For five thousand."

"Very well. What is it worth."

"A minimum of four million and possibly, if someone absolutely cannot live without it, and that depends on who, we might be touching ten million."

"I'll sell it to you for three million."

"Eight hundred thousand to a million," said Feldman.

He folded his hands over his dark vest and let the perfectly groomed and most elegant Dr. Peter Martins squirm in the hard chair in front of the desk.

"But you said it was worth a minimum of four million dollars."

"For those who know what they're doing."

"You're being rather hard," said Dr. Martins.

Norman Feldman laughed at the gall of the man to say that, the sheer chutzpah of it.

"Please. Life is too short. I will probably end up with that stone sooner or later. Unless, of course, someone like Lady Constance Jennings steals it from you."

"Lady Jennings?"

"She lives in Paris, Dr. Martins," said Feldman. He noticed that Dr. Martins's cashmere coat seemed to fit his shoulders better than a suit. The tie had a glistening richness to it. He dressed well, thought Norman Feldman. Of course, lots of people dressed well. Dr. Martins should dress for a living, thought Feldman. This was what he thought that first day in the bank vault with the man from Ohio and the craziness of selling all those big stones in one lump piece as though it were a building or a car or a necklace.

"Are you giving me the name of a buyer?"

"Of course not. Lady Jennings does not like rubies. It's not her stone. Of course, she has some, but not this. This is something else. I would love to deal this stone. I would love to own it for a while. I want it."

"Can you give me some collateral?"

"I will take half the profits. I will give you a large pigeon's blood ruby, the last offer for which was over two million," said Feldman, raising his hand so Dr. Martins would not interrupt. "That ruby is nothing like this, but still it's a great gem. Even you could tell that. I will give you some lesser stones that even you could deal. That would be collateral. When I sell the ruby, you give me back my stones, and I give you your cut."

"But I can't sell your ruby for a good price. I don't know the buyers or any other person who would deal with me on this."

"Probably," said Feldman.

"And what if you run with my stone."

"Don't be a fool. Where am I going to run? Why should I run? I'll leave that to your kind, but let me warn you now. If I sense you're following me in any way, I'm going to kill you."

"What if you kill me not to make a payoff?"

"I have never done that. I leave that to your kind."

"Let me see your stones," said Dr. Martins. When the deal was struck and Dr. Martins had surrendered the large Christ's head ruby, he also added sixteen one-ounce bars of gold.

"What's that?" asked Feldman.

"Your appraisal fee," said Dr. Martins. "My kind pays its bills, sir."

Norman Feldman was amused by Dr. Martins's sense of hurt pride. As he took the gold, he did not respect Dr. Martins one iota more for paying the fee. This was not the coin respect was earned by, although gold was easily the most portable and sellable commodity ever taken from the earth.

BEFORE NATIONS AND BEFORE CALENDARS

The gold in the sixteen small bars had come from dozens of places, from smelters in Scythia and breastplates in Egypt. It had adorned standards of kingdoms not even remembered. Its oldest speck was found before man even used bronze to make tools.

It was first spotted glinting in a stream that the people who hunted and gathered grains in the valley called simply "the water." There were no countries when it was found. There were those who were from the valley, and others. The others had to be repelled.

The man who found it saw the sun glinting back from the water, little shining reflections as though the sun itself hid parts there. He knew what to do. With his hands he scooped up the sand and lay it on a rock, and very carefully, all day long, he picked out what shone from what did not shine.

He could spend the time. The hunt had been good, and there was grain the women and children found in abundance in this valley that had to be protected.

All day, he picked the specks and when he was done he had less than a thin half of a fingernail of the yellow. Many days he came back to this stream looking for the shining specks of sun. Once he found a whole nugget of the yellow metal, and this too he pounded with the other specks; and to hold them together, he pressed them all into a small piece of wood with animal fat. When he died, his tribe put the wood with the pieces of the sun over his eyes so that he might see sunlight in the places he was going, the places after death.

Within a generation, another tribe moved through the valley and dug up all the graves, because they were always a good source of stone knives and spears and other things other tribes buried their people with.

And in his skull, as in the backs of many skulls, they found the gold that had fallen through over the years. And they knew to melt it with the gold they had. And this gold was worn on the bodies of the men to make them strong in battle.

Centuries later, the specks first found in a stream joined other gold hundreds of miles away in earrings that went with a woman in trade, and these earrings lasted a few centuries more until they were melted down to make coins for the great temple in Jerusalem, coins, of course, without graven images, and when the temple was sacked, the coins were melted down to make a drinking goblet, which was melted down for levies to build an army to fight the fierce Scythians, who among all peoples loved gold the most. And this gold, paid a soldier, was taken from his body after a battle and made into a necklace for a warrior, who was buried in it. And when those graves were robbed, the gold went back into the form of coin again, to be paid by a German knight for killing another's slave, in what was called *mangold,* the price of which was used to pay off such debts incurred by accident or anger.

And this gold after many years was paid to the great Charlemagne in taxes and melted down again for rings on the fingers of a Norman lady who naturally brought them with her across the channel to England in 1066.

So important was gold to the Norman nobility that by 1327 King Edward had established an assay office in London and assigned to it a royal charter for the Worshipful Company of Goldsmiths, to regulate all gold and silver in the kingdom, to have provenance over the work of duly charted goldsmiths assuring "such labors of such quality as to do honor to their name and their sovereign." A British goldsmith was infinitely more important than a doctor and, of course, more rigorously trained.

And so as England waited in the grim days before the Spanish

Armada would invade the island, a most worthy goldsmith, Simon Sedgewick, was called to the Tilbury encampment to bring his entire year's allotment of gold and those tools with which he could form a piece for Her Royal Highness, Elizabeth.

He was escorted by a full company of men with pikes, all whispering the horrible news. The Spanish Armada had already set sail, and some wondered if the London goldsmith had been called to prepare an offering for Phillip II.

But when they reached Tilbury, the camp seemed almost to rejoice. The Queen's standards were there, and men talked of welcoming the fight and how already several raids on the Spanish coast had been successful and that while the galleons were big, they were exceeding slow.

Sedgewick was taken directly to the tent of Her Majesty, Elizabeth, Queen of England, France, Ireland, and Virginia. And there the soldiers waited, as her captains and lords exited and Simon Sedgewick stayed.

Inside, Sedgewick could not believe he was alone with his monarch. He did not dare think he was going to be seduced, as rumors had the Queen doing to lords or handsome soldiers. Her Majesty wore a simple frock, yet studded with small pearls and emeralds. The tent gloried in her perfumes.

"How still your tongue, good smith?"

"Like the grave, Your Majesty," said Sedgewick. Would she call a goldsmith for bed when she had thirty thousand younger more active swords in this encampment?

"Then don your smithing apron and make your Prince a work."

"What work, Your Majesty?" asked Sedgewick. So it was not that. But this was stranger still.

"Anything but a chalice," she said and put before him a large gold chalice with an enormous sapphire in its bosom and six diamonds at its base. "To this add you your yearly allotment of gold the better to hide, and to the purpose of that manufacture, you may add from any of treasure here, topaz, jade and lapis lazuli."

Close, he could see how evenly whitened the creams of her face were. But what did she want?

"May I suggest, Your Highness, a great crucifix in honor of our Lord and Saviour for help in victory over God's Spanish enemies."

"We do not know if they be God's enemies, but they certainly are ours. So let us hope we are His allies so that we may deserve this victory. Yet not a crucifix, good smith."

"There is too much gold in my allotment for any gold ornament or vessel."

"Cellars take a goodly measure."

"But they are hollow, Your Majesty."

"Then make me one as solid as your reputation. And add that of painful memory," she said, pointing to a ham-sized box with an alabaster lid.

Simon Sedgewick bowed and took the box. Inside was a great ruby on which Christ's head was engraved. He had heard of this gem, given by Elizabeth's father to Elizabeth's mother, Anne Boleyn, and then taken back again when he beheaded her, never worn by Elizabeth.

"It is a fitting stone for this cellar you will make."

Even more strangely, Her Majesty insisted upon waiting until Sedgewick had melted down the chalice itself, after carefully prying the diamonds and the sapphire from the binding wax setting in the gold itself. Inside, protected by old burned cloth, was a scrap of a clay bowl.

"What would you have me do with this poorish bowl, Your Majesty?" asked Simon Sedgewick, holding it up to candlelight. It was, on closer examination, a crude bowl of common baked clay, pink in color on the outside, and dark with strange lacquer in its bottom.

"It does not seem an impressive thing of princes, does it?" she asked her goldsmith.

"No, Your Majesty."

"Ah well, kings can ride on humble asses and still be kings, can they not?" Elizabeth said, not allowing an answer because she did not want one when she referred to how the Lord of the universe rode into Jerusalem town for the week of His Crucifixion.

It could be, she thought. And it could not be. It did not matter. There was a sense this battle could be won now, and if for nothing else she would never let Phillip II find the bowl again.

"Put the poorish bowl in the bosom of the cellar, make you a listing of every part therein, use no apprentices, and do your work here in this tent. We will secure it shortly."

Sedgewick never saw her again. A great storm in the channel washed the great Armada into helplessness, destroying Spain forever as a power and launching Britain as an empire, while Simon Sedgewick without furnaces or apprentices to work them crafted a massive cellar of rings, and necklaces, coins and medals, crucifixes, and medallions, and all the things that gold fashioned to stay in the form of a cellar until a ring clamp in a New York City apartment would hold the pieces separate again underneath an acetylene torch.

It was four hundred years later and a surgeon now was considered more important than a goldsmith, yet these surgeon's hands were familiar with gold. They had to be to get at the gems.

When Dr. Peter Martins had finished, and all the stones were ready for transport, the hysterical art dealer had come to his apartment and refused to let him leave.

Battissen's hands had fluttered with the uselessness of it all.

Dr. Martins had tried to reason with him. He had explained quite realistically that the woman had no real claim, that the policeman had no charge that could be substantiated. It was clear, Geoffrey Battissen had been pressured out of reason.

Dr. Martins had tried three times to return Battissen to a rational state. He pointed out how well everything had really worked, how the detective and the woman would have to give up eventually because they had no realistic case, and then as the final proof, Dr. Martins had brought the weeping, threatening, hysterical Geoffrey Battissen into the small workroom that still smelled of the ugly sulphur fumes of the acetylene torch and showed in every separate piece, from diamond, to sapphire, to ruby, why the cellar simply could not be returned. When Battissen had insisted on returning the untraceable valuable pieces in hopes of mercy, turning in Dr. Martins for that same ridiculous mercy, there really was no other option. Battissen's hysteria had closed them off.

The pointed graver was there and so was the back of Geoffrey's head. Dr. Martins had gripped the graver in a surgical manner, firm but not knuckle-whitening tight, firm enough for the tissue he had to cut into, actually thrust into, right behind the ear, and up into the posterior cerebral lobe.

Then, of course, to get rid of Geoffrey, who had dropped in place, roughly one hundred and fifty pounds of something that was going to make a worse stink than the acetylene torch. Geoffrey had fit easily into a green plastic lawn bag and was just as easily brought down through the service elevator to the garage beneath the New York apartment and easily driven in the trunk just outside of Queens, where, before heading for Kennedy International Airport, Dr. Martins had left his former partner at a dump to be covered by the rest of the day's waste from one of the largest cities of the world and set about to sell the gems, which proved infinitely harder than he had imagined.

XXIII

For the heart of a knight must be so hard and unrelenting towards his suzerain's foe that nothing in the world can soften it.

—WALTER MAP
Queste del Saint Graal, 1225

Spring hinted not with patches of brown grass coming up through the snow, or crocuses in the yard, or the smell of new life around the corner, but with black-coated slush melting into rivulets carrying a winter of trash along the gutters.

Claire Andrews missed home, and it was the worst day to accommodate a visit by Captain Rawson. For some reason, Arthur could not get mad at him.

"He's just doing his job. That's what he's supposed to do. Britain wants its saltcellar back. He goes after it. It's like sending a gofer out for coffee, except Harry does it all over the world."

"Lying to you. Pretending to be your friend."

"He warned me about a couple of things. There's doing your job and doing your job."

"Why does he want to see you now?"

"Maybe he likes me."

"Now, after all he does is phone every so often? You haven't seen him since Paris."

[311]

"You want to ask him? Ask him."

"I really would prefer not to be in the same room with him," said Claire.

"He wants to take us both out. I think he's leaving New York."

"He's your friend," said Claire.

That was breakfast, and they had been home from England and that awful moment on Westminster Bridge for three days now. Arthur had mentioned that it would be nice to get a bookshelf up on the wall, her wall, the wall from which she had tracked down the Tilbury Cellar hidden by Captain Rawson's government in a most suspicious manner.

She had promised that she would "make the research area part of the living room, instead of vice versa." But she hadn't moved a jot on her wall, and it was still a couch and a few chairs intruding on her research center. She was not home that evening when Rawson arrived, tanned, perfectly groomed, relaxed, and out for a good time as always.

Artie apologized for Claire's not being present, and when he returned to the living room after dressing for the evening, he noticed Rawson had spilled his drink on the worktable set beneath the wall. He apologized for it. He didn't know what to wipe up without disturbing the papers. Neither did Artie.

"What do these lines mean?"

"Ask Claire. I'm out of this thing."

"This one from Jerusalem to Seville to Tilbury. You wouldn't happen to know that one, would you?"

"Yeah," said Artie.

"What?" said Rawson.

"It's pen," said Artie.

"You're joking," said Rawson.

"No, it's pen," said Artie with a big smile. Five times that evening, in one way and another, from one pub to another, Harry Rawson came back to that line from Jerusalem, and Artie, even swimming in the same good champagne they amazingly had in New York as well as Paris, was ready for every one. He gave away nothing and played the easygoing New York detective at peace with the world.

Near the end of the evening, when even the Queen's good captain of the Argyle Sutherlanders was weaving to the moment, Artie pressed him on the thousand-dollar whores.

"You don't deserve to know. And I won't tell you. But for me, one advantage is that you do not love them, Artie. To love is the most dangerous thing anyone can do. Most dangerous."

"You never loved?"

"I suppose, somewhere, sometime, very young."

"Your parents?"

"I had been away from London for almost eight years. My father, whom I had not seen since Sandhurst, did not delay his return to Venice by one day to have dinner with me."

"And your mother?"

"Mother told me that when I grew up I would be a great screw for someone. I was five. She was on her way out of the house with her lover of the moment and never returned."

"You poor bastard," said Artie.

"No. I am privileged. I am very privileged to have a most interesting life, to drink with a fine fellow like you, and to charge the guns of Balaclava, because while you are galloping full steam ahead, you really can't think how meaningless it all is."

"You poor bastard," said Artie.

"To us poor bastards, Artie."

"I'm not a poor bastard," said Artie. "I'm the luckiest guy in the world."

"Charge," said Rawson.

The next day, Artie had a hangover, and Rawson, phoning the apartment from his hotel, was unfairly alert and chipper. He wanted to speak to Claire. It was 8:00 A.M.

"Just a minute," said Artie. He passed the phone across the bed.

Claire angrily shook her head.

"Just act normal," said Artie, covering the receiver.

"That's just what I can't do. I told you that yesterday."

"You never lied?"

"Lying is not the trouble; acting normal is the trouble."

"Don't think about it. It's only trouble when you feel you've got to be perfect and you start analyzing which lie could be unraveled. Other than that, forget it."

"That's what I can't do."

"Then don't talk to him," said Artie, starting to take his hand off the receiver.

"He'll know something," said Claire.

"Right," said Artie.

"Well, don't you think it's strange that they send someone in secret for something they own anyhow?"

"What has that got to do with anything now?"

"I'll be thinking that."

"Don't talk to him then."

"I'll talk to him. Maybe I'll find out something."

"You do know that he is on government business, so this is not some game," said Artie.

"I understand, Arthur. I understand it very well."

"Don't get mad, because when you get mad, you'll do something wild."

"That's not so," she said. But she was certainly mad at Arthur now.

She took the phone and said hello to Harry Rawson while squinting angrily at Arthur. Captain Rawson had a proposal: Why not join forces?

"I think I turned down something like that before," said Claire.

"I couldn't help but be fascinated by your research. It's amazing. Wonderful. I am enthralled. As a matter of fact, I can be a help, you know, if ever you need anything done in England."

"I don't understand," said Claire.

"You know I saw that splendid map of yours yesterday. You really must have done magnificent research, and frankly I was most amazed by Jerusalem."

"Why?"

"Because what does Jerusalem have to do with a British cellar? I assumed the colored dots were where the gems appeared, here and there."

"And what were the Rawsons doing with it in the first place? Do you want to explain how you could have an identical cellar to one owned by the Crown that nobody is allowed to see?"

"Yes. Not identical. Family was nouveau riche in the sixteenth century. Everybody's got to start sometime. They tried to copy what they heard about. I've never seen the Tilbury and neither have they. But by now the Rawson cellar is an heirloom, imitation or not."

"How do I know that?"

"My good woman, it is awfully early to call someone else a liar, and I do have to be about my business. Good day, and good luck, and if you ever do discover something of even passing interest, anything in the list I gave Artie, please do let me know."

"What else is left?"

"Anything. I doubt you will, however."

"What's left? The framework? The poorish bowl? There's nothing left."

"Our tradition is left. Even the poorish bowl," came Rawson's voice, cool and tolerant.

"Maybe I'll find out more than you want to know," said Claire, hanging up, while in bed Artie shook his head and Claire ignored him.

"They're still lying, Arthur, even if you don't want to know about it," she said.

"Right," said Artie.

"Right, what?" said Claire.

"Right, I don't want to know about it," said Artie, who did not want to know about it while brushing his teeth, drinking his orange juice, drinking his coffee, and eating his bagel with bacon and eggs. Not interested.

But that evening he had to be. Just by the way he asked her to go out with him for a hamburger, she knew something was wrong.

But she couldn't get him to explain. He didn't answer her questions normally, and only when they were out of the apartment did he even admit something was amiss, and he asked that she wait until they were far away from the apartment in some noisy area.

In a little neighborhood coffee shop just off of Queens Boulevard, after they had sat down at a formica table with someone else's fresh coffee rings on it and ordered quickly so the waitress wouldn't hover, Artie said: "I'm sorry Claire. Our place is bugged. We're in the midst of something."

"I know that."

"No, the something is watching us this time. Not an exciting self-actualizing exercise anymore. We're a target of someone."

Claire folded a napkin on her lap. She hated when Arthur talked like this because then it became so hard to get the facts through his emotions. But this time, he had it down professionally pat.

Homicide had discovered the tap, when doing surveillance on Norman Feldman on suspicion of the murders. He was, after all, someone who wanted the ruby and did have foreign access and, more importantly, when checked out, was known to be a "dangerous person," something Arthur had discovered only recently.

What Marino and McKiernan found, however, was that not only was Feldman virtually impossible to tail, but that he had hidden under the guise of old phones and a sparse office one of the more modern electronic protection systems they had ever encountered, things only used so far by governments. Not only was he protected, but Marino and McKiernan found out Frauds/Jewels wasn't. Someone with equally advanced equipment had bugged Artie's line. So they checked where he was living, and they found the same kind of advanced eavesdropping surrounding Claire's apartment in Queens.

"Did you tell them our suspicions about Harry Rawson? About the British government? About the questions we had?" asked Claire. "Maybe Harry is behind some of this."

"I mentioned some stuff. That's a very professional job that's been done on us."

"What are we going to do?" asked Claire.

"Ignore the bugs. Ignore everything. Let them go their own way, whoever they are. We stay out."

"How can we ignore the bugs? People will be listening to us. I will be cramped in my private life. I can't act normal."

"Forget they're there."

"While we make love?"

"Especially."

"That's disgusting, Arthur." The way she said it was so adorable that, laughing, Artie had to grab her hands across the table and kiss them, even as she refused to accept the humor in this.

"Well, then, I am certainly not going to stop my research. If it is your friend Rawson, I am going to find out why."

"Fine. It's your right."

"That bug doesn't bother you?"

"No."

"I am bothered by that. I am offended by that. I am bothered that you are not bothered, Arthur."

"Hey, I don't bother with something as big as a country. I get out of its way. Between a country and us, they are going to win in a head-on collision. Let them have everything. You can always go back to your search in ten or twenty years. You don't have to know the answer to everything immediately one hundred percent."

"What is your friend looking for, and why doesn't the Queen announce she has lost the family cellar? Why?"

"My friend," said Artie, as though unfairly shackled with the association.

"You know, that ruby belonged to Henry the Eighth and he gave it to Anne Boleyn. One of my researchers phoned in today with a couplet Henry wrote. It was about the blood of Christ being as eternal as the red of the love and the red of the stone Henry gave to Anne Boleyn. Do you think it's the ruby?"

"I don't want to think," said Artie.

"You've got to admit it's fascinating."

"People are listening to us brush our teeth and screw, and you still think it's a game."

"I'm not taking down the wall right away," said Claire.

"God forbid there should be a killing around here we're not associated with. You gonna finish your french fries?"

"Yes," said Claire.

"You never do."

"I will now," said Claire. "You know that, when it's proved to me that my research is dangerous or in any way encouraging surveillance. Maybe when they installed the bug they thought I might lead them to the jewels. Do we know how long it's been there? Do we?"

Artie was through his hamburger before Claire had taken one bite of hers. She insisted on talking.

"Besides, most importantly besides, I don't want to stop now that

I know of the Tilbury and that for some reason Britain is chasing something in it or on it, possibly a relic. And why do they want this all to be a secret?"

"It's a government. Everything's secret in a government. Toilet paper is classified."

"Not for four hundred years," said Claire.

"You're not going to finish your fries," said Artie.

That night, as she filed away the new information into her computer, a device that now would probably be moved into another room, she found something quite strange.

Certain words on later files had commands on them instead of writing, a mistake she had made early on in using the computer. But not anymore. Someone had entered the Tilbury file and read it while they were out.

She would have asked Arthur but for two things. One, he never went near the computer, and two, her own apartment was not a place she could talk about such things anymore. She did not enter the latest facts concerning the ruby with Christ's head, but kept them in her head. She was not going to stop the research now, least of all now. Not with people listening in on her very orgasms. If she were going to be constrained in her lovemaking, someone was going to pay for it.

If great gems transcended civilizations and borders, they most certainly ignored hatreds and foreign policies and all the things historians thought ruled the world. Norman Feldman understood this.

During the worst of the Arab-Israeli tensions and hatred, Norman Feldman never had trouble entering Arab lands, especially the Gulf sheikdoms. Many of these rulers came from old trading families, whose slow and stately dhows, pitching in the winds of the Persian Gulf and the Red and Arabian seas, had sold pearls and slaves and ivories and incense throughout the east, centuries before oil was discovered under the land. And they knew their gems.

For Norman Feldman, to deal with an Arab was to match wits with one of the few people he considered his equal. They understood bargaining, the traditional way of selling things before the modern phenomenon of fixed prices. And this, of course, was the only way major gems were sold.

But something was wrong. At his first stop in the Gulf, he was driven in the sultan's stretch limousine not to the place in the desert but to the more official residence in the capital, a subtle but significant difference.

In the desert, there was that bedouin obligation of hospitality where there could be no question of Feldman's safety as a guest. In the capital city, while he was still under some protection of hospitality, there could be a question. Still, he was safer here in this sheikdom than on the streets of New York or London.

In the city, he missed the tents and the clean wind out of the desert. Instead, there was German air conditioning that when combined with incense made a room smell slightly rancid, like spiced butter gone awry.

Still, in the office of the Minister of Defense, Ali Hassan Al Hadir, brother of the sultan, there were tiny cups of strong sugared coffee, even though there was no servant woman making it, but a major in the defense forces.

"My friend, Norman," said Ali Hassan Al Hadir, embracing Feldman.

"My friend, Ali Hassan Al Hadir," said Feldman, who returned the embrace. Otherwise, Feldman did not indulge in touching people except for sex, which he got over with as quickly as possible.

They, of course, were not friends, but this was the ritual of the bargain, a subtle but necessary affirmation that they could never let anger openly interfere in a very hostile combat of wits.

There was still a good woven rug on the floor, but not with the same sense of specialness it had when laid over sand. The sofa was a leather thing possibly bought in London or New York.

Both of them knew that a negotiation in this office was different from one in a tent, but neither of them mentioned it right away; instead, there was the half hour of courtesy talk, which Feldman got through mechanically and with great difficulty, until the correct question was asked, by Minister Hadir, exposing the reason they were meeting in his office and not in the desert.

"What is wrong with the ruby?" asked Hadir, too directly for this to be bargaining.

"Nothing," said Feldman.

"No governmental complication?"

"There have been some killings."

"Of government people? Important people?"

Feldman shook his head. "They were just killings," said Feldman. Murders in another country were, of course, of no interest to the head of state armed forces whose sole job was the security of his brother. These were the people who bought gems this size. Something was operating here that someone like a New York detective no matter how shrewd could not comprehend. To him there were laws. Anyone could break a law. But in these countries the people who made the laws were the laws, and no warrant in a foreign country for murder or otherwise was going to affect them. It was blatantly inconsequential that someone had gotten killed over the ruby somewhere else.

"Then I fear you are mixed up with some ugly people. You are being followed, you know? People are asking questions, you know?"

"Which people?"

"Hard to tell, but we have warnings. Are you engaged in any political thing?"

"You would have to believe in some government for that," said Feldman.

"Ah, Norman, these are hard times, when friends who meet to do business must talk of such things. Are you having trouble selling the ruby?" asked Hadir, and Feldman knew the shift from the problem to the negotiations had begun. His answer had been satisfactory.

"Not at all. I may keep it, such is the pleasure of owning it. Still it is such a wonder that when you see it in New York, you will be happy you made a concrete offer now."

"How can one buy what one does not see?" asked Hadir.

"Eighty-seven karats and undiminished dancing power in her belly," said Feldman. "She was luscious. She held her own right through her size. That stone gave me an erection in my soul, friend."

"And you thought of me?" asked Hadir. He was trim, but with a mocha fleshiness about his face, making him appear mildly pleasant in his light blue field marshall's uniform.

"I thought of you as the leading one among many."

"How many?"

"Twenty."

"Ah, Norman, there are twenty now who would buy such a great gem?"

"Twenty who would pay readily," said Feldman.

"Ah, well, at least I am glad my friend has so many clients. I myself unfortunately feel that should I have to resell such a stone, its size would make the sale too prohibitive. I am afraid your list has shrunk to nineteen. I am looking for smaller stones."

"I will send you some for examination. In any case, a visit with my friend Ali Hassan Al Hadir is always worth a trip."

"This too large gem, what are you expecting to get for it?"

"I have turned down ten million," said Feldman.

"Then a mere three million–dollar offer would be useless," said Ali Hassan Al Hadir.

"I could not meet that low price, even for such a one as you. But because I know your word is good, and the other was just a promise, I would sell this ruby for nine and a half million."

"And I would add a hundred thousand dollars to my price, even though such a large ruby would present more problems than it would solve."

"When you see it, you will know nine million dollars is a bargain."

"If you say so, Norman, but I can in good conscience offer only three and a half million dollars."

They talked of prices and gems and the fickleness of fate for the next hour, but the closest they could come was to within three million dollars of each other, with Hadir unwilling to top four million. Feldman made a very casual offer for Hadir to come to New York to see the stone if it hadn't been sold by then.

These were only preliminary negotiations, to see who was interested. The real bargaining would begin after Hadir had held the eighty-seven-karat pigeon's blood in his hand and had seen it in the proper light. Then that three million difference would collapse, Feldman was sure.

It took Feldman four days to get through the sheikdoms, and in one place he heard of one person asking about him, in another it was two, in another it was supposed to be a government. And so, because he was not about to give up his precious list of those who would buy great rubies, he began making stops where he knew he could not sell it to throw off anyone who might be following him.

In Thailand, Feldman mentioned offering the stone to a dealer who now had a virtual monopoly on any good stones coming from the prime ruby region of the world, the Mogok mountains of Burma across the border.

Feldman knew Burma well and still had good contacts there, once even being offered an advisory position in their intelligence service. But this greatest source of rubies had disappeared, under a government takeover, the Burmese reasoning that since the rubies were a natural resource, all the people should profit, instead of a few wealthy men.

This noble intention, taking greed out of mining and assuring all the men who dug for the stones an equal pay no matter what their luck in finding stones, resulted in miners turning in only the lesser gems and smuggling the good ones next door into Thailand.

Thus, the place to buy Burmese rubies became Bangkok, not Kachin, Sagaing, Shan, or, even farther south, Rangoon, where good lapidaries once worked.

Unfortunately, for some reason, the Thais never could cut stones, and while the ruby had no clear cleavage lines, there certainly were preferred directions, none of which the Thai butchers seemed to understand.

This was not the worst situation, since the Thais did cut the stones to leave the largest amount, so that the stones could easily be recut in Europe or America.

What saddened Feldman somewhat was the loss of the Burmese

cutters. Had their skills been lost? Did they die with the passing of a generation? He hated to see competence leave the planet, because there was so damned little of it. Anywhere. In any field. In any country.

He never mentioned this as sadness, however, rather expressing himself in bitterness on one hand and vindication in his contempt for the whole human species on the other.

To the Thai businessman in the white building with a slow fan hardly rustling the humid swelter of the noon-baked day, he got to business virtually on the handshake. And as he expected there was no money the size of the Christ's head, but there were stones for sale, and in a manner more direct than in the Arab world, he made his deal to buy smaller stones.

He made two more stops in Asia, in Hong Kong selling the prestige of the stone, in Taiwan the glamour of its internal power, but only a third of them were real buyers. Everywhere, there was ruthless bargaining. And in many places, he picked up the same warning about being followed. He changed his plans several times, making random side trips, and never spent two nights in the same place. Sometimes he slept on planes, and sometimes he didn't sleep at all.

Finally, he flew to Geneva, saw several industrialists, one of whom might be a buyer, and then hired a driver to take him outside the city to an elegant chalet, Dr. Peter Martins's main home.

It was an hour and a half trip over good but somewhat narrow roads. Coming from the Far East to Switzerland always made him feel that he had stepped into an operating room of a country. He did not exchange one word with the driver during the whole trip and did not mind it.

By making stops in Geneva, Feldman had given Dr. Martins enough time to get home. And he was there, in a silk bathrobe, with perspiration coming from his forehead. Apparently he was exercising. Feldman did not enter.

"Why are you such an idiot?" asked Feldman.

"Won't you come in?" asked Dr. Martins.

"Do you think I can't kill you? Do you think I won't kill you?"

"What are you talking about?"

"I could cut that ruby into three major gems and have them sold in the morning, getting almost five million out of it. But I have too much respect for the Christ's head to do that. Don't press me."

"I don't know what you're talking about."

"If you think you can get my buyers by trailing me, and then possibly doing me harm, forget it. I would have thought that by now you would understand. Don't make me decide between cleaving the Christ's head or yours." Feldman did not wait to hear another denial, which he was sure would come. Feldman had to make sure Dr. Martins was not hanging about when the Christ's head came out into the light for display at the point of sale.

Boarding the Pan Am flight to the United States in Geneva, Feldman felt free for the first time from the entanglements that had been creeping around the borders of his life. They would be gone, he was sure, with the sale, and the transfer of the money to Dr. Martins.

The ruby had been just too big for someone whose only qualification was greed. Feldman slept on the flight because airplanes always were the safest place to shut one's eyes and prepared for the final bidding.

He was always excited by this. Selling a great stone in some way left a share of it with the seller. He could remember it and remember the look in the buyer's face. It was almost a sexual sharing of knowing the insides of the ruby.

Despite his relief, he was as cautious entering his office on Forty-eighth Street as he had been before he had cornered the snake Martins. Before he stepped into the elevator, he knew no one was in his office. No one was waiting outside in the hallway, and no one was waiting in the elevator. The electronics took care of that.

When he put the key into the first lock of the door, he felt it swing away suddenly, almost drawing him into the room, and before he could get his balance, a hand had his hand and was pulling him down to the floor. The crash chipped a tooth and numbed his nose. Pushing off with a hand to get a kick free, Feldman felt the hand yanked away from him, like a helpless thrashing steer, felt someone tie the hand and whip it across his desk, to his chair.

He knew enough to bite at the close neck. With life at stake there were no rules, just what you could use. But his teeth met something gummy, and no sounds came out. His mouth was taped. His arms were taped to the chair, and then he noticed that for the first time, no north light fell into the room. The blinds had been drawn down.

And then the pain began, just under the heart, not a stripping of skin, not a single cut, but a small thrust of a blade, and then wait, and then it went in farther, just a little bit, and then wait, and then just a little bit farther as Feldman writhed in the chair, knowing to his horror he was in the hands of a professional. The tape was going to come off soon. How could he save Artie? Even dying, he had some tricks of his own. Even screaming soundless into tape, he knew he could do something. Eventually, the tape was going to have to come off. That was how it was done. Eventually, he was going to have to talk. When you were in the hands of someone who knew what he was doing, your body was not your own.

One day, it would be known as Burma, but in those years it was at the fringe of civilization, the outer garment of the Middle Kingdom, which the world called China. Thus was the Mogok region known, but the girl who found the large ruby did not know it was Mogok. She knew it was home. She knew her father owned her and owned the ruby because she found it. Her highest hopes were to be given extra portions of food for this great discovery that would make her father rich, perhaps even the meat of the duck that important people ate.

But her father sold her, along with the large ruby, to a merchant who might need sexual company in his travels. The merchant did not take her body, and she thought it was because she was ugly. She had known that a long time. She watched him trim the ruby from the glistening dolomite in which it was found, and still it was an impressive size. If she were allowed to talk to people she would have told everyone she had found it.

Only when the ruby was trimmed of the white rock in which it was found did she understand why such an ugly girl had been bought. He wanted her to swallow it. She could not do this by herself and he put the large stone in her mouth, tilted up her chin, and with a rounded pole, pushed the stone down her throat. She almost strangled on the sharp hard object, but with a punch into her back, the stone went down.

"Little one, if you tell anyone about this, they will cut it out of you. Have you ever been cut?"

She nodded. Her name was Mai.

"It hurts very much and if they should have to look for it in your belly they will cut a thousand times, and you will die, with your belly cut open. You don't want that to happen, do you?"

Mai shook her head.

He made her wear a thick cloth girdle under her dress, and even though it caused redness and chafed little Mai, he would not let her take it off until she had let waste from her bowels. Then he checked the cloth and poked a small stick through her discharge, and when he was satisfied she had not passed the stone, he let her clean the girdle, and then reattached it with a knot in the back that she could not duplicate if she secretly took off the girdle and tried to replace it.

Often, as they traveled toward where the sun set, they were stopped by soldiers, or villagers, and once by bandits, and every time they were searched. Once, angered by no passage money, soldiers wanted to take the girl, but the merchant explained she was so ugly, she would cost more to feed than she was worth. They all agreed and let her go as unworthy even of the taking.

Thus over days and months they passed westward, joining a caravan for safety, and seeing people with round eyes and light skin. Farther west, even stranger people appeared, some with horrible blue eyes, so frightening to the young girl. She heard tales of different gods, of a god of the slaves who died, but conquered death for everyone in so doing.

She asked if this god also helped ugly slave girls, and she was told by one follower, with tears in his eyes, that Mai was the one dearest to His heart because she was poor and pushed about and considered worthless by others. This glory of the universe loved Mai especially. And it was the first time in Mai's life she heard anyone loved her. Of course this was too good to be true. Way too good for little Mai whose main ambition was to get the leftovers from the plates of people who mattered. And so she laughed at it.

She saw jewels on the rich in litters, but none so grand as the one in her belly. Eventually, she came with her master to the largest city in the world, she was told. Rome. They had been traveling months within the empire of this great city.

And there her master gave her a bag of oil to drink and would not let her wear the girdle anymore but made her wear a tunic that only came down to her waist. And every time she had to move her bowels, which was often now, she had to use a pot, which her master examined by tilting and shaking the bowl because now all her discharge was as loose as the oil he forced her to drink. For two days he made her drink, and for two days he waited for the stone to appear.

"Girl, if you do not pass the stone by tomorrow, I am going to have to cut it out. I do not wish to do this. You follow orders, and you follow them with heart. I wish to keep you. But I have no choice. That ruby is my fortune. You must pass the stone by morning."

Now she knew that if the stone had not succumbed to the oil or all the food she had eaten, certainly it would not pass by morning. So Mai prayed to this god who had died by a shameful execution. He was, after all, the only god for poor slave girls. She prayed all night and forced herself to drink more and more oil, and just before dawn, amidst a great trembling in her body, Mai felt something tear at her rectum. The ruby had passed.

Her master washed the stone, and so overjoyed was he at seeing it just as it was back in the hem of the center of the world, as China was known, here in the center of the world, as Rome was known, he offered the girl her freedom.

He sold the ruby to a newly rich Greek who ordered the head of Jupiter carved into it, Jupiter looking suspiciously like the Greek. It was a stone worthy of the pommel of any sword, its redness showing an ability to draw blood and thereby kill.

Little Mai was burned a few years later for refusing to worship the gods of Rome, choosing instead death for her God, now the center of a despised cult among the civilized. But by the time Mai chose death, she had learned much. She had learned that life was precious, that she was precious, and that what she felt and thought and did was important. That life was more than the scraps from the tables, more even than the greatest bounty on the tables themselves. She knew even in her fear that all they could take from her was a body that had been beaten too much and days that had become too long waiting for her God who loved her. With all their legions and all their roads and weapons, all they could do was send Mai to the God who loved her, the God who cherished ugly slave girls more than empresses and the most beautiful courtesan, a God who saw the hearts, not flesh, a God who died for her, just as she chose to die for him, Jesus, the Christ.

The Jupiter carving had an easier time making a religious transition. As Christianity became the state religion three centuries later, another lapidary changed the crown of Jupiter to thorns, and the face to that of Jesus merely by carving in a beard.

Thus with Christ's head in the ruby, it could now be set into the pommel of a sword that would slay Christ's enemies, who happened to be the enemies of every owner of the sword through generations. It slew Visigoth and Gaul, Parsi, and Jew, but mostly it slew Christians because they were the most about. It marched on Jerusalem after the Muslims, tiring of momentary tolerance, leveled Golgotha, where Christ was crucified, cut away the limestone sepulchre where He had lain, and slaughtered every Christian in the city.

And in recapturing Jerusalem, it slew Muslim and Jew before it was lost to the armies of Sal A Din, whereupon it slew Christians and Jews, but mostly Muslims in ensuing generations because they were the most about.

It did not protect an owner from Shiite killers stoked on Islam and hashish who would terrorize the Middle East and give the world the name *assassin*, until Hulagu, grandson of Genghis Khan, found the one way to stop these assassins. It was the Mongol way. He took Baghdad, the home of the Shiite assassins, and slaughtered every Muslim in the city, bringing a rare century of peace to the area.

The Christ's head left the sword because only fools believed it could draw blood, when every Mongol knew its real purpose was to prevent bleeding. If worn around the neck, it could stop the bleeding from the stomach. It fell into the hands of a Mongol Shaman, whose great-grandson traded it to a Persian merchant, who traded it to a Christian knight, where it found itself at the end of a sword again. And knowing it was envied by a baron who would eventually somehow get it, the knight gave this great red stone to a local abbey for the indulgence of not only past sins, but, as the good abbot promised, any sin the knight might commit now or in the future. He gave it away for a guarantee of heaven.

Now this abbey, like many in England, untaxed like subjects of the Crown, became rich in land and jewels. And Henry VIII, who saw the Spanish emperor grow rich from the gold of the Americas, and the Portuguese grow rich from the trade of the Far East, found himself with precious few returns from the leftover colonies of the world, mainly a place called Virginia.

And he was a spendthrift. It did not hurt that he had profound theological differences with Rome. And there were the abbeys, always suspect for allegiances to Rome. In less time than incense rose to the ceilings of Canterbury, royal commissions were sent to the abbeys to assure they practiced true Christianity, to root out such things as homosexuality, licentiousness, gluttony, and Popery. Almost every wealthy abbey and convent, as it turned out, suffered from one of the above, and the great Christ's head ruby quickly found its way into the hands of the King, and shortly thereafter onto the neck of Anne Boleyn, and then back again to Henry's hand before the executioner's sword, and then to his son Edward, who left it to his stepsister Elizabeth, Anne's daughter, for whom it represented an aching memory, only relieved at Tilbury where she found a suitable place for it, forever out of public sight and memory until a janitor in a Forty-eighth Street office building in New York City, smelling something sweetly foul coming from one of the offices, called the police.

NEW YORK CITY, THE PRESENT

With a warrant, they broke in to find a gems dealer, Norman Feldman, sixty-seven, of West Eighty-seventh Street, dead in his office chair, his dark eyes open and cloudy with that stupid look of the dead.

Inside one of the common unlocked drawers was a large red stone labeled and seized by the NYPD, and identified by Frauds/Jewels as an eighty-seven-karat pigeon's blood ruby with enough power in it to set off an industry.

The body was gone when Artie got to the office, but the stench remained, and it was so strong, his clothes would have to be cleaned to get it out. Marino and McKiernan were there. They had in a white lacquered wood box a large red stone big as a jumbo egg with Christ's head engraved on it.

Artie pulled up the blinds, to let in the north light.

"What're you doin'?" asked McKiernan. "People can look in."

"It's the right way to do it," said Artie and his voice cracked. "It's got to be the north light. That's how you see these stones."

As Feldman had showed him so many years before, he put the jeweler's loupe to his eye and looked into the belly of the Christ's head ruby. Now he understood what Norman had been talking about all these years.

There was not just light in that ruby, there was a great energy. It was set ablaze. It danced. It roared big and wild, with all the strength of inner earth. It was not five times the power of a smaller ruby; it was awesomely more powerful.

Suddenly the jeweler's loupe clouded. Artie clasped the ruby in the center of his left palm and removed the loupe with his right. It was wet. What a crazy stupid way to look through a jeweler's loupe, with tears coming out of your eyes.

Artie handed the ruby to Marino.

"It's real," he said. "It's very real."

Marino opened the top of the small wood box.

"Don't put a ruby in a wood box. Don't ever put it there," said Artie. "Rubies are fragile. A drop on wood can crack them. You got to be careful with a ruby." Artie did not look at the black-stained chair of poor Norman Feldman, his friend who obviously never did the killings with the tape, who may have never lied ever to Artie, Artie was realizing now, too late now with Norman's body bloated, swollen, taped, and violated, according to the police pictures Artie had been forced to look at. Norman, whom he never understood. Norman, who hadn't been lying.

"Hey, don't get so hot about a ruby, Modelstein," said McKiernan.

"I'm not fuckin' mad. It's a ruby, asshole. You treat it right. You do things right. Do something right, once. You don't keep a ruby in a wood box where it can rattle around."

"That's how we found it, asshole," said McKiernan.

"Not here, you didn't," said Artie.

"Here," said McKiernan.

"He's right, Artie," said Marino softly, Marino, who understood that human beings were allowed to cry and grieve and that Feldman had been Modelstein's friend and also that Modelstein was ready to tear things apart.

"Couldn't be," said Artie. He did not look at McKiernan. If he did, he might swing.

"It was hidden. Here," said Marino, pulling out a drawer in the desk. "In the box in this drawer."

Artie recognized the box now. It was Feldman's paper clip box. And that was the drawer he kept it in.

Inside the drawer were some letters, an old bottle of Scripps ink, but no paper clips.

"Any paper clips on the floor?" asked Artie.

"What?" asked Marino.

"Paper clips. Paper clips. You see any?"

McKiernan spotted a couple under a radiator. Another paper clip lay against the bookcase, and one lay on one of the shelves of the bookcase.

"I know what happened. The killer opened this drawer. Maybe he sat on the desk as he did the job on Norman," said Artie.

"No," said McKiernan. "He had to stand."

"Why?" asked Artie.

Marino took an envelope out of his pocket and on the back of it drew a staircase.

"Feldman's knife wound wasn't just a knife wound," said Marino. "Sometimes to identify a knife that killed someone, they'll pour liquid metal into the wound. It hardens. Gives the exact shape of the blade."

"That's a strange blade," said Artie.

"That's not the blade," said McKiernan. "That's the imprint the pathologist made."

"So?" said Artie.

McKiernan, pretending he had a knife in his hand, faced it toward Artie and pushed. He pushed the invisible knife, paused, pushed upward again, paused, and pushed upward.

"Somebody walked the knife into Feldman's heart. Push, raise, pause, push again," said McKiernan. "He had to stand in front of him to do it."

Artie felt the room darkening around the edges.

"How far was the desk from the chair?"

"You can't read the chair marks?" said McKiernan, pointing to the floor, where the chair was outlined. It had been next to the desk. "Feldman was taped to the chair. Broke a bone trying to wrench free."

"Close to the desk, huh?" asked Artie.

"You don't look too good," said Marino.

"Better get some fresh air," said McKiernan.

"Okay, the killer is close to the desk, gets the ruby, and looks for a quick place to dispose of it. Finds the box, throws the clips away, and then leaves it for us to believe he never found it."

"You can't prove that in court," said Marino. "Feldman could have put it there."

"I am telling you, Norman Feldman would hide a ruby, that ruby especially. Norman Feldman would swallow it and cut the stone out later. I know the man. I knew the man. I knew a little bit," said Artie, closing his fingers together, "about rubies. You don't put them in wood boxes to rattle around."

"Who in God's name would leave a ruby like that?" asked Sebastiano Marino, who had hit the point square on.

"Somebody who's after revenge," said McKiernan.

"You don't just leave a stone like this," said Artie, taking it back from Marino and holding the red egg-size stone engraved with Jesus in thorns up to eye level, where it seemed to radiate in his hands. "You could cut this baby four ways and retire with four fortunes. Four ways, there's no trace on this thing, and even if there were a trace, in most of the world it wouldn't matter. Whoever has it, owns it."

"That," said Marino, "is scary."

Detective Marino understood what Modelstein had been explaining—that whoever had done the killings was not someone lured by the jewels, but something greater than even this ruby, which Modelstein had described as awesome, more like an event than even a piece of property. He understood that in the killer's scheme of things to be found with that ruby was not worth endangering what he was after. That was why the ruby was left.

"What are they after?"

Artie shrugged. He did not want to think about Claire's research at this time. He did not want to think about many things. He found himself telling Marino and McKiernan he was all right. He was telling them he was all right and then wondering what he was doing with that awful dull light all around him, and they were telling him he was in a squad car, not in the office, and that he had passed out, and that they had caught him, and Artie saw several people looking in the windows of the squad car and he realized he had indeed passed out.

They took him to a place where they could get him a drink in private. It was a dark restaurant, and Artie downed the shot like medicine and McKiernan nursed a beer while Marino had a light Scotch, and they both told him what concerned them.

"We couldn't keep a tail on Feldman, and this guy who killed him, not only killed him but did it at his leisure. If Feldman was out of our league, this guy is way out. He's the Great White shark. And we're tellin' ya, if you're in the water in some way, get out of it, Artie."

"In what way?" asked Artie.

"The girl's apartment. We're thinking now maybe she wasn't bugged because you were living there. Maybe you were bugged at Frauds/Jewels because you were living with her. Same bugs we found on Feldman's place. Top-notch work. We thought it was our own CIA for a while, but you can't get shit out of them."

"So what are you saying?" asked Artie. He refused another drink.

"Leave that crazy lady from Ohio," said Marino.

"Can't do that," said Artie.

"You in love with her?" McKiernan asked, as though Artie had committed some irrational act.

Artie nodded.

"You can fall in love again," said McKiernan.

"C'mon, Denny," said Marino.

"Well, you can," said McKiernan.

"Spoken like someone who's never been in love," said Artie.

And then, after McKiernan had finished his beer, and Marino his Scotch and water, when they were outside on the street amidst plenty of New York City noise, Artie suggested they both investigate Captain Harry Rawson of the Queen's Argyle Sutherlanders. The suspicion was murder. Many of them.

"He's at the Sherry Netherland when he's in town," said Artie.

"We know where he stays," said Marino. "You got anyone else in mind? Someone we can arrest?"

XXIV

So then when the Holy Grail was brought before thee, He found in
thee no fruit, nor good thought, nor good will.

—SIR THOMAS MALORY
Morte d'Arthur, ca. 1470

Norman Feldman was buried from a
Jewish funeral chapel by a rabbi who had never met him and who spoke
for twenty minutes about virtues as alien to Feldman as the inside of a
synagogue. Attending were a few curators, his ex-wife, a son he never
spoke to but had left a multimillionaire, Claire, and Artie.

Artie's was the only face in the almost empty funeral chapel with
a tear on it.

That he shrugged off when Claire squeezed his hand.

As they headed for the cemetery, the ex-Mrs. Feldman and the son
looked angrily at Claire. She had filed a suit against the estate for ownership of the ruby.

It was an even better claim, considering American laws, than the
one she had quietly and routinely filed in France for the sapphire. Under
European law, she didn't have a case, and a lawyer she had hired in Paris
told her that, deriding her instructions.

Dad would have gotten mad at that point. But then Dad was not
quite as calculating. He thought of business as a vindication of himself,

a battle whereby he won himself. For Claire business was business and thrift was thrift, and perhaps because he had assured her she would always come from money, even in a collapsed financial empire, she never felt she had to do anything or spend anything to make someone else believe she was rich. She didn't have to win.

She did business, and understanding through Arthur that Lady Jennings disliked publicity, she knew Lady Jennings just might settle to avoid any notoriety. And she did. It was worth twenty thousand dollars to her for Claire to drop that suit, twenty thousand dollars better in Claire's pocket than Lady Jennings's. She had not told Arthur, who had felt guilty enough already about his part in wresting information from Lady Jennings. He would have gotten emotional about it, and it wasn't that important either way. It was simply business. Quietly done, and quietly concluded.

Interestingly enough, her Paris lawyer told her, Captain Rawson had filed no such claim. Nor, to her knowledge, had he filed claim yet in New York City.

At Woodlawn Cemetery in the Bronx, the funeral cortege was joined by television cameramen, reporters, and photographers. With the last death, the media had finally linked them all for a major story. One of the television reporters tried to interview the ex-Mrs. Feldman about what they were calling "the death cellar" and got only a murky explanation about how her former husband was the most respected man in the gem industry and would never be involved in anything illegal.

She was told that police had said the ruby was part of a cellar stolen from an Ohio heiress and that everyone connected with every jewel from it had suffered horrible death or disgrace.

"It was Norman's ruby," said the widow.

Claire, too, was interviewed.

"I don't know why people are dying. If I knew, I would tell you. You might want to speak to Harry Rawson, of London, who was staying at the Sherry Netherland and for some reason claims the cellar and all the gems are his. He's a very mysterious gentleman, I would say as mysterious as the Queen of England, and probably just as trustworthy," said Claire, the wind catching strands of hair. She knew Arthur would have preferred her to say nothing. But this seemed like such a little thing to do, considering the great big fraud over the Tilbury Cellar, considering Arthur's real grief over his friend's death. It was out in the open now and that was good. As for what they would think in Carney about the cellar and Dad, she realized they would think this Mr. Rawson was the real owner. They would have thought anyone else was the real owner. And did it matter? Probably.

She looked right into the camera when she spoke and did not blink; nor did she fix her hair, which tended to blow too freely at times in the wind. She smiled into the camera and then worried that people might think she was gleeful at a funeral. Of course, she didn't want to seem beaten either. Facing the cameras, she realized now was not the time to think, which of course she was doing all over the place.

A few reporters recognized Artie as the Frauds/Jewels Squad detective who was assigned to assist detectives Marino and McKiernan.

"Do you think your life's endangered?"

"No."

"What do you think is behind this series of horror deaths?"

"See McKiernan and Marino."

"Do you think the jewels are cursed? Are they living out an ancient pharaoh's curse?"

"Pharaoh? What has a pharaoh to do with this?"

"Weren't the jewels robbed from a pyramid?"

"Not to my knowledge."

"Where were they robbed from?"

"The case is still under investigation, and I am afraid at this time I cannot comment."

"Are you planning a wedding? Will you give her an uncursed diamond?"

Artie smiled. He knew that the reporters were not asking stupid questions, even though it sounded like it. What they wanted were the silly answers, and they would leave their questions from the stories, so that if he were foolish enough to answer the last question honestly, they would have a story on him searching for uncursed stones for the wedding ring, hoping the marriage wouldn't be as duly cursed.

He looked over at Claire. Apparently her fresh good looks were going to be a commodity on the television screen. She was trapped by television reporters, a blond head poking through a swarm of cameras. He rescued her by simply taking her arm and leading her away to one of the two black cars in the funeral cortege. The first was reserved for the family Norman Feldman never spoke to.

Inside the car was safe talking. They only had so much time and so many places they could feel free of the surveillance.

"I am certain Harry Rawson is doing the killings," said Claire. She had waited for this stretch of time they would have returning to Manhattan in the limousine.

"You don't know that. Could be lots of people. Could be this guy who's a surgeon. Lots of guys."

"I've tracked this thing, Arthur. I think Norman Feldman was selling it, which was why it was near him and out of a vault, near his good north light. And I think his killer knew it. And I think under torture Norman Feldman would have told him where the ruby was."

"So?" said Artie, who did not tell her how right she was, did not tell her he had found the proof in the ruby being discarded in the white paper clip box, something only the killer would do.

"So, obviously we are not dealing with some gem thief, which leaves out your surgeon, whom you mentioned was a form of society fence for jewels, am I correct? I mean, the ruby was found somewhere in Feldman's office, wasn't it?"

"So maybe it's not them. So? Why do we have to talk about this?"

"Because, Arthur, we can talk freely here without being overheard, something we can't do in our apartment. And more importantly we are already in this thing. Denial of reality is not a form of precaution."

She folded her white gloves over her little black bag. Artie looked down at his hands. She continued.

"Only someone working for a government, someone highly motivated by the highest integrity, would pass up that ruby knowing where it was. I vote Rawson."

"You vote Rawson," said Artie sarcastically. "Could you tell me why?"

"Who else is there?"

"Three billion people in this world," said Artie. "You take away that ruby, there's nothing left."

"Good point, Arthur. If it is not the ruby, what is he after? That is what we really learned from this. It was never the gems, Arthur. And the gold is gone. It was the first thing to go, taking with it the shape of the old Tilbury. The Tilbury Cellar was the first thing not to exist after it was stolen from me."

"Not the Tilbury again," said Artie.

"I have been tracking this thing since Jerusalem."

"We were never in Jerusalem."

"It was. It was in Jerusalem, where it was a lesson for a Muslim, and in Seville, Spain, where it was not of God for a Jew, and in England, where it was worthy of a lie."

"Yeah, what?"

"A poorish bowl. I do believe it. There's nothing left, unless they're looking for jade lions or topaz pieces, which I doubt."

"Why not topaz pieces? If you're going to murder for flatware, why not a piece of jade? C'mon Claire."

"I do believe from the religious comments of others that the poorish bowl is a Christian thing, quite probably some relic."

"That Great Britain is willing to kill for a relic, right? Hey, this ain't the middle ages, Claire."

"No. And that's what puzzles me. But they certainly were willing to lie about the Tilbury in this modern age, weren't they?"

Claire saw Arthur's large hands go up to the roof and his face explode in red flush like a volcano.

"No," screamed Arthur. "No. No Tilbury saltcellar, books, researchers, castles horseshit. No. I buried someone who thought I was his only friend. He had his heart cut into. There are people dying all over the place. Their eyes burned out. Their skin cut. Will you take down that damn wall out of our lives already?"

The driver, separated from the passengers by a thick soundproof glass, looked around to see where the sudden reverberations were coming from. He saw a big man flushed with anger and a calm lady in a black dress, who looked as level as a librarian. The driver turned back to the traffic under the Jerome Avenue elevated line.

"Arthur, we only have a brief time to talk about this. I think we are going to have to talk about it, no matter how unpleasant this is for you."

"Then leave out the Claire Andrews in search of the Tilbury Cellar. Feldman had a knife walked into his heart. This is real. It's a real coffin and a real grave and a real cemetery, and never again will I hear him insult me. Period. Let's talk real. He's dead. Lots of people are dead. And you don't know why and I don't know why. And neither of us knows who's next."

Artie turned angrily to the window to watch the passing of Jerome Avenue, the stores, the movie theaters, the people. This was the Bronx. A few blocks away, he had played stickball and drunk egg creams, and one strange day lost his virginity. Now, he was in love with someone who might get them both killed.

Claire waited until he subsided. She knew he was grieving, and this, in a way, was how he handled it, by trying to avoid what was all around them. It was the way he handled many things. But this was far too dangerous to let go its own way because unless they understood what was happening, they just might be in its way without knowing it. When she saw him turn slightly from the window, she put a hand on his.

"Arthur," she said, "I think this all very much has to do with the Tilbury Cellar and what was in it."

"Norman's body stunk so bad, I could taste it for the day, and I had to use Marino and McKiernan's special cleaners to get the death out of my clothes. Don't talk to me of four-hundred-year-old saltcellars. They walked a knife into his heart."

"All right, then let's talk about torture, Arthur." She felt bad forcing this. She could sense his despair and anger. His words came out with difficulty.

[335]

"I don't want to talk about torture. And I don't want to talk about it with you."

"We've got to. This is our best chance. We've got to resolve things now."

"Will you take down your wall?" His big, beautiful, dark eyes were pleading.

"It's open to discussion, Arthur. I think we should know what we're doing if I do take it down. I want to take it down for a reason."

"I thought we buried one," said Artie.

Claire nodded gravely to let Arthur know she understood the danger.

"Harry Rawson's got diplomatic immunity, Claire. We can't touch him," Artie said finally, with all the draining futility that swirled around all this.

"How do you know?"

"You don't think I mentioned him to Homicide?"

"And?"

"They said they were advised to back off him."

"By whom?"

"What whom? A captain. A superintendent. A word here and there. There's nothing we can do about Rawson, even if we know he did it. He's got immunity. If he shoots someone in Times Square, our government can then ask Britain to remove him from the country afterward. That's diplomatic immunity."

"Of course that does limit things. I'm most glad now I mentioned him and his Queen at the funeral. It makes things public. That's a little bit of protection, don't you think?"

Artie looked as though she had shoved a burning stick into his face. He didn't even bother to honor her question with an answer.

"Arthur, the fact is that only those who have had parts of the cellar were killed," said Claire.

"We're not snatching conversations in funeral processions because they haven't bugged our bathroom," said Artie, shaking his head. "We're in it with those microphones up our ass back at the apartment."

"Unnerving, yes, but possibly just to make sure I don't find what they want first."

"And you want to find it? You want to find it?" screamed Artie.

He dropped his head in his strong hands. He was not angry now. He stayed quiet that way for a few moments, with Claire watching him closely.

Then with more muted motions than she had ever seen in him, he told her, "I can't leave you. I can't protect you. I can't protect us."

"Because of Captain Rawson's immunity?"

"No. I don't even know that he was the one, for sure."

"It's highly probable."

"Yeah, well, probable," said Artie. "The person or persons who're doing this stuff move in ways that we don't know. What I'm saying is, they're beyond us. It could be this man, Dr. Peter Martins, too. He was a very successful gems dealer whom I couldn't touch before and Feldman warned me about. Could be him or someone I don't even know or Great Britain working with our government. I don't know. I don't know, Claire," said Artie without even the force of a shrug, rather with the quiet of surrender.

"Would Martins leave a ruby, Arthur?"

"I don't know who would leave anything, Claire. I know I love you more than anything in my life, and for once nothing I can do can make you safe. It haunts me. It horrifies me. I can't protect you. Please, let these people pass us by. Let go of it all. Please. Let them do what they do away from us, out of our lives."

"I'll take down the materials on the wall, Arthur," said Claire.

"Hell, I don't even know if that's it, but that will make me feel a lot better," said Artie as they drove past Mosholu Parkway and a big square of a building to their right, which was DeWitt Clinton High School and behind it, the playing fields where Artie used to be a star linebacker in the high school leagues, before he got out into the world.

He felt her kiss his cheek and realized he was lucky to have found her, having been such a star, such a wise guy, in the very little world that he had grown up in. And lived in before she came.

"I think Norman Feldman understood your suspicion of him, darling. In fact, I am sure of it. And I am sure he forgave you."

"I never knew what he understood," said Artie.

She did not mention that her computer had been violated, and when they got to their apartment, she made Artie a cup of tea, opened a Cherry Coke for herself, and then, talking as she went, she began stacking the file folders on the table beneath the wall.

"I'd like to get storage for these folders. I want a living room again," she said.

"What will you do with the research?" asked Artie.

"I'll store it somewhere," said Claire for the benefit of all the listening devices. "I'm through. The Feldmans are claiming the last valuable piece. That's it. Let the British and the Feldmans fight for it."

"You gave it a good shot," said Artie. "A great shot."

"I did," said Claire. "I really did." And she folded back a corner of the map, looking at Tilbury one last time, and then folded back another corner, revealing the bare white wall behind it. She had pressed so hard that some of the marks had dug into the wall. Even with the map gone, she could tell an indented line on flat white paint was her old Poseidon

Enthroned coming out of Asia to Alexander. She took down a copy of Count Orofino Desini's drawing and her own four pieces of notebook paper on which she had rapidly sketched a memory from a Carney cellar.

She took down charts of dates, remembering a time when she thought history began with the birth of Christ just because the western calendar did. In the end, the wall was bare again, but it was not barren. She was not the same terrified person who had looked at infinity and an invincible world.

It was all right to take it down now. She had found what she was looking for. It was not Arthur, although he was part of it. She had found herself, and quite simply she was someone she liked. She went into the bedroom and, from a drawer with her sweaters, took out Dad's picture.

Something had to go on the wall, and it was time he had an airing, not a saint, but her father, whom she loved and accepted. She was a woman. She could love people with flaws. She remembered taking the picture in Rome while they were on vacation, Mother staying in the hotel. She was a girl then. She had been a girl so long.

"Good-bye, Dad," she said as Artie held up the picture for placement against the wall. But it didn't belong there. No single small framed photo belonged there, and she took it down to put later on her dresser.

"Why good-bye?" asked Artie.

"To what I thought of him."

"Hey, you said he only tried to leave you richer. That's not all bad," said Artie.

"In a way. But it doesn't matter. I think he would have liked you. I think he would have, Arthur."

"That would've been nice," said Artie, and he hugged Claire. The wall was still bare. It would take a couple of chairs and perhaps a table with a vase of flowers to make it part of the room.

"Yes," said Claire, "I have a table back in Carney we can use here."

"My sister has a table," said Artie, and they laughed, because that was all they could do with someone listening in. That night, at 3:00 A.M., while her man slept warm and oblivious in her sheets, she went out into the living room and looked at the wall so bare, so wall.

"Thank you, wall," she said.

But she couldn't stop thinking about what sort of relic would be so valuable as to kill for in the twentieth century. And the answer was, there wasn't any. This was five hundred years too late for that. And besides, why torture and kill for information one could buy? If Captain Harry Rawson represented the Crown, couldn't he purchase whatever information he needed? A person who could afford to leave the Christ's head ruby could afford to buy most every one of those thieves and dealers.

*

Dr. Peter Martins sealed Feldman's collateral stones in small plastic bags, each no larger than a prune, and swallowed every one of them. He packed his bags and prepared to leave his Swiss chalet forever, the Chinese lacquered chests, the crystal dinnerware, the manservant, the designer drapes, the elegant clothes, the view of the mother of all civilized mountains, the Alps. Leave, too, all the fine dining places in Europe and America that knew him. He would have to leave his life to keep it.

"Peter, what are you doing?" This from an absolutely delicious twenty-two-year-old woman whom he had introduced to the pleasures of her body seven years before, when she had been left in Lucerne for a proper education among girls of her own class. By sixteen, she already enjoyed several other lovers, but insisted Peter Martins had ruined her for life because she would never truly be able to enjoy the techniques of another man like him. Which meant, of course, that by sixteen she had already learned the essential ingredient of a fine affair: the skill to lie properly.

Dr. Peter Martins would be leaving all that, too. She brushed the small hairs on his neck with her lips. Martins felt her body touch his back ever so slightly, just the nipples, then the pelvis, letting the most delicate scent of all, a young woman's body, tantalize him.

They were in the main bedroom, with the ceiling-high windows showing the rising snow peaks in the distance and the flowered fields beneath. He wore the gray slacks to his business suit. A green leather valise lay on the embroidered blue silk puff.

"What are you doing?" she asked. Her name was Maria. She had a minor title from her mother and a major trust from her father. He had hoped to grow older with her, among other such lovely women. Each age had a delight all its own. He wondered if he would abstain from passion because it failed his standards. He assumed not. He wouldn't be running for his life now, if he valued the quality of life above life itself. Funny, how one really discovered oneself only in trauma.

"Maria, I am going to give you a very special gift now, and I hope you will appreciate it."

"I'm more than ready to appreciate it," she said. He felt her hand slip a thumb under his belt buckle.

"Get dressed. Take everything of yours from this house, go away, and tell everyone you know in subtle little ways that you have not seen me for months."

"Oh, this is exciting," she said. "I want to be part of it."

Dr. Martins felt himself laugh lightly. It was more of a sigh. Where he was going, she would be the first to complain, return to her old play spots, and ultimately get him killed, possibly both of them.

"I think not," said Dr. Martins.

"Daddy says you're one of the shrewdest men he knows, and Daddy knows shrewd men."

Dr. Martins smiled. So shrewd, he thought. Killing pathetic Geoffrey Battissen had been an unpleasant necessity, much like making sure an overdue toilet was flushed. Dr. Martins had killed twice before under similar circumstances. These things came up. But then, in disposing of the gems, all his shrewdness, all his cunning turned from one inexplicable failure to another. He knew his world and this was a world he did not know.

The polished diamonds should have been the easiest to dispose of. Diamonds for people who knew them were virtually as liquid as cash. He had hardly given that much thought, until Avril Gotbaum phoned him from New York City, saying he had been arrested. That was the first clue. Dr. Martins had carefully and precisely made sure Gotbaum would not phone his home again leaving a traceable number. He kept in phone contact with him every day, from Gotbaum's high hopes early on to his desperation near the end, with every other word from Gotbaum's mouth being, "Whoever brings Avril Gotbaum the best package will get Avril Gotbaum."

And, of course, the answer was: "Name the package. Let's be reasonable." This was designed to keep Gotbaum on the string until something could be worked out. There were some advantages in New York with the police refusing to make a deal to let the rabbi's son off the hook. That looked perfect.

And then Gotbaum, for no fathomable reason, was tortured to death. Was someone in a hurry? Was someone seeking revenge?

Dr. Martins had stayed away from this precious home for days just to make sure his name had not been given away. And it hadn't. Which was not all that surprising considering that Gotbaum had died not of torture but of a myocardial infarction. But that was too lucky. Dr. Martins did not trust luck.

"Would you get me my red silk shirt?" he asked his young friend.

"I've never seen you wear that before," said Maria. She went to the four drawers set into the wall, which contained his shirts.

"And the Polynesian design, too."

"That was for a costume ball," she said. "Now I am desperately intrigued, darling. Where are you going?"

Maria, if she were ever asked to remember everything under torture or not, would remember those clothes. Dr. Martins had already decided to change bags. She would remember the green bag. He would throw that one away, along with the clothes she would remember. She bounced pertly over to him holding the shirts in front of her and then with the dramatic flair of a stripper, teased the shirts down the front of her body to the green leather valise.

Then she took the shirts away completely. Dr. Martins sighed. Lovely. He would remember that body forever. He packed the shirts.

Other than the diamonds, there were only really two other stones of value, the sapphire and, of course, the great ruby. The secret to wealth and survival was the ability to understand that one should never attempt to make all the profit, only some of it. And so Dr. Martins traded off the sapphire to see what was going on, specifically to know how he could best market the great ruby.

"Green slacks?" asked Maria.

"Yes, the green ones," said Dr. Martins, watching her head for the pants closet. She had such a delightful bottom, he thought. Women lost that firmness first, but only a cad would tell them about it. A cad or an idiot.

Werner Gruenwald offered several advantages. A petty businessman without the courage or skill to be an outright crook, Gruenwald not only lived close by, but, despite that proximity, never touched the world of Dr. Peter Martins. The class difference was so distinct and inviolate here that they both might have been on separate planets.

Gruenwald had resisted at first.

"How do I know this is not some piece of glass from a well-dressed con man. I don't know that. You won't even show me identification."

"The sapphire is its own identification."

"I gotta have my jeweler look at it."

"Fine."

"Leave it."

"Not on your life."

"Is this hot?"

"Burning," Dr. Martins had said.

Gruenwald had merely cocked his head, applied medicine drops to his eyes once more in his abysmal filing cabinet of an office, and called up some apparently quasilegal person with a jeweler's loupe. All the man said was that it was a real sapphire. And Gruenwald, still oblivious to what he really had, bargained the price down a few thousand more, not really changing anything much. And, like the fool he was, he sold it for a pittance to the largest jewelry store he could think of.

Which, of course, was what Dr. Martins knew he would do.

"That tie?" asked Maria.

"That tie," said Dr. Martins. She hung a light blue paisley tantalizingly over one shoulder. Dr. Martins offered the expected comment of lust. What could he tell her? That fear could kill an erection faster than ice water?

And Dr. Martins had waited, holding the ruby to see what, if anything, would happen to Werner Gruenwald. And when it happened, he knew something very dangerous was out there, and because of all the things he had known about Norman Feldman in the trading markets of the east, he was sure it was the ruby dealer after the Christ's head.

So he brought the ruby right to Feldman, the safest, most reasonable thing a man could do in those circumstances. Take less of a profit; let the monster have his way. And then Feldman had come to this chalet and threatened him for the strangest reasons, and the next thing Dr. Martins knew, from reading the Paris edition of the *Herald Tribune*, was that Norman Feldman had not only been tortured to death. The ruby was found in his office. It was never the ruby.

That was twenty minutes ago, and immediately Dr. Martins had swallowed his most sellable stones and begun to pack. Why the killer had not gotten here by now—the death was several days old—Dr. Martins did not know. He could not imagine Feldman protecting him. Something had happened to give him time, and he wasn't wasting it.

Maria, seeing the suitcase was full, sat down on it, and pulled Dr. Martins's belt buckle toward her as she spread her young thighs to receive him. She pulled her head up to his belt, tongued the zipper lightly, and pulled it down, slowly and tantalizingly.

She opened the fly and worked her fingers inside.

"My friend knows me even when you don't, Peter. He's going to rise to meet me. He always does," said Maria.

Dr. Martins stood motionless. He let Maria work for a while until she looked up puzzled. This had never happened before.

Locking eyes with her, Dr. Peter Martins said with paced gravity, "Things are that dangerous."

"Are those slips in the downstairs bathroom mine?" asked Maria, wanting to make sure she left nothing of hers in this place.

"No," said Dr. Martins.

"Thank you," she said and just before leaving added, "I am saying good-bye to someone I can never replace. You were the first and the best, Peter."

"How thoughtful, dear," said Dr. Martins. He couldn't even think of a compliment, not even an adequate lie. His hands were sweating, and he noticed his mouth was dry, but he didn't want water. He wanted something calming, but not so calming that he might, at this most dangerous time, lose his wits. He administered fifty milligrams of chlordiazepoxide into the muscle of his left forearm, avoiding the vein to slow down the sedative's action.

Still, his hands sweat and his mouth perspired, and the pen he used to address the label shook ever so slightly. He copied the name and the address in the *Herald Tribune* onto the label.

Careful not to get his fingerprints on the label, he pressed it onto purple wrapping paper anyone could buy in any store and found a box of biscuits and emptied them into the garbage. Then he took the box in gloved hands to a Chinese lacquered chest of drawers in the south sitting room and carefully removed that strange clay bowl with the dark lacquered stain in the bottom, the one in the belly of the cellar that the *Herald Tribune* indicated might also involve the British Crown in some way, and more thoroughly than he had ever prepared for an operation did Dr. Peter Martins clean the bowl of any possible fingerprints.

And just as carefully he placed it in the box and wrapped the box in the purple paper to which had already been affixed the label; and then he forever left his home and the life he had known.

It had to be the bowl that force, that monster, was looking for, for some strange, incomprehensible reason. All Dr. Martins knew was that to be associated with it would more than likely get him killed most horribly.

His only chance was to offer up some other victim to that beast, who would then for its own reasons get its bowl and possibly search no more for the likes of a man who only wanted the finer things in life.

On the way to the airport, he stopped at a post office in which he had never been before, and a clerk asked Dr. Martins if he had the American zip code for his package.

"I am sorry. I only know it is Queens, New York City, USA," he said. By now he was carrying a gray suitcase and wore a light blue suit. If the force should have caught up with Maria so quickly, she would have given them the wrong description.

"In Her Majesty's very presence, I was asked if indeed we had anything to do with the horrible killings around the world. It has been in so many newspapers. And do you know what I told her?"

Sir Anthony trembled, furious. The little man in the back seat of the uncomfortable car with the darkened closed windows tapped the bowl of his awful smelling pipe against his knuckles. He had come on call to a specified street corner within twenty minutes.

"I told her, no. I told her we have an exceptional person you supplied us. I assured her we were blameless. And she asked why these people were being killed so horribly. Every one of them was in some way connected to the object we sought."

"Oh," said the little man. "You didn't tell me that before."

"Does it make a difference?"

"I think you should know a bit more about this exceptional captain, Harry Rawson. He is discreet. He is most capable of working alone. And he can keep his eye on an objective to a point you might call ruthless. He is exceptionally coordinated and a fine specimen. All things being considered, he was the best candidate."

"What are you saying?" asked Sir Anthony.

"No one human being is perfect. You just don't find everything in someone; courage, resourcefulness, discretion, brilliance and topping it all off a morality that we approve of entirely."

"What are you saying?"

"They were torture murders weren't they?" asked the little man, and Sir Anthony did not even notice anymore when the pipe lit up, and filled the back seat with acrid fumes.

XXV

And the thicket closed behind her and the forest echoed "fool."
—ALFRED, LORD TENNYSON
"Vivien"
Idylls of the King, 1859

It was the day of reckoning, and Claire Andrews had to decide. Christmas had been one thing. Dad had just died, and she had just started on the search. Reverend McAdow could explain that to Mother and everyone, even the McCaffertys. But this Easter measured how far she had gone, how much she intended to stay away, and whether she would come home.

Mother called while Claire was reading a small book titled *The Torah Made Too Simple* in preparation for a seder at Arthur's sister's house. Claire understood what this day meant to the Modelsteins: the highest Jewish holiday celebrated in the home, and also a chance to examine the important woman in Arthur's life.

It was serious, and she had been preparing in the one way she knew how, by studying and researching.

"No, Mother," Claire said. "I'm going to a seder at Arthur's sister's house." Easter and Passover had fallen within two days of each other that year.

"Was that the man who answered your phone twice?"

"Yes, during your monthly call," Claire said, hating herself for being sharp.

Claire was sure she did not feel guilty about living with Arthur. More and more she was thinking about how impossible it would be to live without him. But when Mother asked not too coyly about the man who had answered Claire's phone twice, Claire did feel that somehow she had done something wrong. For this she now felt doubly bad, because she felt she was betraying Arthur, by not telling Mother proudly about it, and Mother, by doing it at all, and herself, by feeling these things in the first place.

Thus, with one simple question from her mother, Claire, the woman who had reduced the awesome New York Public Library to a manageable system for her needs, who had set up an international research team, who had systematically scoured the remnants of worlds gone by for the trails of jewels, who had marched with Alexander, Darius, and Augustus Caesar, who had seen Jerusalem fall and be retaken so many times in the Crusades, who had finally read the great message hidden from the Spanish empire by a Marano Jew, who had trapped the English bulldog in its lie, and who, more importantly, had found herself to be a strong and uniquely capable human being, who had dared to love, now was reduced to a nasty petulant little girl hating herself. She could have said bitterly, "Thank you, Mother."

But that would have perpetuated it. Instead, with great and painful tenacity, she forced herself not to proceed in this line of defense, but to remain quiet and vulnerable, awaiting Mother's traditional silence. Ordinarily, she would attack more, feel more guilty, and then Mother would move in to pick up the pieces.

Omar the Great used a similar tactic in capturing Egypt, Syria, and Byzantine Palestine for Islam. His battlefield timing was supposed to be impeccable. Claire doubted Omar the Great could have taught Lenore McCafferty Andrews a thing.

"Are you going to convert?" her mother finally asked. Funny, that was the same thing Reb Schnauer asked when she had gone to him for instruction for Arthur's family Passover seder.

With Reb Schnauer, however, it was a far cleaner negotiation. Claire had simply said no and then, in hearing about how he had planned to help her, realized it would be like going to a neurosurgeon to find out about a headache. She just wanted to know about seders. So she had gone for the more digestible, if not more detailed, accounts in synopsis books, which felt in a way like cheating after so much original research on the cellar.

"No, Mother, I am not preparing to convert. Why did you ask?"

"I read where so many are doing it."

"Where did you read it?"

"I think there was an article once about it in the *Toledo Blade*."

"Could that have been an article about one woman converting?"

"Yes. It was a lovely story. So many are doing it, that's why I asked."

"I'm not."

"Well, good. Not that I am against any religion. I just feel that the Jewish religion is best for Jews—do you know what I mean?"

Stop. Don't attack. Don't say anything, Claire told herself.

"Do you know what I mean?" Mother repeated.

The answer had to be shrewdly pleasant, letting the thrust pass like Alexander treated the war chariots of Darius.

"Yes, Mother, I know what you mean," she said.

"Oh . . . well . . . good," said Mother.

And it was over. Mother had not only been told about Arthur, but had been informed that he was Jewish and that Claire would not be coming home for Easter. As to living together, Mother had to assume it. And, therefore, it was as good as told.

On the way to the seder in Hazlet, New Jersey, Claire asked Arthur if he were nervous.

"About the killings?" asked Artie.

"No, about seeing your sister Esther. I mean she's like your mother."

"She'd like to be."

"But aren't you nervous about what they'll think of me?"

"I love you. I don't care what they say."

"What could they say?" she asked. She had dressed defensively in a plain blue suit, formal enough for the dinner but in no way exotic. She had swept back her hair tight in a bun so none would fly out, and her white blouse had a delicate collar so the suit would not exude any power. She wore a simple strand of pearls. Arthur's answer was totally insufficient.

"I don't care what they could say. They could say anything," he said.

"Like what?" asked Claire. She grabbed the closest forearm, the one he was using to steer with.

"If we're going to make it there alive, you're going to have to let me steer, sweetheart."

"What could she say specifically?"

"Esther could say anything. She thinks like my mother."

"I hate that. Disapproval from someone who isn't even there."

"What makes you think they're going to disapprove?"

"I'm not Jewish."

[347]

"So?"

"Oh, c'mon Arthur. Don't tell me they wouldn't prefer I was Jewish. I mean, let's be open about this."

"They probably would, so what? But they don't know you. They don't know you yet. Let them meet you."

"This could be the most important dinner of my life. I want to marry you," said Claire.

"Good."

"That's it? Good? Good?"

"They'll love you, Claire."

"We're talking about living together forever, and all you can say is 'good'? Is that the great joyous affirmation of marital union? Is that what we're dealing with?"

"No, we're dealing with your fear, darling," said Artie.

"Then tell me they're going to love me."

"They're going to love you."

"I don't need sarcasm at this time. Now, was the seder better formalized in the Babylonian or the Palestinian Talmud?"

"What?"

"The Talmud. The Talmud. What you're supposed to know and live by. It's supposed to tell you everything."

"Ask my Uncle Mort. He's what we call the *melech.* He actually does the seder."

"You don't know?"

"I know there's a mention of the laws of the Mishnah. I remember Mishnah, if that's part of the Talmud."

"You don't know what the laws of the Mishnah mean, do you?"

"No."

"You're not a good Jew."

"I don't see you go to church on Sunday. How come you're a good Presbyterian?"

"You don't have to go to church to be a Christian."

"Same here."

"Oh, no. Without adherence to the law in every aspect of your life, without the study of the Talmud, you are not a good Jew."

Artie knew where she got that from, the crazies in the black hats from Bensonhurst, Brooklyn, nee Linzer, Poland. But he did not argue with Claire. She never said anything that she didn't seem to be able to back up with several arguments, including her opponent's. And in Judaism there were arguments going on for five thousand years.

The rich fabric of Judaism, the laws and the people, the study and the practice, the constant interpretation of life and law, the meaning today and the history for which Claire had prepared—all came down to a somewhat overfurnished living room in a suburban community, with a Mercedes Benz sedan in the driveway, and the crucial words coming from Esther Modelstein: "So Claire, how long have you and Artie been seeing each other?" Esther, like the rest of the women, wore somewhat conservative dresses but adorned them with heavy jewelry. They all used more makeup than Claire, but Claire understood that if she had dressed as they did, they might find fault. This living room with the wall-length couch and track lighting over original prints and deep pile carpeting was really an examining room, with Claire as the specimen.

"Long enough to appreciate each other," said Claire. She smiled broadly. The test had begun. There was an attempt by Esther, a rather handsome woman, to put down Arthur and see how Claire would react, and Claire did not go for that. She did mention, however, that Arthur had great talent, great potential, and that she saw Arthur using it more fully in the future.

"If running after people to arrest them is a future. I mean who would want to know the people he deals with?" asked Esther with a little laugh. The other women smiled.

Claire smiled. She had to be careful here. She couldn't allow herself to denigrate Arthur in front of the women, but she couldn't directly disagree with reality also.

"Arthur has many options, and I think he is going to be using them more," said Claire. There was talk about homes and children and husbands, and even a few jokes. But the women—there were four others, not all immediate family—understood every loaded question and every precise answer, even though there were smiles all around. And through this Claire Andrews proved herself sufficiently in touch with reality, specifically Artie, to be worthy of proprietary rights to him, heretofore owned by the family women whether Artie knew it or not.

Artie and the rest of the men thought the women were having a polite conversation that was going rather well.

"You've got a winner, Artie," said Esther, giving him a peck on the cheek.

"Yeah, I think she's kind of nice. I love her. We're getting married."

"When?" asked Esther, delighted.

"We haven't set a date yet," said Claire. She was delighted, but she understood that this initial acceptance would be conditional, even precarious until they were legally married.

"So you're sort of engaged?" said Esther.

"Like that. A bit stronger. I'm here," said Claire.

"Yes, you are, and we're glad to have you," said Esther.

If the meeting lacked religious overtones, the seder, with the salt water to mark the Red Sea that opened on the Jewish flight from Egypt and the matzohs commemorating the unleavened bread the Jews were forced to eat, was an absolute desecration.

While Mort conducted the seder in Hebrew, reading from the Haggadah, the rest of the family ignored him and talked of the New York Yankees, the stock market, how much television newscasters were making, women's fashions, international politics, laser technology, bras, furniture that wouldn't hold up, antisemitism, red meat, and cholesterol versus sugar as a danger to the human body.

The only one trying to listen to Arthur's Uncle Mort, and trying to follow the seder ritual, was the Presbyterian from Carney, Ohio. And she kept being interrupted to give her opinions of things. She felt cheated and thought Arthur had been cheated in his upbringing. She wanted to beg them to let the seder be the important event of the evening, but she dared not sound like the prophet Elijah, for whom the silver cup at the head of the table was named. She was here for Arthur.

It was inevitable—the subject that had been in the newspapers and television a few days before finally came up.

"Go ahead, tell them. It's been on their minds," said Artie. "It's okay to talk here, I'm sure."

"Is this really the place and time to discuss it?" asked Claire. Uncle Mort looked up briefly, waved as though the family was a useless part of the ceremony and did not matter, and then went on with his seder.

Reluctantly, and partly because they were going to talk about other things anyhow, Claire laid out her strange findings on the Tilbury Cellar before Arthur's family, while Uncle Mort softly chanted Hebrew prayers, retelling a flight of a people from an empire that ceased to exist more than three thousand years before. And Claire knew this was a ceremony so old Christ Himself had participated in it, presumably with more religious attention.

She told of the strange events leading to her discovery of the Tilbury Cellar, of the pall of death that hung over all who came in contact with its pieces. There were so many mysteries about the saltcellar her father had shown her back in Carney. The greatest was the fact that it had jewels at all. And such great ones.

"Why?" asked Claire. She saw everyone at the table leaning toward her, except Uncle Mort and Arthur, who pried a piece of glistening pastry from a pile in a Wedgwood dish, careful to brush off the white tablecloth.

"Listen to her, Artie," said Esther. "This is interesting."

"I know it," said Artie.

"Shhh," said another aunt.

"What about the curse?" asked Esther.

"Nonsense," said Artie. "You get that much dough involved there are gonna be bodies."

"Shhhh," said Esther. "Let her talk."

"It's not the money and not the jewels," said Claire. She knew the table was rich with ceremonial dishes, but unfortunately she was the real center. Her plain blue suit and plain makeup with the hair defensively in a bun were set among the more ornate Modelstein women.

"Right, they found the ruby still on that dealer after his office was ransacked. Tortured," said a round-cheeked nephew with curly black hair and blue eyes. Claire thought Arthur must have looked like that at his Bar Mitzvah.

Mort stopped his prayers and tapped the dinner plate. He picked up the cup of Elijah and poured out ten drops as everyone joined in pouring out ten drops of their wine, representing the ten plagues God had visited on Egypt forcing Pharaoh to release the Jews.

At this point, Claire wanted so much to stay with the seder, but the family wouldn't let her. So she told them about tracking the gems through history, seeing them come up again and again, until once they joined that which would become the Tilbury, they were never mentioned separately again. The family especially liked the tale of the Seven Eyes of Seville becoming a message of evil, from the perfection of seven to the evil of six.

"How did you know they were the same stones?" asked the nephew. "What if they were other stones?"

"Good question," said Claire, smiling. If only this conversation could have taken place in the living room, she thought. "A friend of mine in Bensonhurst says everything has questions, especially facts. And some have big questions and some have small questions. So for want of any other system I grade each fact according to believability, from highly probable down to highly improbable because on most facts we do not know for sure."

The men were nodding. They liked the way she talked logic to the boy.

"So I would grade my answer to your question as only slightly possible. There were not that many diamonds that size at that time in history. They were not as plentiful as today. They were not a business then.

"And so we take the most probable statement from a Jew that this thing is 'not of God' and add to it another statement from a Muslim toward another of the gems, the one hundred and forty-two–karat Jennings sapphire, the one with Poseidon enthroned. The Muslim was Omar the Great, and he mentioned in his Jerusalem chronicles that this sapphire or something it was attached to was a 'lesson' of some sort. And also attached to this cellar formed in 1588 was the great ruby that we know was given to Elizabeth's mother by her father, Henry the Eighth, who took it back before he executed her."

Even Mort was quiet now, putting down the Haggadah.

"And so a captain in the Royal Argyle Sutherlanders now tells us there are two of these cellars with Christ's head rubies, Poseidon en-throned sapphires, and six polished diamonds, and he has the second one imitated, he says, from the original."

There were several snorting laughs around the table.

"The first one supposedly is still where Britain claims it always was, locked in Windsor Castle without anyone allowed to look at it," said Claire. "I will tell you I had a deuce of a time even finding out what it looked like. How Captain Rawson's ancestors could have copied it, I don't know. The Crown just didn't show it that often, the last time, I believe to a Count Orofino Desini around 1600."

"So they're lying. So what? Governments always lie," said Artie. He didn't want Claire whipping up a crusade at a seder table. It had been hard enough to get Claire to take down the maps and notes from the wall. He didn't want his family pushing her into putting them up again.

"A queen shouldn't lie, not to Claire," said Esther.

"May I ask all of you what it really means to any of us if a queen somewhere for state reasons, whatever they are, tells a lie?" asked Artie.

"Claire's got a claim to this thing, too," said Esther angrily. "That's a big powerful queen there. This is a single lone American girl, someone you're supposed to love, Artie. That's what."

"Whose side are you on?" asked Uncle Mort.

"A lot of people have been getting killed, if none of you noticed already," said Artie.

"You should be catching the murderers and not running away from them," said the nephew.

"Where d'you live, kid?" asked Artie.

"She has every bit as much right to that cellar as the Queen of England herself. The law is the law. That's it. If you don't believe that, get out of the police department. You shouldn't be there anyway, should he, Claire?" asked Esther.

"I never saw Artie as a cop," said Uncle Mort.

"It's your father's cellar," said Esther. "And if you need a good lawyer—"

"It's not my father's cellar, and Arthur had the courage to help me understand that. He can be quite courageous if he has to."

"You're in love," said Esther.

"I am, and contrary to popular opinion, love does not cloud the vision—it enhances it. I think you really mean infatuated, and that only with his good looks. I think he's the handsomest man in the world."

Everyone laughed.

"So what's with the Tilbury Cellar?" asked Esther.

Claire nodded. "Gems mean different things in different ages, such as diamonds meaning love today and wisdom in another age. But only when I was in Bologna did I see the sort of massed gems on a smaller scale that were in the Tilbury Cellar."

Claire paused, fingering her wine glass. Uncle Mort had put aside the silver cup of Elijah reserved for the head of the seder table, the *melech*. "They covered the foot bones of a saint. People didn't so much revere the relic as something holy, but as something powerful. It could do things for them."

"It's an Italian custom," said a knowledgeable uncle.

"No. Not just Italian. All of Europe was like that in the fifteen hundreds. I think the cellar hides a relic important enough to send a captain of the Royal Argyle Sutherlanders around the world searching for it."

"What's around the world about New York?" asked the nephew, reaching for a stuffed prune cake, one of many dishes on the long white linen tablecloth, arrayed like a convoy, heaped with cakes, and fish, and sweets, and fruits, and all the religious condiments, such as the sweet and the sour dishes to portray both the joy and the bitterness of the flight from Egypt.

"From London it's around the world. Go ahead, Claire," said Esther.

"I believe this captain is after something he has never seen, a relic so powerful that it was deemed in 1588, the year, by the way, that Britain defeated the Armada, too valuable to be shown. It had to be disguised and locked away."

"What?" asked the nephew. Even Artie leaned forward on his elbows.

"A poorish bowl," said Claire.

Everyone waited for Claire to continue.

"Well?" asked Esther.

And Claire shrugged. She didn't have the answer. What dinner bowl could have been so important? Did it have something to do with St. George, an important British saint? She didn't know. And thus began a guessing match around the table that left Claire feeling somewhat ashamed of herself. She had contributed to the general carnival atmosphere when she had really wanted to share in the seder. Passover was part of her religion, too.

This seder was the reason Easter and Passover occurred in the same season. The seder was what Christians called the Last Supper. Christ had come to Jerusalem just for this ceremony. Everything at this table was now part of Christianity because of what happened from that meal on.

The matzohs the Modelsteins ate represented what was for Catholics the eucharistic wafer that Christ had said would be His body. The cup of Elijah Uncle Mort used was the cup Christ had used to establish the new covenant. It would hold His blood He had promised to shed, His blood like the wine in the cup for the redemption of all mankind. The only things that were different at this seder table were the forms of the dinnerware, she thought. The plates would not have been so flat or uniform. Probably made of clay, common. Nothing nearly so grand. Humble ware.

She looked over at the silvery cup of Elijah. They didn't have goblets then. The one Uncle Mort used was an imitation of later European styles. Jews would have drunk from something resembling more of a bowl . . . Suddenly, Uncle Mort spilled the blood red wine on the white tablecloth, and Claire didn't know if it was because she was shouting.

"Oh my God. Oh Jesus mercy. Oh no," she cried, pushing herself away from the table. And she knew. She knew everything. She knew what the dates meant and why so many had died, why she and Arthur had to die if she made one false move. She sat there trembling at the Modelstein seder table, shaking her head, saying to herself what she had said on hearing of her father's death.

"No. No. No."

XXVI

If he gives way to fear, he is not in company of true knights.
                    —WALTER MAP
                    Queste del Saint Graal, 1225

Claire refused to answer questions, accept help, or move. Artie, who had never seen Claire frightened before, now witnessed her face whiten and her hands tremble. Esther wanted to call a doctor.

But Claire, straining to the extent of her discipline, forced herself to stand. Arthur's hand was there to help her. The cup of Elijah had been spilled in the turmoil of her scream and the blood red wine stained the white tablecloth.

She would not look at it. She asked Arthur to help her to a bathroom, and even as she left, she heard the shocked mumbling begin.

She motioned Artie to come into the bathroom, where she tried to steady herself with two glasses of water that came right back up.

"No," she said.

"Claire. What?" Artie asked, steadying her with his strong arms.

"Tell everyone I got sick," said Claire. "And let's go. We've got to go."

"I can't do that."

"Do you love them?" she asked, turning up from the sink, facing him. Her blue eyes were reddened and wide, but her lips were hard and tight. She was determined. "Do you love them, Arthur? Answer me."

"Sure," said Artie.

"Then tell them I'm sick," she said, dampening a washcloth to clean her face. "Just tell them."

"What are you afraid of?" asked Artie.

"Tell them."

"Hey, you're the lady who's not afraid of death."

"No, Arthur, I've never not been afraid of death," Claire said, trying to get her breath, trying to get her wits, trying not to let the terror seize and shake her again. "I didn't know we were in danger before."

"How? Who? What?"

"Not here."

"If we leave now, that perfect impression you made is blown. Forget it with my sister."

"If you care about them, about their living, we've got to leave now. Let me get cleaned up."

"Do you really think all my relatives' lives are endangered?"

"Arthur, I don't know how you can seriously bother to ask that question. A few lives? Where have you been?" For the first time Artie saw real disappointment in him in her face. He never wanted to see it again.

"What should I tell them?" he asked.

"Just tell them I got sick, an ulcer, anything."

"Claire—"

"Do it . . . please," said Claire, and she breathed deeply, trying to stop the trembling. She had to think. Panic would do no good. It would feel emotionally valid, but it would be destructive.

Waiting for Arthur to return, she went through several ramifications of what they were up against. Every conclusion came down to the fact that they were helpless and there was no place to hide anywhere in the world. There was nowhere they could turn. They had no friends they would not endanger more by sharing what she knew, no government they could trust for certain.

She refused to tell Arthur what was wrong, even when they drove away from the house. She didn't trust the car. They knew it was his car, just as they knew it was always parked near her apartment, which was bugged. She put a finger to her lips and held up a hand. Because of the apartment, they were practiced now at signaling these things. She could have just suddenly changed the conversation, and he would have known. Ten minutes from the house, she turned on the radio loud and told him to pull over at the earliest convenience.

"I feel like a walk, Arthur," she said.

Several miles onto the New Jersey Turnpike, he turned into a small rest area with wood benches. New York City many miles away blinked its mass across the Hudson River. There were trees and benches here, and Claire sat down at one of the wooden tables.

"Are you all right, honey?" asked Artie.

"I'm rational. Listen, I am going to be brief and I am never going to repeat this or mention it again. You've got to understand this now, before we return to the car. The poorish bowl, the last element in Harry Rawson's list, is the holiest relic in Christendom, the Holy Grail. During the middle ages, thousands of armored men and entire countries sought that thing. No matter what you or I might think, that is the only explanation for why people are dying, and why Harry Rawson, whose family could not have owned the Tilbury, is killing people for it. It belongs to Great Britain. It has since at least 1588, the year they rose to power, and they lost it in the year that began their decline, the date of what I believe must be a phony Scotland Yard report, undoubtedly prepared for Rawson's visit to the United States."

"I can have that checked out."

"No. My God, when I think I asked you to do that! Absolutely not. When I think of how close I came, I think we are lucky to be alive now. The moment Great Britain believes we know that the poorish bowl is the Grail, I think Captain Rawson will have to kill us."

"For just knowing?" asked Artie. He hit the wood table set out for motorists to take respite. Traffic whizzed twenty yards away, people who knew where they were going. Everything moved so quickly. He was still trying to fathom the Holy Grail. All he had really known before was that it was a symbol for unreasonably looking for something impossible to find. And here he was in a turnpike turnoff hearing about it in one sudden, too fast lump.

"That was the only reason they would kill. Why not buy the information? Do you really think a few million dollars mattered to a country?"

"Just to know?" asked Artie. "Just to know?"

"There was no reason he had to kill that Swiss businessman, who would have sold the nails from his mother's coffin for a price."

"Gruenwald was tortured to death. He wasn't bought," said Artie.

"But if he could have been bought, why was he tortured?" asked Claire.

"Okay, something he didn't know about, which might have been who sold him the sapphire. He wasn't part of that world."

"But Norman Feldman was that world. So why was he tortured?"

"Norman wouldn't have cooperated. He could be stubborn. I could see him not telling anything just for not telling."

Claire threw up her hands. They had only the small window of safe time for her to get Arthur to understand what he absolutely had to know if they were to survive.

"Normally, you're the first to see danger. Why are you resisting, Arthur?"

"The Holy Grail. Big deal. This isn't Sir Gawain and the Green Knight and stuff like that. This is today. Harry's a captain in the Argyle Sutherlanders, not Lancelot. I mean just for knowing about it, Claire? So we know. Big deal."

"The reason they were tortured was because they wouldn't tell him something, and the reason they didn't tell him was because they didn't know, and what they didn't know was not where was the ruby, or the sapphire, but the last thing, the poorish bowl. Just to know that he asked put them in danger. I'm sure of it."

"You can't be sure," said Artie. But it was more hope than conviction. She held his hands, and the wind played with the little curly wisps of her hair escaping from the bun, in the darkness, and the quick passing lights gave a sudden flat whiteness to her face, a face of grace and charm, of delicate lips and a perfect nose, and, damnit, a mind that could look at torture and file away all its pertinent details when the likes of McKiernan and Marino were talking about curses. That thing in her head that could codify a death scream was saying things Artie did not want to believe were happening.

Anyone else in the world would be less believable, including official Washington or official anywhere. His little Claire was more official for breakfast than the police manual.

Artie looked away at the traffic on the New Jersey Turnpike.

"Arthur, listen to me. I am not talking about how you think. You happen to be an American. You don't believe in those things. But in Europe there are enough people who do. You should have been in the church of Saint Julian with me. You can believe these things have power. Now I am not going to argue whether the poorish bowl is the Grail or not. It's what people in Britain believe, what the Queen believes."

"I don't know what the hell a queen believes," said Artie.

"And neither do I, to be precise. But someone who sent Captain Rawson on this mission must understand it does not take that many people believing a civilization is over to bring it down, especially not in a country like Great Britain. Through the history of empire, they had that bowl. When it vanished, so did the empire. So did their greatness. From Tilbury field to that Scotland Yard report, do you think it is not worth a few more lives to protect a nation's stature? That island is going under over there, unless of course you happen to be unaware of anything but the Los Angeles Rams and Chicago Bears."

"You don't know," said Artie. "You can't be sure. I mean how did you get to the Grail in the first place? We're sitting at the damned table. You're making a great impression and then screams. What's happening, Claire?"

"The Holy Grail, Arthur, is the cup Christ used at the Last Supper. It was a seder like the one we just left. That cup you still call the Elijah cup was the one he raised to announce the coming of Christianity. The middle ages thought it was the most powerful thing left in this world. The poorish bowl your friend from the Royal Argyle Sutherlanders still said he wanted for family tradition."

"He never made a big deal of it," said Artie.

"If he did, darling, we would be dead," said Claire.

"Do you know that for sure?"

"No," said Claire. "But Harry Rawson was certainly ready to give me a lot of money just to find out what I knew. What could I know, Arthur? Tell me, what could I find out that the British intelligence couldn't? I wasn't chasing the gems, I was chasing information."

"I don't know," said Artie.

"And my apartment was bugged, and people were asking about me in Carney, and someone looked through my computer, broke into the apartment just to find out what I knew."

"You didn't tell me that," said Artie.

"What would you have done? Don't get angry on me, Arthur. What would you have done? Honestly, would you have done anything? Could you have done anything?"

Artie sighed. She was right. He hated her for not telling him, but she was right. He glanced at the cars whizzing by and at the great city across the river, powered by electricity, with satellites overhead, with electronics controlling everything. Would anyone do those things for some superstition about a cup Christ used?

Claire spoke softly and convincingly, and in the end, of course, Artie had to acknowledge it was Claire Andrews, too reasonable Claire Andrews, who presented the facts.

"Arthur, I saw it through history. The Muslims would believe this Christian relic was a lesson because they constantly go about proving Christianity is flawed as well as Judaism. So they would say, 'Look at this, what the Christians worship.' And a Jew during the Inquisition might well signal silently his repressed contempt, 'This is not a thing of God.' And the jewels scream relic. Well hidden in a saltcellar, never allowed to be used by others, but hidden away like an atomic bomb. And shown once to a possible ally to show England's strength. It's a secret as old as Jerusalem, and one we would die for today as sure as in a Spanish court or English dungeon. I'm sorry, Arthur. I'm sorry. I wish it weren't so."

"I don't mind living a kind of a scam, but this is with a gun at our heads. You know. I really don't know what we can do," said Artie.

"What you always said. What we're doing now. We let it go by and never mention it again, and since our apartment is bugged, they will hear us never mention it, and because they will not stop, and because they can move easily throughout the world, they will find their Grail, and then the bugs will be gone, and we will live happily ever after."

Artie thought about that a moment. "Sure," he said.

They returned to the car, pausing for one long intense kiss, with the world whizzing by them in the flash of lights in the darkened night of their twentieth century.

"Okay," said Artie softly.

"Okay," said Claire.

Back at Claire's apartment in Queens, they found a bread box–sized package left for them in the inner hallway of the building. It was wrapped in light purple paper. It was from a Mr. Smith in Geneva, Switzerland. Claire tried to place a Geneva researcher. She didn't have one.

"I'm still sick from this evening," she said, putting the package addressed to her on the kitchen table of her apartment.

"Want something for your stomach?"

"No. That combination of foods at the seder just tore out my stomach," said Claire. "Going to bed?"

"Yeah," said Artie. Knowing she said nothing about the package, he didn't mention it either. They were going to have to be careful for a long time not to bring up random facts that would force them to backtrack obviously away from subjects. It was almost like pinochle. One did not introduce a new suit when the partner had the lead. And Claire had the lead, and he trusted her with it. He would trust her with anything, he realized. More than any other detective, more than anyone, this pretty lady from Carney, Ohio, whom he loved.

He watched her unfold the tissue-light purple wrapping from a reinforced gray cardboard box. She did this slowly to avoid a loud rustle. She removed the cover, revealing, strangely enough, an English-language newspaper used as stuffing. In fact, this was one of the editions about the cursed cellar. It even had her name in it, and address, among the other leading notables such as the latest victim and Artie himself. She pulled aside the wrapping and immediately looked up to Artie, putting her finger over her lips.

Very carefully, careful not to touch the object itself, she lifted the paper, revealing a piece of baked clay with a dark splotch in the middle.

It was rounded like a bowl. A large chip had been taken out of it, partly by a fine saw, the rest cracked away. It faintly reflected the overhead light in a few spots, showing it had once touched gold for a long time.

"I could go for a cup of tea. How about you, Arthur?" she asked.

"Nah, tea keeps me up. I'll have some cocoa," said Artie.

"Cocoa would be good," said Claire, letting the poorish bowl back down into the box. Arthur enveloped her quickly so she would not fall off the chair.

"Do you want cream in your cocoa?" he asked.

"Cream would be good, Arthur," she said, and she began to weep silently into Arthur's broad shoulder.

Sir Anthony did not even wait for the black limousine with the darkened windows to slow down at the designated street corner. He flung open the door and before it was even shut, was yelling at the little man.

"You must stop Rawson now. You've got to help us stop him now. Withdraw him."

"We'll work with you on that."

"This is awful. This is horrible," said Witt-Dawlings, remembering now as he would forever the shock on the face of his monarch, the absolute raging disdain when she heard that indeed in all probability, the horrors were done by the man they had sent after the grail.

She didn't care that it was the grail. More important than what *it* was, was what England was. What the monarchy was. Witt-Dawlings was to put himself into the hands of the Foreign Office, and order the intelligence people to recall that man at once.

"She wanted to know how we ever could have ever employed anyone like that in her service. Or yours for that matter," said Sir Anthony feeling the rage of his helplessness, and venting the force of his despair.

"For one, in the context of a feudal state like Banai, what Captain Rawson did was not out of order. Secondly, I assumed that in a different circumstance, such as return to the western world, Captain Rawson would put aside what he was known to do in Banai. Thirdly, when you send one man alone, you end up without any safeguards or checks. So that is how it was possible, and please do tell Her Majesty that on your return."

"I am not to return to her service," said Sir Anthony.

"Would you like me to open the window?" asked the little man.

"No," said Sir Anthony. "It doesn't really matter. Thank you."

"Perhaps you should see a doctor now," he said buzzing down the motor driven window with a switch.

"Doesn't matter."

"Suicidal thoughts can be treated. I've seen this before."

"Oh no. That's not for me, thank you. Please do shut the window."

"Why?"

"I think I am going to weep, possibly now."

Captain Harry Rawson had no intention of answering the four messages left around the world from Witt-Dawlings. He was too close to getting the poorish bowl. He would return to England with it and without anyone knowing the Crown had ever wanted it.

He would deliver it casually. He allowed himself the luxury of imagining how he would do it. Bring it in a little paper box, and leave it on a table as they spoke, and then, almost as an afterthought, nod to Sir Anthony that 'that was it, if the Queen's secretary still wanted Britain's Holy Grail.'

The cab stalled in the heavy dusty traffic of Cairo. The air was oppressive, and, of course, the car's air conditioning didn't work. If it weren't new, only the basics worked in any car in these countries.

The driver apologized for the delay.

In Arabic, Rawson told him the delay did not matter and recited the old Arabic proverb that patience was faster than haste.

He knew the driver's delight at sharing the language was totally fraudulent. This meant the driver had to watch how he swindled him on price, on what he might ask of a policeman, on what he might say to someone in the street. Certain nonsense would have to be eliminated, nonsense designed to engender a larger tip.

It was good to be in his second home again, and Rawson crossed his legs comfortably. Even though the suit was feather light and designed to breathe, he perspired profusely. The trick with this, as with the pain of a hangover, was just to ignore it.

The cracked leather seat of the taxi smelled of a thousand asses, accumulated gas, the garbage of the streets, and the stench that accompanied many cities of the Third World.

Rawson did not mind. He had come a long way. He had endured much and overcome much, and like any modern knight, his greatest sacrifice would be that it would all be unrecorded. No one had recorded at Balaclava what a man's entrails looked like being pulled along by his fear crazed horse. It was all that and worse, and he had chosen it, and now without sword or Christian purity, but with skills learned in the Banai security headquarters and his ability to use a modern intelligence network, he was close to it.

The ruby dealer, out of persistence, or just the nasty brass of his last breaths, had given him the name of someone quite logical to have stolen the cellar from the art dealer. A fence in Brazil. It had taken a week to ferret that one out as an impossibility. The fence identified by the ruby dealer turned out not to have left Rio for a year. Why Feldman sought to delay, Rawson did not know, unless, of course, it was an old intelligence trick used by men who understood that when a man held your body, you had to provide something, so along with the accurate information, you salted your misleads. But a delay was all the old Jew had bought.

The problem in finding out who had really dealt with Feldman was that Feldman did not use names over the phone, not even of the person he was speaking to, but always assumed someone was listening. And this meant that the many people who did go to his office had to be identified laboriously. It became too much of a strain on an already increasingly skeptical intelligence network, skeptical inasmuch as it was becoming more reluctant to perform extensive work without some explanation.

Fortunately, or perhaps logically, Harry Rawson was not sure that the big ruby had to be paid for by someone. A stone so recently stolen was not going to be entrusted to Feldman by a thief on just a word. This was not some museum or the three known major ruby dealers doing business. This was a thief. Therefore Feldman had to have something for insurance, collateral, if it were not sold outright.

If Feldman had paid cash for the great ruby, Rawson might have taken much longer picking up the trail. But Feldman had paid in kind, in fact with a large ruby that he was known to have. When that surfaced in Cairo for sale, Harry Rawson knew he had his man.

There was a whole slew of rubies suddenly for sale, not as great as the Christ's head, but most certainly of significant gem quality. All for sale in Cairo and all by Peter Thorsen, recently of Switzerland and recently of another name.

The taxi arrived at the exclusive address just outside the main city. Here large white buildings separated by luxurious distances straddled the Nile banks. Here the air was clean. Here were patios and white-coated servants and broom-swept streets for the cars. He took one look at the large single-story house with the iron gates and told the driver to return him to Cairo. He obviously had the wrong address, he said.

That night, at about 11:00 p.m., when parties were just getting going in such a rich neighborhood, Rawson returned in a rented car. The gate was locked, but there was a speaker system with a buzzer. He was surprised when it worked.

"Yes?" came the voice.

"I'm looking for Mr. Thorsen," said Rawson.

"Who are you?"

"A mutual friend said you had some fine stones to sell."

"Come back in the morning."

"If you say so, but really, I hate to carry so much money on me. I was hoping, after all, to have gems to bring with me."

"Drive in, but when you come to the door, stand away," came the voice. The gate opened with a buzz, and Harry Rawson pushed it open, returned to his car, and drove through as the gate closed behind him.

He stood at the entrance. Electronic devices with camera eyes and possibly x-ray souls set into the entablature over the driveway scanned his body. The system was a crude German make. They were all so much alike, however. As soon as they were manufactured, every intelligence agency had their flaws catalogued. They were, in effect, only useful against local thieves and local police.

"Turn around," came the voice, and Rawson did a small pirouette, humoring the man.

"Is that little penknife in your left pocket the only weapon you're carrying?"

"I would hardly consider this a weapon," said Rawson, taking the knife out of his pocket and opening the little blades, even the one with the scissors. The man apparently had infinite faith in electronics, the armor of the latter part of the twentieth century. Rawson knew the system could not detect nonmetal objects.

"All right," said the man called Thorsen, and clicked open the door.

Thorsen sat with a .357 Magnum in front of him on an elegant little marble table. Rawson raised his hands, and Thorsen nodded him to a seat much more than an arm's length away. Rawson shut the door behind him.

"I didn't see your other pocket. What's the bulge?" asked Thorsen.

"Nothing," smiled Rawson, taking the box of two-inch hospital adhesive tape out of his left pocket and offering it for inspection right over Dr. Peter Martins's gun, which was made suddenly useless by foolishly letting a well-trained British agent get closer to it than its former owner.

It was not a hard move, and he was surprised that Martins was so slow. He was sure now that this was the one who had delivered that professional blow, but he had to make sure, as he had made sure with Feldman. It was not Feldman who had killed the art dealer with that alarmingly professional stroke.

Martins did little more than squirm as Rawson taped his hands to the arms of a chair; probably, like most he thought he could talk his way out. The purpose initially was to break the will, and talking was a waste of time. One made the subject sure the pain would go on forever, and then as a sudden arbitrary blessing, it would stop and the tape be removed.

Harry Rawson opened the knife and used the scissors to snip a cut between earlobe and jaw. He wiped the blade off on Dr. Martins's shirt, put it back in his pocket, and slowly pulled the ear away from the cheek to maximize subject's pain. Pull. Wait. Pull. Wait. Subject's eyes widen, subject tries to bend with ear, to lessen tear, subject screams silently, pupils dilating full, body heaving in chair attempting to keep head still to preserve ear.

"Shh," said Rawson. Release subject's ear. "Shh."

Establish authority over subject. "You will tell me things." Subject nods head. Touch hanging ear. See pupils dilate.

"You will not scream."

Eyes tear. Head nods slightly, trying not to move ear.

It had begun as it had begun so many times. Now the tape could be removed slightly from subject's mouth. Information: Dr. Martins was the one who had killed Geoffrey Battissen with the professional blow. Not trained for that, but surgery. Graver was handy, so was back of head. More of an accident than anything else. Subject had set up Feldman as decoy. Subject had indeed found poorish bowl but had sent it off. By mail. To address and person now being named. Why her?

To save subject what he was enduring now.

And Rawson asked the question. He asked it in English. And he asked it in French. And the man groaned, and cried, and strained in his bonds, and Rawson forced himself to remember that this was just a subject.

The most necessary question had yet to be answered.

Why did subject think anyone would be tortured over knowledge of a bowl?

"You're after the bowl. I don't have it. I don't know anything about it. I don't want it. I don't know. I won't know," groaned Martins, closing his eyes against pain. They did that. So many did that.

Subject knew it was the bowl, and if he lived he would know it was the bowl, and no one could be allowed that. To know it was the bowl Great Britain was after or to know it was a "poorish bowl" someone would kill for, to know how important a seemingly lowly bowl was was to ask that first right question that could lead to the one answer Rawson had promised he would never allow. The Crown could not allow the question to be answered.

Why the bowl?

Why that bowl?

This was realistically the most dangerous risk of exposure of Her Majesty's secret . . .

Subject had to die. Gotbaum had not gotten that far before his heart gave out. And Gruenwald did know the identity of the man who sold him the sapphire, only proved after the torture began. But he did know Rawson, so he had to die. Especially after the bodyguard had to be disposed of to get to him in the first place. And then, of course, Feldman. Crafty Feldman with the misinformation. He knew it was the bowl because there were more questions after he had offered up the ruby. And he, of course, knew Rawson.

They all had to die. Vern Andrews was an accident of the Foreign Office. Battissen the work of Martins. But the rest, all seemed to get going like this. They always got going.

It happened in these times, no matter how hard Rawson tried to be professional, no matter how he told himself he was dealing with a subject and not a person, it almost always became a person, a groaning person, a person open to everything you wanted to give it, excruciating, teasing suffering that could seize Rawson with a passion that consumed will and even presence of mind.

It had started almost as soon as his revulsion subsided in those early days in the Banai security headquarters, where he learned how Hadir kept slaves honest and couriers more honest, where the truth could be tickled and banged and grabbed and torn out of a person, where he felt his own body tasting the pain, licking the groans like a hungry dog. It was evil. It was vile. And more often than not, he would leave the headquarters with an exhilarating sense of release and a sticky stain in his pants.

As others in the headquarters assured him, this was not unmanly, but a sign of manhood. Many torturers felt that, the good ones at least.

And he had become good.

And so he took Dr. Peter Martins in the expensive suburb of Cairo, and in the morning, Dr. Martins was found with the tape over his mouth, both ears torn off, and his belly opened over his pants, while Harry Rawson was in flight to New York City.

XXVII

He who was the paragon of knighthood strove so furiously that he drove his opponents back, doing them such damage with his keen sword-edge that no armour could prevent his spilling their bodies blood.   —WALTER MAP
Queste del Saint Graal, 1225

"Gee, is it good to hear from you, Harry," said Artie.

"Yes, what's happening, old boy? You've been phoning me at the Sherry Netherland. You've phoned my London flat. You've even left word at the embassy."

"Yeah, Harry. I've got good news," said Artie, keeping the voice not too upbeat, even faking a smile at his end of the telephone at Frauds.

"Must be," said Rawson. "I say, where is Claire? Has she forgiven me yet?"

"Don't you wanna hear my good news?"

"Decidedly."

"I think I've run across your poorish bowl. I can try to get it as a collar, in which case we may lose it. Or I can set up a buy for you, some secluded place and they hand you the bowl."

"I should rather the latter."

"Let's meet for dinner tonight," said Artie.

"What about lunch?"

"Tight. We'd have to make it about one-thirty or two."

"Fine. I'm at the Sherry Netherland. Do bring Claire. I think I can come to some arrangement that would be satisfactory to all parties involved. I never did wish to prove her father a thief, you know. Tell her that, if you would."

"Sure. And good to have you back," said Artie, who knew now that Rawson had tried to reach Claire first. "I'll do that. And you do want her to come for lunch then?"

"If she's willing."

"Sure," said Artie and hung up. He saw wet blotches on the black receiver. Sweat. If he smoked, he would have lit up now. He noticed his hand was shaking when he reached for a pencil.

He wrote down the time Rawson had phoned. It was 10:22. Claire should be in the air by now, that is if she had gotten to the airplane, that is if everything were working according to plan. Plan? It wasn't a plan. It was a path through a nightmare. And the nightmare was being awake, hearing Claire explain what was going on in the world, what had been going on in the world.

In a nightmare he could wake up. Claire had awakened him to this one. What could he do? Go back to sleep? He had been sleeping. She was the only one awake.

He had wanted to reach out for the protection of the police. He was a policeman. He could call on that. But Claire had pointed out too convincingly that it was more probable his own government would back Rawson over Arthur. And this included the police force, not necessarily his brother officers, but certainly the superiors. The higher up one went in the police department the more vulnerable the person was to government pressure. Arthur just could not count on them.

She had thought it all through. They had to reach Rawson first. They had to get Rawson going in the only direction he could, and still it was all too chancy. Artie wished he had learned to reason. He was sure there had to be a safer way. It was just that he could not think of it. And, more important, neither could Claire.

The night before she had been weeping silently in his arms. They both knew they were dead, and they could not talk about it because the place was bugged, and between them was the poorish bowl, the mention of whose name had killed so many. Her Majesty's Holy Grail, Great Britain's lease on greatness. Tell me where it is, old boy, and then die because you know I asked. Die because just telling me who was down the road was not enough. Die if you tell me what I want to know, old boy, old chap. Charge. Ours not to reason why.

Who had sent it? Someone who knew what Artie and Claire knew and hoped the monster would take them as his last sacrifice.

When Claire had stopped trembling, she gave Artie a quick kiss as though she were off to the office and then got a yellow legal pad and a pen and sat down in the living room. She used the sofa, away from a window, scribbling, pausing to think, and then going on.

She asked for tea and gave him a smile. The fear was still in her eyes, but there was that courage he used to think was insanity. He saw her tilt her head back and forth, weighing something and then scribbling some more.

She looked up at him once, at the chair on whose edge he had been sitting so long it cut into his buttocks, and gave him a wink. He walked over to the couch to see what she was writing and then he shook his head violently at her. She raised a hand, signaling everything was all right. Artie put his hand to his forehead. What he had seen was words like *Grail, Empire, Death, Survival, Torture, Advantages, Benefits, Losses, Risks*, and, of course, her weighted probables and improbables. They were subject headings. She was putting them into writing, all under the four levels of probability she used to find her way through history. He thought putting it into writing was too much of a risk, but her hand signaled she somehow had taken care of that.

About three o'clock, Artie dozed off with his head in her lap while she used his chest as a pad rest. His gun, instead of in the closet where he usually put it when off duty, rested on the floor near his right hand. The "tulip" he had given her for Christmas was ready nearby in case somehow someone might get in and force him to surrender his own weapon.

He awoke to Claire's lips kissing his forehead. The pad was filled, and getting off the couch Artie almost stepped on the .38.

"Let's go out for some breakfast," she said. She had that no-sleep energy she used in Bologna, only this time, her eyes were considerably redder.

"Yeah," said Artie. "Lemme shave."

"Oh, you can do that later. I'm just hungry, that's all."

"Good," said Artie, and they went out into the quiet streets, with the new red sun over nearby Queens Boulevard, hearing their leather soles on empty concrete, Claire holding her coat where Artie had seen her stuff the pad, and Artie with his gun in his unbuckled holster under his jacket ready to shoot at footsteps.

"Arthur, I wrote everything down because I think best on paper," she said. "It will be all right."

"How you gonna get rid of your notes? You got to get rid of them

[369]

somewhere, and if you get rid of them, they can be found. You can't even burn it without them reconstructing the writing nowadays. Even a police department can do that and you got *Grail* and *empire* on those pages. I saw. They'll know and it'll be all over. Even having the bowl may not be as final as those notes."

"It will be taken care of, Arthur. I've worked it out. Also, darling, if I could have figured out some way to get you safely away from this thing, a way you would be safe, I would do it. But Arthur, once they killed me, they would kill you."

"I'm not leaving, so go ahead."

She had calculated like a geometry formula. Given that they were up against the British government, and that it would never stop looking for its Grail until it had it, and that it had already killed in that quest, how could Claire and Artie assure their survival, considering that because the bowl was sent to them the British were probably on their way already.

If they did absolutely nothing, they were waiting to die, probably soon. Feldman had been tortured, it was clear now, not to find the ruby but to find the bowl. Feldman might not even have known about the bowl, but the man he got the ruby from would have. Feldman was tortured to reveal that name. It was that person who had sent the Grail. And the reason he did so obviously was to make Claire the sacrificial lamb. That person must have realized what he was up against and probably thought Rawson could find him.

Considering how Rawson so easily found the sapphire in a gray world where thievery was hardly even noticed, considering how he had cornered Feldman, a person even Arthur's colleagues couldn't tail, the man who sent the bowl had undoubtedly made the right decision.

Which brought up the question, could they just keep their mouths shut and drop Britain's Grail in the first Dempsy Dumpster they saw at a construction site?

"I don't think so," said Claire. "Maybe that man was counting on me to be stupid enough to talk about my strange package. But that doesn't matter. I've seen nothing from the way Harry Rawson operates to lead me to believe he would not find that man also. And make him talk if he has to make him. And when he talks, he will tell who has the bowl. It's not a question of whether, really. It's when. To assume otherwise is self-delusion."

At this point in the early morning street, with every car heard distinctly even blocks away, Claire brought up what she called the very crucial facts of what they did not know. They did not know that Rawson would not kill them if they contacted him and gave him the poorish bowl sent from Geneva with the wrapping, claiming the receipt of the bowl was a mystery to them. They did not know that they would not disappear some night if they sent the bowl to the British Embassy or the Queen herself. In fact, given how everyone had died, it was probable that they would die. To know was to die.

There was a possibility of some short-term protection, this from going to the news media and announcing all their suspicions, laying out all their facts. At that point, Britain would probably sit back, righteously scoff at the whole thing, and then, after many years had passed, make sure Arthur and Claire, who would by then be known as certified nuts, disappeared on some boat trip somewhere, as Rawson or someone else took the poorish bowl back to Windsor and England. That is, if Rawson were not waiting for them at the house now. Which was more probable than their reaching a press conference alive. Time now was so crucial. They had to assume Rawson was close on the heels of that bowl.

What they needed was for Britain to get its Grail and to know that they would have to pay a dear price for killing them. It had to be in Britain's self-interest to keep them alive.

For this very dangerous transfer, she was going to need two safe days. And there was only one way to get them.

"You have to make Rawson believe he is getting the poorish bowl. As long as he thinks you are getting it for him, you're safe. I am probably safe."

"How do we make him believe that? I mean this guy's gone in and out of countries, buildings, everything, like a zip code. This is not some little fence somewhere, the guys I'm used to dealing with."

"Since he's been around, Arthur, he will more easily recognize greed than any other motive. Look at yourself and your colleagues at One Police Plaza. The last thing they would look for in suspects is heroism, love, nobility, a sense of honor, even though they might have it themselves."

Artie knew the weight of logic was falling on Claire's side. Still his stomach said run, his stomach said yell the whole thing from the rooftops and circle the wagons as well as the New York Police Department. He never altogether trusted logic.

He felt cold this spring morning, with the traffic picking up on Queens Boulevard and the smell of freshly brewed coffee coming from a luncheonette down the street. But she was right. Rawson would believe Artie was setting up a buy for her, trying to make some money on Great Britain, possibly even sure Artie felt safe because he was a policeman. That would hold him, and she was right. But not for long, of course. Even down to the maximum of two days holding off Rawson, she was right.

She was right.

"Shit," said Detective Arthur C. Modelstein of the New York City

Police Department, looking up and down Queens Boulevard for the charge of the light brigade or the redcoats or the Royal Air Force in the person of a British gentleman who knew how to take the flesh off people. "Good. Okay. Yeah. What are you going to do?"

"I'll be all right. I'll be in Carney, where they tried and did not succeed in running a check on me without my knowing. Bob Truet, who owns the newspaper, told me. So did our police chief, Frank Broyles. They're all friends of the family. I'll be safer there. I wish you could have the same protection in New York City."

He didn't know how long they had to live, and there was something he had to say if he were going to be the one not to make it.

"Look, I want you to know that if I knew everything was going to turn out like this at the beginning, I was thinking this morning that I would have done it even sooner, no matter what. That's what I was thinking, Claire."

Claire's jaw stiffened, her lips trembled, and she was crying.

"Arthur, don't say that. Not now. We have work to do. Don't say that."

"But I love you."

"That's what I don't want you to say. Not now. I know you love me. Let's keep our heads about us. All right?"

"Okay," said Artie, and seeing her cry, he was crying, and they were both crying in the middle of Queens Boulevard, like two idiots, ready to take on the British Empire.

They embraced and kissed, and he tasted the salt from her tears, and he too was a lunatic, because despite it all he was the happiest man in the world.

She hailed a cab for herself, and he asked where she was going.

"To the airport," she said. "I told you he might be waiting for us back at the apartment. If he is, he probably has broken in, in which case he will see the empty box and the Geneva postmark."

"You've got it?"

"You don't think I'd leave it with you in New York. You'd be dead. The most dangerous time is when he thinks he has it in his hands. Make your phone calls to where he might be. It's better that he thinks you're on the make for dough. Good-bye. I love you," she said, giving him a peck on the cheek. "Oh, if he's at the apartment, don't shoot him, but don't let him near you; start talking deal."

"Wait. Like that you're going to Carney? No bags, nothing?"

"Safest way to leave an apartment. Good-bye, Arthur. I've got to run. I'll be phoning you as a Mrs. Donaldson. That's my message that I'm home."

"When?" he had asked.

"Noon," she had said.

And she had driven off at 6:45 A.M., with Artie realizing she had solved the problem of disposing of the notes also, very cleanly and logically taking them with her. She had achieved a solution based on a ruthless analysis of the facts they knew. He had seen in a few hours the transformation that had taken months, from the time Claire was a distraught and helpless woman at her father's death to when she became the woman whose powerful mind had broken a four-hundred-year-old secret.

Artie had made the calls and had gotten one back from Rawson, and now in his squad room the clock minute hand went past twelve, taking his heart with it.

If she were dead, he was going to shoot Rawson in the face. Right out in front of the British Embassy. For Claire. For Feldman. Even for the damned cat. Right out there, unloading the gun very close, where he couldn't miss.

But he didn't even want that. He wanted Claire safe, and when the second hand made it 12:03 and forty-seven seconds on the clock on the wall, and a woman, not Claire, said she was Mrs. Donaldson reporting the switch of her engagement ring stone by a local jeweler, Artie felt his life was handed back to him again. He had enough discipline not to thank the woman over and over. Now to push back lunch to supper, giving Claire her first full day.

"You're not in trouble, are you, dear?" asked Claire's mother, adjusting the daffodil bouquet she always kept in the main parlor on the cherrywood end table that the original McCaffertys had brought with them to the Ohio Territory in 1702.

"No. Everything is all right. Thank you. It's fine."

"You're not selling drugs, are you, dear?"

"No, Mother. It was just a way I can reach Arthur. He is on special assignment now. They know I'm his girlfriend there, and he's not supposed to take calls from me at this time."

"Because if you are somehow caught up in drugs, there are wonderful programs I have been reading about."

"No, Mother. Thank you for making the call," said Claire. The house was as light as she remembered; the white curtains were the same, covering the same tall windows over the yard where now crocuses had bloomed and tulips pushed up green through dark earth laden with the water of the melted snow. The white Victorian house on Maple Hill was home, the home of memories, the place you went when you needed a certain kind of safety even though it was no longer the kind of home you would live in. That had left with her childhood and should have

[373]

left many years before it really did. Before New York. Before Dad's going. Before everything.

Claire borrowed one of the family cars and drove to Ohio State, where she had a small conference with the head of the archeology department, and then drove back to Carney, where she had coffee in Bob Truet's office. He asked her about her life and about the detective he had heard she had fallen in love with.

"I'm sorry, Bob, I have."

"To be honest, Claire, I don't know why you didn't fall in love with me," he said in that tepid way of his. He was so comfortable in the soft tweed jacket and the oxford shirt and the paisley tie, being the most secure man in Carney, and keeping it that way. Everything about him was rounded and balanced. There was not a corner in the man. Placid lips. Placid brown hair.

"It certainly would have made life easier," she said.

"You use more makeup now in some places and less in others. It's attractive. More attractive. But I like you the other way better, I must say," said Bob.

Funny, she could hear his twang now and realized, because of that, that her own Ohio accent had to have softened. She had been afraid that perhaps Bob Truet might seem awfully attractive now, with that patina of safety, the old times. But she had to agree with Arthur, even if she knew everything were going to turn out this way, she would have done the same thing, but maybe sooner. And possibly stop the research a bit earlier.

"I want a favor, Bob," she said.

He leaned back in his large swivel chair in the largest office in Carney, and did not say, as he had always said before, that all she had to do was name it.

"I would like to borrow your office tomorrow or possibly the next day," she said.

"Why?"

"Because I want to meet an Englishman here in a newspaper office. It adds a certain authority."

"About what?"

"Private business," said Claire.

"I'm afraid, Claire, that the *Carney Daily News* engages in a public trust of providing the news. Even if I knew what your business was, I don't think I would give over this office to you."

"This is the most important thing in my life, Bob. It will in no way cause any harm to your newspaper, which I might add was extraordinarily discreet with the stories concerning my father."

"What do you mean by that?"

"I don't buy your public trust when it serves me only when you think you have a chance with me. But let me be more specific. I would consider your denying this thing I need, which will cause you no harm, an attack on me. Understand this now. This is not a game, and there will not be years of gossip. This is a matter of life and death, and I have got to have it."

"No."

"I can't believe you said that, Bob."

"I'm sorry it has to be this way," said Bob Truet, at the door of his office.

Claire did not answer him.

It was a short ride home, interrupted by hellos from old friends who had to be greeted.

By the time she got to the great white house with its large yard and the new dog running in the back, Claire had asked herself just how much did she need to have a local newspaper. It was an awful lot.

Her mother answered the door herself and grabbed Claire's arm immediately, pulling her inside.

"I just spoke with Bob Truet. He said you came to him, desperate for the use of his office, and said you were in trouble. He said he had turned you down."

"He's hurt, I think."

"That worm isn't hurt. You've got an office when you need it. And he'll have it cleaned if you want. The place is never dusted. He's got all those silly awards that are just magnets for dust, actually his protection against someone saying he is a sniveling little worm. Did you really tell him your life depended on it?"

"In a way, yes."

"You'll have it," said her mother. "Come, you need a stiff drink."

"I could use some sleep," said Claire.

"You're home, dear. You're among your own."

"I know," said Claire, who hugged her mother, and found perhaps she knew her for the first time.

When Claire awoke before supper, she found out her mother had told Bob Truet, and by implication all the Truets, that if any harm came to Claire, the McCaffertys, every one of them, would consider Bob Truet responsible. He would be starting a feud in this small town that certainly would not end in his lifetime, at least.

"Now, dear," her mother said. "What sort of trouble are you in?"

"It's not trouble like you think it's trouble. It's something I have to do that is dangerous, because if I don't, I could be killed."

"Do you want to tell me?"

"I would decidedly not like to. Trust me."

"You sound like your father."

"No. I think things through a bit more carefully."

"That's our side," said her mother and did not bring up the subject again, except to assure Claire that if she wanted to store a package in Bob Truet's safe, she most certainly could count on him. For just about anything.

They had a long talk that evening, and Claire realized she had never known her mother, even though she could spot most of her reactions in advance. She had never known her mother as a woman.

And she discovered this as she described Arthur, and her mother asked questions about him, some quite knowledgeable for someone Claire thought had been just a guilt-dispensing overseer of the past.

It was a hard conversation because Claire was worried about Arthur. And her mother spotted this.

"He's a policeman, but he really drifted into that job because it was easier than pressing on in school," said Claire.

"Lacks ambition?"

"He doesn't want trouble from the world."

"I don't know what world he thought he was born into," said Lenore McCafferty Andrews, who poured a white wine for Claire and a double martini for herself.

"I love him."

"I can see your face, Claire. You know, you really couldn't come back here to live if you married him. I don't think he would feel comfortable."

"Him or you?" asked Claire.

"Him. I already love him," said her mother.

"He is a doll. He gets so excited about things," said Claire, shaking her head. "And over the wrong things."

"Men always do. You know, I think I will visit you often in New York. I may get an apartment there . . . No, don't worry, I'm not going to be a mother-in-law close by. I have been thinking about having an affair."

"With whom?"

"I don't know yet, but I've seriously been thinking about having one for quite a while."

"How long?" asked Claire.

"Twenty years," said her mother, laughing hysterically, and Claire joined her.

Artie checked the chambers of the "tulip" he had given Claire for Christmas. It looked good. There were no obstructions. Besides, he always had his own gun for backup.

He was not going to let Claire face Rawson alone. There was going to be no Harry Rawson. He was too dangerous. He would try to use the tulip to kill Rawson, and if that failed, if the gun did not fire well, he would use his own pistol and drop the .38 he had picked up off the kids near Houston Street on Rawson's chest and claim the British agent tried to kill him. Or beat him to death with his hands. He was not going to let Rawson near Claire.

That was the worst case. The best was that he would shoot Rawson's head in with the gun that would be untraceable, then throw the tulip away, and call Claire at her Carney home. Yes, he knew she wanted to do it her way. He knew her way was logical. But she had never dealt with killers. There was no talk. There was no reason. They killed. That's what he knew from the streets.

Artie would not admit it to himself, but he had panicked.

"Looking good, Harry," Artie said when they met that evening for dinner at Rawson's Sherry Netherland suite.

"Where's Claire?" asked Rawson. He wore a light suit, without a vest but with a regimental tie. The suit was cut a bit closer than American fashion. His hair, as ever, was styled perfectly.

"She's going to meet us later for drinks. Look, I have the buy on the bowl if you still want it. They've got a couple of jade lions and lapis lazuli chips, too."

"I might. How much?"

"Could you go for two hundred thousand dollars?"

"Not on such short notice, Artie. I am landed, but not flush."

"What could you go for?"

"On a moment's notice?"

"Yeah. Tonight."

"Maybe twenty-five thousand dollars."

"I don't know if I could swing that," said Artie.

"Thirty-five."

"I think they'll go for fifty. That's what I'm hearing."

"We'd have to wait. I don't know if I could get it."

"Let me see if they'll go for thirty-five," said Artie.

It was clear enough now to Rawson that Artie was really doing the negotiation.

"You can use these phones, Artie. A drink?"

"No on that. And I have to meet this guy."

"He's waiting nearby?"

"Not with the stuff."

"Well, do hurry. And thank you, Artie," said Rawson.

"Yeah, I'll hurry back," said Artie, who phoned the suite fifteen minutes later to say there was no deal. "Guy's got to have fifty."

"Would he take traveler's checks?"

"Are you kidding?" said Artie, and after another proper lapse of time, he phoned back Rawson to say thirty-five thousand would do, but the seller had to set up the buy in his own territory. Rawson asked where that was, and Artie said he didn't know yet, but would find out on the way. He didn't want to give Rawson a chance to set up something. He felt bad when he saw Rawson and almost decided to do things Claire's way. But when he thought of Claire, and he thought of all the victims, he knew at last he could kill a man for one simple reason. He was scared witless. Looking at Rawson come down the street in his Burberry raincoat, twirling his umbrella and whistling, Artie understood revenge never would have been enough.

"Charge," said Rawson on the corner of Forty-seventh Street and Madison Avenue.

"I got to phone the guy to find the place," said Artie, reminding himself to keep his back away from the man who had killed Feldman. The main thing Artie had going for him was the fact that Rawson thought he was going to get his Grail. Until then, he had at least one free shot. He walked Rawson around a few blocks until they found a pay phone, which Artie used to dial his old telephone number. The tulip felt heavy in his side pocket. Strange how tight even his jaw was. He forced himself not to show it.

"Okay, I've got the place. It's near Bed Stuy," said Artie.

"Negro section?" asked Rawson.

"Nearby," said Artie. He hailed a cab and tried to see if Rawson had someone tailing them, some extra muscle. He didn't see it, but that didn't mean it wasn't there. When they left the cab, he took Rawson through a park where they could notice anyone nearby. They safely passed a few small gangs of blacks, who now owned the park at night. They would undoubtedly think both of them were police.

"Are we getting near?"

"A coupla blocks," said Artie.

When Artie was almost certain no one was following them, he suddenly turned into one of the many abandoned buildings.

"He's in here," said Artie.

"After you," said Rawson.

"Sure," said Artie. He walked carefully through the debris, lit only randomly with the light that could make it in from the the street, shadowy light, slivers of light, and lots of bottles and garbage underneath.

Artie stopped.

"Shhhh," he said, as he reached into his side jacket pocket and got a good grip on the tulip, hiding the motion with his body. There was no worry about prints. They never got prints from handles of guns. Nor

[378]

from triggers. Only if someone grabbed a flat metal part or the barrel would the oils that made the prints be able to adhere correctly.

"I don't hear anything," said Rawson.

Artie had the tulip out, hidden in front of his stomach, and still running the scam, said "Back there" as he turned smoothly and fired. A shot went wildly into a wall, as the gun disappeared. Something painful had ripped into his wrist, and Artie felt a tearing yank at his shoulder as he felt himself hurtle over the Burberry raincoat.

He landed cracking on his back, with his ear and face cut by glass and Rawson diving on him. But Artie had powerful legs, and he smashed them upward at Rawson, who took the blow and got his own kick excruciatingly into Artie's groin. Rawson proved a gutter fighter of the first rank. Everywhere Artie swung, Rawson seemed to be able to glance by it and deliver pain. Then there was the knee into Artie's face, and the flashing lights, and waking up in a place with a dulled flashlight and no windows.

Knives tore at his wrists. Someone was piercing knives into each wrist and into one leg too. He was pinned by the knives, and he screamed, but the scream choked him, choked in his throat right back into his stomach. His mouth was held by a slab of tape that just let him breathe through his nose. The flashlight shone on one wrist and then the other. It was then that Artie saw the nails.

"Artie, there is no way I can not kill you now," came the voice from behind the flashlight that had showed him the nails. It was Rawson. He was speaking with a softened voice, but some urgency. "You understand that, of course. I am going to have to have certain information. When I get it, I will let you go peacefully. There will be no pain. The pain will end. I've seen death. We're all having it sooner or later, and there is nothing bad in the death itself. At worst, old boy, it's the best sleep ever. I'm sorry about this really. I liked you. I would have loved to have done the world with you. Do you understand? Blink if you do."

Artie shut his eyes. He felt the spike in his left hand tear tendons and he screamed. There was no sound.

"Artie, please. Please don't make me do this, not with you. I don't want to have to do this. Do you understand?"

Artie blinked.

"Good. Now, I am going to have to know two things. Where is Claire Andrews and where is the poorish bowl?"

Artie blinked.

"Does that mean you're going to tell me?"

Artie blinked.

Rawson reached over and carefully lifted up the adhesive, strangely careful not to cause more pain.

"Where?"

"She's here in Brooklyn. She's got it."

Rawson gently rolled back the tape, and merely shook Artie's right hand like a limp hello to send Artie writhing against the nails, screaming back into his own throat and then quivering to a halt, trying desperately not to move anything, lest the nails cause pain again.

"Artie, I know when you're telling the truth and when you're not. There is a fairly set pattern to these things. You don't know the pattern, so you don't know how to lie to me. Really you don't. This is beyond what you know. Artie, I don't want to hurt you. I don't want to do this to you."

Artie did not blink. He thought, If with one yank I can get both hands free, maybe I can get out of this, or force a fight, or even get killed. But the hands he thought about were the ones he dared not move, not a fraction, not a speck, because that was where his hell was.

He was had. There was no way he was getting out of this, until Rawson put him out for good.

Rawson shook hands again. Artie wrenched again. He was crying and sobbing, but no one heard the sobs. And Rawson wrenched again, and Artie quivered, and screamed the soundless scream.

He felt water on his forehead. Rawson was gently bathing his forehead.

"You know, I should tell you the secret of the thousand-dollar whore, old boy. They are not different in any way from your five-pound screw. They give you the illusion that you're not paying for it, really that they enjoy you. And of course they're prettier and younger and that's about it. So do not think I would let you die without knowing that."

Had Artie told? He had passed out, he was sure. He didn't remember Rawson starting to bathe his head. Was Claire going to die now, too?

"Look, just a couple of more details, if you would. What sort of shape was the bowl in when you got it? You already told me where she is, so you can tell me that. Blink if you are going to make us go through this again."

Artie did not blink. He felt the tape come off, and he spat out blood, and got some water, and then the tape went back on, and the pain came again to his left wrist. He had not talked. Even in the pain, he knew that making someone believe their information was not really needed that badly was a way to get it through the back door.

He felt the water on his head again. He had passed out again, he knew.

"One word, tell me one word, Artie. Is she still in New York? Yes or no?"

Thank God. He hadn't told. But he did not know if he could go on. He would go on for the next moment. That's all he promised himself. Just the next moment, he would go on. He would give Claire, precious Claire, that moment of safety. And thinking that, he saw her face in front of him, that precious courageous face that he wished he could merely die for. He knew he could do that now, but he did not know if he could last another instant of pain. He screamed back into his throat, trying to control the convulsion so the leg and other arm would not tear from him.

XXVIII

"**H**e's not there," said Claire's mother.

Claire put down the morning coffee that Cissy, the cook, had made, that awful family favorite with chicory.

"You phoned as Mrs. Donaldson?"

"Yes."

"All right, thank you," said Claire.

"Something has gone wrong?"

"I believe," said Claire.

"We can always get Frank Broyles to phone the New York City Police Department," said Mother, referring to the police chief of Carney.

"No. No," said Claire. "Phone my home in New York and see if he answers."

"There is a problem," said Mother.

"Yes. Please phone."

Her mother was about to ask Claire if she were sure this were the right thing, but she saw a desperate strength in her daughter, a knowledge of worlds her young girl could not share with her immediately, if ever. She had just found her daughter as a friend the night before. Now she might be losing her, as a friend and as her only child. Lenore McCafferty Andrews felt helpless.

Claire's voice on her machine answered the phone. Lenore put her hand over the receiver.

"He's not there. Do you want me to leave a message?"

"No. Phone the Sherry Netherland. Find out if a Harry Rawson has checked in."

"Are you all right?"

"I don't think so, Mother," said Claire. "We'll find out."

Claire finished her coffee. She could phone McKiernan and Marino in Homicide. They would be more likely to help, but that was all. Just more likely, and not definite, considering what they were up against. There was no one in any large government office she could trust not to be influenced by the British. She had perfected the technique of operating with unknowns and calculated presumptions while she had tracked the coming together of the Tilbury Cellar through history.

"They say he checked in from Cairo yesterday morning," Mother said.

There was no point in waiting any longer.

"I'll take it, thank you," said Claire, getting up from the white tablecloth with the April sun streaming onto the dining room table, casting shadows from the buds on the trees, so that spotted patterns made the cloth look as though Rusty had run across a hundred times leaving paw prints.

"I'd like to speak to Mr. Rawson," said Claire, when she got the phone.

"He does not seem to be in his room. You may leave a message. He does check in roughly every two hours."

"Yes, tell Mr. Rawson that Claire Andrews has what he wants, and she is at home in Carney, Ohio," she said and gave her home phone number. Then she asked Mother if Frank Broyles might not stop over for a while and keep someone about.

"Are we in danger?"

"Yes, but I don't think anything will happen yet. If you can ask Mr. Broyles if any more people are calling about us, I would appreciate that, too. I think Arthur might be in trouble."

"Oh, dear," said her mother.

"We'll be all right."

"Your father used to say that, but not as kindly. He would get angry when you questioned him. I think you're stronger than he was."

"The McCafferty blood, Mom?" asked Claire.

"Well, I was thinking that. You're not going to get angry about that, are you?"

"Later, Mom. I don't have time."

Everything was ready, and when Mother said a very pleasant English gentleman was on the phone, Claire knew Rawson had gotten the message. She took the call in her bedroom, and while looking at Puffy, the stuffed dragon, and the Carney C she had gotten when she made cheerleader in her junior year at high school, she went head to head with one of the more ruthless killers of the world.

"So nice of you to phone, Claire," said Rawson.

"I have what you want," said Claire.

"The bowl?"

"The Holy Grail," said Claire.

There was a pause on the line. Finally, Rawson said, most cheerily for someone who had to be taken aback, "Well, none of us really does know about that for certain, do we? So let us establish a price if we can and get this thing over with, happily for one and all."

"I want Arthur to be nearby."

"That might be a bit difficult."

Claire felt her body grow numb. But all she had heard was Rawson imply that Arthur was dead. If he were dead, then there was nothing she could do. On the other hand, Rawson might be feeling her out to see if he could finish Arthur off with impunity. She did not know either as fact. But she had to work on the latter possibility. It was the only thing she had.

"That's too bad, because without Arthur, you are never getting the Holy Grail," said Claire.

"We're talking price. Let's at least negotiate."

"He is not negotiable."

"Well let's say, he would be impossible. What's done is done, and nothing can bring him back. Then do you really wish to pass up the small fortune?"

"Without question and absolutely."

"Well, then, we'll just have to make sure Arthur is about, won't we?"

"I would say," said Claire, feeling her body release almost to tears, yet knowing, on the other hand, that this is what Rawson would have to say, even if Arthur were dead. She told Rawson he would be met at the airport and hung up.

She met him as planned, in Bob Truet's office after Frank Broyles escorted the British visitor up through the newsroom. Bob Truet himself brought up the box she had asked him to hold in the main safe of the

Carney Daily News. It was a black gift box from the local jewelry store for something the size of a toaster. Two pieces of clear adhesive tape held down the edges.

Captain Harry Rawson of Her Majesty's Argyle Sutherlanders wore a light tweed suit with a vest, regimental tie, and polished cordovan shoes. He was shaved, fresh, immaculately groomed. And he had arrived without Arthur.

Claire could find nothing at home but a frilly blouse from Mother. It didn't matter. She didn't need a power suit when there was so much blood on the table already.

She could have worn her Carney C sweater.

"Well, here we are," said Rawson, looking around the large corner room with the view of Main Street shops and the church at the corner and the civic and news awards against the wall.

"It's in the box," said Claire.

"May I?" said Rawson.

Claire nodded. She felt weak. She felt tired. She felt angry. She felt frightened. And she didn't care. She was here. She had prepared everything, and she was never going to be in a better place or a better time. If it were going to work, it would work. And if it weren't, there was nothing she could do now.

"Looks somewhat pitiful. One has to say, as one says upon first sex, is that all there is?"

"That's it," said Claire.

"Well, then, let's get on with things. What do you want for it?"

"Two and a half million dollars."

"The money is no problem. There will be no difficulty with that. There is some difficulty with your boyfriend. I am afraid he's dead."

Claire didn't know how she was able to answer, but she heard the words come clearly from her mouth, hard words, words she had prepared and hoped she would never have to use.

"Then you lose, Captain Rawson. We have a news story already prepared about Britain's killings for the Holy Grail, and we will run a picture of it, just as we will run the picture taken of you when you entered, Captain Harry Rawson of the Queen's Argyle Sutherlanders, coming to make the deal on the Grail. You're in Ohio now, Captain, not some international city. Ohio, America. It will be the biggest story here ever, and let me tell you how newspapers work. There is a service called the World Associated Press, of which this newspaper is a member. That wire service goes all over the world, as you can imagine. And the nice thing is, it will take the story as written, and there are some very good facts, including maps showing what Britain was when you had the Grail and what you are now without it. I am sorry it came to this."

"Five million," said Rawson. "Without Artie."

"You knew the terms."

"All right. You will have him when I have our mutual bowl safe."

She felt something in her want to dance joy before the heavens, and yet something else, that calculating reason that had brought her through to this, told her that any relaxation could lose Arthur if, indeed, he still were alive. She had to be very careful to get him through now. There was still danger if Great Britain didn't know exactly what she wanted.

"No," said Claire. "You're going to have to bring him here. I want to see him. I want to hold him. A promise will do no good. I'm not selling his life. I don't want your bloody five million. You heard my price."

"There is going to be some difficulty getting him. He is alive. He has been injured."

"How much?"

"He has all his functions. He is in pain. You really shouldn't have put him in that spot you know. He really was not equipped to kill me."

Poor Arthur. He had tried to do it his way. He had panicked. She could strangle him if she didn't love him so much.

"He is going to be here within three hours, or there is no deal."

"That's impossible."

"There are no negotiations on this point, Captain."

"My dear Miss Andrews."

"You're losing time," she said. If she had that gun Arthur had given her, she knew she could kill this man now. Although she wouldn't. It was as though all her most violent feelings were only whispers far off, while her mind worked this thing.

"There is a problem in getting him here. I would have to for discretionary reasons use my embassy. There might be some difficulty there," said Rawson.

At that moment, Claire Andrews knew she had him. He might try something more, but he was done for. There was nothing more.

Now, the moment he admitted possible lack of support from his own people, he had given up negotiating and was pleading. No matter what he said from here on, it would be begging. There was even another offer of higher money and a threat to let Arthur die, but it was all meaningless.

Eventually he got on the telephone with his embassy and described some New York basement and Arthur's condition, including, to Claire's horror, nails in Arthur's arms and one leg.

"It does not kill. Only if they're upright so the arms won't let them breathe does it kill. You damned well better know. He's all right. I have that arranged here. You can check out my priorities. . . . Well, I did have them. . . . It really is up to you, old boy. I am here. I have what I was sent for; I employed my commission with the judgment I used all my life. If at this time, it seems inappropriate . . . you're wasting time."

Captain Rawson hung up. Claire Andrews said they would both wait in the publisher's office.

"Arthur will have to go to a hospital, I believe. May I smoke?"

"No. I don't like smoke," said Claire.

"Someone here smokes a pipe. I can smell it."

"I don't," said Claire, and it was then that Captain Rawson rose and gave Claire Andrews a stiff and formal salute.

"I congratulate you," he said.

She did not answer, but turned away, embarrassed that someone would say something like that after all this blood and suffering. They waited three and a half hours in silence, and she didn't let him smoke and she didn't let him leave and every once in a while she locked eyes with him and it was not Claire Andrews who blinked.

When Captain Rawson took the clay bowl later that afternoon, apparently under some sort of detention by his own embassy staff, she did say good-bye.

It was agreed, with an abject apology from the British Embassy, that Her Majesty's government would make any amends required. It was requested that Miss Andrews and Mr. Modelstein not press charges, that Her Majesty's government wished to settle this matter of utmost embarrassment discreetly. Claire knew the words and it was not that she didn't believe them; she didn't care whether the Brits meant them or not. Arthur had been flown to Ohio with a British doctor in a private plane, accompanied by embassy officials. He was here. He was alive. He was going to be well.

She told them to leave and take their damned clay cup with them.

Artie did not have to be hospitalized, but he did have to stay in bed, and the bed he stayed in was Claire's in her mother's house, which posed a problem for Mrs. Andrews.

New York City was one thing, but Carney was another.

"Everyone's doing it, Mother."

"We're not everyone."

"I am."

"No. You're not."

"Haven't we had this conversation before?" asked Claire.

"No, but we should have. You just never brought anyone home to sleep in your room," said Lenore, laughing. "Not my fault you were so inactive."

[387]

Artie met Mrs. Andrews with his wrists bandaged and his foot encased in something stiff, all done expertly by a British doctor.

She thought Claire's Arthur was so brave in not wanting to talk about his injuries. He was the strong silent type. Claire knew otherwise. Arthur didn't want to talk about it because it made him sick.

"At least you found out how truly brave you were," Claire's mother had said.

"I coulda done without it real nice," said Artie.

Claire promised no one would bring it up again, but she knew one day Arthur would have to talk about it.

In England Sir Anthony Witt-Dawlings had one last assignment. A piece of rounded orangish clay, in a bowl shape, was given him with instructions to tell no one and to deposit it in the Round Tower at Windsor. No one was quite sure what to do with it after all. He returned it to the passage in the Round Tower, which he had once given Captain Rawson permission to enter, and not knowing in which cell exactly to place it, he stumbled with a search beam past several cells until he found one whose heathstone floor seemed to have been hacked at recently, disfiguring an engraving. It was the cell Captain Rawson had presumed he had made safe for England's secret. On a dark stone pedestal a faint round mist of gold reflected the beam, the Tilbury's golden fingerprint, taken over four centuries.

Sir Anthony put the poorish bowl in the middle of the faint gold circle and left it for as many more centuries as Windsor would choose.

Then he went to the funeral of Captain Harry Rawson, Royal Argyle Sutherlanders, who upon his return to the Gulf was killed when trying to teach friendly troops the use of grenades.

In Carney, Claire Andrews received a package from the Ohio State archeology department and promptly bought a large can of green enamel paint the hardware store assured her would never chip but would wear for years.

In the basement where she had first seen the Tilbury Cellar, she opened the box from the archeology department and put aside the two-page letter of explanation. That could be handled later. Quickly, she reached into the packing and removed an orangish bowl with a lacquered dark bottom, reflecting faintly in small spots the glow of the basement light. Then with a cheap brush she lathered on the thick green paint over Great Britain's Holy Grail, smothering it in ugly layers, making it unworthwhile for anyone to steal, a common, ugly sort of ashtray she intended to leave out on some table or desk.

It was hers and it was America's for whatever it was worth. Captain

Rawson had admitted he didn't know what it looked like during the dinner back in New York. And if he did recognize he had a substitute, she would have sent for this from Ohio State archeology. But he hadn't.

It felt dangerous, but in no way did it add to the risk. She knew that. She understood Rawson's war for the Grail. There were no morals. No one was punished for lying and cheating, only losing. That was the sadness she felt for so much of this.

She put the green wet thing on a brick to dry. She would give it another coat in the afternoon. She would not hide it, but keep it out in the open and if someone stole it, they could have it. She had won a greater prize than she had set out for. She had won herself.

The archeology department at Ohio State was more than helpful. They appreciated not only her donation to them, but also her interest in the field. They had supplied the clay bowl of the Roman period that went to Britain. It had come from a find in Israel. They were so common they were even sold in dozens of antiquities shops in that country.

As the paint dried, Claire read the letter under a bare light bulb. The clay, as they had told her informally on first sight, was the typical orange of the Roman occupation of Judea. But clay, as Claire had been told, could not be carbon dated. Fortunately, the black substance at the bottom of the bowl was organic and did date to 50 c.e., Christian Era, plus or minus fifty years.

Claire smiled. She had determined that if the clay bowl was dated at the time of Christ, then it was just a bare possibility this was the cup of the Last Supper, the Grail, this thing she had tracked in Jewish comments coming to England from Spain and Muslim comments coming to Spain from Jerusalem.

And this was because the saving of relics other than the bones of the saints only started several centuries after Christ's death. The inclination to create a forgery at the time of Christ would therefore be less.

Of course, who would have saved it in the beginning? she wondered, putting down the first page of the two-page letter.

Those at Christ's seder were all disciples who did not stand up to the Romans seizing Jesus. Would they rescue a cup? Judas had betrayed him. Peter denied him three times, and there was no indication any of the others did anything but flee in panic. Except there was one who doubted everything: Thomas, who had even put his fingers into Christ's wounds to make sure the resurrection was not an illusion. He would have done it. He would have been curious about what there was to the mysterious words about the cup, that this would be the cup of the blood of the new covenant. He might have saved it to examine it, if the Gospels were accurate as to his behavior and the other events.

She glanced down at the green painted thing drying on the brick.

Maybe, she thought. And then she turned to the second sheet from the archeology department. They were puzzled by their analysis of the bowl they had returned because human sacrifices in the Canaanite, Judean, later Palestinian area had ceased many centuries before. And yet in this bowl of 50 c.e. the dark stain in the bottom was that of human blood.

Claire tore up the letter in the basement, careful to save the pieces. She capped the paint and put the brush into turpentine so she would not have to buy another for the second coat and went upstairs to Arthur.

"Anything doing today?" asked Artie, glad to see her.

"Nothing," she said.

"It's a beautiful town but kind of dead, you know," said Artie.

"Sometimes," said Claire, and kissed him, and fluffed up his pillow. And later that day she burned the fragments of the letter in the compost pile behind the house where Jed had collected winter refuse to decompose in the flower beds of the big white Victorian house on Maple Hill.